BITCHEN CHASE

BOB MOODY
with
DIANA HOWELL GALLAGHER

BANYAN · TREE · PRESS

an imprint of
Hugo House Publishers, Ltd.
Denver Colorado, Austin Texas.

ACKNOWLEDGEMENT

To Diana Howell Gallagher

Lifelong Friend and Muse

Diana's talent, tenacity, and diligence turned an otherwise rough draft into a compelling and easy read. Her abilities with sentence structure, punctuation, continuity, and creative contributions enable the story to flow. She's one of the very few people I've ever known who gets me and my twisted take on life because she possesses the same sense of the absurd. Without Diana's participation, it would not be the polished work you now hold in your hands.

With mucho affection, mi amiga

Bob

MORE COMMENTS ABOUT *BITCHEN CHASE*

"I really liked the characters and identified with *Murdock* right away, especially when days are long and life gets tough. The friendships between the male characters are very well done, and the women in their lives realistic. With my curiosity in full gear throughout, the plot kept me entertained, laughing, and at times, blown away."

SSG Todd Fisher

"Once I got halfway through the first chapter, I couldn't stop reading the book. The plots move fast with twists and turns every few pages. I was sad, mad, dying laughing, shocked, and touched over and over again. Great beach, vacation or anytime read."

D. Lozano

"*Bitchen Chase* definitely got our attention. We were hooked right away on the bitchen characters, their irreverent humor, and their determination to live a full, quality life no matter what they faced. Both of us laughed out loud often and enjoyed the undeniable swag."

Kim and Jerry Hart

"So glad I found this hilarious, heartwarming book while still in my fifties. Dreading I might follow most folks who pretty much wither away as they age, I found a new perspective about what's ahead for me after I turn sixty. I can't get rid of the problems I'll face, but I can have the time of my life if I so choose."

J. Aiken

Bitchen Chase by Bob Moody with Diana Howell Gallagher

ISBN: 978-1-948261-48-7

Library of Congress Control Number: 2021922973

Cover and Text Design by: Christa Mella

BANYAN · TREE · PRESS

Published 2021 by Banyan Tree Press,
an imprint of Hugo House Publishers, Ltd.
Denver Colorado, Austin Texas.

DEDICATED TO

ALL BITCHEN COTTONHEADS

CONTENTS

PREFACE

Bitchen Chase is the second novel in our *Chase Murdock Series*, which explores the two-year raucous transition of our protagonist, Chase Murdock, into senior citizenship as he crashes into his early sixties. Our first novel, *Dirt Nap Chase*, introduces Murdock finalizing his suicide plan after his personal and professional lives ran off the rails. The day described in the last chapter is the same day *Bitchen Chase* begins. Who says tragedy can't usher in a perfect destiny?

We weaved our preferred vernacular from 1960s Southern California throughout our *Chase Murdock Series*. For example, taking a "dirt nap" is the equivalent of being six feet under. In case readers are unaware of what *bitchen* means, we have provided a current definition below:

Definition of **bitchen**; American English; Adjective, slang; Also, bitchin'**: **marvelous; wonderful**. Word Reference: Random House Unabridged Dictionary of American English © 2021; **amazing** and **fantabulous**. Word reference: Urban Dictionary © 2021.

**Author's note: An alternate spelling may have evolved over the years from the British or other non-American publishers, who possibly decided we Americans, whose Southern California surfers coined *bitchen*, surely didn't mean to spell bitchen like kitchen. These word-snatchers also tied bitchen to the ugly, opposite meaning word, bitching, the meaning of which centers around excessive complaining. Spelled correctly, bitchen emphasizes a happy moment. For those of us who were there during the original onset of bitchen and its wildfire adoption by high school and college students in the early 1960s, b-i-t-c-h-e-n is the ONLY correct spelling. Example: This is a really bitchen kitchen. We think it's time to bring bitchen back into American conversations.

BITCHEN CHASE

CHAPTER I

BACK AMONG THE LIVING

Richard Bodine scurried up the steps of his yellow Mediterranean-style home. He blasted through the front door with a shout, "Chaser's on board, baby. I got the man I wanted to replace him."

His live-in girlfriend, Doctor Jenna 'Talia' Gorman, rushed out from their bedroom, dressed in a black thong and bra. She squinted her eyes, "How many cocktails have you had? Whatever's happening must be exciting because what you just said makes no sense."

"Sure, it does. He's the man I wanted for the same job he had before at Eye Cue, and he accepted tonight. Mmmm, you look downright edible. No matter how many times I catch the different stages of you undressing, it never gets old."

Talia smiled, rolling her eyes, running her tongue over shiny red, glossy lips, then winked at Bodine. "Easy, Stud. I ran out because of your four-alarm entrance. So, let me get this straight. Same job, same guy. You have a peculiar way of communicating sometimes, Bo. But I'm thrilled the one and only Mr. Murdock is back on the team. With him in the mix, your chances of turning Eye Cue around just improved dramatically. But surely, he's still reeling from Donna's death, right?"

"Yeah, he definitely is. The difficult part is it hasn't been that long. But I'll keep him so fucking busy he won't find time for any depressed bedwetter mode. Plus, I already worked on a compensation package with executive status which I never mentioned. He'll probably shit nickels in the HR office when he gets it from Brenda."

Talia quipped, "That conjures up a vision." They both giggled.

Talia retreated to the bedroom; Bodine eyed her strides in full admiration of her natural beauty, projected from the front or rear, clothed or stark naked. After an essential nose job, her face emerged flawless shrouded by cascading, golden blonde hair. He recognized her glamourous appeal as one in a league of few. Deep inside, he knew he could commit to her one day.

Bodine plopped down in his tan leather recliner, kicking off his shoes while extending the footrest. He closed his eyes, pondering his decision to rehire Murdock. The man was right for the job. His uncertainty revolved around Murdock's fragile psyche. Could he fend off pressures, focusing on the challenge of righting a floundering ship? He'd know two weeks from now if he made the best choice rehiring his closest friend.

After driving home in a daze from the blurring sequence of the day's events, Chase Murdock got out of his car, shut the door, then stared at Pearl, his faithful 10-year-old white Cadillac. He patted Pearl's hood, showing gratitude for her magical autopilot abilities carrying him home in one piece. Replacing Pearl with another car remained out of the question. Moving his face near her windshield, he whispered, "Miss Pearl, I will protect you and keep you in top shape until my geezerhood requires my residence at the state home for the unwanted."

Wiping both eyes, he ambled toward his apartment's brown, paint-chipped front door, tediously unlocked the wobbly deadbolt, and swung the door wide open. He stood at the entrance, scanning the room as if he arrived there for the first time. If things worked out the way he plotted earlier for the day, his lifeless body would be located in a refrigerated room at the Ventura County morgue by now, encased in an insulated body bag for stench protection.

He shuffled to his bedroom, stopping in front of the full-length mirror. The reflection outlined his disheveled, lanky, six-foot frame with unkempt, sandy-brown hair above a contorted face. He peered closer, noticing his gray eyes barely contrasted his uncharacteristic pale skin. As he stared at his image, his mind strayed. He considered himself borderline attractive rather than handsome like his striking friend Bodine.

Moving to his living room, he flopped down on the stained beige microfiber couch. Bodine knew nothing of his original plan for the day. It would stay that way. The only two people ever aware of his ongoing despair were his best friend, Ted Zachary, and his deceased lover, Donna Alvarez.

His pensive mood shifted with a sudden thought. Without warning to his ex-wife, Kathleen, he had mailed his will to her earlier that morning in anticipation of her executing it in the near future. His only option was to text her first thing before with an apology in case he alarmed her by sending the will unannounced. By explaining it was sent as a mere update of the document, perhaps the normal bout of drama might be eliminated.

Pushing forward, he focused on a good night's sleep and getting himself psyched up for the work force pace where he thrived. The promise of a new job and a fresh start mandated he give life another shot. After all, meeting Donna and falling crazy in love with her proved something as good or even better might be just around the corner. Mourning for Donna owned a permanent residence in his soul. As he closed his eyes, brushing off the new tears, an obnoxious, yet familiar, rap at his front door broke the moment.

The front door cracked open. "Chase, hey, I just saw you walk in. Care to have a cold one and catch up on our conversation at the hardware store?" babbled Johnny Dunne, his nuisance of a neighbor and the sole human in existence who caused the inadvertent towing of his car, the effect of which created a triggering of the events sparing his life.

His eyes still wet, he needed all the energy he could muster to stave off the onslaught of grief. For a few seconds, he considered screaming every profane word in the book at Dunne. Instead, he summoned his voice, but all he could manage was, "Not tonight, Johnny. Not feeling well. I'll catch up with you tomorrow maybe."

"Dunne deal," Dunne shouted, using the worn out catch phrase which long ago became annoying. "Hope you're feeling better." Dunne slammed the door as usual. As he heard the man-child's feet padding away from his apartment, his solitude returned.

Even with his job and life handed back, the distressing thoughts returned with a vengeance. The one thing he cherished most vanished forever in a heap of mangled metal. Instead of the alcohol consumption with Bodine deadening his emotions, it intensified the sadness and overwhelmed him. "Oh Donna," he cried, "what will I ever do without you?"

He sat motionless on his couch. Without warning, his body convulsed into weeping, tears streaming onto the carpet at his feet. He contemplated the monumental task before him to resurrect his once upbeat persona. It required a pasted smile on his face to conceal his expanding post-traumatic stress, a state of mind he recognized too well from his soldiering in Vietnam. With Bodine relying on him for top level performance to bring Eye Cue back into prominence, what choice did he have? Bodine gave him the miracle of another chance, appointing him to co-lead a prime mission in the arena he loved. He vowed he would never fail him. In reality, for a healing strong enough to overtake the debilitating depression, manning up remained the most viable first step.

He forced himself up from the couch and wobbled to the kitchen for the beer and food remnants in his refrigerator. A vision of Johnny Dunne helping himself to another free beer in the fridge disrupted his pity party. Euphoria suddenly ransacked his emotional and physical exhaustion, replacing it with hope. "Johnny Dunne may well be expendable," he announced to the refrigerator. "Once I'm settled in my new job, I'll just move to a new place. I'll be done with Dunne and this rathole apartment."

Smirking, he closed the fridge door. Sleeping was more vital than leftovers and beer. He headed for his bedroom, undressing and throwing clothing on the floor between strides. He wilted onto his bed, scrunched his pillow, and pulled a small portion of his never-been-washed, bluish comforter over his butt and legs. With the smirk still on his face, he imagined a serene world minus one Johnny Dunne as he fell into a deep slumber.

A dream materialized at the moment of unconsciousness. He stood motionless on the shoreline at his favorite spot in Westward Beach. It was the middle of the night as he walked barefoot with his pants rolled up high above his ankles. Under a soft, supernatural luminance over the water line cast by a full moon, he scanned the barren beach. He gazed on the horizon, oblivious to the cold breakwater lapping over his feet. Several yards beyond, he spotted what appeared to be a woman with blonde hair floating on her back splashing in the shallow water.

He cupped his hands around his mouth, yelling, "Hey! Are you all right?" The woman rolled over and began treading water. She stared directly at him without responding. The moonlight brightened after a cloud passed, allowing him clear sight. It was Donna. He dropped to his knees in an uncontrollable shiver. His entire body trembled. He heard her voice whisper a distinct melody, as if she were standing right beside him. "Come join me, baby, in my endless sleep."

He jerked awake, heart racing, tears running down his cheeks. He threw off his sweat-soaked comforter gulping for air. As he sucked the oxygen into his lungs, the gasping relented, turning into a sob. "Oh God, Donna. Oh God. I saw your face; I heard your voice. Where have they taken you? Please come back. I'm dying a slow death here. If I had answered one, just one of your calls, you wouldn't have worried, you wouldn't have come looking for me. It's all my fault. Forgive me, Donna, oh God, please forgive me."

CHAPTER 2

DÉJÀ VIEW

Murdock's new job started in ten days, allowing him time to regroup and giving Bodine extra days for establishing himself as the new CEO while formulating urgent priorities. Murdock spent two days on his laptop analyzing the competition for clues disclosing the extent Eye Cue Technologies lagged the rest of the industry. The more he read, the more disappointed he became. Eye Cue's stock had nosedived in the wake of the previous president's death. Operating as a telemarketing entity only, Murdock surmised the company handed its industry edge over to its mediocre competitors. His juices flowed, flooding his mind with new approaches and strategies.

Craving the fast-lane life again, he chomped at the bit for his entrance back in the game. He pestered Bodine for sales reports and current product performance matrixes, wearing down Bodine's resistance. On day four of the job countdown, his future boss gave him a password for the Eye Cue remote access website. Once Murdock downloaded the computer reports on his laptop, he delved into their details for hours at a time.

Since Murdock's firing from the company, the sales numbers steadily trended downward in lockstep with Eye Cue's share prices. Although Bodine immediately reinstated every independent sales rep terminated, the sales results remained lifeless. Bullet points for lighting a fire under the rep's asses paraded through his mind, at times making him snicker as he listed them. For now, all he could do was observe, but he would turn up the heat on the reps with his trusty motivational blowtorch early during his first day back.

Exasperated as the days crawled by with only sales monitoring and note taking on his itinerary, he crabbed at Bodine, "Bo, why am I waiting so long to start? Three times a day I'm tracking sales and nothing's happening."

Bodine reassured him, "Look Chaser, I don't want you showing up until we both can hit the ground in a full sprint. I know business sucks for us right now, but by the time you walk back in our front door, I'll be locked and loaded with *all* the personnel we need. I have a few more I's to dot and T's to cross. You just keep psyching yourself up for the major ass-kicking I've put at the top of your agenda, okay? I'll have you so fucking busy, you won't have time to scratch your huevos."

"Okay, okay. I think the walls of my apartment are closing in on me because I'm so eager to do you proud."

"I'm counting on it. Just be patient and wait for the bell."

He spent the last three countdown days shopping for new clothes, chilling at the beach, getting a haircut, and restocking his kitchen with food, beer and tequila. Spotting a new pudge in his midsection from all his favorite bagged snacks and beer meals, he added a long jog to his morning routine around his unremarkable neighborhood where he knew no one. Each night, he prayed for no repeats of the Donna nightmare until he dropped off into a sound sleep.

When his first workday at Eye Cue arrived, energy thundered through him. After a hurried coffee and leftover beef burrito, he darted to the shower. Every millimeter of his body was scrubbed with special attention to stench areas. Each whisker met its demise under the driven razor. He positioned his eyes two inches from the rusted-out medicine cabinet mirror to scrutinize his eyebrows and ears. Tweezed wild and miscolored brow hairs joined by sprouts of ear hairs soon joined the whiskers and shaving cream littering the bathroom sink. He slathered whitening toothpaste, which tasted like baking soda, onto the toothbrush and challenged the remaining enamel on his teeth for several minutes, spitting into the already trashed up sink before washing it all down at once. Slicking back his hair with a bit of styling creme and dabbing on his favorite Calvin Klein cologne completed the primping. Running out of time, he grabbed his new slate-blue suit, the crisp white shirt he adorned with mother-of-pearl cufflinks mounted inside solid silver square frames, a burgundy silk tie threaded by angled white stitching, burgundy socks, and matching bourbon-colored Italian leather belt and shoes.

After one last check in the full-length mirror, he bolted out the front door. He hopped into his aging Cadillac, saying out loud, "Alright, Ms. Pearl. The sales rep's keesters have lined up for my golden kick. Let's not keep the supreme Mr. Bodine waiting."

<hr />

Honoring his promise to Bodine, Murdock bounded up the steps at the main entrance of Eye Cue Technologies at precisely 8:45 a.m. Monday morning. He smiled at his first encounter, relieved Gina Morgan, the receptionist, remained in the fold.

"Welcome back, Chase," Gina beamed, extending her hand. "We're all excited about your return. Mr. Bodine requested you see him right away. He's in the conference room."

Gina's face, hands, and entire body were slimmer. She flashed a trendy short hairdo of highlighted chestnut brown hair, enhanced by minimal make-up. His gawking located a prominent tan line on her left ring finger where a wedding ring formerly resided. Intrigued, he added a mental task for learning what prompted her striking makeover.

"Thanks, Gina, you look terrific," was all he could utter for an answer.

When he opened the conference room door, a throng of employees yelled, "Surprise!" Humbled by the welcoming, tears filled his eyes. Drying his eyes as he regained his composure, he observed the room brimmed with his former co-workers to kick-start his new beginning. Their warm fellowship toward him permeated the room, offering his nerves a welcome rest. Humbled by all the attention, he produced a sheepish smile, uttering under his breath, "Oh boy, I'll get you for this, Bo."

Bodine, standing off to the side, sent him a royal highness wave. "Welcome home, Chaser. Just thought we'd make it official by giving you an informal re-meet and re-greet. It's not too early for a little celebratory cake, is it?"

As if on cue, everyone stared at him. His smile dropped, replaced by wide eyes atop a long face, knowing they were expecting a speech. After a nervous giggle, he spoke up, "I sincerely appreciate everyone here making me feel so at home, but I can't take the job."

The chatter ceased. All attendees, above all, his target, Bodine, expressed utter disbelief on their faces. He held back a laugh when the silence suffocated the frivolity. After an awkward pause, he said, "JFWY…. You know, 'Just fucking with ya.' Now quit wasting valuable company time, folks. Get back to work." Laughter shattered the silence as each employee filed by to shake his hand, hug him, or pat him on the back.

Bodine approached him last, shaking his head in mock disgust. His new boss pointed his middle finger at him shielded by their handshake, "You've got major brass huevos, Chaser. Even I didn't see that one coming. I don't know whether I should kiss you on the lips to start a rumor or simply chalk it up as Murdock madness."

"Hah! That'll teach you to make me a spectacle. Seriously, though, I can't thank you enough for bringing me back. It seems almost everybody is still here. Bottom line, I am raring to go on a full tank at high speed." He paused, feeling his throat tighten again from emotion. *In the last few hours, I've journeyed through a hellish nightmare, then smack into Bo giving me another chance.*

Spotting Murdock's eyes well up again, Bodine broke a smile, "Excellent, just keep your twisted sense of the absurd under wraps at least until we get you re-oriented. Before we start talking shop, visit Brenda King in HR." Murdock raised his eyebrows, surprised at hearing the former widow-maker's name. "Yeah, she is still here guarding your papers for signature on the dotted line, so to speak."

He nodded, shaking Bodine's hand. Before heading for King's office, he asked, "Oh yeah, what about Gina Morgan? What the hell brought her butterfly out of the chubby larva I remember?"

Bodine let out a loud guffaw, "Long story. Her self-esteem is on a steep rise. She's dating the very handsome, soon-to-be wealthy son of one of our new investors. So, don't go getting any ideas. Besides, she's way too young for you, no offense." Murdock bristled at the reality check as he headed for the HR office.

King brandished a broad grin followed by a cute sigh when she spotted him. "Oh Chase, I'm so happy you're back," she gushed. "This place would never have been the same without you."

He grinned at King, warmed by her unchanged frumpiness and bland attire. "Well, if you make me sit through another new hire orientation, I may take a long bathroom break."

"Not so fast, Chase, that won't be necessary. Just sign the requisite tax forms, and of course, your new contract. I'll bring you the other benefit forms later today."

She laid the contract in front of him. He studied each page with precision until he spotted the hidden treasures. There they were, the magic words describing his stock options, fully vested on date of contract signature. After several minutes more, he looked up, staring at King with eyes glazed and mouth open.

"Vice President of Sales?" he crooned. "And a 30% increase in base pay over what I got before? Plus commission, potential bonuses, *even* vested stock options day one in the Executive Benefit Package?"

"It's all accurate, Chase. Mr. Bodine spent hours with me making sure you got the package he feels you deserve".

"Well I could kiss you, Brenda, but I know you'd have me written up before I could find my office. I guess I'll have to go kiss Bo." King started laughing, but this time unfettered, accompanied by a sideshow from her leftover pudgy midsection shaking like a Jell-O mold. Recalling her stoic behavior before Donnelly died, he never heard her belt out a full-blown belly laugh, ever. Through his own chuckling, he thanked her, departing with her still giggling. Brenda confirmed his inkling. The office culture had shifted toward a more positive vibe than he remembered.

Entering Bodine's office, he closed the door before he approached the new President's desk. Bodine gave him a sly grin but said nothing. "Bo, I feel like such a schmuck for what I did in the conference room. This compensation package is beyond generous. I'm blown away you would…"

Bodine cut him off, raising his hand. "You're not being compensated because of the crushing hell you've been through personally. That package is purely my vote of confidence in your abilities plus me knowing I got the right man for the job. On a personal level, I love you like a brother. A much older brother, true, but a brother, nonetheless."

They both smiled at the smack. Murdock took comfort in validating his new boss kept the former light atmosphere between them. With a deep breath, he swore lifelong reciprocation for Bo's limitless kindness and friendship with his version of the same.

Bodine continued, "But on a professional level, I can't imagine anyone filling this position who matches your talent or qualifications. You deserve this, Chaser. As such, it's best you understand I'll be riding you hard. It won't be easy turning things around here. I'm counting on you kicking ass and taking many names on massive purchase orders. That's why you were the only choice for me."

Overcome with gratitude, Murdock's throat knotted. His eyes reddened. He quashed the urge to hug Bodine fearing he might start bawling. Not a good impression for his first day back on the job. Instead, he offered his hand to the man who rendered him a restored life with renewed purpose. With his lower lip trembling, all he could whisper was, "Thank you so much, man."

He walked toward the door. Bodine shouted, "Make me proud, Chaser." He wheeled around, giving Bo two thumbs up, still unable to articulate a thing.

While walking toward his office, his mind took off in high gear. Eye Cue required a promotion campaign, one which would grandstand their new President in the limelight. Murdock made his top goal to educate the business sector how Eye Cue would bounce back stronger than ever under Bodine's visionary guidance. Their stock had taken a beating in the weeks following the death of their former president, Bob Donnelly. Industry peers knew Donnelly as a capable administrator but mediocre leader. His reluctance for travel compounded by his stagnant leadership with the reps hindered the company's growth potential. In general, he rode on the coattails of the tenacious Bodine's marketing talent. Bodine loved business travel, showing little or no tolerance for the weaker reps. Where Donnelly preferred a passive approach, Bodine's persona used the in-your-face manager tactic. The reps respected yet feared him. Murdock resolved to inform the business world, especially Wall Street, how the revitalized Eye Cue emerged back on track, headed in the right direction, run by a forward-thinking leader. In fact, he would present a campaign leaving industry leaders feeling behind the 8-ball, wondering how they missed Bodine's rise.

Besides, Murdock reasoned, Bodine possessed a natural panache conducive to ad campaigns, unlike Bob Donnelly or any other pasty-faced, balding, out-of-shape executives openly avoiding the spotlight or asserting their prominence. Bodine carried a striking, leading man's appearance with thick, pitch-black hair and espresso-brown eyes, exuding a dynamic persona which attracted people. Murdock counted on Bodine's engaging personality coupled with his keen sense of Eye Cue's business to entice both industry frontrunners and the general public. Anyone around Bodine recognized his full embrace for the aggressive, talented top executive role, essential for Eye Cue restoring their industry frontrunner status.

He leaned back in his chair, muttering the last rationale piece a tad above a whisper, "No, my doing an effective job in publicizing the charismatic Bodine within the business community will not be a stretch. It will be a cinch positioning Bodine's image center stage as the new face of the company. Bedwetting competitors beware!"

Murdock's promotional strategy kept racing through his mind, too fast for his typing fingers to keep up. He was grinning like an idiot.

CHAPTER 3

BACK IN THE SADDLE

Murdock zipped through listing bullet points from his Eye Cue marketing plan starring its dashing President. He held the belief how basic, even easy, the anticipated project implementation would manifest. In turn, Eye Cue would reap dual outcomes, splendid sales results and a sorely needed new image. He sensed its success from head to toe, which increased his impatience toward getting the ads live.

Richard "Bo" Bodine represented the consummate professional. Exhibiting striking features, skillful articulation, sincere, meaningful responses during questioning, and a bullet-speed wit, Eye Cue's President supplied the ideal focus for compelling marketing copy in brochures, even more dramatic on live media. Murdock's enthusiasm generated the steam he needed for planting the campaign rollout's rough draft on Bodine's desk by his third day on the job.

After he finished enough notes for a jumpstart the following morning, he set out on a full office tour, including the warehouse. Garnering employee support, a vital ingredient in meeting Bodine's future expectations, mandated he relearn the current facility layout. Also, it opened an opportunity for meeting new hires while greeting former cohorts.

Noticing the same worn flooring and drab wall decor, he mumbled, "This place could use a facelift. But first things first. Gotta get Bo on the launching pad before I start whining about our lack of feng shui in the office."

He peeked into the office adjacent to his own. A large framed, middle-aged man, gray hair trimming the sides and back of his head, stood up, and put on his thin, silver framed glasses. Murdock extended his hand, "Hello, I'm Chase Murdock. I don't believe we've met."

"Mr. Murdock, I'm Rex Sullivan, your new Sales Manager. It's code for righthand man," Sullivan chuckled. "I am so happy meeting you finally after hearing so much about you. Please have a seat."

"Right-hand man? I don't understand."

"Yes, sir. Mr. Bodine hired me as the Sales Manager under your direction. It's my understanding this is a new position in the company. The job requires I be at your disposal whether you are in or out of the office. Also, I'll be assisting you in running projects or assignments as smooth as possible," Sullivan paused, lowering his voice, "so I earn my pay, which then gives my landlord no reason for changing the door locks." He smirked at his new boss.

"I'll be damned," Murdock snickered. "Bo never said anything about me having a sales manager. Well, so nice having you on board, Rex. We definitely will work together to keep your landlord at bay."

Bodine came out, saw the two men talking, and hurried over to Sullivan's desk. "Chaser, I forgot to introduce you and Rex. He attended your welcome party this morning where you nearly gave us all a heart attack, so I spaced the new folks' introductions." Everyone chuckled. "Rex was hired as the sales manager, an extension of you badgering reps for business, keeping things flowing internally while you're out of the office, and acting as inside sales manager supporting your VP duties. A rather supercharged man-Friday, if you will, complete with manager's authority over the reps to maintain our business flow. His resume reads like a road map for successful sales strategies capped off by supervisory and admin experience."

"What an unexpected luxury, Bo, *and* very much appreciated. Rex, I welcome your expertise in all areas. I think the first order of business is assigning Rex a nickname or two to get his feet wet. How about Casual Rex?" Bodine and Sullivan busted up.

Bodine countered, "Considering the competition we're up against, what do you think of Unprotected Rex?" More cackles followed. Murdock caught Sullivan's playful expression, an indication the new manager enjoyed the repartee his bosses shared.

Murdock added, "I know… when he raises hell among the reps, he'll become Unsafe Rex. When everything is going well, we'll call him Consensual Rex. The man will have many moods bringing forth many names, depending on how business is going. Consider this an element in your job security, Safe Rex." All three laughed as Bodine excused himself back to his office.

"I'm pleased you're on the A-team with Bodine and me, Rex. As soon as I get re-acclimated with the sales and marketing reports, we'll meet to talk about priorities."

Sullivan smiled, offering another handshake, "Whenever you're ready, Boss." Before Murdock exited the door, his man-gift from Bodine resumed his work on the computer.

Murdock glanced over his shoulder, assuring Sullivan, "No need to call me Boss, Rex. There's only one boss here, but it ain't me. Chase will be fine, thanks." Sullivan nodded in the affirmative.

He stopped just outside his office, eyeing his gold nameplate. The first line read, "Vice President of Sales," followed by a fancy-lettered, all caps, "CHASE MURDOCK." He closed the door, took a seat at his desk, then swiveled his chair until he faced the back wall, preventing any passersby eye contact. Eliminating the distraction from his office window, which overlooked the main floor, afforded him time in assembling his thoughts about his first day on the job. Resting both elbows on the luxurious African Blackwood credenza against the wall, he brought his hands up to support both sides of his jaw. He closed his eyes, slowing his racing thoughts. The day's euphoric musings oozed out, replaced by a flashback to his chilling nightmare during the wee morning hours. He relived the pain at seeing Donna's face gazing at him, pleading he join her. He shuddered as the scene in his mind diminished. Simply recognizing his location, occupying the Eye Cue Vice President of Sales office, curtained the punishing past from his view. Combing through the marketing plan stages, he detected ample signs his future workdays would consume most of his waking hours.

He shifted gears. Knowing Donna's memory might hit him without warning, he imagined himself on a mountain top under a warm sun, dancing while lip-syncing Donna Summer's

"I Will Survive." He swung his chair back around so fast he went sliding into the desk, whacking his kneecap on the drawer he left open. A loud pitched "Son-of-a-bitch, shit" exited his vocal cords. Catching his slip, he peeked through the office window where he counted five people gaping at him from the main floor. His face flushed bright red. He waved at everyone, squinting above a giant grin. Yep, he was back. He sucked up the blazing pain in his knee by reaching for the reports Sullivan stacked on his desk.

After a few moments passed, his cell phone rang. Still massaging his knee, he picked up the phone to the voice of Kevin Alvarez, Donna's oldest son, "Hey Chase, it's Kevin. I'm checking in to see how you're doing."

Remorse flooded his mind. He couldn't remember the last time he spoke with Kevin or his younger brother, John, whom he considered the sons he never had. No doubt they missed her as much as he did. He gritted his teeth at his thoughtlessness, smiled broadly, and sputtered, "Kevin, my boy, how's the head of the Alvarez clan holding up?"

"Well, I needed proof you were okay. Since Mom's been gone such a short time, I hope you're not too overwhelmed or anything. I know I'm having rough times every day. Frankly, I just wanted to hear your voice."

Murdock shook his head, recalling the well-mannered, considerate character each Alvarez brother possessed. In his mind, this call gave him further proof they regarded him as a father figure, since several years ago the Alvarez boys' father committed suicide. After their mother's brutal death, he was the only person close to their mother they knew. How could he be so insensitive? He closed his eyes, mouthing a private promise for staying connected while watching over them throughout whatever time he had left.

"You know, I'm doing ok, Kevin. I apologize I haven't called you or John on a regular basis. I've been in a whirlwind since Bo threw me a new lifeline. You won't believe this. I got my old job back at Eye Cue, except as the Vice President of Sales, including top executive benefits. As you can imagine, it came through at a perfect time. Missing your mom has been devastating for me, too. How are you guys doing?"

"That's amazing about your job, Chase. Congratulations. John and I are fine. John hesitates to call you because I think he's still having a bad time. It doesn't help that we're working through the details in settling mom's estate. But I do have good news.

Fortunately, Mom's estate more than covered all our financial needs. Also, I set aside various photos of Mom my aunt gave me. I'm sure you'll want them. Two pictures are of you and Mom." Kevin choked up on the last word.

No doubt, the pictures would trigger more pain. No matter, Murdock had to have them. During the short time he spent with Donna, why did he neglect taking phone pictures or selfies when he had the opportunity? These two photos represented the sole physical evidence he would possess of her presence in his life. His voice finally cracked, "Thanks so much, Kevin, and please thank John, too, for even thinking of me. Really, it's a wonderful gift."

Kevin sniffed. "I don't think you've met my Aunt Barbara. The last thing I remember was at Mom's house the day after she died. I mentioned to you she and my grandmother were coming over soon, but you left before they arrived."

"Your Aunt Barbara? Wait, your mother *had* a sister? Wow, the connection must not have clicked when you said her name. Whoa!"

"Hardly a surprise. She and my mom had a bad fight quite a while ago. Over what, I don't know. Mom never would talk about it, never even said her name during the last two or three years. She also kept us from mentioning her, always cutting off any reference we made. Aunt Barbara attended her memorial, but she didn't know much about you. John and I decided we wouldn't tell you about her being there either. It wasn't the time, you know?"

"Sure, I understand. I'm grateful you handled that for me. You know, Kev, I can't imagine your mother ever doing something hateful against her own sister. Did Barbara cause it?"

"I still don't know. Like I said, mom stayed completely silent on the subject. Never talked about Barbara, ever. My brother and I love our aunt. We always enjoyed being around her, even though it required our sneaking around when visiting her. Kind of strange considering how devoted they once were to each other. The frustrating thing is Aunt Barbara won't discuss their issue either, so John and I are clueless."

"It's a sad mystery for sure. So, give me the quick skinny on Barbara. Older? Younger? Married? Divorced? Kids? She's probably much less attractive than your mother, right? Maybe it's why she resented her sister so much. It would make sense if she were a borderline skank, right?"

"On the contrary, Barbara's every bit as beautiful as mom was. She's a couple years older, a bit shorter than Mom, maybe not quite as slender, divorced, and has no children. Her last name is Conley, her and Mom's maiden name. I thought it best you knew about the other woman alongside my mom in the pictures I'm giving you."

"Thank you. You boys are beyond kind giving me those pictures. I love you guys."

"Love you, too, Chase."

The wheels in his mind raced over Barbara, interrupted by a rap on his office door. Bodine walked in talking, "Lose the call. I'm taking the new kid out for lunch. Let's go."

"Kevin, I've gotta go. The boss is in my office. By the way, he's a rude, impatient prick. I'll call you after I get off work, okay? You got my curiosity up about the Barbara Conley saga."

Kevin chuckled, "Okay, Chase, anytime this evening is fine. Take care."

As soon as he hung up, Bodine pounced, "Who the hell is Barbara Conley? Chaser, you should turn down your speakerphone volume. Innocent conversations become juicy tidbits that morph into wild rumors around here overnight."

Murdock leaned toward Bodine. "Well I found out Donna had an estranged sister from a falling out long ago. I never knew she existed until just now."

Bodine raised his eyebrows then scrunched his nose. "Interesting indeed. Probably the runt of the litter, right? I mean, who could hold a candle to Donna?"

"Agreed, but her son, Kevin, has them neck-and-neck in the allure department."

"This I've gotta see," Bodine replied.

"Well, it won't happen anytime soon, Bo. I'm working through a mountain of grief, as you already know."

Bodine nodded. They headed out toward the parking lot on their quest for a lunch fix.

Bodine led Murdock to the familiar specialty burger grill across the street they frequented during their former days at Eye Cue. Bodine ordered his usual cheese-dripping, rare-grilled baconburger, then ordered Murdock's usual avocado burger covered with melted provolone, both orders with waffle fries. In between chomps, Bodine advised Murdock what he wanted accomplished in the next 3-4 weeks. Murdock interjected,

"I've already started drafting a marketing strategy targeted for delivery on your desk two days from now. I can certainly incorporate everything you've mentioned."

"Fucking A," Bodine smiled with food covering his teeth.

Murdock leaned across the table. "Lose the food on your teeth, heathen."

Back at the office, Murdock called his other best friend, Ted Zachary, to update him on current events at their favorite sports bar. "Hey Teddy, are you available for a get-together this evening at Mandrake's? Everything's changed since I last saw you."

Zachary relaxed hearing the jovial tone in his friend's voice. "Sounds great, Chase. It'll be good to catch up. See you at six."

CHAPTER 4

GETTING A TED FIX

Murdock pulled into Mandrake's, his official man den where he, Bodine, and his lifelong friend, Ted Zachary, arranged many an evening meeting to solve the world's problems. After he shut off Pearl's engine, he looked around the parking lot where cars flowed in from all sides. As he opened the car door, the people noise buzzing from inside the bar comforted him as he weaved through the incoming traffic to the entrance.

Recalling their sacred ritual, initiated through an automatic response caused by sitting down on a barstool at these gatherings, uplifted his mood. The routine included disparaging humanity while suggesting profound cure-alls, ordering multiple cocktails until serious inebriation occurred, and uninterrupted leering at the waitresses. The three amigos rated their servers' desirability by a thumbs up or down. Waiters won the scorn bucket, becoming victims from the contest judges' unapologetic, blatant gender bias display. At tip time, the group released their generosity through an unbiased lens, redeeming themselves with all the employees.

He spied Zachary sitting at the bar, wearing a new Tommy Bahama palm tree shirt with a white background, freshly shaved and looking sharp as he nursed a margarita while staring at his phone. "Zachary, party of pathetic, your table is not ready and never will be. Now get out," he said in his best announcer's voice.

Zachary spun around on his stool, "Ah, another unwelcomed intrusion, yet it's strangely good to see you, Chase."

He gave Zachary a hug before taking a seat beside him. The man deserved a full report since Donna's memorial service, his botched dirt nap plan to gulp exhaust fumes, and his subsequent rehiring at Eye Cue.

"Teddy, it is damn good to see you, my most bestest pal in the universe. It's been almost three weeks, but it feels like months."

Staring at Zachary's beaming face contrasted by his thick salt and pepper hair, Murdock choked up, his eyes reddening, as he recalled his friend assuming control the day Donna got killed. He stepped up after Murdock called him with the shocking news, handling every single thing on his behalf, including all the memorial service details. The gratitude for Zachary in his life inspired his dismissing any further verbal potshots at the man during their get together.

Zachary studied him, started to speak, stopped himself, then uttered, "You should order a drink, a stiff one, because I have to tell you something."

"Yes, immediately, Commander Zachary," he said while flagging down a waitress. He ordered a double Don Julio on the rocks then faced his friend. *This can't be good.* "Is there something wrong, Teddy?"

"Actually, the 'something' is now incredibly right, and I intend for it to stay that way." Zachary clasped his hands as he laid them on the bar, throwing a serious stare at Murdock. "I thought you should know who orchestrated your rescue at the hardware store."

A chill quivered Murdock's body as he connected the dots. How could Zachary have known anything about his intended final act before Johnny Dunne's nauseating prattle at the hardware store salvaged him? He took a long pull from his drink. His entire body shaking, he set down the glass using both hands. "Talk to me, Teddy."

Zachary drew a short breath before he continued. "I knew you were at hell's gates every moment of every day after Donna died. You were in the deepest depression I'd ever seen, so bad I feared the worst. That fear consumed me, so I started doing a little covert surveillance around your apartment. I learned about Johnny Dunne from your chronic carping about him, so I looked him up. I paid him to call me whenever he saw you coming or going. Each time you left the complex, I had him follow you. The day you headed for the hardware store, I made sure he was in your rear-view mirror. When Pearl entered the handicapped parking space, he called me. Right after he saw you with the garden hose and duct tape under your arm, he called me again. I told him to stall you as long as possible, which gave me time to call the tow truck."

Time froze as Murdock leaned back in his stool, noting his friend's intense stare still in place. As he kept his eyes on Zachary, a warm gratitude overtook him. He sucked in Zachary's words through a long, deep breath. It all made sense. Zachary's invincible call of duty in the guardian angel department facilitated his deliverance through the witless Johnny Dunne. He finished the tequila.

He opened his mouth, thinking he could speak. The full force from what he learned hit him; without his best friend's loving concern, he wouldn't be enjoying his company at Mandrake's. He would be packed inside an urn decorating his ex-wife's mantle. He inspected his empty glass. Tears filled his eyes. A wild juddering racked his body. He held his breath, stifling a wail shrill enough for Mandrake's patrons to hit the parking lot.

He forced several deep breaths, bringing back some composure. Facing his friend, he squeezed out a whisper, "You'll never know how much I love you, Teddy. What you did was the greatest gift.... I just cannot put into words...."

Zachary leaned forward, wrapped his arm around Murdock's neck, "I told you about this so you *understand* I will never stop caring about you. I'll always have your back. Look, there are many other people who like having you around, too. You can't let depression or tragedy overtake your mind. Promise me you'll scrap that thinking. Forever."

After wiping his eyes with a bar napkin, he stared into Zachary's eyes, "Deal, Teddy."

"That Johnny Dunne is a piece of work, isn't he?" Zachary asked.

"Yeah, now I'm bothered by what a shit I've been, doing everything in my power to avoid him." Murdock went pale. "Wait, you didn't tell him what my end game plan was, did you, Teddy?"

"No way. Once I determined what a simpleton he is, I just told him Donna's death threw you into major stress. I requested he make multiple call-in reports, so I knew you hadn't taken any unannounced road trips. Even though he saw what was on your shopping list, he never connected the dots."

"Thank God. Otherwise, I'd find myself new digs overnight. At least now I'll be prepared for any questions if I run into him. Tell me what I owe you for his detective work."

"Don't be ridiculous. No payback necessary, Chase. You're paid in full if you just stay among the living."

"Okay, Teddy. Let's change the subject. Answer a question for me. Did you know Donna had a sister who was at the memorial service?"

Zachary cocked his head, eyeballing the ceiling as he cupped his chin in one hand. "I didn't know she had a sister. I did notice a woman at the service who resembled her though. Quite a beauty, too. You were in no shape for making any new friends, so I didn't bother introducing myself. I just showed her to her seat."

"I'll be damned. Do you remember if she was sitting by an older lady?"

"Can't recall. I do remember thinking how attractive she was, even wondered if she was Donna's friend or relative. The entire day was a blur, so much going on. In your fragile state, I kept one eye on you at all times while playing usher."

"Well, I bet it was her. Name's Barbara Conley, Conley being her and Donna's maiden name."

Zachary had a muted smile on his face, "Well, have you met or called her?"

"No and no. I just found out she existed today after a phone call with Donna's son, Kevin. He brought up Barbara because she gave him photos of Donna she thought he and John might appreciate. Get this, both boys are sharing some of those precious photos with me. Donna never mentioned Barbara in our conversations. Kevin said they were estranged for many years. Nobody knows why because neither sister ever told anyone about their predicament."

"Intriguing," Zachary muttered. "Maybe you should meet this woman. I mean, she's quite the looker and..."

Murdock raised his hand, cutting off his friend. "My greatest love has been gone less than a month, Teddy. I don't know if I can socialize with another woman ever again, especially Donna's look-alike sister. I suppose I'll meet Barbara one day, but not anytime soon."

"Understood. I was just curious, that's all. Besides, you'll have plenty keeping your mind off anything not business related. By the way, I'll be following Bo's progress as he rights the ship at Eye Cue. I saw a newspaper article last week in the business section about his promotion. I guess I'll address him as President Bo next time I see him."

"Bo will hate that, Teddy. I think he'll do fine. The previous boss wasn't dynamic at all. He avoided confrontations, even business travel. Bodine is the exact opposite. And...," Murdock mimicked a drumroll, "he just hired me as the Vice President of Sales. Can you believe it? It happened during the fiasco at the hardware store. I called him for a ride once I realized Pearl got towed. That's when he gave me the offer on the phone, then picked me up to get Pearl at the impound lot. We discussed the details during the drive. After he finished and before I could ask a single question, he asked me to start ten days later. Between you two, I went from nearly dead into a promising future almost overnight."

"Pretty unbelievable. You landed on both feet with a dozen roses sticking out your ass. Congratulations, man. You had one helluva day." Zachary slapped him on top of his head Three Stooges style.

Murdock waved over their waitress. "Hey Teddy, looks like we have a new waitress, and I think she left her chesticles in the car." Zachary choked on his final swig giving the new hire a thumbs down. "I'm famished. Let's get some appetizers."

"Done deal," Zachary resonated.

"Please, promise me you will never use that phrase again. If you catch me using it, slap me hard. Johnny Dunne uses it constantly because it sounds like his last name."

"Oh geez, no problem, mi amigo," Zachary remarked from behind a food menu.

—◦◦◦—

Later, sitting on his bed at home, he dwelled on Zachary's shocking news. None other than Johnny Dunne, his perpetual irritant, facilitated his reprieve from the crematory's dust catcher. His best friend, Ted Zachary, masterminded the entire scheme. A few minutes before 10:00 p.m., he remembered Kevin Alvarez, and placed the call.

"Hey, Kevin. Sorry I'm calling so late. I had dinner with Ted tonight. Like with you and John, I hadn't even spoken to the man since your mom's memorial."

"Not a problem, Chase. John and I just got back from having dinner with Aunt Barbara. She gave us the box of photos I told you about. When I asked if she minded if I gave you a few, she was fine with it. And, by the way, she'd like to meet you sometime."

"You know, Kevin, it will take us a while to work through this mind-numbing sadness we all have. Until there's considerable progress on my end, I can't meet Barbara. Please tell her thanks for the pics. I would like to meet her, too, eventually. Tell her I sincerely hope she understands."

"She does and is in no hurry. She loves the fact you, John, and I have bonded. Maybe she's lonely, though. Since mom's gone, I get the feeling Barbara wants more involvement in our lives."

"Makes perfect sense, Kevin. So, tell me, how could a woman as lovely as your mother be lonely? Surely some quality gentlemen out there hit on her all the time. I can't imagine a woman with Donna's striking appearance hurting in the social activity area. Kevin, is your aunt personality challenged or does she harbor contempt for men since her divorce?"

Kevin giggled. "No, no, nothing like that, Chase. I remember Mom was like that, too, after Dad died. When we were kids, she and mom were always the party queens, keeping things hopping with their fun personalities. Aunt Barbara's bright, witty, and has a wicked sense of humor. She's still friendly with her ex-husband, Will, who I still consider my uncle. Great guy. They just decided they couldn't live together. It happens."

Murdock recalled Donna describing her disinterest in dating before she met him, how he felt about her story. He had reacted the same way with Donna as the feeling he got from Kevin's description, as if something just didn't add up. He remembered his becoming the invisible man whenever he and Donna were out in public. Men seldom acknowledged his presence the second she came into view. She illuminated every room she entered. He became accustomed running into rubbernecking men with sly smiles who couldn't take their eyes off her. She never made eye contact with the oglers; he accepted being ignored, proud he was the one she chose. Reminiscing about Donna again triggered his yearning for her, causing another sobbing episode. He gasped through the gushing tears.

"Chase, are you alright?" Kevin's voice made him realize he was still on the phone.

"I'm sorry, Kevin. I just flashed back on your mom, how proud she made me feel, how other men gawked at her no matter where we went. You know, I could have been stark naked beside her wherever we were without anyone noticing." Kevin chuckled. "She was the ultimate middle-aged head-turner. I loved her more than I can express in mere words. At the time you mentioned Barbara might be lonely, I considered her seclusion as self-imposed. But it seems to me, any woman blessed with your mother's personal characteristics who chooses seclusion must have good reason."

Kevin also choked up, then sputtered, "Mom was one in a billion, Chase. I can't imagine our lives without her. Somehow, we'll go on living. With all the stupid, violent, hateful, and destructive people in the world, her life is taken while the useless slackers continue roaming the earth. Barbara's very cool, though. John and I want her more involved with us. Every time she smiles or laughs, it's a little like being with mom again."

Meeting Donna's older sister, a woman who possessed the same qualities as the one true love he lost, seemed unfathomable. No, he required a process for grieving, like crawling under the covers every night to nurse his wounds, which so far showed little signs of healing. "Kevin, why don't we get together for dinner. Are you guys available this weekend?"

"I am. I'll make sure John is, too."

"Great. I'll text you when I figure out a spot where we can meet. Oh, by the way, don't surprise me with any special guests, okay?"

"I wouldn't spring Aunt Barbara on you like that. You both need a proper introduction down the road."

"I'm not worried you'd pull a stunt like that, Kevin. I meant another cougar conquest date. Remember, you little butthole?" His playfulness resurfaced as he retold the time he threw a birthday party for Donna. Kevin brought a Bodine discard as his date to the affair.

"Oh God, Chase, that Rachel Jordan was something else, wasn't she?"

"I never told you this, but my boss, Richard Bodine, had a one-night stand with her way before you met her. Later, they had a public falling out with an enraged Rachel giving Bo a cocktail shower. Apparently, she expected a follow-up date, which never happened because Bo was, at the time, a bed 'em and forget 'em serial womanizer. Angry words were flying loud enough so everyone inside the club could hear. They made such a scene the band held off starting their next set so they could catch what was going down. At the end, Bo strongly suggested she hop on her broom so she could fly the hell away from the Carousel."

"This happened at the Carousel?"

"Yeah, so Rachel spots me laughing as the whole deal unfolds. You can imagine she was none too happy running into me at your mom's birthday party. I give her credit, though. She kept her mouth shut at the party, although she shredded me outside near the valet stand. She didn't appreciate my comment about the cougar sightings in the area."

"Holy crap. Well I learned myself she could be a hot head. No worries, Chase. John and I prefer we spend time with you, no other distractions. Just send me that text with the location."

"Excellent. You'll hear from me soon. Take care, Kevin. Goodnight."

He obsessed about Barbara Conley. Without his courage, how could he consider enduring an introduction in the near term? Rather than an anti-social desire for isolation, his hesitance toward meeting the woman surfaced from a fear she would spark a crushing meltdown the moment he saw her versus giving her a simple, "Hello, nice to meet you."

CHAPTER 5

DIGGING IN

Walking toward his office, Murdock noticed three people standing over Rex Sullivan's desk. Sullivan waved him in. "I hope you're happy, Chase. Seems everyone is on your nickname bandwagon now that you've tagged a few on me ."

"Oh good. I thought you might have customer issues, or worse yet, a crisis. So, let me hear them."

The people crowding the office, caught wasting company time by the new VP, greeted Murdock on their way out of Sullivan's office. "Well, I'm now Group Rex or Anal Rex. My theme song is Rexual Healing. Cute, huh?"

"Consider yourself Contributor of the Day in support of Eye Cue's camaraderie culture. You're a team builder, Rexuality. We don't want no stuffy, cover-your-ass corporate attitude around here, right?"

"You made sure *that* won't happen, for which I thank you. I worried about the company culture when I took the job. My performance maintains a higher tempo in a relaxed setting rather than feeling like my undies shrink a couple sizes as the day wears on."

Murdock smirked, "Bo will not cause intentional undie contraction around here. What will keep our president mellow is grabbing market share amid rapid sales growth, reportable to the Board in the next 30-45 days. If we fail, we *will* experience the wrath from his unintentional side. So, here's your first official assignment. Please determine Ventura County's best magazines, newspapers and online media suitable for promoting our upgraded, results-oriented President. I'll start working on copy strategy. We'll worry about the rest of Southern California plus the other major markets after we create a groundswell of awareness in our own backyard. I'll create the profile on our new dynamic leader. You weren't here under the previous president. His missing-in-action reputation developed from a profoundly lackluster style of leadership compared to Bodine. Each day, his top priority required avoiding interaction with media, clients, reps, even employees whenever possible."

"I get the picture. I'm on it, Chase. You'll have a list on your desk asap."

"Oh, don't forget the advertising rates. I'll need them when I make my pitch to Bo. Hopefully, he will have the Board hand over a proper budget. Do me a favor, Rex. I prefer typed reports the old-fashioned way, labeled manila file folders holding the printed information inside."

"Done deal, Chase."

The second he heard it, Murdock recoiled. Another personal moment corrupted by Johnny Dunne when Sullivan spoke his ragtag catch phrase, "Dunne Deal."

Sullivan stiffened, perplexed by his boss's weird reaction. "What's wrong, Chase?"

"I'm fine, my well-meaning friend. Long story not worth mentioning unless you use the phrase 'Dunne deal' again. I'd appreciate this assignment becoming your top priority today." Sullivan gave him a tight-lipped nod.

Murdock excused himself back to his own office. His pitch promised Bodine a short deadline. Under the gun, he gathered all his positive spin experience for a promotion designed to catapult Bodine and Eye Cue to maximum industry prominence. The business pace still struggled. Bodine and Sullivan, both new on their respective jobs, grappled with their respective learning curves. Murdock owned this project top to bottom. He dove into the daily sales reports, making side notes. After placing the appropriate reports alongside his legal pad, he called all the sales reps around the country.

He poured a third coffee before reviewing his copious notes written on the legal pad. The reps confirmed unilateral approval during upbeat comments for his and Bodine's return to Eye Cue. He suspected the approval involved a collective relief after learning Bodine's promotion precluded his making frequent field visits. Murdock admired Bodine's balanced management style, a volatile cop persona supplanted by his more even-keeled, one-of-the-boys personality. The style kept the underachievers in the field at a minimum. He spent the remainder of the day catching up with every principal of Eye Cue's sales rep organizations. When he sank into Pearl, familiar feelings of fulfillment mixed within a mild exhaustion confirmed he resettled back in the loop.

Famished upon arriving home, Murdock hit his kitchen. He crafted a thick ham sandwich while gulping down a beer. Between sandwich bites, he prioritized the props within the steps outlined for the Bo promo. First, a splashy photo by the right pro would propel Bodine's image, superseding the black hole left by the previous president. Where Donnelly withdrew from the spotlight, Bodine thrived in it. The overweight Donnelly's flaccid, pale appearance projected a first impression caught between the *before* picture on a physical fitness poster and the *after* shot of the pudgy squealer in the movie *Deliverance*. Conversely, Bodine could be mistaken for a celebrity. His full head of black hair, dark chocolate brown eyes, brawny yet trim physique, amplified by chiseled facial features and six-foot, two-inch height made men cautious and women swoon. Bodine's personality traits featured a quick wit, a steady, positive disposition boosted by a fearless persona when confronted. The Bodine image projected rock-solid confidence without arrogance.

Working up the profile reconfirmed Murdock's choice for the perfect spotlight in the official Eye-Cue re-launch. Every bullet point he jotted down fed his enthusiasm. One of the points piqued his further attention. Most decision makers of his marketing targets were men. If the opposite gender occupied more of the ranks, Eye Cue's ad launch might reach its goal as an overnight event. Women found Bodine irresistible, a notion he saved for later consideration.

The next morning, he fast-tracked through the parking lot straight for Bodine's office, still psyched about the pitch he prepared. As President/CEO, if Bodine saw merit in the project, he would employ his direct line to the Board in budget creation for items greater than just sales promotions. Tapping on Bodine's closed office door, he let himself in. "Good morning, Chief. How's the leader of the not-so-free world doing on this fine day?"

"Hey Chaser. Another day at the salt mines. What's up?"

"I have a proposal for you, a promotional vehicle to help re-establish Eye Cue as a major player in the industry." He described his idea using ads of Bodine as the new head rooster at Eye Cue enriched by photos, a flattering profile, and the new direction for the company. "Donnelly was a near invisible President. We never came across any media folks called in for interviews or grand tours. It left Eye Cue zero opportunity for good press. We can change that situation in record time. I've got Casual Rex gathering the best industry media vehicles' ad rates. All it takes is a budget."

Bodine leaned back in his chair, eyes pointed up toward the ceiling, a blank expression on his face. He steadied his gaze on Murdock. "I like the idea, Chaser. The way I see it, you should hit the road talking up our renewed mission statement with our customers. I probably sound like a hard ass, but you'll have to perform any such promotional work on your own time. Our top priority is to play catch up. Since Donnelly's death nosedived the company into a brief tailspin, I think our sales network should receive a shot of confidence through defined direction first."

"Already on it, Bo." He handed Bodine a single sheet of paper. "Here's the outline of main discussion points. I personally called all the reps followed by the principals of their companies yesterday. What could be a better shot of confidence for our reps, employees and customers than to promote our new direction by utilizing a media splash right away? Plus, it puts our competitors on notice. The entire industry will know we, under your command, are not fucking around. Visibility through you as the dapper head of the company becomes the number one priority. I'll prepare the details remotely at home, on airplanes, even in hotel rooms, routing all the results through Conjugal Rex. The method puts us on center stage in a few days. Just earmark some funding for me. I'll make it happen, Bo."

"Okay, let's do it. Give me a day or two. I'll figure out what we can afford. In the meantime, quit fucking around. Go sell something."

He glanced at his watch, astonished two hours passed since he left Bodine's office, not the few minutes he assumed. Bodine strolled in wearing smiling eyes, "Okay, I scrounged up a couple grand for the promo piece. I even drained our petty cash. At least, it's a start."

"Did you really just say 'a couple grand'? That's it? May I remind you, your Bo-nificense, Southern California is the hotbed of advertising. I'd estimate it's a tad more expensive than rates we might find in, say, Monkey's Eyebrow, Kentucky. And yes, Monkey's Eyebrow is for real. One of the reps drove me through the town. Alright then. I'll show you my notes for Plan B."

He shuffled some papers until he found a mock outline he worked up on a lark while getting motivated for the task. "Ah, here it is. Serial womanizer, Richard 'Bo' Bodine, was promoted to President/CEO of Eye Cue Technologies due to the untimely death of their previous President, Bob Donnelly. While Donnelly's porn addiction may have caused his premature demise, Bodine prefers the real deal. His deviant behavior earned him the prized moniker of The Skank Whisperer. He's rung so many women's bells, it forced continual replacements of the notch-worn dashboards in his cars. Bodine weathered the occasional cocktail shower he experienced when women assumed they deserved a second date. In his quest to bed the maximum number of skanks possible, several condom brands solicited him as their spokesman. Currently leading a more responsible lifestyle, Bodine settled into a somewhat committed relationship shared by the striking Doctor Jenna Talia, a woman sporting a rack so bodacious she could start a chain of retail stores specializing in spices. Shall I continue?"

Bodine let out a wild laugh, pointing both middle fingers in the air. "You are such a righteous asshole. Okay, I get it. It's not enough. Things are tight right now, Chaser, so I…"

"Hold up there, let's check out what the Unsafe one can add before we continue down this path." He dialed Sullivan's extension. "Casual Rex, would you please join us for a moment in my office?" Sullivan arrived at his door as he set the phone in its cradle. "Ah, welcome, my Unprotected friend. Please inform Mr. Bodine of the advertising budget the media visibility project entails."

Sullivan paused, eyes wide sensing a setup, "Well, I found about a half dozen viable sources. A couple of trade magazines, notably Consumer Electronics Daily, a Ventura County monthly magazine, and two online sites targeting local business. For a modest additional fee, the online sites will give us national exposure."

"Good work, Rexuality. What kind of a budget do these vehicles demand on a one-shot basis?"

"Getting the right scale, meaning four-color plus a full page or screen shot, without the national fees, I'd say somewhere between seven and ten thousand dollars."

Bodine slumped in his chair, a scowl on his face. "Okay, you both know this requires Board of Directors approval. I'll request a market development budget in the range you suggested."

Murdock rolled his eyes. He stood up facing Bodine, underscoring his next point. Sullivan, frontrunning the signal, quietly excused himself. Murdock stepped toward Bodine's desk. "Bo, don't ask them. Tell them. *Sell* them. It's not like this is a new concept. The campaign is a crucial element in re-establishing Eye Cue by getting the edge on the competition. The milquetoast days of Donnelly are over. Don't *ask* them for 7k, *tell* them we need 10k minimum. If the Board expects a sales spike sooner than later, I'm sure they'll find the money. Maybe we can check out the budget together, marking non-essential things we can cut or delay. You know, it wouldn't hurt if you nabbed a kudo from the Board after they witness your real skill in running this company. C'mon, this is easy doings for you, my most charismatic friend. Let them hear the power of Reverend Bodine. Let them feel your thunder."

Bodine rose from his chair, "Nice sales job, oh tenacious one. I believe you're right on the money, pun intended. I *will* press them hard by releasing some of the thunder. You're right, I've been holding back. We do indeed have a new direction. We'll give every damn business involved in our industry the flashing yellow caution light. Always a winning tactic to keep the rivals off balance."

Murdock whispered, "Magnificent One, so grateful you returned from the crypt."

A re-energized Bodine spoke, "Stand up, peasant. Get a photographer in here asap. You and Random Rex fine tune your copy. I'll mark up a copy of the budget where I think we have some wiggle room. Be ready in an hour for a strategy session. I'm not walking into a Board meeting emptyhanded. By the way, plan on being my date. Two heads and all that."

Murdock retorted, "Thank you for the privilege, Your Grace. Perhaps you should warn the members of my unpredictability. I'd like them feeling a morsel of trepidation."

CHAPTER 6

SALES PITCH

With the Board member meeting scheduled for 10 a.m., Murdock and Bodine took a walk a few minutes early over to the Eye Cue conference room. Expecting a full house, each carried a half dozen handouts supporting their case, both displaying their mutual confidence as they stepped into the room.

"Hey, why don't we..." Murdock stopped as he watched Bodine's eyes widen in surprise, if not shock. He turned his head in the direction of Bodine's stare. He spotted one person in the room, a striking forty-something woman, smartly dressed, long, chestnut hair, and makeup spotlighting her beauty. Her shamrock green eyes perched above her high cheekbones and symmetrical nose. A stylish pair of Chanel glasses complemented her elegance. *This woman may be a former beauty queen.*

"Well... hello, Nadine," Bodine said as he turned toward her. He cleared his throat, smiled and continued, "This is Chase Murdock, my new VP of Sales. Chase, this is Nadine Curtis. She's one of the Board directors. Where is everybody?"

Sensing the tension, a grinning Murdock gently shook Curtis's hand.

Curtis returned his smile, "Pleasure, Mr. Murdock," then turned toward Bodine after losing the smile. "Bo, you don't get the A team until I hear you out first, assuming I'm convinced your proposal has merit." She ended with a smile and a wink at Bodine.

Murdock raised his eyebrows. *I knew it. They've shared bedsheets during their business association. This prior relationship could work to our advantage if Bo didn't kick her to the curb like the rest of his roadkill. Oh crap, he can't keep eye contact. Probably lost his confidence.*

Murdock stepped in, "Ms. Curtis, we respectfully request the Board's approval for a modest budget so we can embark on the essential promotion of Eye Cue using our industry media; a re-launching, if you will, advising our business rivals there's a new, improved leader at the helm. The previous president had no visibility or presence outside this office. As a result, the company lacked any kind of dynamic reputation or growth. With Mr. Bodine now in charge, we have a leader who can make our existing accounts, as well as new and potential ones, sit up and take notice. By focusing on Mr. Bodine in the promotion, we deliver our competition a strong message showing we're not sitting on our hands waiting for the phones to ring or the e-mails to pour in."

The blank look on Curtis's face told him she was not impressed. He groped for a Plan B.

Bodine sat upright in his chair, projecting renewed confidence in his manner as he locked eyes with Curtis. "Nadine, this isn't about some trumped-up dog and pony show. Eye Cue must diversify, pull away from the bandwagon approach so many companies in this business have lapsed into. We'll lead the way, introducing not just new products, but entire new product categories. We'll escape Donnelly's status quo approach for simply more of the same thing we've offered for years. You know, Nadine, I don't know why they picked you as the gatekeeper here since we had a personal relationship at one time. Maybe you made it known to them I was a scoundrel, or even worse. Perhaps they thought you'd be the perfect foil, so I would retreat to my office, whimpering with my tail between my legs. It's important to all of us here you understand our motive. The way Chase and I see it, Eye Cue will rise from the ashes, so to speak, by generating more meaningful revenue plus a cutting-edge reputation. All we're requesting is ten thousand dollars for funding the kickstart. If we don't deliver a noticeable increase in business within 90 days, I would expect the Board to react accordingly, maybe hitting my compensation, *and only my compensation*, with the cost of the expenditures."

A palpable silence engulfed the room. Bodine held a riveting gaze at Curtis until she relented by breaking the stare-down. She picked up the handout, reviewing the bullet points Murdock prepared.

Several long, silent minutes passed before she took her high-end glasses off and set them down on the table. "You know, Bo, you weren't very nice to me," she jeered. "*Yes, I volunteered* for this meeting because I wanted to see you squirm a little." She sighed with annoyance, bringing back a more amiable tone. "But it's clear you have a deep conviction in turning around the company. I'm surprised your proposal is so reasonable. So, I will inform the other Board members you're not such a self-absorbed prick after all."

Murdock couldn't contain himself, bursting into laughter, taking the opportunity to pile on. "And here I thought *I* was the only one who knew Bo that well."

Both Curtis and Bodine laughed hard. Although it took what seemed an eternity, he scored the ice-melting one-liner.

Curtis stood up, then gathered her things. "OK boys, I'll see what I can do."

All three exchanged farewell handshakes. As she pivoted, leaving the room at a brisk pace, her stunning figure awoke Murdock's man juices. She possessed all his favorite features, tall, slender, and well-endowed. Bo may have earned his reputation as the 'The Skank Whisperer,' but Curtis was lightyears from skankdom.

When the door closed behind her, he threw a bear hug around Bodine, "I've never been so fucking proud of you in my entire life. Just when I thought you would wet the bed and soak the carpet, you rallied. You certainly impressed the hell out of Nadine even though she came in here hating your guts. That was white hot shit, Bo."

Bodine put on a muted smile, "Thanks, Chaser. But it ain't over until that stone fox sings. We need her coming back with the right answer. Let's get some work done while we wait for her call. Hopefully, it'll be later today."

"Well, they've got nothing to lose with your ballsy impromptu guarantee, so I'm thinking you nailed it."

He stopped at Sullivan's office after leaving the conference room. "Hey Chase, how'd it go?"

"We don't know just yet, but you and I are going to proceed as if the stony fox has sung in the affirmative." Sullivan squinted, cocking his head with a question mark hanging over it. "That was a Bo-ism describing the woman who made us sweat bullets in the conference room. But no matter. Find a good pro photographer and set up an appointment with them here. I'll make sure Bo wears a *Hollywood Nights* suit for the shoot. Also, contact the three or four strongest media concerns you tracked down. Have them call me for an appointment asap. I'll start working on a press release."

"Done deal, Chase."

His head spun in disgust. "If I hear that phrase one more time, you'll be on permanent probation." He then smiled, giving Sullivan a wink. "Let me give you the backstory. I have a twit of a neighbor whose last name is Dunne, D-U-N-N-E. He says 'Dunne deal' to me ad nauseum, thinking it's the cleverest thing anyone ever thought of. So, you see, my Rexually unenlightened friend, I cringe every time I hear anyone utter it." He almost made the mistake of telling Sullivan how Dunne saved his life. Sullivan nodded, smiled, made a zip-the-lip sign but said nothing. "Good, we're on the same page then." Sullivan saluted as Murdock left for his own office.

As he looked at his watch for the twentieth time even though a mere hour had passed, he obsessed on when or if Bodine received word from the Board on their proposal. At 4:30 pm, his phone rang, the receptionist saying a Ms. Curtis was on the line.

"Hello, Ms. Curtis, this is Chase Murdock."

"Hello, Chase. I hope Bo and I didn't get too personal during the meeting this morning. I didn't know you'd be taking part, and he did lay things out in the open."

"It's okay, Ms. Curtis. Things said between folks are their business, not mine."

"Please, call me Nadine."

"Sure thing, Nadine. I'd like to share something with you. Knowing Bo over many years, I can say with certainty he's a changed man. He's serious about his new position. Honestly, his personal life has become quite stable, more focused than in the past. He's even involved in a committed relationship if you can believe it."

"I can't, but that's beside the point. The Board requested you have a follow-up promotional plan in place. I just sent Bo an e-mail approving the ten grand. You should know, if your plan bears fruit within 60, not 90, days, we will follow it up with another ten. We think you're onto something."

"Well, hot shit, er, I mean hot spit, Nadine. Great news." Curtis giggled at the slip.

Without warning, Bodine threw his office door open, bellowing, "The ice lady came through, Chaser. Whoever's on the phone, tell them you'll call them back."

Murdock put his index finger against his lips, a futile attempt in silencing Bodine. He shook his head recognizing the damage had already been done.

Having heard every word of Bodine's outburst, Curtis hissed, "Ice lady, huh? Tell that smartass rooster we weren't going to consider docking his pay if the promo plan doesn't fly, but after his undeserved smack, all bets are off now. Goodbye, Chase."

He looked at Bodine then closed his eyes as he set the phone down. "That was the ice lady herself on the phone, and yes, she heard the exact phrase you used to reference her. You just lost your get-out-of-jail free card with that crack."

"What get-out-of-jail free card?"

"The one that said you don't have to cover the damages if the promo fails."

CHAPTER 7

A BREAK IN THE ACTION

"You know, Bo, if I am on the phone when you walk in, *do not talk to me out loud.* Your 'Ice Lady' rip may have just hammered the coffin nail on our proposal per your former, very nasty paramour." Murdock squinted his eyes at Bodine for emphasis.

"It was a mild faux pas, Chaser. However, I will admit I'm sometimes infected by the Dumbass Virus. By the way, Ice Lady is her nickname among all employees, including the Board. Believe me, she knows all about it. Let's hit Mandrake's tonight to celebrate. Invite Consensual Rex, too."

Murdock liked the idea of Sullivan joining them at Mandrake's. He appreciated Sullivan's sense of urgency, which boosted his trust in the man's abilities. He recognized Eye Cue had reached a crucial stage in its rebirth where saving time came at the expense of strategy meetings. The quicker he became more dependent on Sullivan, the faster they could produce the campaign. More than acknowledging Sullivan as an executive team member, he desired a unified bond between them as the basis for their mutual success. He would focus on learning more about his righthand man at the celebration.

He stuck his head inside Sullivan's office. "Cocktails on the boss man at Mandrake's after work. You in?"

"I was just thinking how great a cold one might taste after dealing with all these media vultures today. Thanks, and hell yes, I'm in. Oh, we have three of said vultures scheduled to be here tomorrow."

"You just put a damper on my swilling activity this evening, unsafe one. Can't be showing up hungover before such an important task as vulture interaction."

The three formed a caravan to Mandrake's. Happy Hour, still in full swing when they arrived, kept the place jumping. Sullivan said in a loud voice, "I haven't been here in ages. Can't believe the scenery hasn't changed. I often took my old girlfriend here years ago."

"I knew I'd seen you somewhere before. This place became Bo's and my haunt long ago. In fact, Bo met his current squeeze here." As soon as the words were out of his mouth, Dr. Jenna 'Talia' Gorman made her entrance.

Not knowing who she was, Sullivan's gaze locked in on the voluptuous beauty, his mouth agape, his tongue threatening full exposure. Gorman sported a very low-cut, tight-fitting black blouse exposing a minimum three inches of her protruding cleavage. "Will you look at the front porch on that. How can a woman with such an exquisite rack have such a slender waist? They must be bolt-ons."

Bodine stood, cleared his throat, grinning as he tossed a side glance at Sullivan. He opened his arms for a hug, saying "Hey baby," before planting an eyes-closed kiss on the woman in question. Gorman also hugged Murdock, smiling as she looked at Sullivan, who had difficulty finding his line of sight. "Jenna, this is Rex Sullivan, our new sales manager. He works for Chaser. Oh, he suspects you've had some work done."

Mortified, a bright crimson crept over Sullivan's face. He stammered, "Now Bo, wait, I uh..." He stood facing Bodine's significant other, incapable of cobbling together the right words for damage control. Murdock howled while Bodine chuckled at Sullivan's baptism by fire.

Gorman's playful spirit kicked in. "Oh, my pleasure, Rex. You must have a keen eye since you spotted my nose job. Hey, I'm also thinking of having a breast reduction procedure. What do you think?"

Sullivan, still in shock, glanced at her abundance again. His eyes darted back to hers. Before he formulated a response, Murdock shouted, "I think I speak for all of us when I say, no fucking way will you desecrate that bodacious bounty." All four cracked up, Sullivan's face recovering its natural color.

Murdock signaled their waitress to take a drink order from the new arrival.

By inviting Gorman, Bodine made it clear the shop talk should be minimal. "Glad you could join us, baby. How's work been?"

Gorman rolled her eyes. "You'd think some of these women, knowing they will bare their lotus patches during an exam, would tidy up a bit down there, right? Maybe I should buy a couple of HAZMAT suits for the office. I could give the offenders skull and crossbones sticky labels for their belly."

Bodine and Murdock roared, laughing in unison. Murdock elbowed Bodine, directing him toward Sullivan staring at the floor stifling a laugh. "Apparently, Random Rex never experienced the company of such a modern woman," Murdock whispered.

The laughter brought Sullivan back in the conversation. Still in awkward mode, he blurted, "Jenna, what exactly is your profession?"

"Stench management. Sometimes it stinks, but the money's good."

Murdock choked down a laugh, offering clarification. "Rexuality, you are in the presence of the esteemed Dr. Jenna 'Talia' Gorman, OBGYN. She's one of the least uptight doctors you will ever meet."

Gorman smiled, gifting Murdock a peck on the cheek. He swore if Bodine ever did her wrong... then caught himself. Bodine played a major part saving his life. The act alone kept all his character flaws immune from Murdock's judgement. He hoped Bodine recognized Talia as the perfect partner for him.

Sullivan chuckled as the others gazed over his way. "I'm assuming Talia is not your middle name. I don't even have to ask you who coined it."

"Oh no," Gorman deadpanned. "My real middle name is Rose, but I like how Chase created Talia. It better suits my line of work, doncha think?" Everybody giggled.

After musing, Murdock jumped in, "Let's talk a little biz before we get too inebriated, folks. Tomorrow we are scheduled for three media reps along with a photographer to shape Bo into the perfect image of the industry stallion he is. Sullivan can handle the reps while Bo sits pretty in the shoot. Bo, wear your most dynamic, studly suit. Use just the right power tie nestled on a dark colored shirt. No white shirt. Remember, white shirts with a side of bland carried the Donnelly brand." Bodine nodded.

Talia added, "Don't worry, Chase. I'll handle the quality control. As for you, Mr. Bodine, it's safe to assume you'll have to appear relaxed. I'll make it happen with a little cooperation from you tonight, definitely in the morning. Of course, I am talking about a healthy dinner and breakfast." She smiled with a wink at the group, noticing Murdock and Sullivan both required drool checks.

Talia's tantalizing charm often conjured up Murdock's memories of Donna. A twinge of sadness pierced his heart. He continued, "T-Rex, grind the media reps, bring us a better deal before I meet with them. Tell them we're considering a follow-up campaign, so they best sharpen their pencils. I have a quasi-commitment from the Board for additional funding. Make these reps understand the first round must be a homerun, generating instant measurable results. It's the only way we obtain further commitments from the Board. "

"On it, Chase," Sullivan confirmed.

"Well at least you didn't say the forbidden 'd-d' phrase. Thanks for remembering." Gorman took a restroom break when Sullivan got a phone call. As soon as she was out of earshot, Murdock addressed Bodine. "So, what's the progress report on you two? You've been exclusive quite a while. Bo, in my most humble opinion, she's a keeper with a capital K."

"Yeah, she sure is. She's kept me out of the bars, gave me some much-needed stability in my life. It's just...," he paused, "she wants a kid." Bodine gave Murdock a solemn glance, "I can't imagine fatherhood at this stage of the game. Besides, after my first marriage went south, I swore I'd never fall so hard for a woman again. Still, I can't imagine my life without Jenna in it, so I'm kind of at a crossroads. It's probably why I seem so distracted lately. I'm in the midst of soul searching, you know, in between my past experiences and my knowing she is the one."

"So glad she's the one. You know, before I met Donna, I believed I would spend the rest of my days alone drinking beer, pretending all the internet porn babes made up my personal harem. I never knew I could feel so empty. At the risk of sounding melodramatic, Donna renewed me. Even though I didn't have her very long, I never imagined such a profound love with someone. I'll always be grateful for every second we spent together."

It dawned on him Sullivan's phone call had ended. He and Bodine were discussing some very personal information in front of a man whom both of them barely knew. "Sorry we entered the way-too-personal realm in your presence, Rex. Oh hey, here comes the Doctor, so we'll spare you any additional discomfort." He was deliberate in calling Sullivan by his actual name.

"No apology necessary, Chase. I'd just like the backstory on both of you some day. I'll be happy to share mine. Should only take about three or four sentences." Murdock grinned, giving him a quick nod, valuing him more by the minute.

Gorman took her seat, "What backstory? What did I miss?"

Bodine smirked at her, "You didn't miss a thing you don't already know, baby. We were lamenting Chaser's loss of Donna plus talking about how lucky I am having you to love."

Gorman always had a quip or humorous retort at the ready. This time, her expression softened. She glanced at each of the men, then focused on Bodine, a tear in her eye. "No, baby, I'm the lucky one. Being with you makes me happier each day, more than I deserve." She took Bodine's face in her hands. Showing visible tenderness, she kissed him.

Murdock barked, breaking the tension. "Is there a preacher in the house?" He turned to Sullivan. "Had enough personal shit this evening, Rexuality? Now it will be impossible for me to put you on probation."

Sullivan smiled "I guess I'll consider that a fringe benefit."

CHAPTER 8

GAME ON

Murdock strolled into the office at 7:30 a.m. The reception area appeared crowded with media participants for the Eye Cue promotional session scheduled at 8:00 a.m. He sped through the lobby without acknowledging anyone's existence, curious why all the media reps showed up so early.

Before they left Mandrake's the prior night, he and Sullivan agreed upon wearing power ensembles, a first impression tactic to school the media reps on their inferiority against the Eye Cue team. He spotted his righthand man dressed in a sharp black suit, white cufflinked shirt, and bold royal blue silk tie. Nearing Bodine's office, he glanced at his own navy-blue suit, white cufflinked shirt, and crimson red silk tie. Murdock saw Bodine in full primp mode near the front of his desk. He bellowed from the walkway, "You look fan-fucking-tastic, Bo. I've never seen that suit before. Wow, a faintly pinstriped black suit, a black polished cotton shirt, and a lush purple silk tie. Perfecto, mi amigo. Man, it reeks of self-assurance, even more impressive, intimidation."

"Yeah, Jenna picked out the entire ensemble, even worked on my hair."

"Well, it's kickass, my friend. Those expecting another dowdy, pasty-faced Donnelly will be taken aback. I hope your mind-blowing proofs arrive later today. I really can't wait." The trio nailed their power outfits. Murdock smiled, aware how well his team set the stage ahead of the upcoming meetings.

Sullivan peeked in the door. "The first media rep is already waiting. In fact, all the media reps have arrived already. I don't know what's going on. They may be checking each other out."

Murdock's smugness showed up. "I noticed them, too. My office is a little too cozy, not conducive for brow beating. I'll be over in a few minutes. We don't want those reps thinking we're in any rush on their behalf. So have Gina take the first rep to the conference room, consensual one. Also, ask her to bring coffee and bottled water. Just wait in your office until I call you."

"On it," Sullivan chortled.

"Oh, one more thing, Rexuality. Have you ever in your entire life seen a more handsome, virile-looking stud than Bo?"

Sullivan echoed what Murdock thought all along. "No. Too bad there aren't more women in our industry to clamor for his attention. It would be a mob scene."

Bodine frowned, "Knock it off, you two. I can't be distracted before a photo shoot."

Murdock quizzed Sullivan, "What's the rundown on the first rep?"

"His name's Billy Green from MediaTronics. They handle advertising in several publications, both print and online. These guys can create a domino effect which increases exposure with competitors we can't afford just yet."

"Billy? Seriously? What full-grown man calls himself Billy? Never mind. I like your strategy accompanied by your T-rex power garments. Like I said, get him in the conference room, then wait for my call."

Murdock killed some time in Bodine's office, letting Billy Green stew a bit. Exactly five minutes later, he bolted. Murdock stepped into the conference room heading straight for Green. He introduced himself, shook his hand, then took the seat directly across from him. He turned his back on Green as he picked up the phone on the credenza behind the table. He dialed Sullivan's extension. "Where the hell are you, my elusive friend?"

Sullivan replied, "Just waiting for the 'Green' light, Chase." Murdock kept quiet after the pun. "You should know, Mr. Green and I didn't hit it off too well on the phone. I kept grinding for a better rate. He finally got agitated, raised his voice, then accused me of being said grinder and unreasonable."

Murdock swiveled to face Green, smiled, then began laughing, noting his attire was as bland as his middle-aged face, mousy brown hair, and tie. His choice of small, frameless glasses could have been stylish if he were John Lennon. "All the more reason your presence is required here, Group Rex. I want your input on the rates, especially how they compare with the other companies we're considering. Besides, you're the Sales Manager, and as such, will record the meeting minutes in bullet points for our analysis later."

Green, only hearing one side of the conversation, seemed confused while under Murdock's stare. As he hung up the phone, Green asked, "Who's Group Rex? Is that Mr. Sullivan?"

"Yes, the man has many terms of endearment. Seems to me he's not too fond of you, so I asked him here to direct traffic." He then turned on the office intercom, piping the proceedings into Bodine's office. Green remained none the wiser.

Green stammered, "It wasn't my intention to offend the man, but he was relentless in pursuit of a deal I couldn't offer."

Murdock scribbled words on a small note pad. Without making eye contact, he asked, "Then why are you here, Mr. Green?" The question hung in the air like a slow-motion slap in the face. "I'm sure my colleague described in detail the desired outcome we will create from this promotion." Sullivan walked in the room. Murdock jumped up, handing Sullivan the note before he could take another step. It said, "Don't shake his hand, look pissed." Sullivan's pleasant face changed to a scowl, confirming he endorsed his leader's scheme, happy to play along.

Billy Green stood up, extending his hand toward Sullivan, who left him standing with a handful of nothing. He sat back down. Sullivan sneered at him while he took a seat beside his boss. Before any more words could be exchanged, Bodine walked into the conference room. His annoyed expression showed him in on the ruse. He barked, "What the hell's going on in here?"

Seeing the Cajun Adonis President decked out in corporate muscle threads, Green clutched a water bottle. He caught sight of Murdock and Sullivan glaring at him. His hand shook so badly, he put down the water. As planned, the exclamation point in the engineered proceedings arrived with Bodine's menacing presence. The predicted effect set Green in backpedal mode before the meeting commenced.

Murdock called out, "Mr. Billy Green, meet our President, Mr. Richard Bodine." Again, Green stood, ready for a handshake not offered. "Mr. Bodine, Mr. Green came here this morning, apparently to spin our wheels. Says he can't provide what we need from the budget you worked so hard to secure."

Bodine's eyes turned to slits as they threw daggers at Green. "You're telling me you drove here this morning just to give us the finger?"

Green tried to rally. "Gentlemen, please, please understand Mr. Sullivan's initial request was not possible... uh, at least at the time. However, if you'll give me a few minutes, I'll call my office to inquire about the possibility we can offer a better rate." He walked toward the door, adding in a flustered tone, "I have to go to my car. I'll be right back."

The minute he was gone, the three men eyed each other. Bodine laughed through his nose prompting muted giggling from the other two, all trying to prevent their glee from escaping outside the door. Murdock mused, "Line cast, hook set. All we have to do is let Billy Green reel himself in."

Sullivan nodded. He glanced at the door, then lowered his head, keeping his voice soft, "We need MediaTronics's broad reach more than everyone else we've scheduled. They can generate more impressions in the numbers game than almost all the others put together. I suggest we lighten up a tad should Green offer a better rate."

Murdock queried, "Exactly what amount and how many total publications did Green quote you?"

"$7500 for the top four."

"What amount were you after?"

"5k. I wanted enough left to spread around or hold back, if necessary."

"Say, you are a superb master grinder. No wonder he got pissed at you over the phone. You asked him for a 33% discount." Murdock slapped his knee while Bodine snickered.

"There's deep water in these rates, Chase. I knew he had wiggle room, but he dug in. You get kudos, however, making him squirm. And thanks, Bo, for assuring he came close to wetting himself."

Giving Sullivan a wide grin after witnessing his tenacity, Murdock phoned the receptionist. "Gina, hi. When you see Billy Green heading back into the conference room, wait exactly one minute, then call me on the intercom and say Consumer Electronics Daily is on the phone. Great, thanks." He snarked to the team, "Let's watch how Billy boy reacts hearing the top media outlet in the country is on the phone. And put a lid on your exuberance, both of you."

In the next minute, they heard a tap on the door. Green let himself back into the conference room. "OK, gentlemen, I think we have something a little more palatable." He entered the room confident, perhaps more self-righteous. As soon as he took his seat, the announcement came over the intercom.

Murdock watched Green's cocky demeanor wilt. He smiled at Green, "Can't wait for your good news, Billy, right after I take this call."

He picked up the dead phone line. "Mr. Weston? Hi, Chase Murdock here. We're hoping you have good news regarding our counter proposal. You guys are pricy, however, I'm sure you want in on this. Oh? Oh really? Excellent, that's more like it. We sincerely appreciate you going to the well to get our business. Remember, if we experience a great outcome from you, we may want a follow-up campaign. Bottom line, you can amortize the reduction in your rate. Thanks for the quick response. Mr. Sullivan will contact you today so he can arrange sending you the copy and photos. Alright, take care. Bye now." After an uncomfortable pause writing notes, Murdock gazed at the prey, "You were saying, Billy?"

Murdock watched Bodine and Sullivan as Green caved in, matching Sullivan's asking price, delivered by a monotone voice with a toddler sad face. Green stood up, gathered his things, bid the Eye Cue team a pleasant day, and left the room.

Bodine spoke first, "It's my turn to be proud, Chaser. Poor guy had no idea he was dealing with the master manipulator."

Sullivan clapped followed by a bow to Murdock, "Your highness."

Murdock rocketed through the office for the scheduled photo shoot. He caught sight of Gina Morgan escorting Jenna Talia toward Bodine's office. Everyone in the vicinity, men and women, stared at her. With genuine affection, she smiled at everyone she greeted. He scrutinized the details comprising her outfit, a tailored black, pencil-skirted suit, a rose pink, slightly opened silky blouse, all presented atop black leather, open toe, slingback four-inch heels. Her golden blonde hair loosely pulled back in a trendy bun style softened by occasional ringlets of hair around her face and dangling, rose-pink crystal earrings boosted her rating to eye-popping. Murdock stopped his sprint. His throat constricted as she approached him, shrinking his voice to a squeaky whisper, "I don't think I can breathe."

He wheezed, "What a great surprise, Dr. Talia. I don't think Bo will mind my saying you are more lovely than I've ever seen you before. What's the occasion?"

"Thanks, Chase. Bo suggested we have our portrait done while the professional photographer is here. You know Bo adores Elvis, right? Well rose pink and black were his favorite colors, so voila! Here I am. I hope you don't think my outfit's too boring." She whispered the last word with pursed lips.

"The word is breathtaking, Jenna. Nothing *boring* about it." He mimicked her whisper for the word boring. "I'm most impressed how you nailed the famous 'Elvis rose pink' created by Cadillac for his special ordered car in 1955. Elvis would definitely approve."

"Aw, thanks Chase. You know your Elvis stuff, too. Of course, you love Elvis, or Bo would have thrown you to the curb years ago. We'll show you the proofs when we get them. Bye for now."

In the midst of thinking how surreal it might feel watching the couple in a professional photo session, Sullivan peered around the corner from his office focused on Jenna Talia's backside. After the enticing beauty left their view, Sullivan muttered, "Life just isn't fair for us commoners, is it, Chase?"

"Yeah, but both deserve what they have. When's the next media rep appointment?"

"I cancelled them all. Since we got the hot screaming deal from Billy Green, it's worth a shot at getting what we can out of Consumer Electronics Daily. I think money will be better spent on them."

"Superior strategy, Unprotected one. I like the way you think on the fly. You're right, it will fit Bo's promo directive better. You know, maybe good things *are* falling into place here. If the promo succeeds as planned by splashing Bo's pearly whites everywhere, our neglected switchboard will light up like a disco ball."

Sullivan chuckled, "Yeah, that would make our world, as you would say, pretty fucking bitchen."

CHAPTER 9

LIFT OFF

Three days after the Bodine photo proofs were hand-delivered by the photographer to the Eye Cue conference room, Murdock's exhilaration caused his anxiety to hit maximum level. The striking poses emitted confidence to Bodine's dashing elegance, and the angles used by the photographer brought forth the indisputable image of a leader. In unison, the portrait of Bodine with Jenna Talia stunned the photographer, Murdock, Bodine, and Sullivan. Right after the photographer left, the men stood speechless viewing the electrifying picture.

Murdock suggested the couple's portrait become part of the company's promotional piece. He reminded his colleagues about their marketing targets for the media blitz. The portrait served as an insurance policy for attracting maximum male gazes, gender fluid or straight, throughout their industry. Talia's impeccable beauty framed by the heartthrob Eye Cue President improved the chances for drawing in the escalating number of female executives and salespeople in their trade. Without discussion, they all agreed.

Right before Sullivan sent Billy Green the photos and copy, the executive team made another last-minute decision. Using the rest of the budget, they agreed the online ad campaign would run at a national level without any local test run. Minutes later, Sullivan advised the team Green expanded the scope of the campaign and confirmed receipt of the final selection of finished shots, plus the word copy Murdock prepared. Sullivan mentioned Green promised the promotion would go live in the next online editions of four media companies within 48 hours. Murdock's apprehension ramped up. Sweat beads peppered his forehead as he paced the hallways searching for brief distractions, worried their bet of the entire budget on the first run carried too high a risk. His entire crew shared his edginess, not knowing what to expect.

During the 50th hour of the 48-hour waiting period, the online versions hit the internet. The three executives rushed to the lobby to observe activity on the switchboard. The phone lines lit up all at once. The volume of calls exploded, a spectacle no one predicted. Gina Morgan, the receptionist, punched the first line with a simple, "Hold, please," before she caught the next line and the next. Murdock felt faint, his knees folding. He grabbed Sullivan by the arm, as they charged back to their offices behind Bodine.

Existing customers bringing new orders waited on hold, uttering no complaints about the delay. When Murdock took the phones to help, some of their old customers mentioned how the confidence given off from Bodine's swagger inspired, even excited them about Eye Cue again. Aspiring new accounts also tolerated the hold times for opening accounts then placing orders; in fact, many employees reported the callers sounded enthused when finally greeted. The positivity astounded Murdock into momentary giddiness.

Following the flood of service calls came an onslaught of curious outsiders, caring nothing about the company, inquiring only about Bodine, or the gorgeous couple from the ads. Some audacious people simply asked for a personal appointment with Bodine or Dr. Talia's address and phone number. This separate novel interest in Eye Cue's President, which no one saw coming, proved the ads would blow the tops off their competitors. From the outset, it was Murdock who recognized the marketing opportunity Bodine and Talia together presented as head-turning media magnets.

On the third day after the media release, Murdock found Sullivan near the bathroom, complaining while grinning how he and Bodine skipped lunch plus dinner breaks the past two days working the phones. They entered adjoining stalls in the restroom, continuing the conversation. Sullivan acknowledged he also fielded the barrage of phone orders. He mentioned he almost forgot to go home the first night, adding an apology for not having time to say hello. After they speed-peed, they blasted out the doors headed in the same direction to their offices.

The sudden call volume creating a bombardment of orders flung Eye Cue systems out of control. Bodine entered Murdock's office. "Now do you see why I had so much confidence in you, Chaser? I can't imagine anyone except you pulling this off. We're running out of product because of this wild response. I had to give our suppliers several humungous emergency orders. You may end up avoiding airplane travel for the foreseeable future. The reps have orders up the ass, wondering what just hit them. Now I'm thinking I probably missed a ton of orders because of all those groupie-like callers. They acted as if they were talking to a celebrity when I got on the line. What's the matter with people?"

"You know how whacked out people are these days. Thanks for all the Atta boys, Bo, but right now, it's essential we follow through on the claims we made during all the hype at the Board meeting. I'll be on an airplane soon, but not for customer visits. Instead, I'll visit the factories where I can shop for new products. Bringing back new categories will take our sales momentum up a couple of notches. It's one thing giving lip service about diversification, another delivering on it."

Bodine smiled. "Sounds like a plan. Well, Director Curtis called me this morning. Seems the Board can't quite wrap their heads around our sudden burst of success. She requested I let you know how much the campaign impressed her. I think you're a person of interest now. How do I know this? Because she asked what your situation is, if you know what I mean. Is it too early to throw your line back in the water, Chaser? She's very hot."

"Ya' know, Bo, I still miss Donna so much I can't even think about dating. If I were on the prowl, she'd be the first woman I'd call."

"I'll certainly let her know…"

Murdock waived his hands, "You do, and I'll reveal the dating body count you've left in your wake over the years. I'm sure Talia would be none too pleased knowing how many dashboards you've had replaced."

"Ok, Ok. Don't get snotty. What I'm trying to get through your head is how special Nadine is. She's smart, witty, sexier than hell. She would be a wonderful escape from your mourning. Did I mention what an excellent relief valve for all that backed up testosterone she could be? Just sayin'."

"You know, Bo, here you are, the President/CEO of the company. You're standing here pimping Nadine, a Director of the Board, to me. I think you better get the fuck out of my office so you can get back to basking in the glow of your newfound celebrity."

"Alright, Chaser, I feel your venom trying to block this subject. Understand this. It's obvious women like Nadine are in high demand. She won't be available forever. Plus, she likes smart men and already digs you. It won't be a start-from-scratch scenario for you. Get the picture?"

"Get out." Bodine threw up his arms and left. Murdock pictured himself on a double date with Nadine, Bodine, and Talia. Men nearby the couples drooled over Nadine and Talia. The women made goo-goo eyes at Bodine. He laughed out loud when his fantasy valet at the restaurant mistook him for the trio's chauffeur. The ringing phone broke his daydream.

"Hi Chase, this is Nadine Curtis." *Well, how's this for a coincidence?* "I wanted you to know how thrilled the Board is with your ad campaign. I wondered if we could get together so we can discuss the follow-up campaign over cocktails, maybe dinner one of these evenings."

"Sure thing, Nadine. That would be great. I'll have Bo and Rex Sullivan, my sales manager, join us."

"Hmmm. That isn't what I had in mind, Chase. I hoped I'd have a chance to know you a little better. Anything more than two would be a crowd."

He knew where this was going, suspecting he had been set up. *That prick Bodine. I hope my explanation doesn't piss her off.* "Uh, Nadine, I lost the woman I loved deeply a few weeks ago and…"

"I know. Bo told me about Donna. Chase, it's a very tragic story. I'm so sorry for your terrible loss. He also mentioned you're not ready yet for considering a new relationship. Believe me, I understand. However, I'm kind of an old-fashioned girl. I'm not looking for more than casual conversation away from the office setting. I think it's helpful understanding work partners better on a personal level, especially since it appears we'll be working together more. Never hurts to have a friend on the Board either."

"Well, okay then, sure, Nadine. Which evening do you prefer?"

"How about Saturday night? I know a nice, low-key piano bar in Moorpark called 88's, only a fifteen-minute drive from your office. Does that work?"

Murdock paused, leaning back in his chair, swiveling back and forth. *Bingo. This is no quasi-business meeting she wants, but I can't risk offending her. She's key for our getting the budgets we need to create a more dynamic company. If I blow this, I'll suffer the wrath of Bodine.*

"That sounds fine, Nadine. How about we meet at seven?"

"That's perfect, Chase. See you then."

He threw down the phone and jogged toward Bodine's office. "You sidewinding viper."

Bodine looked up from a pile of papers. "What?"

"Guess who I just got off the phone with? Yeah, that's right. You orchestrated this whole Nadine thing, didn't you? She asked me if she and I could have dinner and drinks while we discussed the follow-up ad campaign... at a piano bar... on Saturday night. When I suggested you and Sullivan should attend, she pooh-poohed it straight out."

"I don't know what the fuck you're talking about. When she asked me about you, I told her you're still mourning the loss of Donna, not ready for anything new. Listen to me, I told you she's smart. I also told you she's into you. The worst that could happen is you spend a kickass evening in the company of a woman who's an absolute knockout. Here's a thought, you could even avoid sitting home alone drinking by yourself, spinning your ancient vinyl LPs you've heard a thousand times. It's time you stop wallowing, Chaser. Let Nadine show you the way out of your depression. You can set her straight at dinner if that's what you really want. Me? I'd rather be filling my nostrils full of her magnificent fragrance, scrutinizing every inch of her substantial bustline, D cups, by the way, while marveling at her perfect figure or gorgeous face. Nah, you're probably better off getting hammered all alone, putting In-A-Gadda-Da-Vida on auto-repeat until you pass out. Oh, let's not forget Johnny Dunne, who will be sure he stops by to talk your ear off about nothing. Yeah, you should stay home."

"Ok, ok, Bo, I'm worried things could get complicated overnight. I can't risk offending one of our Board members. What if she comes on to me?"

"I don't think that will happen. She has too much self-control. I'm sure she'll monitor you for signs of thawing. However, after you've had a cocktail or two while inhaling her charms for a couple of hours, you may be the one doing the oncoming. Either way, it's a win for you, Chaser. Relax. Have a good time. Go there without any expectations. Let the evening unfold before you judge the situation."

88's piano bar already had a low-key buzz on when he arrived. Once inside, he surveyed a cozy room bathed in soft light with cherrywood walls garnished with large, black-framed, autographed photo collages of over a dozen famous contemporary piano performers. Between each pair of collages on three walls, a crescent-shaped, chocolate-brown leather booth allowed parties up to four people to face the pianist in the center of the room. In front of the fourth wall in the back was a solid cherrywood bar with swivel captain seats above thick cherrywood legs, and a full-length mirror supported on its sides by two columns attached to the wall. Enthralled by 88's elegance, Murdock guessed all seats required a reservation with fee.

He spotted Nadine as she stood up from a booth to his left placed between collages of Jerry Lee Lewis and Billy Joel, two of Murdock's most revered performers. He gave her an uncontrolled, wide-eyed smile as he observed her short, tight-fitting crimson dress accentuated by a revealing, brocaded neckline, loudly inappropriate for an executive meeting. Almost as well-endowed as Talia, he tallied her features: a chiseled face offering luscious, glossy crimson lips bordered by long, glistening, chestnut brown hair draped over her right shoulder. Her tiny waist flared into perfect hips bolstered by sculptured, tanned legs. French-tipped fingernails and black patent leather heels overlaid with a red patent trim finished off her business attire. His mouth went dry as he tried not to hurry over to her.

"Hi Chase. Right on time. What do you think of this place?"

"Nadine, may I say you look sensational? No one would ever guess you are an uptight corporate type. And wow, this place is beyond classy."

Nadine glowed as she hugged him before they sat down next to each other, each entering from opposite sides of the booth before meeting in the middle. She answered, "Yeah, I like that it's design is rather unexpected from the parking lot view. And, *Chase*, I'm anything but uptight. That corporate persona is a necessary image. Just get to know me."

She reminds me of my sweet Donna with the poise and air of confidence few women possess. I'm right back feeling invisible around all these men, even those creeps with dates, leering at her the same way as when I walked around with Donna. I don't blame them. Nadine is a bona fide goddess wearing a "look at me" outfit.

It took less than five minutes before her charms engulfed him. She engaged him in spirited conversation, the chat pausing only for brief drink sips and food bites. She got his jokes, even offered a couple of her own, punctuated by an infectious laugh. Bo was right. He wasted too many Saturday nights alone. Nadine gave out more than a breath of fresh air; she emptied a charged tank of pure oxygen.

Mesmerized by their mutual chemistry, Murdock glanced at the time. Two hours flew by without one word of the campaign being discussed. He snapped back to reality. His fear over this meeting compelled him to broach the subject. "So, Nadine, should we talk a little biz before I get too loopy on our cocktails?"

"Let's not." She leaned in toward him. "I'm enjoying your personal side too much. Besides, we have nothing to discuss. As long as Eye Cue keeps pumping out the product, the Board will back any promotional plans you deliver. Truly, they are impressed as hell the way you generated such a sales spike under so modest a budget. They think you're a genie. Suffice it to say, there's more money where that came from. On a personal note, I find your kind of smarts very sexy."

The guilt overwhelmed him as heavy as the infatuation warmed him, as if he were betraying Donna's memory. *Give me some kind of sign, baby. Tell me it's okay.*

Curtis continued, "I think you're pretty bitchen, Chase, and just so you know, I am a valley girl, *for sure.*"

"But do you think I'm titties?" She cocked her head, letting out a slow chuckle, which morphed into a full-blown roar. "Oh yeah, well, I'm a valley boy, too. When I was a young dude, there was good, then great. Better than great was bitchen. Better than bitchen was titties. The rare rating that eclipsed titties was nipples. Are you getting a whiff of what I'm stepping in?"

Curtis started laughing so hard she had trouble catching her breath, grabbing her napkin to wipe her eyes. She howled at his inherent, brazen lack of inhibition. She regained her composure, "If I can do *anything* helpful so you can work through your, ya' know, situation, let me know. Here's my business card. I wrote my personal cell number on the back. I hope you call."

They left the club arm in arm. He walked her to the car, then bowed, "Madam Board member, your ride awaits."

Upon returning home, he turned on his audio system, rifled through his LP collection, ultimately placing "In-A-Gadda-Da-Vida" by the Iron Butterfly on the turntable. He had to sort out all the feelings racing through him.

CHAPTER 10

CONFLICTED

Murdock sipped his second cup of coffee Sunday morning. His phone rang at exactly 9:00 a.m. The musical ringtone on his phone, Jimmy Buffett's "Margaritaville," announced the caller, Ted Zachary.

"Am I suddenly a human discard? I pulled you from the edge of self-annihilation, and all I've heard from you is nada, nothing, zilch, zero. Jesus, Chase, I'm considering hiring Johnny Dunne again to snap a picture of you, so I'll remember what the hell you look like."

"Teddy, you don't understand. I've been insanely busy at work since we launched the Bodine promotion. I haven't even called Kevin or John Alvarez for several weeks after inviting them for a weekend dinner. Can you please forgive me?"

"It's okay, Chase," Ted said chuckling. "More than anything, I'm simply taking your temperature as verification no demons took residence inside your head. You know how I worry. Besides, I haven't completely healed yet from your last foray into becoming incinerator fuel, you know."

"I know, Teddy. Of course, I still dwell on Donna most evenings. The good news is I don't have time for any depression because I'm focused on dozens of complex issues during my sixteen-hour days. Plus, a wonderful distraction, a woman who's a mere Eye Cue Board Director came my way last night. She's apparently interested in me. Did I mention she passes for a ten plus?"

"Titties."

"She's got those in spades, plus she thinks I'm near the nipples category as well."

"She actually said nipples?"

"She used bitchen followed by *for sure*. Then I introduced her to *titties* and clued her in on nipples, which completed her update on the rankings above bitchen. Turns out she's from the San Fernando Valley just like me. She genuinely digs me, Teddy. But I don't feel ready for the responsibility a relationship requires right now or the potential work conflict."

"Yeah? Remember the time you picked up a pretty woman, then took her back to your apartment? She was primed to sample your pulp stick, then you sent her packing without so much as a goodnight kiss."

"Yeah. What does she have to do with anything?"

"You have a propensity for rejecting quality women, though Bo leads the pack in that category."

"Remember the circumstances, Teddy. It was Donna then and it's Donna now."

"Are you exaggerating about this woman.... what's her name?"

"Nadine."

"About Nadine being a ten?"

"Not in the least. She's so fine, she makes your wife look like a toothless hag. Just kidding, I think Cindy's superb, and you know it. I can't find the right words for how incredible Nadine is, both in looks and personality."

"You can't find the right words, so you took a swipe at Cindy. An extremely cheap shot, but then considering the source, not unexpected."

"I *said* just kidding. Don't go acting like a hyper-sensitive bedwetter on me."

"I'll let that one slide. Let me recommend you not try so hard making your point next time. You know Cindy is off limits, period. Have you forgotten how anything other than profound adoration translates into fighting words?"

"Sorry, Teddy. You know I worship at the altar of Cindy. I'm suffering from infatuation hangover. Last night was the first time since Donna died I didn't cry until I fell asleep."

"Ah, then Nadine good, Murdock sense of humor still sucky."

"Fair enough. Hey, when can we get together? I miss my little Teddy bear. Bring Cindy along, too. I'd love the opportunity to show her my undying devotion to her magnificent existence."

"Why don't we all meet for dinner at a swank place next weekend? And bring Nadine."

"I don't know, Teddy. I had guilt flashes during the entire time we were together last night. It was as if Donna sat right beside me, watching me get worked up over Nadine. I made a silent plea for her approval without receiving any affirmation."

"The truth is you'll never totally shake Donna's loss. Without exaggeration, she was in a league of her own. Chase, you've gotta know how upset she'd be if you don't get back on your horse. If the situation were switched, you'd want the same for her. It doesn't matter if the poonettes are relationship material or not. You've had the restrictors on for too many months already. Let yourself have some fun. God knows you shouldn't sit at home every night by yourself. Have you worn out your LP collection yet?"

"Bo made a similar crack, skewering the Iron Butterfly, of all things."

"Maybe this Nadine leads you out of the celibacy cave. If she's a ten inside-out, I vote for Nadine therapy. Besides, I'm curious now about a woman who can make my wife look like a skank."

"You better not tell Cindy what I said, or I'll hire Johnny Dunne to flatten all four of your tires. Give me a day or two. I need more time for mulling it over. Even if I don't bring Nadine, are we still on?"

"Sure, although I'll be disappointed if I can't meet this ultra-babe. You know how well Cindy rewards me with envy sex when you show up with someone she perceives as competitive eye candy. How old is she, anyway?"

"Don't know. Hmm, I'd say 50-ish decked out with a 20-ish body. I hope my own age isn't a deal breaker with her."

"That's just plain dumb thinking. Make it happen, Chase. She sounds like a jewel. Maybe her charms yank you out of your doldrums."

"Teddy, would you mind if I also invited Kevin and John Alvarez? I'm way overdue with them, too."

"Sure, bring them along. I'd love a good catch-up chat with those boys. Invite Bo, too. I haven't seen him in ages."

"Not a good idea. Bad blood between him and Nadine."

"Don't tell me, another victim of his bed 'em and forget 'em conquests?"

"Yeah, his love life played like a broken record for too long. After spending time with Nadine, I can't figure out why he kicked her to the curb. She's the antithesis of skankdom. If memory serves me, you tagged him with the 'skank whisperer' moniker. He'd wait until almost closing time at the bars when desperate women were all that remained. If you ask me, meeting the incredible Talia reversed his error in letting Nadine go. The man always captured any woman's heart he wanted."

As soon as his conversation with Zachary ended, Bodine called. *Ah, he wants the dirt on my date. I'll back a dump truck of it all over him.* "Good morning, Bo. Curious you're calling me on a Sunday. I can't imagine why."

"You know damn well why. Give it to me, Chaser. Spill your guts for your President. I want all the details about your bogus business meeting last night."

"Oh, big surprise. Well, you know from experience how Nadine can be a passionate woman. Then again, since you've partaken in so much 'tang, I'm downright shocked she didn't warrant an entire dashboard's worth of notches."

"You can stop with the psychoanalysis, Doctor Fraud. I've often wondered why myself. If the good doctor hadn't entered my life, I would have taken another shot at Nadine. Now nix the small talk and give me the dirt."

"As you can imagine, no business was discussed. By the way, we have a blank check for more promo funds if things keep cooking like they have."

"Yeah, yeah, yeah, saw that coming, but I'm waiting for the real story."

"Okay, get this. We had a couple of cocktails when, out of the blue, she invites me over to her place. She pours some wine, then excuses herself for a powder room break. When she returns, she's dressed in a see-through, black negligee covering a black bra and matching thong holding a tube of raspberry-flavored gel and a couple of toys in her hands. She kept on the black patent leather high heels from our date. We ended up having a pretty good time."

"Stop fucking around, Chaser. It's a nice appetizer, but it ain't anywhere near paydirt."

"Alright. We never made it to her bedroom. She took me right there on the living room floor. Nadine is the only woman I've ever known, other than Donna, who looks better naked than she does with clothes on. By the way, she's extremely flexible. We did things I never attempted before. We both endured multiple rug burns. I had trouble walking out of there. My knees still throb this morning. I sure appreciate your encouraging me to pursue her, Bo. It felt great blowing off all that pent-up energy. *Twice*. She was on fire, man."

"Twice?"

"Ok, enough of this nonsense, Bo. Nothing happened. She portrayed the consummate lady and I showed her as much gentleman as I could muster, although I did educate her on some locker room jargon. She's flat out terrific. Truth is, however, I still have trouble seeing myself with someone else so soon."

"You had me going there, Chaser. I even wondered why I hadn't ever been thrown on the floor by her. I do hear what you're saying, though. She's a lady, alright, but with the ability to turn into an animal when it comes to splitting the uprights."

"Jesus, Bo. You're making me feel like I folded my cards too early last night. Let's change the subject before I hang up on you and race to Nadine's place. Teddy and I are getting together for dinner next Saturday. After telling him about Nadine, he invited her, too. He requested you and Talia join us, but don't worry. I told him it wasn't a good idea for obvious reasons."

"Perfect. Just consider Nadine as worth throwing your trepidation out the window, Chaser. She can help you ease back into the mainstream. Really, I can't imagine a better companion for your sexual reawakening. And you won't find a more intelligent or interesting woman out there."

"I'm giving it serious consideration. All the rug-burn bullshit is actually stuff I've fantasized about ever since I saw her last night. You should have seen her, by the way. Jaw dropping, beyond stony. Wrapping my face and hands in glow-in-the-dark gauze would have been insufficient for the men there to notice my presence. She gave me her personal cell number and said she hopes I'll call. Right at this moment, I don't know what I'll do."

"There's only one play when a woman like Nadine serves. You must volley. Get in the game again, Chaser. She's not a commodity. Few men ever experience the luxury of a woman with her brains and pulchritude."

There was a familiar rap on his front door, setting off his 'Dunne deal' alarm.

"Much appreciate the advice, Bo. Gotta run. I think Johnny Dunne just knocked on my door. Of course, I've been avoiding him. I owe the man some face time."

"Good luck with that. See ya' tomorrow."

He opened the door where the giant hobbit stood before him. Sincere gratitude for Dunne's role in saving his life softened his expression. "C'mon in, Johnny. Care for a cold one?"

CHAPTER 11

FROM OUT OF LEFT FIELD

Unaware the time just passed 8:00 p.m., Murdock marveled at his success story at Eye Cue over the past few weeks. He assumed the 'I'm so bitchen' position in his office with feet on the desk, chair swung back as far as it would go, and a toothy grin from ear to ear. The whole approach of the marketing blast was his brainchild; he merited extra rights for wallowing in the joy. His idea of the campaign focusing on Bodine, then later adding Talia, seemed so simplistic, yet exploded into such instant success. The team's boldness with the meager budget spurred an unexpected deluge of product demand, the results of which prompted pure pandemonium in the warehouse. Only one exposure of Richard Bodine beside Dr. Jenna Talia Gorman superimposed over the catchy Eye Cue Technologies logo drove sales up overnight, creating an order processing level difficult to sustain.

He recalled his happiness when he and Sullivan dropped their own workload to help the warehouse employees pull orders. The move gave the staff a small pause during the breakneck pace. Rolling up their sleeves to fill the orders with the warehouse employees felt good. It provided some relief for the mounting delivery pressure while building morale. Without being asked, Sullivan joined him daily, embracing their mutual struggle to juggle their manual labor between answering calls on their cell phones. They kept pads and pens at the ready. Murdock saw Rex as a treasured gift from Bodine. His close friend selected with precision the exact person required for his attaining personal success as a top Eye Cue executive.

He made mental notes of what it took for their staff packaging then loading the onslaught of orders for shipment. The unintended consequence of the self-inflicted chaos allowed him and Sullivan an opportunity for analyzing the operational flaws. From the analysis, they could discover smarter ways for staff deployment. This information would become his opening for an upcoming presentation justifying funds for hiring new part-time workers, which he and Bodine would offer the Board of Directors. These workers could earn their way into full time positions if higher demand warranted more headcount. Their proposed hiring method would generate a cost-effective growth model for the company driven by product demand.

Sullivan approached him during his smiling session with the ceiling. "Chase, glad you're still here. I've received a lot of calls from the reps. They have customers who want your personal reassurances Eye Cue can support the spike in demand with no supply disruptions. Without exception, Chase, the reps expressed strong concern about signing up new customers for fear we're setting ourselves up for a nasty backorder situation."

"Anal Rex, please tell those candy-assed, diaper-wearing wimps their President Bodine has rush orders already on the water with more on the way. Every account will get what they need, but only if the customers have the huevos to step up with orders. Anyone who holds back will be left wishing they'd strapped on a pair when they had the chance. If I hear of any reps bowing or scraping to their accounts because they lack confidence in what we're doing, you'll be sending them strike one letters. We can't have their whiney lack of sacks slowing us down."

Sullivan nodded, "It'll be my pleasure turning up the heat on them. I've already had a few hotshots from our competitors inquiring about the availability of the line."

"Excellent. Explain that tidbit to any Eye Cue reps who may require rubber sheets on their beds."

"Great approach. I'll get right on it. I'll email you with the notable responses from the reps." Murdock nodded in approval as Sullivan left.

As the week wore on, it became evident everything was falling into place for the Saturday night soiree with the Zacharys. His earlier text inviting the Alvarez brothers prompted their quick acceptance responses with cheery phrases from both. The last and stickiest task left, a final decision on whether he should invite Nadine, forced his hand. He was keen to show her off to his best buddy. He picked up the phone.

"Hi Nadine, Chase Murdock."

"Well, hello Chase. So glad to hear from you. I had such a fabulous time with you last weekend. Do you have another in mind?"

"I do, but it will be more of a group setting, at least in the beginning. I'd like you to have dinner Saturday night with me and my best friend in the universe, Ted Zachary, and his wife, Cindy. The late Donna's two sons will also be there. They've become the children I never had. I love them dearly. Keep in mind we can hang out somewhere else after dinner, provided you don't OD on the twisted way we view life."

"If Ted's anything like you, I won't be disappointed. Count me in."

"Wonderful. Please give me your address. I'll pick you up at 6:30." Nadine's voice sounded overly willing, which excited and disturbed him at the same time.

Okay, invitation made and accepted. He exhaled, elated he took the first step toward dating someone. In record time, he managed a swing from fearing making the call to feeling like he couldn't wait to see her. *I can do this.*

Saturday arrived. As he dressed for the evening dinner, wrestling with his anxiety, he wiped his face and checked his pits. He slowed to a crawl pulling onto Nadine's driveway, soaking up the details of her nicely appointed townhome in one of the more upscale areas in eastside Simi Valley. When she opened the door, his heartrate accelerated. He resisted giving her a big hello hug until she stepped forward, wrapping her arms around him, holding him for an extra moment, placing a tender kiss on his cheek. Her sublime perfume filled his nostrils, acting as an instant aphrodisiac. *This is only our second date. I'm already hooked.* He turned so she could walk in front of him while he adjusted his trouser package, while he eyed her backside. The black cocktail dress cut above the knee did not disappoint; her shapely legs enhanced by a pair of black heels bejeweled with a cluster of small, cultured pearls on the toes made her irresistible.

When they arrived at the steakhouse, the hostess led them to the reserved table only occupied by the Zacharys. As the couple approached the table, Ted stood up with a warm smile on his face, extending his hand to Curtis. "Chase told me you were a knockout, so I assumed he'd be bringing you here on a stretcher. Nadine, this is my wife, Cindy. And a hearty hello to you, Mr. Murdock. So glad we could make this happen."

"Teddy, you're as cute as ever. Cindy, lovely as usual. I've missed you two. I know, I know I've been a shitty friend. I won't let so much time go by again before we get together. By the way, Teddy, I hope the food here is as classic as the Andy Warhol and Peter Max prints on the walls."

Zachary quipped with one eyebrow lifted, "Oh yes, the entrees are the same price as the prints per plate." Murdock winced. Nadine and Cindy chuckled.

———

Murdock eyed Cindy, who could not keep her eyes off Nadine. He couldn't avoid obsessing if Ted leaked to Cindy the undeserved insult he dropped on her during their last conversation. The hostess seated them, then took their order for a round of cocktails. Just as the cocktails arrived, in walked the Alvarez brothers. Murdock took a swig, spotting Kevin and John nearing their table. Kevin's gaze fixed on Nadine as she chatted with Cindy. Curtis turned in her chair, flinched, then managed an artificial smile. Murdock witnessed the full scene.

Before introductions could be made, Kevin blurted, "Nadine?" It was more a statement than a question.

Nadine's smile disappeared. "Hello, Kevin. How have you been?"

Murdock went into instant shock, followed by a crestfallen expression before he turned away in disgust. He rose stiffly, "Excuse me, folks, I need a restroom break." He sped past the hostess out the front door onto the parking lot. Zachary broke into a swift jog behind him.

"What the hell's going on, Chase?" Zachary huffed, aware his friend's mood flipped into the dark place.

"I'll tell you what's going on, Teddy. That fuck stain of a stepson of mine has carnal knowledge of Nadine. I bet he picked her up at the Carousel one night, you know, the cougar haven I told you about. Christ, what a tawdry fucking barfly. I should have known she was too good to be true. Why would a woman so smart, so beautiful troll for the schlong of men half her age? And who knows how many others there have been? You know, I'm sure it's the reason Donna didn't give me the cosmic OK about her. I think I understand now why Bo lost interest in her. Goddamnit, she's just a gorgeous hose bag."

"C'mon, Chase. Don't let it spoil your evening. Get your composure together. Best you go back in there. Just ride it out, okay?"

"No fucking way, Teddy. I'll take Nadine home and come back solo. It's not Kevin's fault, nor is it Nadine's, but if you think I could be comfortable sitting at a table making nice with her..."

"Alright, I understand. Why don't I get Nadine? Let me take her home instead. You're in no condition. Make yourself scarce until you see us leave."

"Thanks, Teddy. Tell her something, anything, just get her the hell out of there. Make sure you apologize to the others for me. I'll go back in as soon as I know you're gone."

He positioned himself several yards around the side of the entrance, standing behind a tree, making sure he had a clear view of the front door. When Ted and Nadine emerged, Ted frowned when he spotted Murdock right away, giving him the 'get lost' wave. Nadine's head was down. Her hand clutched a tissue dabbing her eyes. When they were out of sight, Murdock went back inside.

Kevin and John stood up when he arrived at the table. John grinned. Kevin's expression resembled a boy waiting for punishment. He greeted them, "So happy you both came. I'm sorry for the drama." He shook their hands followed by hugs. "Funny thing, your mom wouldn't give me the thumbs up on Nadine when I asked her the other day. Looks like she's still watching out for my best interest. Now, on the subject of cougars, Kevin, are there *any* of them whose account you haven't serviced?"

Kevin cringed, glancing sideways at Cindy, who was texting on her phone. "Let's hope not. This is so awkward, Chase. Seeing her sitting there really shocked me. Funny, I actually think Nadine's a super lady. Sorry for such a stupid coincidence. Maybe Mom meant the message about Nadine for both of us."

"Probably all three of us," John blurted.

Murdock choked on his drink, giving John a wide-eyed stare. "John, I, uh, suppose that makes sense." He smiled back at Kevin. "Bet you're right about the message, Kev. Better I found out now before I had a chance to fall for her. Awkward or not, I believe you and your mom saved me. It's all good. Now let's have some fun."

Cindy, having taken in the entire incident, burst out, "You mean you had an affair with Chase's date, Kevin? She's closer to my age than yours, for God's sake." John ordered another round of drinks as they waited in silence for Zachary's return.

Before Zachary reached the table, Murdock started grilling him. "What did you tell her, Teddy?"

"I said you had crawled over better-looking women than her just searching for a place to self-pleasure." Any tension still hanging over their table evaporated as all five cracked up laughing.

"Seriously, Teddy, what did you say?"

"I told her you were allergic to animal hair, especially that of the feline variety."

"Damnit, Teddy."

"I told her the truth; you just couldn't handle her dating proclivities. She didn't say anything, rather showed an air of resignation about it."

"OK. Perfect. I'm starved." Murdock signaled for the waiter. Everyone clapped as a welcome sign to a party mood.

After midnight Murdock crawled in bed. A profound sense of sadness gripped him. Through the tears he cried, "There's no replacing you, Donna. I shouldn't have even tried. Goodnight, sweetheart."

CHAPTER 12

TONYA

Murdock arrived at Mandrake's on Sunday evening. He analyzed an area devoid of lingering people. Locating the proper seating granted him the luxury to drink and think, alone. He chose a space at the bar where his back faced the street, putting Mandrake's open-air patio entrance full of loud-talking customers at least thirty feet behind him. Jason, the bartender, recognized him as he approached the bar. A beer appeared on the counter as he sat down.

"Hey, Jason, thanks for reading my mind. Can you do me a favor? Keep the barflies out of my vicinity." He reached in his pocket, then handed Jason a crisp twenty-dollar bill, ordering another Corona at the same time. As if he was alone with no eyes on him, he guzzled the beer in hand, then reached across the bar for a napkin to wipe the evidence off his mouth. During the first sip of his second Corona, blinding lights from a car pulling into a parking space flooded the bar area. The headlights' blazing beam bounced off the large mirror behind the rows of bottles lining the bar shelves. He squinted at the intrusion, wheeling around on his barstool to identify who needed a lesson in headlight settings.

The guilty party drove a brand-new black Audi SUV displaying its temporary registration taped on the front windshield. He fixed his gaze on the clueless driver's door just as the car's lights went out, creating a temporary patch of stars blocking his vision. His eyes blinked faster than hummingbird wings until his line of sight returned. He focused on the woman stepping out of the vehicle.

His disdain melted into interest. She became a welcomed package, wrapped in a pretty, smooth-skinned face, minimal makeup, and a slender, youthful body. Her shoulder-length brown hair caught the ceiling lights, showing an expensive gloss on her straight hairstyle. Though her pants obscured her shoes, her gait told him she wore at least three-inch heels. He pegged her height at five feet, eight inches, aided by the lift.

He turned back to follow her reflection cast in the large mirror facing him. She stopped near the half-filled bar for a scan of its patrons. He dismissed her as a barfly there meeting another barfly. She approached the empty stool beside him, "Excuse me, is anyone sitting here?"

He peeked over his shoulder at her, fighting an impulse for a caustic response describing his newfound vision problem, courtesy of her headlights. So far, he confirmed her basics included pretty, polite, and well-dressed, a far superior option than any other candidate sitting around the bar. *Why risk driving her away before her seat is even warm?* He smiled at her, signifying the official cancellation of his human distancing decree. "It's all yours, madam," he stated, giving her an affirmative nod.

"Madam? How cute. I don't hear that one used much anymore."

She perched on her seat. He examined her face, finishing his profiling game by guessing her age. *She either has exceptional genes or has taken great care of herself, maybe a combination of both.* In a rare moment, no age range popped in his head. She could be 40 or mid-50's. No matter, she seemed lovelier than he first observed from a distance, another unusual event. His past profiling experiences often proved disappointing if not shocking.

"Well 'ma'am' is a tad old-fashioned and 'Ms.' just never sounds natural, like 'fizz' with an 'm,' so 'madam' seems like a good alternative, don't you think?"

"I think it's charming, really." She thrust her right hand toward him. "I'm Tonya Turner, by the way."

"It's a pleasure, Tonya," he responded, shaking her hand. "Chase, Chase Murdock." He waved the bartender over their way. "Jason, Tonya here is dying of thirst."

Jason remained his favorite barkeep, a handsome man in his early 30's, in good shape with a winning smile always at the ready. "You got it, Chase. What'll it be, Tonya?"

Again, showing a smile, she offered Jason her hand, who beamed back at her as he gently shook it, setting a basket of tortilla chips with a small salsa bowl in front of her. After giving Jason an order for a Cadillac margarita, she started on the chips. She made rapid salsa dips, gingerly stuffing the loaded chips inside her small mouth.

Murdock asked, "So what brought you to Mandrake's?"

She paused to swallow a mouthful of chips. "Oh gosh, well, I've never been here before. I just picked up my new car, and this looked like the perfect place for a quick celebration before I go home. I'm a little nervous because I don't know what does what on the thing yet." Her voice rose as she put extra emphasis on the last few words. Jason set down her margarita. Murdock watched her take a long pull on it.

"Well, now I know why you lit up this place like a maximum-security prison lockdown when you pulled up. Congratulations, nonetheless. It's a beauty"

"Oh God," she groaned. "Was it that bad? You know, I wondered why the roads seemed brighter than usual. I definitely should read the owner's manual right away." After a second large swill of the cocktail, not much remained in the glass.

"Good idea. Your grand entrance reminded me of the paparazzi at a star-sighting. I may even be suffering from retina burn."

She scrunched her nose, which narrowed her eyes, before cutting loose a solid laugh. "I guess it was pretty bad after all. Oh man, I'm sorry, Chase." She flagged Jason down and ordered another round.

During the laughter, he noticed her flawless, bright-white upper teeth. On the contrary, the bottom teeth, not so white and crooked, showed obvious imperfections. This leveled the playing field for him to move forward. The flaw enhanced her appeal, made her seem more natural, even approachable, than others who relied on multiple enhancements. Her laughing at one of his lighthearted cracks raised his comfort level.

Since his last glimpse verified no ring on her finger, he opened the probing. "Already over the temporary blindness, Tonya. I'm curious why you picked that particular model car. Is it the new 'Duty' SUV they just came out with?"

Already guzzling her second margarita, a puzzled expression came over her face. "The Duty?" Murdock snickered when he heard the incredulous tone in her voice. The moment the words came out of her mouth, she stared at him, wide-eyed. "Hah! The Audi Duty," she howled, loud enough for everyone in the bar to hear. "Well, Audi Duty to you, too. Too hysterical, Chase. You're either hilarious or this tequila is stronger than I thought."

He demurred. "I vote for the tequila. You're the first person who's laughed at it after years of trying."

"Still, I think it's very clever." She caught Jason's attention waving the high sign for a third 'Cadi,' a nickname used for the potent elixir she just inhaled.

On his third beer, Murdock detected his early buzz stage. Watching her behavior, he presumed she either felt too comfortable in his presence, or perhaps, craved a heavy buzz in the shortest time possible. *I may suggest she leave her brand-new car parked for the night, or I could talk her into chugging coffee instead. Her rate of alcohol consumption is a bit scary.* On alert over her alcohol behavior, he toned down the conversation to a simple chat.

During their talk about life in Ventura County, including what fun activities they liked, he asked, "What line of work are you in, Tonya?"

"I'm a literary agent. I've noticed it's much tougher making a go of it out here. The east coast, New York City in particular, is where most of the action is."

"Well, I know one way you can get more attention. Change your name to Paige."

"Paige?" she asked, the inflection in her voice again indicating uncertainty. "Why Paige?"

"Don't you think the perfect name for a literary agent would be Paige Turner?" She finished the name with him, having caught the pun.

This time she shook from laughter, setting down her drink to prevent spilling it. "Where do you come up with this stuff? You just crack me up." She kept the smile on and leaned in near his face, lowering her voice. "Would you care join me for a smoke out back?"

"Oh, thanks, I don't smoke, but I'll keep you company while you burn one."

"Great." She turned toward Jason, "Hey, will you please save our seats? We'll be back in five."

He followed her out the rear door into the parking lot, verifying her stride could pass a sobriety test. After another drink or two, he estimated she would hit the official hammered zone. She cautioned, "We better move away from the door. I don't want any customers getting a whiff of this."

They headed for the alley, turned right, then walked behind a deserted building alongside the restaurant. She reached in her purse, pulling out a silver cigarette case. When she opened it, he saw why secondhand smoke might worry her. She plucked a fat joint from the case. Murdock, impressed by the perfect shape of the doobie, concluded an expert rolled it. His radar went off. *Oh, great. She's at least two sheets to the wind on booze already, so now she wants more buzz.*

"I know you said you don't smoke but….?," she prodded, stretching out the word 'but.' She held the joint in front of his face, almost touching his nose with it.

Having given up pot-smoking for several years, Tonya's subtle urging caught him off guard. He worried he might come across too old or stodgy to let his hair down for a little fun. "Oh well, sure, since I get what you mean by 'smoke.' I'll share a little reefer with you."

Suddenly self-conscious, he feared she could tell how out of touch he was with the present-day weed scene. She smiled, produced a lighter, fired up the hefty joint, and took a long drag before handing it over. The thick, pungent aroma was sweet, jarring his sense of smell and old memories. Her exhaled smoke covered his face, as it had many times during the days from another era. Back then, he got loaded with his buddies while sampling the latest record album one of them just bought.

She handed him the joint. Her eyes followed its journey to his lips. When he finished the longest drag his lungs could tolerate, a tiny fraction of the long one she took, she asked, "What do you think, Mr. Murdock?"

His response began a conversation which lasted far longer than the 'five minutes' she told Jason they would be gone. He got higher quicker than he desired, bringing on stoner paranoia, climaxing in a bout of fear and anxiety. If he were alone, he could crawl into his car until the rush subsided.

His curiosity about Tonya overpowered his inclination to whimper. Stabilizing his stupor required total concentration. They talked about music, movies, traveling, books, whatever crossed their minds. He mentioned his reclamation from the unemployment scrapheap, the catalyst for his subsequent renewal on life. During the unrestrained conversation courtesy of the mutual weed buzz, he almost revealed his loss of Donna. He used a clever diversion by describing instead a car wreck he once experienced, but his stomach churned from the brief recollection of Donna's tragedy.

By the time they finished her oversized joint, they had been talking for 45 minutes. "Oh crap," she said. "I wonder if Jason saved our seats. Let's go see if our drinks are still at the bar. I really *am* dying of thirst now."

They walked back into the restaurant. Murdock worried his eyes glowed stop-sign red. Jason glanced up from one of his concoctions forcing a grin. "Nice five minutes, guys. I put your drinks behind the bar, but I had to give up your stools."

"I wish you hadn't done that, Jason," Murdock clamored. "I planned to take mine to the doctor tomorrow. He asked for a sample but didn't specify from which bar." Jason rolled his eyes.

Tonya slapped him on the arm, cackling, "You're insane, Chase".

She downed the last of Cadi number three. "I better get going. It's been fun meeting you. I had a great time." She reached into her purse and pulled out a business card. "My cell's on there, so give me a call any time. Maybe we can do this again."

"Sure thing, Tonya. Your company made my evening a blast." He put his arms around her as she leaned into him while they hugged in front of the bar. *I could get used to this.* The embrace went on a little longer than he expected. When she released her hold, he took the cue to escort her outside.

As they reached her car, he suggested, "Let me help you with those brights. The last thing you want is attention after what we've consumed." He found the headlight switch and set it to low beams right after he opened the car door. "There. Now your neighbors won't think you're an incoming spaceship when you arrive home."

"Thanks so much, Chase." She put her right hand on his neck followed by gently pulling his face down to hers. After giving him a light kiss, she got in the car.

When she drove away, he hoped she wasn't too loaded to drive or wouldn't forget all about meeting him when she woke up the next day. In spite of her propensity for Cadi's before a weed chaser, he rated her as normal, possessing entertaining qualities. At his stage of life, meeting women as attractive as Tonya who interested him involved sheer luck.

He entered the bar, then decided he had enough for the night. He gave Jason an adios. Jason returned a knowing smile, putting both thumbs up. He located the keys in his pocket as he headed for the parking lot. During the walk, he gazed skyward, "What do you think of Tonya, sweetheart?"

In the middle of pulling out of the parking lot behind Mandrake's, a delayed rush of the dizzying effects from the marijuana overcame him. He rolled down the windows, sucking cool air into his lungs. He contemplated stopping the car until his head cleared, but he was so close to home. He surveyed the empty streets. Confident he could make it home without incident, he pointed Pearl west in the slow lane for the short ride. Less than three miles later, flashing red and white lights in his rearview mirror forced his eyes to slits. A cop appeared from nowhere tailgating his bumper. He froze. Without moving his head, he glanced at his speedometer, barking, "This is bullshit. No way I was speeding." Indeed, the numbers glowing back at him confirmed he did not break the speed limit, going all of 20-mph in a 45-mph zone.

"Fuck," he cursed as he pulled over, stopping his car near the curb. He had to think quick. A DUI required taking out a second mortgage, a lending option negated by his rental status. "I can't just sit here. I gotta do something now," he screamed through a whisper. "Wait, cliché or not, the best defense is a good offense."

Before the cop opened the door of his patrol car, Murdock popped the hood release. He got out of Pearl, shaking his head, wearing a deliberate frown during his walk to the front of the car. When he raised the hood, he viewed the engine compartment, staring at nothing. Hearing the cop approaching, he reached for a random part, saying loud enough for the cop, "Must be these damned fuel injectors."

The cop, his ticket book in hand, reached the front of his car. "You know you worried me when you got out of the car. So, what seems to be the problem?"

"Good evening, Officer. Sorry I worried you. Well, they told me I might have problems from the fuel injectors *after* I bought the car, of course. Then, sure enough, I'm cruising along at fifty, and all of a sudden, it loses power. I must have looked like an overly cautious geezer when you saw me." He trailed the statement with a nervous laugh.

The cop eyed him using his flashlight then pointed the beam into the engine compartment. "May I have your license and registration, please?"

Oh shit, he's not buying it. "Oh, sure thing." As he walked toward the passenger side, he pulled his license out of his wallet. He opened the door and grabbed his registration from the glove box, handing the cop both items.

The cop's tone remained the same, "Stay put. I'll be right back after I run a check on you and the vehicle."

Taking as many deep breaths through his mouth as he could, he busied himself under the hood, pretending he knew what he was doing. While his VIN and license numbers traveled through the Ventura County PD's computer system, the deep breathing calmed him down, letting him focus in the moment. *Just need a get-out-of-jail-free for this one. There'll be time for thinking later.*

The cop returned grinning, returning his documents, "If you want, I can call a tow truck for you, Mr. Murdock?"

He went limp with relief. "Oh, gosh, Officer. Let me start the car up again, just in case. It's a recurring issue lately. It usually works itself out after a rest, so maybe I get lucky one more time."

He hopped back into his car. He gave it a few revs, nodded his head, rolling his window down. "Sounds okay now, Officer. I sure appreciate your concern. I'll have this damned thing checked out first thing in the morning."

"Alright then, Mr. Murdock. I didn't give you a warning for your hazardous slow speed. I'm trusting you to get your car fixed as soon as possible." Murdock nodded, maintaining his concerned demeanor. "Take it easy getting home." The cop returned to his patrol car.

Having just dodged a massive bullet, he waited until the cop drove off before re-entering traffic. He cursed himself for trying to impress Tonya by partaking in her overstuffed joint. He swore he would never put himself in a position again where he got behind the wheel of his car after consuming anything other than a beer or two. After the cop took off, he eased back out into the light traffic. To insure against being pulled over for driving in slo-mo again, he set his cruise control to 40 mph. Having never used it before on surface streets, it felt weird.

The steady ride dissolved his brain fog. The debacle involving Nadine Curtis the night before unnerved him; meeting Tonya encouraged him. Even though no cougar alarm went off during their time together, being scammed twice in the past year lay fresh in his mind, so anything was possible. *I should have asked Tonya if she knew Kevin Alvarez.* In spite of the fact men his age were not in high demand, he considered scoring Tonya's phone number without even asking a victory of sorts. At this point, the pros led the cons.

Back at his apartment, he had a one-way conversation with Donna while he undressed. "Sweetness, there will never be another you, and I know it. However, I can't become a hermit when I'm not working. I need some company of the female variety. When we were together, I walked on air. I treasured our talks, especially the banter with all the laughter, and the closeness I experienced being your only man. The chemical sparks we shared amazed me, maybe one in a billion odds for me to experience. I don't imagine I can ever expect love again at the level we had. All I'm thinking is maybe someone can come close again. I'm not sure living alone is for me. If you were still here, I would be okay because we'd be planning our wedding. But life has a random way of picking its spots, doesn't it, baby? If there's a heaven, I'm positive you're in it. I know it sounds absurd, yet I hope you will give me a sign should the right woman come along. By the way, sweetheart, did you have that cop deliver me your warning sign on Tonya?"

CHAPTER 13

TIME TO EXPAND

Monday Morning, Gina, the Eye Cue receptionist, stopped Murdock after he entered the building. "Mr. Bodine wants you in his office first thing." Murdock gave Gina a big grin and the peace sign as he walked away.

Entering the boss's office, Bodine interrupted his attempted hello, "What the hell happened at round two with Nadine?"

"Wait, what? Who told you?"

"She did. Called me as soon as I got here. Claims it was a misunderstanding."

"Oh yeah? Well, besides yourself and who knows how many others, the woman had a pork fest with Kevin Alvarez, who, as you know, is young enough to call her Mommy. She's probably had a few dashboards replaced ala the great Bodini. You know, I can't believe how she tattles to you about every mishap with me. It's nuts. "

"Yeah, I hear you." Bodine sounded sympathetic.

"Bo, why is a woman with her incredible attributes trolling for twenty-five-year-olds? She doesn't have one of those teacher/ student complexes, does she?"

Without skipping a breath, Bodine softened his tone, "Why would someone like the great Bodini do what he did for so long before Jenna Talia came into his life? Sure, Nadine may have done the cougar thing for a bit simply because dating men more age appropriate didn't match the excitement level she desired. Most guys her age view her arsenal of charms, confidence, not to mention immeasurable sex appeal, as intimidating. When she senses meekness from a potential suitor, it's an automatic sayonara. Then you came along and didn't flinch. You didn't hit on her or make her feel objectified. In fact, you showed no fear when in her presence. She not only admired you, she had a genuine crush on you. You should put a governor on your tendency for judging people so harshly and reconsider her. You probably won't meet another woman with her qualities again, ever. *Plus,* she still digs you. Just get over yourself. Stop being so hypersensitive. Try putting yourself in her stilettos. She's state-of-the-art, man."

"I don't know. She sure had me hooked, but I have a thing about women who sleep around while I am dating them. The cougar part of it makes it worse."

"I get it. It's okay for us, but when a woman does it..."

"Okay, okay, I get it. I'll think about it. Thanks for your assessment. Hey, I met a real nice lady at Mandrake's last night,"

"Does she put the stone in fox the way Nadine does?"

"Well, not really."

"Is she as smart or engaging with the ability to dish as well as she takes?"

"Probably not."

"Does she sport D cups that can stand at attention untethered?"

"I wouldn't know, but I doubt it."

"Nadine places all of those appetizers on your table. Any other shortcomings you can think of with this babe you met last night?"

"Points taken. She did drink like a sailor on shore leave topped off immediately by smoking a giant joint."

"Without further comment, your honor, the defense rests." Murdock nodded then left.

Bodine made him realize the 'shoot now, ask questions later' attitude toward Nadine released the ugly double standard bias he still held. He knew his tendency for jealousy with instant rejection displayed an insensitivity he would find intolerable if the roles were reversed. Bo was right. The best option for both of them required he give her the benefit of the doubt by making a simple phone call. They would either clear the air, or not. Part of him hoped she swayed him over her way. Her allure remained undeniable.

Before his final step out of the office, Bodine reminded him of their appointment in a half-hour with two gentlemen, Mr. Hwang and Mr. Woo, from a reputable Taiwan factory. They requested a formal U. S. meeting specifically with Bodine to learn about Eye Cue's facility and distribution reach. Most noteworthy, they advised Bodine their chief interest lay in learning who orchestrated the recent promotional campaign for the company, which brought Eye Cue to their attention.

On his way to the conference room, Murdock picked up Bodine, who gave him a ten-second refresher course on Taiwanese introductory customs. As the host, Bodine introduced himself and Murdock, followed quickly by two slightly bowed head-nods from their visitors. Murdock nodded slightly back at both men, giving both handshakes. "How was your flight?"

Mr. Woo appeared agitated, "Fright not van nize."

Murdock countered without filter, "What's so frightening about Van Nuys?"

Bodine clarified through a whisper, "He said the flight was not very nice." His head tilted toward Mr. Woo.

"Oh, well, at least he knows some English," Murdock whispered back.

Bodine admonished him using a weary tone, "Don't go there, Chaser." With a cheerier tone, he continued, "Moving along, these distinguished gentlemen will show us their wares, probably ask questions. Later we'll get them shit-faced at Mandrake's." Bodine ended with a broad grin.

Mr. Hwang asked, "What shit-faced?"

Having confirmed their limited comprehension, Murdock seized the moment offering his reply in a calm, business-like voice, "That's when we get you so fucking wasted, you'll meet every demand we make. In fact, by the time you head back to Taiwan, *you'll* owe *us* money."

Mr. Hwang raised his eyebrows, "What wasted?"

Mr. Woo chimed in with a broad grin, "American actors say 'fu king' all time. Must rike food." Bodine put on a plastic smile, preserving his composure.

Murdock answered, "Mr. Woo, 'fu king' is what we do in America after the food. Mr. Hwang, 'wasted' means feeling so good, you'll love doing business with us." *These boys are clearly out of their element. We'll have them caving in by midnight.*

Bodine gave Murdock one of his classic 'watch it, asshole' looks from the corner of his eye. He kept the phony look pasted on his face, nodding his head in agreement with Murdock's declaration. Mr. Woo and Mr. Hwang followed suit, smiling, nodding, oblivious of the nuances in play.

"We happy get 'wasted' with you, ok? We tour Eye Cue now?" Mr. Hwang maintained his ear-to-ear grin as he spoke.

Soon after the early evening happy hour started, the four men walked into a crowded Mandrake's behind a party of fifty or more tourists who had spent the day at the Ronald Reagan Library. Bodine grabbed the last empty table. Woo and Hwang showed their excitement pointing out the attractive Asian women in the Reagan tour group. A few moments later, their jaws dropped as they spotted the waitress in her final approach toward their table.

"Hi, my name's Laura. I'll be taking care of you gentlemen this evening." The two visitors froze, awestruck at the young, pretty Laura's near six-foot height. Her stature and V-neck black top supplied them with frequent flashing of her plentiful bosom as she delivered the cocktail napkins.

Murdock cracked, "I'll bet you don't have many like Laura back home, right?"

With smitten written on his face, Mr. Woo uttered. "Van Nize, Mr. Murdock."

Mr. Hwang responded, equally impressed, "So pretty, so *big*."

Bodine corrected him. "Laura is pretty and *tall*, Mr. Hwang, not big." Mr. Hwang bobbed his head with a sheepish grin, still fixated on the statuesque amazon's chest.

Laura smiled at the compliment. "Why thanks so much, guys. What can I get you?"

After Mr. Woo asked for "a Singapore Sring, prease," Mr. Hwang ordered "a Mud Sride." Bodine palmed a twenty-dollar bill into Laura's hand. "May their glasses never be empty." He ordered Coronas with shots of tequila for him and Murdock, to whom he whispered, "Pace yourself, Chaser. Can't have you forgetting a word said tonight." Murdock nodded.

As the evening unfolded, each guest's consumption rate steadily increased at the same pace their inhibitions lost restraint. After his third cocktail, Mr. Woo said, "I rike dis prace. So many bootifur women, so fun we here."

Mr. Hwang changed his drink order so it matched the Eye Cue executives. Laura delivered the round. Hwang slurred, "Never see anyting rike Raura in Taiwan. You Americans rucky."

After three hours of steady drinking, Bodine readied himself for business talk. Earlier, the Taiwanese businessmen offered an impressive product presentation at the office along with uninspiring price quotes. He leaned toward the two men. "Your excellent products would fit easily into Eye Cue's offerings. While I like most of what you showed us today, gentlemen, I feel your pricing is way too high."

Before Bodine could make a counteroffer, Mr. Woo added, "We give you twenty percent off for big order, deriver forty-five to sixty days."

Bodine, knowing their first offer was a bluff, countered, "How about thirty percent off for two big orders delivered in thirty to forty days ?" Mr. Woo faced Mr. Hwang. They began an exchange using their native tongue, leaving Bodine and Murdock in limbo.

The dialog went on for a few minutes. Murdock, frustrated at being locked out of their communication, spoke up, "I hate when you guys pull this shit. How about fifty percent off on *three* big orders?" Mr. Woo looked insulted; an inebriated Mr. Hwang showed signs of trouble staying upright while he serial-burped.

Finally, Mr. Woo said, "Best price thirty-seven percent off three big orders."

Bodine took control. "We'll do *two* big orders, not three, for thirty seven percent off with a thirty-to-forty-day delivery."

Mr. Woo paused for a moment then extended his hand, "Very good, preased we do business."

They drove the two men back to their hotel, leaving behind the pair's rental car in the Eye Cue parking lot. Bodine told them he would pick them up first thing the next morning. He and Murdock exchanged chuckles watching the duo stagger toward the entrance. Once they made it safely inside, Bodine frowned at Murdock. "Who in the hell said you could run roughshod on my negotiations?"

"Bo, they went from twenty up to a thirty percent discount in a matter of seconds. I knew there was more water in their pricing, and I exposed it. If I hadn't pressed the issue, we'd have lost the additional seven percent. You can thank me later. Anyway, you showed them the Bodini magnificence when you slid in the earlier delivery terms. The deal's stellar." Murdock stared at Bodine.

"Yeah, Chaser, you're spot on there. Just don't do it again without a high-sign."

"Ok, how 'bout this one?" Murdock flipped him the finger. Bodine frowned but let a chuckle slip.

Murdock reached for his phone soon after he got home. His thoughts of Curtis consumed his concentration throughout the evening. He would discuss Nadine Curtis with Kevin Alvarez right away, clearing the air clouding their close relationship. Maybe the conversation would increase his chances for a good night's rest. Near midnight, he dialed Kevin's number, relieved the young man picked up on the third ring. "Sorry to be calling so late, Kevin. I'd just like to ease the tension between us. If you don't mind, could you explain what the extent of your relationship is or was with Nadine?"

"It's okay, Chase. I'm glad you called. That fiasco at the steakhouse was fucked up. The straight answer is we only had a one-nighter. At some point, I'd drank enough at The Carousel to think the hookup with her was a good idea. But it's important you understand what a quality woman Nadine is. Outside of my mom and aunt, she's the most beautiful woman I've ever met."

"Are you still seeing her, or do you plan to see her again?"

"No, no way. We only got together once."

"What happened?"

"Before she left, she told me she made a mistake by hooking up with me. Said it was the first and last time she would experiment with such an affair. Here I was falling for her only to have it end on our first and what turned into our last date. It seemed harsh at first, yet I knew nothing could ever come of it anyway, ya know? Look, Nadine is the ultimate lady, Chase. I'd love it if I met someone smokin' hot like her nearer my age who also had maturity."

"Thanks, Kevin. I feel like I slapped her in the face by sending her home. Obviously, my temper and insecurity took over. I assumed she was a wanton cougar, constantly on the prowl for young king snake. From what you've told me, maybe she was repulsed by the whole thing."

"Yeah, she was bummed when Ted told her he had to take her home. I'd say from what I saw she's lit whenever she looks at you. You should give her another chance, Chase. The woman is a great catch. And that body? My God, I've never..."

"Okay, okay, Kevin. Don't start painting porn pictures in my mind. I just felt so shitty knowing I wanted what you already had experienced. Then again, better it be you than anyone else.

By the way, when you said, "she's lit," what are you telling me? 'Lit' means drunk or high or something having a flame put to it like a cigarette, right?"

"Yeah, I know the old meanings from Mom and Dad. The way it's used now is like something's on fire in a good way like a party or a feeling. So I was saying she's on fire when she looks at you. In other words, she's hot for you."

"Aha, it's official. I have entered the millennial zone, and I like it. So now, I can reply to what you said with, Hey Kev, that's really bitchen."

"Exactly, Chase."

"Cool, man. Thanks so much for your honesty about the Nadine issue. I'll let you go. Goodnight."

After ending the call, he checked his voice messages for the first time in several hours. Nadine had left a message. "Hello, Chase. I don't know what you think of me, but I'm no cougar. We all make mistakes." Click.

CHAPTER 14

A NIBBLE OF CROW

The following day, Murdock called Nadine while on his lunch break. Before she could say 'hello,' he blurted, "I feel like an asshole for the way I treated you Saturday night. You didn't deserve that."

"Well, hello to you, too, Mr. Murdock. I don't think I did either, especially with no chance to explain."

"Kevin Alvarez told me it was an ill-advised venture for you, but I jumped to conclusions assuming it was a lifestyle choice. For a bonus, he also vouched for your character, which made me feel even worse. I'm so sorry I embarrassed you at the restaurant in front of everyone. It's just, when Kevin walked into the room, the way you two stared at each other, I felt, uh, well... I couldn't imagine why a woman like you would prefer dating men so young."

"Not that you deserve an explanation after serving me up for public humiliation, Chase, but here's the story. I was married for fifteen years. I've been divorced for ten. Would I like to meet a man near my age with whom I can share a relationship on a level playing field? Absolutely. However, I've had a steady stream of potential men cross my path who without exception have disappointed me."

"In what ways, if I may ask?"

"Too pushy, too needy, too horny, too contrary, too timid. You name it. You are the first man I've met in years who impressed me with the way you carry yourself. You are self-assured without being arrogant. You have a very engaging personality, also funnier than hell. Plus, you didn't make a fool of yourself when we first met. Too many men with a high school mentality hit on me. It turns me off every time it happens. They trip over their tongues, saying awkward things, making their testosterone-fueled intentions known almost immediately. They can't conceive a slower approach, having casual and intellectual conversations, or just the old getting-to-know each other technique. I've been asking myself, 'where are all the fine gentlemen' for years. I got so fed up, I couldn't see straight, so I joined my girlfriend for a night at the Carousel, which is where I met Kevin. He flashed more class with more sensitivity toward a woman than the bozos I've met since my divorce. I could still get what I wanted, what I thought I needed, and Kevin fit the profile. I've suffered strong regret from that lapse in judgement. Kevin was so charming, so polite, and down to earth. That young man is wise beyond his years. He knows the treatment women desire. Truth is, I hadn't been with a man in so long I was craving male attention. I knew it couldn't go anywhere with Kevin. Later, I felt guilty as hell for my selfishness. Honestly, Chase, you are the first man in my age range who's captured my imagination because you're so genuine. I thought I'd finally met a *really bitchen* kindred spirit."

Murdock smiled, "Ya know, Nadine, Bo is actually the one who gave me clarity about you. He thinks you're aces. Kevin just reinforced it. I feel so badly about the way I behaved last Saturday night. I'm asking you for wholesale forgiveness, which includes my unattractive tendencies for instant judgement and conviction. I had no idea when we met the first time you saw me as anything other than a business associate."

"I don't wear that slinky red dress for any business associate. I think you're special, Chase. Just don't cast me out on the streets or anything resembling harsh treatment like that again. I forgive you under the assumption all this goes in the past and stays there."

"Agreed. Glad we had this chat, Nadine. We'll talk soon."

Her forgiveness reframed his perspective toward her character. She didn't hate his guts, nor did she tell him to lose her number. He rushed to Bodine's office. "She still likes me, Bo. Even after what I did, she still wants to see me."

"Good deal, Chaser. Just don't treat her like an indiscriminate floozy again because there won't be a round three. She's no patsy."

Once again, muddled with feelings about Nadine, he ambled back toward his office. He respected how Bodine's friendship plus Kevin's maturity adjusted his attitude where Nadine was concerned. He would show her a special time on their next date, making sure she knew how much he appreciated her. His knee-jerk judgement calls were history.

<hr>

Rex Sullivan came into his office later in the afternoon. "Got a minute, Chase?"

"Sure thing, Casual one, what's up?"

"Well, I've heard you use the term 'bedwetter' on a few occasions. I'm quite sure it's not a good thing. I want certainty though, so how do you define the term?"

Murdock leaned back in his chair with his hands locked behind his head, closing his eyes as if this were a critical lesson in Sullivan's development with the company. "I'm glad you recognize how important our internal code is, Rexuality. Your commendable observation skills will serve you well here. Let me fully address your question, including the degrees we've assigned to bedwetting.

"First off, we are not criticizing young children who wet their beds. Most children get over it. No, we are talking about adults who develop a pattern of behavior that repulses us. An adult bedwetter frequently does or says something causing severe disappointment or consistently drops the ball. He or she doesn't deliver on a promise or they do or say something stupid, causing senseless problems."

Murdock leaned forward clasping his hands on his desk. "As a factual matter, there are four intensity levels used to determine the severity of the wetness. Level One is slight, a light misting of the sheets causing dampness without further damage. A Level One bedwetter is harmless but warrants frequent monitoring. They're prone to minor letdowns, seldom making the same mistake twice. Level Two involves soaking the sheets plus the mattress cover. A Level Two bedwetter is cause for concern because their behavior is more bothersome, even chronic. They are challenged in learning from their mistakes. In other words, there is no guarantee they won't repeat it down the road. A Level Three bedwetter is dangerous. They fatally soak the mattress and box springs requiring immediate removal and require a strong warning. As you can imagine, you can never eliminate the stench from the saturation. A Level Three bedwetter at the very least must always be kept at arm's length and be called out for their infractions because their behavior is beyond chronic and could easily morph into Level Four."

Sullivan started out chuckling, hitting a full belly laugh by Level Three. "Oh shit, Chase, you are one twisted mister. I can't wait to hear what Level Four is about."

Like a professor lecturing law students, underscoring his serious subject, he stood up behind his desk. "You must avoid a Level Four bedwetter at all cost because the saturation exceeds the entire bed's containment capacity for the urine volume emanating from said wetter. It ends up running in torrents off the bed frame onto the floor, destroying the carpet or hardwood beneath it." Sullivan laughed till he gasped. "I know you'll find this difficult to believe, Unsafe one, but I wet the bed last Saturday night."

Sullivan cried, "I can't believe you're admitting this, Chase. What level?"

"In all honesty, I believe I qualified for a Level Two rating, and I'm not proud of it." He described his banishing Nadine from the steakhouse along with the pain he later felt after blindsiding her in such a public spectacle. "I will make it up to her, however. We patched things up over the phone today. I learned an important lesson there, my Consensual friend."

Sullivan stood, trusting the conversation stopped there. "One more thing. The boss man is familiar with the rating system. If you should encounter anyone on the phone who is a clear bedwetter and demands an audience with him, give him a heads-up what their level is before you forward the call."

A brief time later, Sullivan called from the main floor. "Rebecca Varner asked if you're available. She's concerned about our delivery abilities. Level One."

"You catch on quickly, Conjugal one. Thanks." Murdock recalled Varner, their rep in the southwest, as an attractive woman, seasoned in the industry for over fifteen years. Everyone considered her a capable, efficient, and valued Eye Cue asset. Flashing back to the affair she shared with the former Eye Cue President, Murdock gagged picturing the flabby, overweight Donnelly mixing it up with such a pretty woman. *So many things simply defy explanation.* He picked up the call. "How's young Becky Varner?"

"Young? Don't yew go sweet talkin' me, Chase." Varner had a gentle Texas twang, always offering easy conversation. "I'm shore sorry to bother yew, but Rex is so new. I just wanted a quick word with yew directly. We have a bunch of orders comin' in from my customers, who are worried about backorders if they place more."

"Becky, I recall the affair you had with Bob Donnelly."

"Now why in the hell would yew bring such a thing up, Chase?" She sounded exasperated.

"Because I know how much you regretted that indiscretion, Becky. You're a strong person with a sharp understanding of your customers. You'll regret even more letting your weak-kneed accounts browbeat you about our delivering capabilities. Bo already moved past the curve on the supply issue. The Board of Directors gave him a blank checkbook. He stepped up and can order whatever quantities of product he deems necessary. Let me assure you he's not being timid about it. Damn it, Becky, be assertive with your customers. Tell them if they hold back on their orders, they'll be left standing at the station, watching the train pull away."

"I guess I just needed some reassurance, Chase. I like yore bullet points and will use them. The demand for our products has risen so dramatically. The promos yew've done have improved Eye Cue's profile so much I'm turning away business until I can hire more reps."

"Get 'em hired asap, Becky girl," Murdock responded with his best Texas drawl. "The wave nationwide continues to gather momentum. Don't turn away any more business without clearing with Rex first. Let your lily-livered customers know we have new product categories coming down the pipe as well. We should have a whole new batch of goodies for our sales offerings within the next two months. Tell your accounts they could get stuck on the outside looking stupid. Look, I'll have HR in contact shortly about your requesting two sales reps. Would two be enough for now?"

Becky's whole tone changed. "Jeezus, Chase, two would be perfect. If I can get them on board and trained within the next six weeks, we could have a real bump in our sales production out here with a banner year to boot. Can yew pass that on to HR? I'll let them know the territories for the reps when they call me."

"I like your thinking there, Ms. Becky. I'll call HR as soon as we hang up."

During the hours after Becky's call, Murdock found himself bolstering the confidence for the remaining sales force. Becky's attitude seemed effortless compared with others, whose bedwetting levels ranged from two to three. The escalation in demand for their products approached fever pitch, showing no signs of subsiding. Mildly exhausted by day's end, he craved alone time with his vinyl record collection, an expensive bottle of tequila, and serious introspection. Nadine was an authentic marvel. While encouraged by their reconciliation, he wouldn't allow himself a full throttle pursuit. The memory of Donna's demise remained too fresh.

CHAPTER 15

CONTEMPLATION

On his way home, Murdock picked up a bottle of Don Julio tequila along with a six-pack of Corona beer. With Donna gone, his first love digressed into seeking comfort from his favorite music while downing beer and tequila shots. Neither Zachary nor Bodine ever appreciated how his feeding on a song's melody or phrase provided the channel for releasing his troubles and relaxing. Once inside his apartment, he locked the door. By turning down the light low enough, he protected his solitude from a would-be visitor's knock.

Heading straight for the fridge, he put the beer minus two bottles inside. With his favorite shot glass for three-finger shots and the beers in hand, he placed them all on the coffee table on the way to his bedroom. Yanking off his tie with his half-unbuttoned shirt over his head while kicking off his shoes, he dropped everything alongside the other two piles of clothes on his floor. After stepping out of his trousers atop the new clothes pile, he shuffled to the living room couch. He assumed the proper drinking position wearing only his t-shirt, boxers, and socks. He chugged the entire first beer. With expert precision, he poured the tequila to the rim of the glass, then guzzled the liquid gold. He finished the routine by selecting the perfect record album for his cerebral consumption. Steely Dan fit the bill with their unique styling on "Rikki Don't Lose That Number." Despite the puzzling lyrics raising questionable interpretations for decades, Rikki had a rough decision brewing. He/she would be good company.

With the rushed buzz settling in, he took his center channel listening position. After a deep breath, he closed his eyes, shifting his mind to autopilot. So much had happened since Donna's death. He welcomed the frenzy at work with his new duties at Eye Cue. It left him no time for dwelling on the crippling effect of his lingering sadness. Being exhausted at the end of each day with only time for food then bed recharged his focus for the next day on keeping the ship at high speed pointed in the right direction. For the first time in a long while, a feeling of accomplishment warmed him with added hope, even anticipation for a brighter future. On his behalf, his best friends, Zachary and Bodine, shaped the catalysts for his new life. Remembering how he almost threw all of it away, he refilled his shot glass before grabbing the second beer. He stood, then raised his glass toward the ceiling. "To the best pals in the universe, this chug's for you." He gulped down the liquor in one swallow. Becoming overwhelmed by fear or depression again had no place in his future. "So be it," he murmured, ending the ceremony by welcoming his new perspective with a long draw from the second beer.

As his reflection resumed, the number one issue, Nadine Curtis, came forward. She had been an incredible surprise for him, although an unexpected complication. Could he even consider a relationship with her being a Board director? If he pursued one, would she remain interested or determine he wasn't what she wanted after all? One thing was certain; no way she could break his heart. His invincibility fending off any potential rejection lived in his belief no woman alive could touch him the way Donna did. Still, the primal urges would always beckon him, so who better to stoke the flames than Nadine? Most men could only dream of having a lady with her amenities. He stood again, gesturing with the bottle of residual beer as if toasting, "Life certainly can deal from a deck of puzzles, Ms. Curtis. Here's to solving our puzzle naked."

Where he saw himself as an everyman, resembling the Joe lunch bucket type, he saw Zachary as much smarter, Richard Bodine as a notch above handsome and near brilliant. Even as a garden variety type, he shared romance with a spectacular woman like Donna. Now another extremely rare beauty, the savvy Nadine, not only showed interest in him, but she also came onto him, hard. He recognized the 'better to be lucky than good' syndrome. His job awarded him an opportunity beyond golden. At the rate things were developing, he may well buy his own home in a couple of months, hollering a loud adios to apartment life. His upcoming bonus money easily covered a down payment.

Hell, he might get the dog he wanted, a sweet black Labrador he would name Rikki. He pictured his home showing off an authentic wood-burning fireplace, not one of those fake gas jobs. He saw Pearl parked in a garage sporting the deserved protection she deserved. The modern kitchen where he practiced gourmet cooking, merging into a dining room large enough for a dozen people, finished off the major features he fancied. He imagined throwing a welcome party, inviting everyone in his close circle over for a feast.

The eight hundred square foot apartment walls pinched his sense of space, seeming more and more suffocating. He leaned forward, using a louder than normal voice, "I *will* search for a more legitimate residence the moment I get my bonus. What kind of a Director of Sales still lives in a one-bedroom apartment the size of a walk-in closet?"

The next priority involved scheduling more time with Kevin and John Álvarez. He wondered how they tackled coping with their grief. Fortunately, they had a loving aunt who lived nearby. And what about the aunt, Barbara Conley? When will he find the courage to meet her? If she reminded him too much of Donna, it would disintegrate his composure. He discarded any thoughts of Barbara in terms of romance. However, if she mirrored Donna right down to her effervescent personality, how could he not weigh the possibility? The prospects she represented felt too daunting for any further attention for now.

Before he picked another album, he poured another shot of Don Julio and cracked open another Corona, taking a long first swig to savor its initial chill. After shuffling through his LP's, he picked a Bruce Springsteen album with the song, "Pink Cadillac." He loved the line, "Well they tempt you, man, with silver, and they tempt you, sir, with gold, and they tempt you with the pleasures that the flesh does surely hold." *Ah, now this is therapy.*

Nadine popped backed into his mind. He fantasized about seeing her completely naked for the first time. Reaching for his shot glass, he selected four more LP's. *Get your mind off Nadine, you perv.* There would be no calling her tonight, no matter how much an elixir of lust the tequila became.

He lifted the tequila to his lips just as his phone rang. He fumbled the shot glass, splashing half of it on his t-shirt. His reverie in the alternative state, created by the music, liquor, and streaming of random thoughts, shattered as he crash-landed into real time. He gulped down the rest of the shot.

"Damnit, shit, what the fuck," he snarled as he glared at the phone. Nadine's name on the screen put a smile on his face, yet he cautioned himself. After having consumed three shots and almost three beers, he couldn't risk any irresponsible jaw-flapping. "What a coincidence, Nadine. I was just sitting here wondering what you looked like in your birthday suit." *So much for being responsible.* He opened a bottled water in the kitchen, muted his phone, then gulped down the water to diffuse the alcohol buzz while she responded.

"I have it on right now, if you must know, Chase. I must say, it's a perfect fit."

"I can only imagine. Seriously, though, what's up?"

"I hope I'm not bothering you this late, but there's been a development with the Board. We've been tracking Eye Cue's sales. The question arose how you'll sustain the present pace based on the size of your current facilities and manpower."

"Crap, Nadine. I hoped you called for a round of hot phone sex."

"Now you're sounding like every other horndog I run across. Can I have a raincheck on the pillow talk?"

"I apologize. This was my night for playing music and getting lost in it for travel to an alternate reality. I'm being too forward with you, and I haven't earned the right."

"It's okay, Chase. I'd be lying if I said you offended me. I'm learning you're capable of saying anything. I love your boldness. However, your sales success caught their attention. The Board wants details on how you and Bo will manage the expansion necessary for the demand you've created. It's a high-class problem looming over all our heads. We worry if this is not addressed in a timely fashion, you guys will be cornered into turning away business. Take it from me, that isn't an option the Board will oblige."

Murdock recalled Becky Varner's mentioning her turning away business. "Have you talked to Bo about this?"

"Not yet. I'm giving you an insider's tip because I trust your instincts. Besides, Bo would probably just blow me off by saying everything's fine and under control. I have a difficult time being civil with him anyway." She tempered her voice. "You're the one who can float the plan. He'll listen to you."

"Nadine, are you still harboring feelings for Bo?"

"I was…until I met you. Now my only concerns are keeping Eye Cue's stock on the rise while I learn what makes Chase Murdock tick. We're calling a meeting with the two of you for day after tomorrow. Even though Bo's the President of the company, the Board is just as interested in your ideas. You're the one who orchestrated Eye Cue's newfound success. Bo has merely been along for the ride. Think succession planning, Chase. You can jump on the fast track with this company if you choose to go for it."

"You should understand something, Nadine. My background is purely in sales. Bo is a marketing whiz and the absolute leader of this company. He makes all the things he does appear so easy, but it doesn't mean he isn't putting in the hard labor. I will *never* undermine his authority, so I look good or make him look bad. There's only one position at Eye Cue higher than mine *and it's his.* I'm not after his job."

"I'm not suggesting you are, Chase. Just think about the big picture. There are other companies out there that could use a man with your smarts. If Eye Cue keeps cooking the way it has, you can write your own ticket."

He detected a red flag. "That's not what you said, Ms. Curtis." He hoped the formality would sink in. "Your exact words were 'succession planning to be on the fast track with *this* company.' I'm getting a mixed message from you now, and I don't like the implications. All of a sudden, I don't see you lying in bed in your birthday suit. I envision you lying in bed all decked out in your business suit, giving me one of your smug looks. What the hell's going on here?"

"Chase, please calm down. At the risk of sounding critical, you're showing your naivete here. *This* company, *that* company, it doesn't matter. You have what it takes for becoming whatever you want."

"Bo dragged me out of the sewer, Nadine. I may share our history with you someday *but understand this.*" His voice lowered to a growl. "I will never jump ship. Everything I do for Eye Cue I do for him. Enjoy your business slumber party of one."

He ended the call without saying goodbye. He dialed Bodine whose phone went to voicemail. "Bo, we have a hot problem brewing. Nadine just called me. The Board has gone Level 4."

CHAPTER 16

FEET TO THE FIRE

Incensed, Bodine paced behind his desk, roaring in his loud voice, "Why in the hell didn't Nadine call me first?" Earlier, Murdock awakened abruptly to a terse phone call from Bodine with instructions to meet in his office at 7:00 a.m. sharp.

Murdock treaded lightly. "She didn't think you'd take her seriously, feeling you'd dismiss the Board's concern as being frivolous. She also has a tough time playing nice with you. May I ask a personal question?"

"Shoot."

"What *exactly* happened between you and her?" *So much for playing it safe.*

Bodine stopped pacing, sat down, covering his face with his hands. "Oh shit, Chaser. I guess I made her feel like a whore. I met another woman whose sexuality was incredibly adventurous. So, I asked Nadine if she would participate in a threesome. That ended us, right on the spot. Honestly, she was not only hurt by it, she was thoroughly disgusted."

Murdock got animated, "Had you binged on John Lennon chanting 'Come Together?' You regarded this goddess as nothing more than a pornish game hen? Were you brain dead or just wrapped up in the World of Bodini, indulging his every whim from every woman?" He took a breath as he shut the office door. In a subdued voice, he griped, "What could be finer than a night with Nadine *alone*? No wonder she hates your guts. What's the other woman's name? Don't tell me. It doesn't matter. We'll just call her Taudrey."

When Bodine peered up at him, his fraught expression bordered on pure fright. "Not only is that totally hypocritical from you based on your recent behavior, but I'm in no state for a grilling by you or the Board. They'll be hurling one tough question after another at me, wanting quick responses with complex solutions. Chaser, what in the hell can we do? I mean, why are they springing this meeting on us giving such little notice?"

"It's a test, Bo. They want evidence their new President can front-run unforeseen deluges of orders while overcoming any labor gap within his managers, reps, staff, and warehouse workers. We have a huge task ahead and a deadline giving us less than 24 hours. You get a copy of Eye Cue's land lease. See if it allows breaking ground on any expansion."

Bodine's expression relaxed. "Bingo, Chaser. That's the one thing Bob Donnelly did years ago which might save our asses. He bought the commercial property outright. At this point, with the revenue wind at our back, we can give the Board a proper justification for whatever the hell we want by leveraging our current success."

"With kudos for our late leader and zebra hunter, our task becomes even simpler. Just have the plans doubling the warehouse space drawn up here today. The employees can park on the street until we get the project done. Get a draftsman in here who can complete the blueprints today. We don't want the Board thinking we're winging it. I'll create a manpower analysis based on doubling sales within the next twelve months. I'm betting Nadine doesn't think we'll be ready."

"Fuck her," Bodine groused.

"I was working on that, but since I told her off last night for giving me shady career advice, it's on hold again."

"Huh, I see. Well, it's probably a good thing, Chaser. Just leave her be. We should be on guard probing her every word in that meeting." Murdock nodded.

With phone calls blocked by Gina Morgan and only bathroom breaks, they sat across from each other in Bodine's office, bouncing off ideas while the draftsman designed the blueprints in Murdock's office. They brought in Sullivan for brainstorming after ordering lunch delivered, scattering sandwich, empty containers, and potato chip remnants on Bodine's desk and over the carpet. Right before 9:00 p.m., they finished. Before he left, Murdock sent all department heads an email requiring their attendance at the Board meeting the next morning.

———

Well before the scheduled meeting time, the seven Board members seated themselves in the conference room. Nadine Curtis advertised her number two catbird position on the Board by occupying the only seat beside Chairman Lawrence Davis. Murdock noted she was the only female member on the Board, thinking about the countless 'Nadines' still excluded from American boardrooms.

Bodine leaned over in his chair as he whispered to Murdock, "Davis is a blowhard. He'll try to intimidate us using contrived bullshit rhetoric. He runs his own national fertilizer company showing the same negative disposition. It's amazing the shareholders keep him in charge with their stock performing like a crippled ballerina. Hopefully, he doesn't let Nadine speak."

Murdock responded, "I hope he does. Then we'll see who's side she's on." He glanced on the sly at Nadine who showed off her classic smug image, as if she may soon witness two hillbillies on the scramble. He smirked with renewed motivation to wow the room.

Davis opened the proceedings. "Mr. Bodine, is there a specific reason you've invited all these other people to this meeting?"

Bodine stood up. "Yes, there is, Mr. Davis. Our new mission statement includes product diversity with strong organic growth. These lead managers are key to our success during every step of that endeavor. It's vital they be in the loop on everything we do." He introduced every manager by name and department.

"Very well. You know the reason we're here today, correct?" Davis had a condescending pout on his face. Nadine stared straight ahead without eye contact, now displaying a solemn expression.

"I do. You have reservations about our abilities to manage the escalating demand for our products. Mr. Chase Murdock and I have prepared a presentation we feel confident will quell your fears. I've already added a new man, Mr. Rex Sullivan, covering the Sales Manager duties supporting Mr. Murdock. Rex, please give the Board a wave, so they know who you are."

Sullivan complied. "Our expansion plan includes doubling our warehouse space. May I show you the blueprint of what we have in mind?" Bodine walked over, handing Davis the fresh document. Nadine's eyes widened in surprise. "Barring major construction issues but including the new essential equipment and software installations, we're looking at an estimated six months for completion. This additional space will give us tremendous support toward doubling our sales volume within twelve months. We lose the unsightly portion of the parking lot. However, we gain the requisite space for housing two additional loading docks in tech-smart modern buildings."

Murdock squinted, following Davis as he scrutinized each fellow Board member around the conference table. No one expressed exception for Bodine's rationale. He continued, "The cost for this undertaking, assuming no changes or enhancements, is estimated at $200,000 to $225,000. If we can break ground within the next month and finish within the projected time frame, our present sales revenue forecast shows our paying for the addition in 90 days once it's up and running." Every manager on the Eye Cue team clapped; a couple whistled.

Davis opened his mouth to say something but was interrupted by a Mr. James Terwilliger, CEO of a prominent healthcare insurance provider. "Gentlemen, that's very impressive. I think the only other thing we're interested in is how you will address the additional manpower you'll need."

Bodine leaned over again toward Murdock, "Terwilliger's the only cool one in the group. I already know he's in our corner."

Murdock stood, looked at his people, and informed them, "I've got this." Turning back, he addressed the Board. "Your imperial Boardship, thank you for including me in this firing line chat." A swell of chuckles arose from the crowd, including all the Board members except Mr. Davis and Ms. Curtis. "The day I got underway on the plan to promote Mr. Bodine and Eye Cue, I reviewed every sales territory in the country, noting where we could improve representation, especially in the highest population hubs. While it's true we might have a handful of bedwetters in our ranks..." Laughter filled the room. "...we can offer the proper motivation for their increased productivity. Failing that, we'll show them the door. In fact, Mr. Sullivan already scheduled and will continue scheduling interviews for new reps who will fill our identified regional sales voids. Our current reps are in preparation for training the rookies. Before we roll out any new products slated within the next 60 days, we expect every viable territory in the country will have adequate sales rep coverage."

Davis couldn't resist the urge to needle. "You haven't said anything about adding home office headcount."

"Well, that's because you threw me your jab before I had a chance to, Mr. Davis." His boldness delivered through a lighthearted tone caused more snickers from the partisan crowd. "We do not plan on doubling our office or warehouse staff. Rather, beginning Monday, we will conduct time studies in the warehouse in tandem with employee workload studies for the office staff to determine the appropriate number of employees we should hire immediately. Additionally, those studies will help us monitor our new construction's growth adaptability, adjusting hiring plans when and where warranted. Our department heads you see in this room are combing the industry for quality personnel, the kind who can hit the ground running. These dedicated individuals will identify local supervisors from Amazon, Walmart, and the like by offering them an attractive package above their current compensation without paying excessive premiums. To facilitate this hiring process, we assigned HR with designing competitive salary and benefit packages, including stock options. As I speak, we have stacks of resumes from pre-qualified individuals who would love working for The Great Bodini." This time, the laughter included hoots and whistles. Nadine's somber countenance swiftly became a smiley face. Even Director James Terwilliger beamed as he started clapping. The Eye Cue faithful followed suit. Murdock finished, "We have nothing further, your honors." The managers laughed even louder, then cheered followed by more applause. Bodine caught Terwilliger chuckling while clapping.

Davis's face and tone displayed clear displeasure from the upstaging by Murdock. "We'll consider your strategy. *You'll* hear directly from me, Mr. Bodine."

Murdock bit his tongue. Bodine took exception. "What do you need to consider, Mr. Davis? We just laid it out in detail. What's left for discussion? Maybe when you can make us squander more valuable work time for another unnecessary meeting?"

Davis narrowed his eyes, ready to publicly admonish his brash underling. Murdock jumped in. "I think Mr. Bodine suggests we have this problem under control with the expansion plans already well in process. Our department heads are on board, motivated and productive. We'll proceed under the strong hope your positive answer reaches us before the weekend."

Bodine stood, facing his people, shouting, "Drinks on me tonight at Mandrake's. Tell 'em you're on the Bodini tab." His proclamation triggered a standing ovation. In his opinion, they emerged victorious.

Clearly put off by Bodine's bravado intensified by Murdock's cheeky tone, Davis spoke up, "This meeting is adjourned."

Murdock held both hands up, addressing the Eye Cue department heads. "Hang back a moment, folks. I'd like a short, more meaningful meeting with you."

Davis glared at him. "Don't push it, Mr. Murdock. You don't want this Board coming down on you with both feet. You may be enjoying a bit of success at this moment, but rest assured, you're now under our microscope. This wouldn't be the time to stub your or your boss's toe." He along with the other Board members exited the conference room.

As soon as the door closed behind them, Murdock approached the group. "You might be interested in knowing this meeting was a contrived ambush. You couldn't know this, but Bo and I had less than 24 hours for preparation. Why? The Board is nervous because they don't comprehend the success we're enjoying right now. They've never seen anything like it. Their first instinct was slinging us questions whether it can be sustained because they're in uncharted waters. Bo and I threw our presentation together on the fly. The expansion blueprint was drawn up only yesterday. By the way, I embellished the backlog of resumes you're sitting on. Making my statement a reality becomes your top priority during the next week. We *will* prove we don't need no stinking Board hovering over our shoulders while we exceed their goals. Please ramp up your recruiting skills so we can quickly accumulate those top-notch candidates waiting in the wings. Bo will tell you when you can pull the trigger. We'll see you all at Mandrake's tonight." The frontline managers cheered one more time as they left the conference room.

As Murdock walked into his office, he spotted Nadine postured in a guest chair in front of his desk. He stood in the doorway, glowering at her as she faced him. He spoke in a low, monotone voice, "You drop by to see if Bo and I require any more babysitting?" He walked behind his desk and sat down, keeping his eyes glued on her.

"No, Chase. You both did a very commendable job at the meeting, although you could have refrained from all the barbs you two threw at Larry Davis."

"He's a windbag, Nadine, and a pompous one at that. We didn't appreciate the last-minute fire drill you dropped on us. It was a waste of everyone's time."

"No, it wasn't. Like I told you the other night, the Board seeks visible proof of your and Bo's acumen. Based on this company's recent history plus the executive changeovers, we had every reason to call a short notice meeting. Like it or not, we are this publicly traded company's governance. Fortunately, you both came through quite convincingly. *Unfortunately*, you both tweaked Larry's ego. We're giving you the go-ahead on your plan to facilitate the expansion. However, be careful going forward. Larry's exact words were, 'Let's see if those cocky sons-a-bitches can pull this off'." She relaxed her expression. "What I really came by to ask was why you hung up on me the other night?"

"I was relaxing, having a couple of drinks, listening to music, playing air guitar to a throng of thousands. You call dishing out these mixed messages like succession planning, fast track, writing my own ticket, inferring I could move into Bo's position if I wanted it. I simply didn't care for the tone of what you said, or the serious damper you put on my evening by talking business shit."

"I'm usually pretty concise when talking business *shit*, but I can see how you would look at our discussion as bothersome. I apologize. I should have been more buttoned up."

He winked as he tossed her a smile, "It's alright, Nadine. Today's meeting gave me a much clearer view of what I'm dealing with here. Bo and I will show more reverence toward Mr. Davis. Just ask him not to micro-manage us, okay?"

"Okay."

"By the way, were you really completely naked when you called me the other night?"

"Not a stitch."

He took a deep breath, shaking his head as he stared into her eyes.

CHAPTER 17

MANDRAKE'S MADNESS

As soon as Nadine left his office, Murdock called Ted and Cindy Zachary followed by the Alvarez brothers giving them personal invitations for the Eye Cue party that evening. Along with Bodine and Jenna Talia, they comprised his entire family. Sharing the celebration of another Eye Cue Board of Directors milestone conveyed his love for the ones who never gave up on him. Fortunately, it was Friday, so folks could cut loose.

A few hours later, he drove into Mandrake's packed parking lot. He poked around without finding a single spot. As he rolled past the bar's entrance, he saw folks crammed inside, no doubt exploiting Bodine's open tab. Ten minutes later, having exhausted every foul word he could invoke, he parked across the street almost two blocks down from Mandrake's. He hurried up the street, slowing down to a stroll as he walked through the doorway. After surveying the crowd, he confirmed most Eye Cue staff had arrived. He spotted Bodine and Talia sitting with the Zacharys. At a nearby table, he saw Kevin and John Alvarez holding court at a large table with several young women. He headed for the Bodine/Zachary table.

"Hey kids, good crowd, huh?" Leaning toward Bodine, he mentioned, "I hope you don't mind my spicing up the evening with a few additional invitees. I felt we needed additional support from our outside Eye Cue advisors." He shook hands with Zachary before hugging Cindy and Talia.

Bodine smiled. "Makes perfect sense, Chaser. I already asked for Ted's oversight since he's the most objective one of us. He does not share our frivolous risk tendencies like this open tab. It might be a dangerous thing. Let the shredding of my credit card begin."

"Great, I'll be right back after I welcome the Alvarez boys over there," he said, waving at John.

Approaching their table, he smirked. Both young men carried on simultaneous conversations with four beautiful women. He greeted the two with handshakes and hugs. "So glad you could make it, boys. Looks like you're preoccupied. Any of your lady friends looking for some uninvited advice from Mr. Mature? I also give complimentary mammograms." Kevin and John laughed out loud, while the women glared at him with tepid smiles. He leaned down between the brothers. "These women act like they've never seen a fun-loving senior citizen. At least they didn't say, 'Ok Boomer.'" Both boys cracked up.

Kevin faced the ladies, "It's okay, girls. This is our stepfather, Chase Murdock. His entrance is always unpredictable but quite entertaining."

The young women seemed more relaxed after Kevin's assurances, giving Murdock their best phony smiles. Murdock moseyed around the table shaking their hands after introducing himself while issuing compliments. "Beautiful dress," "Love your hair," "What stunning eyes." He then announced, "Stick around, folks, things should get interesting. Kevin, John, thanks so much for coming. Enjoy yourselves and your riveting company. It's been a pleasure, ladies. Maybe I'll see you on the dancefloor."

A woman sitting across from him piped up. "But there is no dancefloor."

Murdock replied, "Not yet there isn't, but it's early." The women all looked at each other with quizzical expressions. He continued, "You're forgiven because you've never attended one of our parties here. Believe me, you'll be dancing."

Murdock headed back, mumbling under his breath, "Wow, no wonder Kevin goes for the seasoned cougars. I've talked to tree stumps with more savvy." Since he arrived, he observed almost everyone from Eye Cue was in tow. With standing room only, several revelers danced in the aisles from the blaring music programmed by a local DJ named Mind Field. Eye Cue employees paraded by their table, congratulating him and Bodine for a fine showing at the Board meeting. Rex Sullivan showed up last. As he walked in, Bodine waved, pointing at the lone empty seat at their table. Sullivan met the Zacharys as their waitress came over for his drink order.

Murdock greeted his sales manager, "Ah, Casual Rex. Glad you could make it. As you can see, the party's already in full swing."

Sullivan eyed the room. "Are all these people from Eye Cue?"

Before anyone could answer his question, everyone's eyes opened wide in surprise. Murdock didn't see why until he felt a warm, soft hand on his neck accompanied by the familiar whiff of Chanel No. 5. He spun around. Nadine Curtis stood behind him, saucy as ever, her eyes smiling at him. Facing Bodine's direction, she chirped, "I hope I'm not crashing the party, folks."

Murdock stood up, turning his chair around for her. "Nonsense, Nadine. We're all friends here. Besides, we're always in need of higher-class clientele at Mandrake's. And now look at us. We have the three finest looking women in the place sitting at our table. I'll feel badly for any skanks who might walk in tonight. Oh, Nadine, you know everyone here except the doctor. Nadine Curtis, this is Dr. Jenna Talia."

Talia smiled as the two women exchanged hellos. Curtis looked stumped. "You're a doctor and your name's Jenna Talia?"

"My last name is actually Gorman. Our man Chase gave me that term of endearment when he learned I am an OBGYN."

Curtis laughed along with everyone else at the table. Focusing on Murdock, she snapped, "Why am I *not* surprised?"

Any tension which might have been brought on by Curtis's arrival quickly dissolved. Having no luck spotting a waitress, Murdock took Curtis's drink order to the bar. While there, he asked the DJ to play an up-tempo rocker followed by a slow dance number. The moment he got back, the opening strains of Paul McCartney's "Smile Away" blared from the speakers. Mandrake's had no official dance floor, so he improvised.

He commandeered the area in front of the bar, ignoring the people waiting in line. He danced while playing air guitar accompanied by expert lip-syncing for every word. The people in the bar line gave him distance. He pointed at Bodine when the line, "Man, I can smell your feet a mile away," shot through the room. The entire place erupted in laughter while people streamed into the novel dance area. Before he knew it, at least two dozen people were dancing, laughing, a few playing their own air guitars. He looked at Curtis, beckoning her with a finger hook. She jumped up from her chair. She hurried over, busting many nice moves on the way, merging with ease into the mania he created. Her natural rhythm attracted him, drawing him toward her. She rocked out with abandon, shaking her exquisite keester in his direction. Even without a spotlight, the Eye Cue folks were locked in on the two of them. When the second verse arrived, he pointed at Zachary just when McCartney delivered, "Man, I can smell your breath a mile away." Another bolt of laughter from the crowd with more people joining them on the makeshift dancefloor. The scene almost got out of hand when the song finally ended.

The next song, Smokey Robinson's gentle ballad, "Being with You," restored order. The younger people who rocked with him on the previous tune slowly left the dance area. With his arms extended straight out, he lured Curtis in for the slow dance. At first, he assumed the conventional waltz mode. As the song progressed, he wrapped both arms around her, squeezing her against him. As they glided gracefully around the floor, his hands slowly slid down until they enveloped her posterior cheeks, giving them tender squeezes. She whispered, "This is over the line, Mr. Murdock. Remember who's watching." Murdock left his hands in place. He felt her stiffen, but she did not resist.

As the song ended, they were the only couple still dancing as the decibel level dropped substantially. Murdock bellowed toward the crowd, "I'm afraid there's something wrong with your bottom, Ms. Curtis."

She grabbed his hands, shoving them away. "What the hell are you talking about, Chase? What's wrong with my ass?" By now, every ear in the room was cupped.

Murdock, with his eyebrows raised blurted, "It's got a crack in it."

Laughter exploded into the room. Curtis's angry look disappeared as, she too, howled with laughter. He leaned in, lowering his voice, "Ms. Curtis, your ass just experienced one of the oldest jokes known to man."

He followed behind her, pointing at her swaying butt while grinning toward the Eye-Cue crowd. As they neared their table, phone cameras flashed all around the Bodines. Swarming people taking selfies with the trending couple had formed a line blocking the aisles. Groupies not even affiliated with Eye Cue created a madhouse photo shoot with Talia alone. No one asked permission from the couple for their pictures; they just barged up and snapped away. Murdock watched Zachary's attempt at crowd control failing among the alcohol-inflicted masses.

As he walked over, Zachary yelped, "Hey Chase, I texted Uber and Lyft to send cars. We're outta here. I'm giving the waiter the signal when the cars arrive so he can send their bouncers over to carve the Bodines and us a clear path to the parking lot." Murdock nodded, locking arms with Curtis amid the chaos. They found a quiet spot on the sidewalk outside the building.

He took her in his arms, promising, "No more butt jokes. Besides, from what I could detect, yours is indeed perfection."

"Thanks for the clarification. Just for that one split second, you had me wondering what defect I suffered."

"From where I'm standing, you don't have a single one. Hey, are you sober enough to drive? I've had one too many and could use a ride home."

"I've only had a couple drinks, so sure. I have a better idea. Let's head to my place. I'll make coffee so we can both decompress. This was one raucous party Bo threw."

"Thanks, I would love a little pampering at chez Curtis. And yeah, I'm dying to find out the grand tab on his credit card."

As she drove toward her house, he stared at her profile while they chatted. He marveled how remarkable she looked from any angle, comparing how she captured his imagination in the same way as Donna. She pulled onto her driveway. The spontaneity of the situation aroused him. His precious Donna was gone, yet Nadine, lovelier than words he could summon, served as a pinch hitter extraordinaire.

Just as they entered the living room, she said, "Make yourself comfortable. I'll be right back with the java. How do you like your coffee?"

"If it's alright with you, I'll join you in the kitchen. I didn't get enough of your sweet essence on the dance floor," he purred with the best sultry voice he could contrive.

She swung around, draping her arms around him. "I really could use your help in there." She raised her head with lips open, his face already on the move toward hers. Their first kiss lingered for several seconds, both savoring the sensations. He kissed her cheek, then her neck, then her soft mouth again while she ran her hands over his back. He felt his pulse racing, knowing his face glowed hot pink from the excitement. She pushed back, still holding him.

Murdock smiled. "Maybe we should forego the coffee. I know a better way we can stay alert." His voice cracked like a schoolboy as he spoke the last word.

She frowned. "Don't you think this is going too fast, Mr. Murdock?"

He froze at her serious tone, bringing him to full sobriety. A telling smile came over her face as she snickered, took his hand, guiding him toward her bedroom, kicking off her shoes on the way.

Starting with her blouse, button by button, he undressed her. She returned the favor by removing his tie, then unbuttoning his shirt. His eyes became riveted on her overflowing black bra accompanied by a sensation his horns must be scraping the ceiling. As she reached around her back to untether her bounty from its confines, he stopped her. "Please, allow me." She inched her backside up against him. He unlatched the first hook, kissing her shoulders and neck while methodically releasing each hook. As he lowered the straps off her shoulders, she faced him. Awestruck at her well preserved, gravity-defying breasts, his automatic reaction kicked in, demanding he verify their authenticity. He gently caressed them, curious if they had been enhanced. Nadine watched his eyes glaze as he learned they were quite real. He quivered in anticipation.

"Chase, if you're going to finish undressing me, you'll have to take your eyes off my tits," Curtis teased.

He sat on the bed, drawing her forward, kissing each natural wonder, then looking her in the eyes. "I'm sorry, love. I've simply never seen anything like them. You possess the most incredible chesticals I've ever seen. And that tiny waist. You are majestically constructed, a situation blocking my focus from anything else."

She cooed, "I'm so happy you're impressed. Just lucky, I guess. Um, how long does this stage last?"

"Almost done."

By the time she lay naked, sheer lust took over, his passion for Nadine arriving so pronounced, he felt faint. After she brought on a simultaneous, toe-curling climax, they collapsed, smiling, kissing, and finally falling asleep with their bodies entwined.

They spent the entire weekend together, venturing out only on Saturday for Murdock to pick up Pearl at Mandrake's. He drove home, packed clean clothes along with toiletries, then sped back. Over the weekend she exposed her sensuous side where she emerged erotic, witty, glamourous, fun-loving, and most pleasing to him, an irresistible naughty side. He felt enchanted, touching, holding, or kissing her wherever they were. Somehow, Nadine restored the virility of his man parts to a thirty-year-old status. He accepted how their relationship had rebloomed despite his poor behavior the prior weekend. He woke up Monday morning revived and pumped about the future.

Bouncing into his office, his butt just touched his chair when a pair of prying ears charged through his doorway. "So how was your weekend, Chaser? I noticed you left Mandrake's Friday night with Nadine. I called Ted both Saturday and Sunday. No one knew your whereabouts."

"Clearly a deliberate ploy on my part. You know, Bo, first, let me thank you again for straightening me out about Nadine. She's a real prize. Second, she is one relentless love machine. She just couldn't get enough, kept coming back for more. I kept her busy, even tried wearing her down. *It all* amazed me. Needless to say, my divining rod, formerly known as pink steel, is officially in tatters."

"Now *that's* exactly how it should be. I expect you'll match that relentless stamina at work today. No fantasy time either, you stallion. The more you get done, the sooner you can frolic with Nadine."

CHAPTER 18

EUPHORIA EXIT, STAGE RIGHT

During the next month, Murdock and Curtis shared quarters at least twice a week plus weekends. Since Nadine stayed insatiable, Murdock discovered his desire for her cranked into overdrive with each encounter. She showed a fondness for the kinky realm, which suited his predilection for the untried. After gathering assorted toys during their outings, the new habit morphed into a mutually exhilarating game of keeping each other guessing. He reflected how he rarely indulged intimate extremes as a younger man the way he now did with her. A patent latecomer for exploring the wild side, he now fashioned himself as a Boomer porn star when in her arms. It was as if the universe had kept a running list of all his fantasies, releasing them one by one through Nadine.

During the *down* times, they spent their hours together like an ordinary couple, binge-watching addictive TV series, cooking meals together, driving along the coast, hitting a few favorite restaurants, and seeing the occasional live concert. His attraction was past fondness, slowly creeping into the danger zone. He knew she was withholding expressing her feelings as was he. From her affectionate touches, amorous kisses, loving nature, and especially her facial expressions when they spoke or made love, he sensed she was at the same level. Still, his thoughts drifted back to Donna, drawing the inevitable comparisons. Could he love Nadine feeling the same intensity? He hesitated to rule out the possibility since their relationship needed more time before making such a judgement.

Late one afternoon at work, Bodine came by his office. "Hey Chaser, guess who's back in town?"

"Let me guess. Was it Taudrey, that harlot who ruined your relationship with Nadine?"

"Nice try, asshole. No, Chuck Ponzi and the Schemers are back at the Carousel. They haven't played there since last year. Are you free tonight? They're only in town a couple more days, so Ms. Talia and I are going there tonight."

"Yeah, I'm free. Sounds like a blast. I hope your scorned rejects don't start crawling out of the woodwork. I'd hate it if you got another cocktail soaking again, especially in front of Talia."

"Nah, it won't happen since she'll be with me. She's never seen the band before. Why don't you have Nadine join us? I'd like to see any of my past wild things get past either of those two."

"Good point. We were together just last night, so I 'm taking a necessary break. My johnson almost requires a splint. The woman is relentless, although I'm not complaining one bit."

"Excellent. Talia's meeting us here. I'll drive."

***

Murdock noticed The Carousel offered the same gaudy neon sign, the same stream of cougars entering the front door, and the same random drunks from "Happy Hour" shuffling out. As Bodine reached for the door, various people made their way out, so they all held back. A tall young man with striking good looks appeared, holding the door open for someone else. Out sashayed a grinning Nadine Curtis. The moment she spotted Murdock beside the Bodine party waiting to get in, the wide smile disintegrated.

Murdock glowered at her, spewing his disgust, "I guess exclusivity doesn't reside in your vocabulary, does it, Nadine?"

She scowled back at him in defiance. "And just what are you doing here, Mr. Murdock? Trolling for new meat?"

"I thought I already had all I could handle from you... but clearly, you have a different opinion. Who's the boy toy? Another fresh kill?"

The young man stepped toward him. Bodine intervened, "Don't think about it, sonny." The man sized up Bodine's daunting presence, stopped, and took a step backward. His gaze locked on Talia, dressed in a short mini with the usual display of enticing cleavage. Bodine caught the young man leering at Talia's amenities along with his arrogant expression. Bodine squinted, moving in closer. "The fact you think you have the class or enough cash to handle this genuine woman is downright absurd. Now back it up and save your drool for the one you're with." As the young man retreated toward Nadine, Bodine resumed his position with Talia.

Murdock continued, having never taken his eyes off his new *ex*-girlfriend. "Unlike you, Nadine, I just came here to enjoy the band with my friends."

Curtis flushed with embarrassment. She took the man's hand, "Come on, Tony. Let's get out of here."

As the two were walking away, Murdock couldn't resist, shouting after them, "Tell Tony not to use my toothbrush." Under any other circumstances, the quip would have been funny. Now, it exposed the empty realization his brief, extraordinary affair with Nadine Curtis shifted into past tense. He spoke to Bodine and Talia, "I have remarkable clarity now, folks. The woman is a blatant, card-carrying nympho."

Bodine winced at him, lowering his head. "I didn't tell you this before, Chaser, but I saw Nadine in here several times when I was on the prowl. That dalliance with Kevin Alvarez was no one-time lapse in judgement. I thought she might have changed once I saw her with you, but…"

They continued toward the entrance when Murdock stopped. "It's ok, Bo. She fooled me, too. You two go ahead. I'm not much in the mood for entertainment now. I'll get an Uber for a ride back to my car."

Bo gave him a bear hug, whispering, "I promise you, she's in for nothing but shit puddles whenever she's around me. Forgive me for pushing her into your life."

Murdock whispered back, "No harm, buddy, a leopard doesn't change its spots. She's a professional trickster. Get inside with your wonderful woman who for some reason loves you."

Driving home, he started another one-sided conversation with Donna Alvarez. "I should have known she was bad news when you didn't give me the sign, baby. God, I miss you now more than ever. You never would have pulled a stunt like that." Tears streamed down his face. Crying enabled a release for his anger from Nadine's betrayal and his broken heart left threadbare from Donna's senseless death. He wiped his eyes. The crying spasms lasted for the entire drive, ending when his exhaustion became slumber.

The next morning, he checked the time on his phone. Two missed calls plus a text from Curtis showed on the screen. "I'm so sorry, Chase. I guess I'm just in a bad way right now. I hope you'll forgive me. You can stop by for your things whenever."

He responded with a text, "Just box my stuff up and send it to the office. I don't want any further personal contact with you. So much for Kevin Alvarez being an isolated aberration in your lifestyle. Lose my number."

Over the next two weeks, his social life consisted of the occasional weeknight dinner meetings with Zachary or getting together with Bodine for cocktails after work. He spent the weekends walking along the beaches of Malibu, watching movies alone, or sitting in his small apartment drinking beer and tequila shots relying on his music for company.

Late one Saturday evening, the solitude finally wore thin. He bolted off his couch. The blame for loneliness belonged solely to him. As the fog left his mind, he realized he had to end the self-induced isolation. He turned off the music, brushed his teeth, then hit the bed knowing the morning signaled the time for his recharge.

He awoke Sunday morning, starting the day on the couch with coffee and his laptop opened to an unsolicited marketing email he discarded daily before reading. The message started with a question, "Are you home alone every night?" It piqued his interest for the first time. "Yes, I am," he admitted out loud as he opened the message. The website revealed a dating service designed for people aged 50 plus years called MLC.com, the initials for Mid Life Companion. Colorful photos parading appealing men and women, unlikely active members, streamed continually mid-screen. He mumbled at the computer screen, "Where are the pictures of the skank members who didn't make the cut for the promo page? Bet I can find them in two clicks."

Intrusive thoughts involving Nadine and Donna paused further progress on the website. Where he eternally labelled Nadine Curtis in the bitter disappointment category, he likewise believed Donna's essence remained near coaching him through the loneliness, coaxing him to move on. While the desire to satisfy his primal urges existed, his motivation for meeting someone stemmed from the pleasure a quality woman could offer him. He yearned for companionship with the right features, like mutual concern, admiration, witty banter, and genuine affection. Bottom line, he loved sharing time with a likeminded woman.

He clicked the "Join Now" tab, entered his credit card number, then began the arduous task of creating his personal profile. As he forged ahead, forcing himself to write, he found self-promotion difficult for fear he might come off sounding boastful. Composing a compelling, truthful description for strangers proved a daunting exercise. He wrote and re-wrote until he stalled in exasperation. Just for giggles, he dabbled at an experimental A/B approach; description A would describe an alternate reality used by many current members, while description B would capture his truer essence.

He kickstarted the concept using the frivolous approach first. By lampooning himself, he hoped to ease his anxiety before writing the true version. "Mid 60-year-old male, tall, slender, extremely virile, works out two hours and runs five miles daily, leaves men young enough to pass for his son in the dust. Not sexually over-aggressive (unless you like that sort of thing). Hobbies include running a nudist colony on weekends for attractive, well-endowed women (less than C-cups need not apply). Authored successful fiction and non-fiction books, doesn't pander to lowest common denominator readers of banal trash, refuses to blow someone for a publishing contract. Frequent A-lister in the New York Times Bestseller list. Plays electric lead guitar in a style reminiscent of George Harrison. Successful day trader whose stock tips have enabled early retirement for friends and relatives. Desires a seasoned woman with a stunning appearance who passes for half her age, keeps an edgy sense of humor, achieved accreditation as a gourmet cook, and golfs using a miniscule handicap. An insatiable sexual appetite preferred but might consider minimal compromise. Allergic to skanks."

He grabbed a cold beer. Having emptied all the bullshit from his system, lively phrases for the real profile flowed onto the computer screen. "Mid-60-year-old, tall, slender male who takes pride in his appearance, not overly fanatic. Stays in shape through low-impact workouts, powerwalking and golf. Will never be mistaken for a gym rat. Marketing/Sales Executive for a successful firm. Loves live music, great stand-up comics, baseball. Attempting gourmet cooking. Authored two self-published books only bought and read by family members and friends. Divorced for several years, no children, dog would be ok. Looking for an attractive, well-grounded woman sporting an active lifestyle, an edgy sense of humor, and a vivid imagination. A golfer would be a plus but not a prerequisite. Doesn't indulge in much wanderlust, only Tahiti and Australia appear on my bucket list so far. I am ready for a long-term, exclusive relationship."

Mentally exhausted, he ended the profile. It would suffice for the time being. Once the profile went live, he planned for finetuning its website filters. His results-driven marketing protocols were second nature for him, and he enjoyed using the process for profiling results.

"Oh shit, I need photos," he moaned. No worthwhile women bothered clicking on a profile missing a mugshot. Unable to find a single close-up of just himself on his phone or computer, he tried taking selfies. He held his phone at arm's length, snapping various expressions he judged acceptable. They weren't. Not even one. In fact, he hated every picture so much he scrapped being the DIY photo guy. Since he finished the profile's written part, he saved the file without activating it. Either he got decent shots of his kisser or the whole idea got deleted.

He typed "professional photographer nearby" in his browser. Locating one right away, he printed the website screen. He followed his gut when viewing the website, reasoning a woman photographer may have better instincts for shooting a man than another man. The next day, he enlisted the services of a local pro from the website, a lady named Monica. She offered him the first morning appointment at her studio the following Saturday.

Murdock responded, "Sounds good. I don't want the images seeming too slick. No electronic airbrushing or retouching. The photos should show me as natural as possible."

"No problem there, Mr. Murdock. Bring a few different shirts and a at least two jackets to provide variety in your poses."

The next Saturday, he dallied forty-five minutes in primp mode, barely arriving on time for the photo session. The shoot lasted over an hour as Monica snapped one shot after another, giving him posing instructions and telling him when to change outfits. When the photo session finished, she promised an afternoon pick-up for the photo stick to load the images onto his computer. As he reached his car, he murmured under his breath, "I better not have to reject the entire lot, not after plunking down $150 for the service. I bet she thinks I'm as photogenic as roadkill. Man, I can't believe how nerve-racking this is."

During the evening hours before he picked up the photo stick, he glided over hundreds of pictures and profiles on the dating site. He found patterns in the women he rated more attractive than others and helpful profile tips when he studied men's profiles. When the photographer texted him to pick up the stick, he asked her if he could view the photos before he left the shop. Monica's talent for capturing his best angles far exceeded his expectations. His natural photos afforded *something* credible for his dating site profile. He raced home, jamming the stick into the computer as he sat on his couch. From all the images displayed on his computer screen, he picked out a half dozen, uploaded them onto his profile, and clicked the "Activate Profile" tab.

"And there it is, folks. Welcome to the world of internet dating, Mr. Murdock," he announced to himself. Having no inkling what lay ahead, his mind swirled over wishful outcomes, none of them rational.

CHAPTER 19

FOOL ME ONCE

Three weeks passed with no sparks flying on the dating site. Murdock focused on the chaos at Eye Cue created by the overwhelming numbers of daily orders. Sales continued on a steady ascent while the new warehouse construction took off in full swing. Bodine received notification from Mr. Hwang at the Taiwan factory about Eye Cue's first *big order* of new product being shipped within a month. Murdock received instruction from Bodine to rent temporary warehouse space for the anticipated new inventory. With the crunch for filling several sales rep positions in their national territory, he and Rex Sullivan juggled resumes and interviews. The relentless pressure from working 16-hour days kept him distracted from his conflicts. If there was any time for indulging his woes, it happened when he arrived home. Fortunately, he scarcely had the energy to eat, much less dwell on the problems.

During the weekends, he spent late afternoons into late evenings scanning dating profiles on MLC.com. Although the breakneck pace at work severely diminished his stamina, curiosity combined with yearning overcame his fatigue. Almost a month passed with no connections with any women. He battled constant mood swings from high hopes to despondency whenever he searched the sight. The women with *personalities* he preferred showed profile pictures capable of shaming a family for generations. The ones with alluring photos wrote vague descriptions or stated unrealistic expectations. The more appealing the photo, the more his suspicions of its accuracy surfaced.

Checking his e-mail on a Sunday evening, an electronic beep rang out directing his eyes to a message from a woman named Natalie from MLC. When he opened the message, the face of a full-figured, wrinkled woman stared back at him. "Mom! Still on your diet of an extra meal per day I see," he screeched, deleting the message without reading or responding. He skimmed more profiles, one uninspiring presentation after another. *What happened to all the fetching babes featured on their promo page?*

As his mood waffled, he worried if his profile instilled the same piss-poor impression in the women who opened it. Judging from the piddly messages or "Hi there" beeps he received so far, his profile might lack the catchy language inviting ladies to contact him. On the other hand, he pondered the "Hi there" feature, which he defined as an abbreviated means for reaching out without sending a written message. He presumed anyone using the automated hello button fell into the category of lazy chicken shits; they technically made the first move by clicking a screen button, not by attempting human conversation. He reasoned most auto-greetings he received were from women like Natalie, or worse. He let out an exaggerated sigh as he kept searching for a promising face.

He came upon a profile marked as "New!" picturing a beautiful blonde named Linda, whose joyful smile beamed back at him. Using his propensity for instant profiling, he pegged her at about 45 years old. Too young. As he moved his cursor toward the "Close Profile" button, he caught a glimpse of her stated age. "62?" he shouted. "No way. That's a stinking typo. 50, max, maaaaaaybe." Even though she appeared quite younger than him, the captivating face served as an effective lure. He opened the profile, curious if she posted any full-length body shots. Linda did not disappoint. The second photo showed her standing beside a tall potted plant in what could be her living room. Linda's photo showed her enviable twenty-something figure as slender yet shapely, dressed in tight jeans with a snug-fitting black blouse, standing in tasteful black heels. He could not detect an ounce of excess anywhere on her body. A toothy grin appeared on his face. "Linda, you took damned good care of yourself,"

As he continued scanning her profile, he realized Linda resembled a girl he had a crush on in junior high school. Coincidentally, he remembered this Linda, last name Riley, as a slender blonde with the same crystal green eyes. Online, Linda stated her residence as being in Simi Valley, a town west of where he and little Linda attended JHS together. An eerie feeling came over him. "Is this even remotely possible?" he asked the photo on the screen. "Could this be my little crush from junior high? Nah," he bellowed. "This woman makes most other women my age look like candidates for assisted living."

The small chance this dating site woman shared a past era with him sent a quiver over his body making his hands flinch over the keyboard. He began typing a message. He had to know. "Could you possibly be the same Linda Riley from Patrick Henry Junior High? My name's Chase, and I had a classmate named Linda who I adored but haven't seen since. Just curious. A response would be appreciated." He remained awestruck by the chance she was the same person. Satisfied he may have scored an interest, he paused from scouring profiles. He obsessed about her responding, giving frequent glances at his incoming e-mails while going about his routine fixing dinner and playing his music. Late in the evening the yawning started. He ended the vigil, shut down his computer, and slid into bed. "C'mon Linda," he said as he fell into bed. "Talk to me."

As soon as he awoke the next morning, he turned on his computer before heading for the shower. When he opened his e-mail, he spied a message from Linda via MLC.com: "Chase Murdock?! I can't believe it's you! And I can't believe we're both on this dating site. Wowee! I just became a member yesterday and there you were, sending me your message. What a coincidence! Please call me asap." She left her number. He danced around his bedroom like a dervish.

"Small world, huh, Little Linda? I'll call tonight after work. Dying to know what you've been up to for the past 50 years!" As soon as he sent the message, his mind raced at the possibility of an in-person encounter with her. Provided her photos weren't 15 years old or she didn't suffer from terminal halitosis, he felt destined for a reunion with serious potential. Having a conversation with her on the phone, then meeting her for a cocktail while staring into those magnificent green eyes set him on a high he sustained the entire day.

Dreading waiting out the day at the office, he selected music from his middle school days as a distraction for the drive to work. He placed a custom collage of early Elvis in his CD player.

Swooning with the King as he drove, he recalled Linda loved Elvis. He prayed the day would scream through the hours.

After work, he raced home ready to bring in the proper mood before calling. He popped a beer, took a tequila shot, put on a light classical music album, and dialed her number. As soon as she answered, he asked, "Is this the living doll who always watched me get in trouble for throwing spit wads at the clock in homeroom?"

Linda laughed, replying, "Is this the lanky redhead who flirted with me every single day?"

"Well, the red is gone from my hair but not my inclination for flirting with beautiful girls, uh, women."

Sounding as fun-loving, even vivacious, as he remembered from all those years ago, she showed him the old engaging spark in her personality. She enticed him once again to pursue her. Even more exciting, she ended the conversation with, "I can't wait till I see you in person."

They made a date for the upcoming Saturday night to meet at the Islands restaurant in the Simi Mall. He stayed giddy about the possibilities all week. If they hit it off, he could abandon the internet dating ordeal altogether. For the brief period he had been on the dating website, his time and effort produced no favorable results until now. The upcoming weekend distracted him daily at work. When Friday night arrived, he had trouble falling asleep from the anticipation of meeting her the next day.

He sprung out of bed Saturday morning headed to the bathroom. Moving his face close to the mirror with tweezers in hand, he scoped for wild hairs in his nose, ears and eyebrows as he whistled "Gimme Some Lovin" by The Spencer Davis Group. After putting a selection of shirts and pants on the bed for later, he threw on jogging shorts and a T-shirt and headed off to the barber. Everything about his shape and looks had to rock her first impression upon seeing him. After the haircut, he went on a light jog for two miles, then circled back to stop at his favorite outdoor coffee bar and ordered an iced coffee for his wind-down walk home. During the walk, he thought of tasks he would do to pass the time before his date with Linda.

Every time he hit a red light on the way to meet his junior high crush, he checked his face in the rearview mirror. "You are being driven by one handsome devil, Pearl," he said at the last red light before his turn into the parking lot. As he walked into the tavern Linda recommended for them to meet, an unappealing, spiked-haired blonde woman wafted toward him, plastic hoop earrings in full swing, peeping at him sideways from the corner of her tired eyes while grinning at him through a glossy pucker. Her arms revealed weathered skin with long, thick creases on her biceps. *Geez, is she really wearing a sleeveless top? God, it's excruciating. Maybe she gained a lot of weight at one time then lost it all last week.* As she got closer, he guessed she spent too many hours at the tanning salon as the overhead lights caught the grooves on her withered flesh. Her pursed lips exposed a failed lip enhancement. *Ewww, that's way beyond puffy on the lips, more like air inflated. If it weren't for those piercing green eyes peering through the slits, I would never have recognized her.*

"Hey there, good-lookin'," Linda said too loud.

Murdock glanced around the place fearful he would spot a familiar face. "Hey Linda, look...at...you," he said faking a sincere tone.

He struggled keeping up the small talk while giving off the illusion he cared. As they sat down in the nearest booth with Murdock praying she needed a bathroom break, he managed to pose a question, "So, what have you been doing all these years?"

While she rattled off her life history, he could scarcely concentrate on the dull details. All his thoughts circled back to how she obliterated all expectations he had for his Saturday night. What he *wanted* to ask her was, "How could you be so incredibly deceptive as to post those ancient photos on the MLC website? Did you have no idea the minute any man laid his eyes on you, they would be profoundly disappointed, maybe even pissed, and probably nauseated like me? What in the hell were you thinking?" The more he thought about the dishonesty, the angrier he got, not hearing a word as she rambled on about her two ex-husbands and spoiled kids.

An hour passed as he drank three beers during her endless prattling. He abruptly changed the subject to his work situation requiring 16-hour days. Standing up, and putting cash on the tab tray, he announced, "Unfortunately, sweet Linda, my boss called right before I got here and asked, no, demanded I meet him at the office at 6:00 a.m. tomorrow."

She put on her sad face, stood up, hugged him, then said sheepishly. "I really enjoyed seeing you again, Chase. I hope we can do it again soon. I always had a secret crush on you."

Murdock gagged as he pulled away from her. "It was good catching up with you, too. Glad you still have those gorgeous green eyes." *Everything else is scarcely recognizable.*

Stomping back to his car, he scratched off Linda Riley with an emphatic "X". She confirmed the exact circumstance he feared the most. After the shock she caused him coupled with the tedious conversation, he admired himself a bit for being civil instead of going off on her like his hair was on fire.

He slammed his car door shut, shouting, "Piece of shit dating site. MLC must stand for More Life Calamities. How hard is it for people who go online to show some good faith? Is it me or am I the only one noticing there is no verification of information on these dating sites whatsoever?" He cringed as he whispered, "If I can be this deceived by an old friend, what can I expect from total strangers?"

As he pulled in his parking spot at home, he had no recollection of the drive. His anguish during the rotten date quieted when he left her as a permanently deleted event, but his mind remained in overdrive. Without missing a step to the fridge, he grabbed a beer and the tequila bottle. He required something antiseptic for erasing his infected memory.

He leaned toward his computer, muttering, "Man, I am so fucking gullible. From now on, I'll meet them first before I make a move for even a phone number. I'll never risk another chance for public humiliation like that again."

He lifted his computer lid; the dating site came on full screen. He clicked the Menu icon, then clicked Account, selected the Cancel Subscription button, then mashed his pointer finger on the mouse clicking the Submit button. "Subscription has been successfully cancelled, you lying, cheating, butt-hair-braiding profile fakers!"

He downed a tequila shot before he chugged half his beer. With his eyes closed, he sang a line from a popular song by The Who, "We won't get fooled again." He chanted the one line softly until he finished his beer, then fetched another round from the fridge.

CHAPTER 20

COACH TED

While sifting through his junk drawer, he came across the business card from Tonya, the lady he met at Mandrake's and later shared a joint with several weeks back. He dialed her number, encouraged he at least knew how she looked. Assuming she remembered him, they would not be starting from square one. He got her voicemail. "Tonya, hi, this is Chase Murdock. I'm the guy you met at Mandrake's the day you got your new car. Hope it's running fab and you've figured out the headlights by now. Please call when you can. Bye."

As he ended the call, Ted Zachary called. "Cindy's going out with a girlfriend tonight, so why don't you come over after work. I'll feed you along with the usual adult beverages. Need you to catch me up on a few things."

"Sure thing, Teddy. I've been spending too much time at Mandrake's anyway, so your place will be a nice retreat from the clusters of lonely drunks. No noise, meaningless conversation, or distractions. It's sounds dreamy."

His mood elevated as he drove toward Zachary's, knowing how well he would be treated in his ultimate safe zone. *There is no one in my life like Teddy. He is the only human who holds my unwavering trust.* Murdock planned on telling Zachary about the Nadine Curtis letdown and his new involvement with internet dating. Zachary would serve as his best sounding board and personal advisor on both subjects.

When he walked into the Zachary family room festive with Cindy's latest fresh flower arrangements, his host had a cold beer waiting for him with the usual munchies. He spotted his favorite oversized tan leather chair placed to the left of where Zachary sat on the matching sofa. The half-inch thick, bevel-edged glass coffee table held up by a sprawling, California redwood stump had spicy chips, a veggie tray with a hummus mound in the center, and a bowl of mixed nuts not including peanuts, a Zachary favorite. Murdock estimated the coffee table alone cost more than what he paid for Pearl.

As he took his first swig of cold beer and reached for a handful of nuts, Zachary started grilling him. "So, what's been going on? Business good? You patch things up with Nadine? How's the Bo-promo going?"

Murdock swallowed his half-chewed nuts. "Teddy, slow down. Try to ask me one question at a time. You know how my short-term memory is fading. Now, what did you want to know? Just kidding. First, Nadine revealed herself as the bed-hopping trollop, gutter-slut, barfly, tramp I suspected."

Ted dipped a celery stick in the hummus. "You left out harlot, whore, cunt, crack, bitch and sleazebag. Seriously, that's too bad. She is an exceptional looking woman."

"Say, we've identified the contenders for Nadine's personal acronym, but we don't have enough vowels. And, Teddy, you used two C-words. I'll bet you keep a lid on that kind of talk around Cindy." Murdock helped himself to two beers in the nearby mini fridge, handed one of them to Zachary, and scooted the bowls of chips and salsa over to him before sitting down.

"Of course. On the other hand, consider what women call us; sex fiends, dicks, cocks, horndogs, scrotum-cheeked, dildo-nosed assholes, and my favorite, self-absorbed motherfuckers." Ted finished his first beer.

"All true. It's unfortunate I discovered an unhinged nymphomaniac as the real Nadine. Caught her leaving the Carousel with another young pup after we had the hots for each other for about a month. I'd be lying if I said I wasn't disappointed. I doubt I'll find another woman having her intellect, wit and sheer physical appeal. I've never known a woman with a body like hers, not even Donna. Considering her radical kinky levels, we could have made a movie. I swear, Teddy, she would try anything in the sack and…"

"C'mon, Chase. With your luck, someone, somehow would figure out a way for streaming the 'Nasty Nadine and the Geezer' porn flick on the internet."

"It was almost worth it…but not quite. Anyway, she's history, so I'm trying this internet dating thing. My first experience involved an old friend from junior high school. Beautiful photos, which I discovered were taken from a former decade."

"I hear it's common in the online world. I take it she didn't look so hot in the here and now?"

"Quite haggard, actually. A mere plump shadow of her cuteness days."

"Why don't you start hitting the Carousel again like you did with Bo before you met Donna?"

"The operative word there is 'Bo.' I could do no wrong when I was out with him. I think the women I met there gravitated toward me only because I sat beside the quintessential clit magnet. If you touched the hem of his garment, you were gold. No, the women who frequent that place are too young for me, or they're cougars, and I'm *still* too old for them."

"Well, I hear it takes a pretty thick skin to endure i-net dating. You witnessed the deception firsthand, so it must be rampant."

"Well, I made sure it won't happen again. I deleted my account from the dating site to eliminate any future blatant deception. To answer your last question, Eye Cue is riding a sales wave like they've never seen. My media promotion for Bo and the company became an eye-popping overnight success. I'm even thinking about buying my own place."

"Eye-popping?"

"Sales are through the roof, Teddy. Bo is now regarded as a rock star in the industry; even Jenna Talia has her own fans. We're expanding the warehouse plus adding more employees to accommodate the demand. It's unbelievable. I've been working 16-hour days along with Unsafe Rex and Bo. The Board of Directors gave us carte blanche to continue the promotion, but frankly, I wonder how long this ridiculous success can last."

"You just hit the nail on the head, Chase. You know what they say about what goes up. If I were you, I'd take a hard look at where you are versus where you'll be in, say, six months."

"I feel so naïve, Teddy. We haven't faced any adversity so far. I get the feeling we may be getting lulled into complacency."

"May I make a suggestion?"

"Absolutely. I trust your business instincts more than anyone I know."

"Shut down the promotions for a while. Let sales stabilize to the point where you can *accurately* anticipate demand going forward. Have a heart-to-heart talk with Bo. Tell him you both should need to wrap your arms around the current sales pace, then run a forecast on how long it can be sustained. Ask for a copy of the sales budget Bo's established based on your current pace. If he hasn't revised it, you'll know he's flying blind. You guys *cannot* afford acting fat and happy while running the company shooting from the hip. And what about your Board of Directors? Aren't they monitoring every single thing going on at the company right now?"

"We got a little flippant with them at our last meeting. Told them in so many words we didn't need their looking over our shoulders. So far, not a peep from them."

"I guarantee you they are not simply going about their business by letting you and Bo do whatever the hell you want. You think they're perfectly okay leaving you alone? That isn't how a Board of Directors operates. They are watching every move you guys make. At the first hiccup in sales, they will be crawling up your respective asses. These people don't become Board members because they're laid back or complacent. They have strong fiduciary regulations to follow, so compliance is at the top of their list. It will be your two asses before any one of theirs is hammered."

"Yeah, the senior member indicated I shouldn't be stubbing any toes. They're probably just lying in the weeds, waiting for the first fuck-up, aren't they, Teddy?"

"If they're not, they're a weak governing body. Just assume they have their eyes trained on the entire operation. I suggest you and Bo meet right away, like tomorrow. Find out how well-versed he is on sales, P&L, forecasting, purchasing, and every other thing under his control. Remember, Bo was a marketing phenom before taking this position, bearing no leadership experience for running an entire company. Who was the former president, you know, the guy with the escort addiction?"

"Bob Donnelly."

"Yeah, Donnelly. He may not have been the fan favorite Bo is, however, I suspect he possessed a higher, more appropriate skill level for overseeing a large company. Do you remember Donnelly ever being controversial?"

"No."

"Did he ever mouth off to the Board?"

"I can't imagine a guy like him doing that."

"You and Bo better tone down your cocksure attitudes. Shareholders don't give a shit about bravado or wit. All they care about is results, aka, money in their pocket from a steadily growing stock. If you've already pissed off the number one man on the Board, the other directors won't hesitate to clean house. Whether you like it or not, you and Bo are obligated to the Board. As such, you must consistently provide them proof they hired the right men as Eye Cue's top executives, the key word being *consistently*. After you two are in sync, I suggest you request a meeting with the main man on the Board. Show some contrition. Seek his input on any actions he recommends be managed first. You don't have to kiss his ass; instead, show him the respect he deserves. Look, the Board must be in your corner, Chase, so instruct Bo of his and your executive roles in partnering with them."

"God, Teddy. I came over here to party with you, but what you've said is very sobering. I guess we have been a little too full of ourselves. I'm grateful you always get me a front seat on the reality train."

Zachary chuckled. "No better time than now. Show them you are, in fact, controlling this runaway sales frenzy. What's the name of the senior Board member?"

"Lawrence Davis. Bo says he's a blowhard."

"So, ditch the attitude regarding Mr. Davis. Target him as your prime ally. Whatever you two said or did that pissed him off, I can assure you it was a serious error in judgement."

"Yeah, I hear you. As an even more thrilling tidbit, Nadine is his right-hand bitch, uh, woman, uh Board Director. Oh man, I can't imagine being pleasant when I'm around her now. How should I deal with that seedy nympho?"

"Same way you're going to treat Mr. Davis, showing them both the due respect called for by their positions. Keep a vacuum-sealed lid on your sarcastic tendencies toward both of them. Their bullshit detectors will be set to max. And remember, stay away from anything remotely personal. I think you'll impress the hell out of Nadine especially. She might even realize what a mistake she made by treating you as one of her disposable sport fucks."

"No, Teddy. I forgave her behavior once because I was the one who handled things poorly. Her betrayal, which played out in front of Bo and Talia, ends it forever." Zachary nodded.

On his way home, Murdock called Bodine. Zachary's insights and advice made him understand he and Bodine, as Eye Cue's top executives, took a frivolous approach toward the Board.

Furthermore, it unwittingly landed them the top positions on the Board's shit list. "Hi Bo. May I have your complete attention first thing tomorrow morning?"

"Give it to me now, Chaser. I hate suspense."

"Too much to cover on the phone. I'll just say Ted opened my eyes about a few critical things. We need an overhaul on our approach in dealing with the Board."

"I'll be waiting."

CHAPTER 21

BOOTLICK, PARTY OF TWO

Bodine rolled away from the computer when Murdock arrived at his office the following morning. "Okay, Chaser, tell me about the fire Ted lit under you last night?"

"Just some commonsense issues we've glossed over since sales started going through the roof. Teddy lectured me, and rightfully so. You and I will dig into every facet of the company's business, making sure we understand everything about the expenses, sales and office staff, warehouse space, cash flow, and vendors. Then we determine if our current growth velocity is sustainable, factoring in the lag time before the new warehouse is finished. When we're certain we have a handle on all these areas, we'll call a meeting with Larry Davis. Per Teddy, we must treat him as our business guru by seeking his help on occasion. In turn, he'll realize from an inside view we have our shit together. By keeping him and the Board in the loop on everything we're doing without any smart-ass remarks, it proves we deserve our ranks as Eye Cue's top executives."

"I'm not ever kissing that guy's ass."

"Me either because it won't be necessary. We just can't give him any reason to make our lives miserable. Keep in mind the Board can fire us at will. Ted insisted we demonstrate the proper respect toward Davis's position as Chairman by proving we're competent, not just a couple of hotshots riding this temporary wave of success. Believe me, Ted opened my eyes about things we've overlooked, including how we dug ourselves into a deep hole of distrust with the Board."

"Maybe we should offer Ted a job. He'd make a great V.P. of operations."

"He's got the job he wants. Besides, we couldn't afford him."

"Okay, my born-again Zachary business protégé. Where do we start?"

"I'll have consensual Rex put a hold on any further marketing promotions. You call a meeting with the heads of finance and operations. We'll go over purchasing, credit, and the latest P&L statement. Hell, I have no idea who's current, past due, or over their credit line. When's the last time you revised our sales budget?"

"My Director of Sales provides that report quarterly as I recall. Let's change that to monthly for now."

"I should have seen that coming. Of course, you don't have it because that's my job. Okay, at least now we're getting somewhere. I'll look at the last print-out, then adjust the numbers after every rep in the country gives me an update on their 90-day account projections. I'll call the reps after we finish. Let me know when we can meet with those department heads."

"Hey, Chaser, who the hell's running this company anyway?"

"You are and always will, Bo. I'm just injecting some Zachary urgency into the proceedings. Look, our former positions at Eye-Cue gave us freedom from the overall duties in running an entire organization. Neither of us thought in macro terms, just the micro areas of the departments we ran. Ted made me realize we hadn't changed our thinking. We're crisis-managing as things pop up. In other words, if we change our habits through focusing on the financial and operational areas, we front-run potential wildfires. We could even scrutiny-proof ourselves from the Board." He paused to think about how that sounded. "Well, that won't happen, but we better lead them to a proper confidence level in us. We definitely haven't enjoyed that yet."

Bodine mulled over their mutual wakeup call. "Ok, ok. Ted cleared the fog for both of us. We'll send timely communications to the Board, like projected promotion summaries with schedules, hiring plans with timetables, and quarterly budget projections with explanations. It's true, Chaser. We absolutely were in survival mode from day one. Now we should shift into profit sustainability for our shareholders along with protecting the wellbeing of our Board and employees. I'll call you as soon as I get the other department heads together. You start calling the reps. Tell the Unsafe One to shut down the promos pronto temporarily. I'll call Ted now and give him my personal thank you."

"Yeah, we both get the voice of reason from our Teddy. Don't worry, we'll persuade the Board we're airtight. I'm on it."

Murdock poked his head in the doorway of Rex Sullivan's office. "Suspend the promos, Rexuality, effective immediately." Without waiting for a response, he continued on to his own office.

Sullivan jumped out of his chair, knocking over his coffee cup. "Shit." After he wiped up the spill, he dashed out to his leader's office. "What the hell's going on, Chase?"

"Don't be alarmed, my casual friend. Sales are fine, almost too good, in fact. We're just pulling back the reigns a little to review the scope of our operations. We've been flying without a compass since the first wave of sales hit. Bo and I don't want to hand the Board an excuse for meddling, that's all."

"But we have ongoing commitments with these media companies. How do we pull the plug on them midstream?"

"We're not cancelling those commitments, just rescheduling them. If any of them complain, I'm hoping you keep them at bay because I'm up to my nostril hairs in deadlines. And they better understand. Their promos have been an outrageous success. Surely, we can expect their consideration while we analyze their promo results before setting our schedules in the next campaigns. I'll explain our whole thought process later. Meanwhile, get on the horn to these media folks right away. Put the ball in their court. Act surprised, even annoyed, if you don't get the exact response we need."

"Okay, Chase. Understood."

He spent the remainder of the morning hounding Eye Cue's sales reps for updated sales projections. After two straight hours of calls, he rubbed his eyes, leaning back in his chair. *I hate this part of the job, which is why I didn't put such critical tasks on my calendar. This fire drill is as much my doing as it is Bo's. We've been flying blind. Like it or not, it's time to get professional.*

He soldiered on until every rep had their marching orders under an unrealistic deadline, finishing each call by saying "And I need these updates yesterday." Noontime passed without a word from Bodine regarding the department heads meeting. He dialed his extension.

"What's going on, Bo? I was hoping we could meet with the rest of the brain trust this afternoon."

"Not happening today, Chaser. The soonest everyone's available is tomorrow morning. Sorry."

"That's alright. It'll give me time for more preparation. And, hey, would you mind letting me be the one who calls Larry Davis?" A prolonged silence fell on the line.

"Listen, Chaser, it wouldn't look good, and you know why."

"True, but he might be suffering from a bad case of ultra-dapper stallionitis after you dissed him in front of every one of our department heads. That *is* a medical condition, you know." His lame attempt at levity fell flat. He sensed it in Bodine's pause of silence. "Bo, you're the playboy's playboy, the ballplayer's ballplayer, the supreme notcher of dashboards. I'm guessing he doesn't take you seriously enough yet, a problem you know you caused. Davis has a flashing caution light on around you at the moment, and every Board member sees it. I have the edge because he, at least, barely tolerates me. The way I see it, while we're selling the living shit out of everything we have coming in, he won't have an opportunity to pounce. I'll use my softer touch, so my normal testosterone level relaxes him a bit. Think about it and let me know."

"No." Bodine took a deep breath. "I don't need to think about it. You'll state our case at the meeting. I'll back you up whenever you give me an opening. Cheerleading always reduces my testosterone."

He realized he offended his friend by asking to take the lead in contacting Davis. Bodine was right; it wouldn't look like the company's president ran the show. "I'm sorry, Bo. I've just been so caught up in this since I saw Ted last night. I'm out of bounds giving you that request. I just think setting the meeting appointment with Davis is our top priority. It's essential we start winning this guy over. Don't you agree?"

"I do. But listen, don't try steamrolling over my ranking within this organization again. I was the impetuous one when I was in marketing, so I understand your impulsiveness. It's critical we maintain the pecking order here, and especially, when we're dealing with the Board." Bodine glared at Murdock, punctuating his angst.

"I won't cross that line again, Bo, I assure you."

"Good. Let's continue prepping for our internal meeting tomorrow morning."

The meeting with the department heads went much smoother than he anticipated. Eye Cue remained in the black showing a handful of customers being at or over their credit lines or past due on a few invoices. Even all the vendors' invoices surfaced as paid early showing the conventional 2% discount off the total, which easily offset the less than 1% delinquency rate. For a company running at such an unchecked pace, the ledger turned out surprisingly clean. Bodine praised each department head's outstanding performance before he closed the meeting, giving them deserved credit for the crucial oversight in their respective areas.

Bodine let out a long sigh after the meeting concluded, then addressed Murdock, "I must admit we had some dumb luck there. I expected a lot worse. This whole exercise has opened my eyes. You and I will never allow ourselves another lapse into complacency again, right?"

"No kidding. I feel like I've approached our business like some oblivious amateur. I'm much more confident about the Davis meeting."

"Speaking of which, we're on with the man tomorrow afternoon. Let's get buttoned up."

They arrived ten minutes before the 2:00 p.m. scheduled meeting at Lawrence Davis's office in Thousand Oaks. Despite their prayers, Nadine Curtis attended, sitting near Davis. Murdock recalled Ted Zachary's caution about staying professional, not letting anything personal hinder delivering their message. They all exchanged handshakes, taking seats around Davis's large hand-carved mahogany desk.

The senior Board member began, "Gentlemen, it hasn't been that long since we last met. Everything I've seen says your business is cooking in the right direction. Tell us why you called this meeting."

Bodine leaned forward. "Mr. Davis, Ms. Curtis, our business plan has morphed into a moving target from the unprecedented product demand. While Mr. Murdock and I hold pre-scheduled meetings with our department heads, we've not cemented such scheduling with the Board. We ask for your date preferences in our quarterly meetings, giving us preset targets for our Board reporting. From this point forward, we will keep you better informed of our successes along with our obstacles. It's important you know we welcome, in fact encourage, your skilled input. In case you found us a bit cocky at our last meeting, we are here in a humble effort to secure your advice on a regular basis."

Davis' eyes opened wide in surprise. "I got the impression you two had it all figured out, didn't need us sticking our noses in your business."

Murdock smiled, then added, "In hindsight, Mr. Davis, we both acknowledge we were a tad overzealous." Davis cracked a smile; Curtis didn't flinch. "Mr. Bodine and I recognize we're much better off gaining the Board's insight and guidance. We hope together we can create strategies, so we share a mutual understanding of Eye Cue's direction. Our Board members offer a collective treasure of business experience which we hope to tap into as often as permitted. We realized how severely our access to the Board members could be limited if everyone felt they would be confronted by a couple of prima donnas."

Davis seemed to relax somewhat after hearing the statement. "Okay then, what's the plan?"

Bodine stood up, handing Davis and Curtis bullet points printed on a single sheet. "Runaway sales sounds nice, but in order to enjoy a sustainable success, the company requires the wherewithal to manage the pace. While we place large orders daily with our suppliers due to our robust product demand, Mr. Murdock and I have a growing concern about quality control. If we push the factories too hard, we run the risk of our QC suffering as a result. In order to avoid that, we've temporarily paused the media promotion schedule."

Curtis sounded incredulous, "You're not going to promote the company anymore?"

Murdock pitched in, "We won't stop altogether; we're just putting the promos on the backburner pending our stabilizing demand until the warehouse expansion is completed. We're experiencing extra costs for storage space rentals plus the outside carriers for delivery. As you both know very well, these costs cut into our profit margins, so we'd like those expenses eliminated swiftly. We're aiming at taking back the workload and having ample inhouse space available again in the least time possible. First, since we're making excellent profits for the time being, we implemented frequent scrutiny of our margins focusing all eyes on keeping them plump. Next we'll determine how we not only sustain the pace but grow this company through careful forecasting and smart marketing. Our major obstacle, we believe, is an unforeseen QC glitch or any delays in shipping. We firmly believe a QC event could erode our revenue overnight, creating a domino effect in our operations and a chokehold on our growth."

Davis sounded impressed, "You two *are* businessmen after all. You were right about me. After our last meeting, I couldn't be sure either of you had a firm grasp on anything. Nadine will get back to you with quarterly meeting dates over the next 12 months. Glad I'm hearing a down-to-earth tone from you two. I consider it highly professional, in fact, very courageous you called this meeting. I applaud your efforts."

Bodine looked directly at Lawrence Davis. "Thank you very much, Mr. Davis. I assure you and Ms. Curtis we will embrace your and the Board's counsel at the currently scheduled meetings or whatever intervals you determine."

Five minutes into their drive back, Murdock received a text message from Nadine Curtis. "Bitchen bootlick. It worked!"

CHAPTER 22

THE CONLEY PARADOX

A text he received the next morning from Tonya made him realize internet dating remained the most viable option. "Hi Chase, sorry it's taken me so long to respond, but I've moved. Now living in the Big Apple! Yeah, I just couldn't get anything going in SoCal as a literary agent, so I went back where the action is. I regret we couldn't get together. My best to you!"

"Crap!" he carped, knowing he'd been tossed back onto the MLC.com treadmill. "Tonya would have been just right," he whined.

His thoughts of Tonya changed to creating coulda, woulda, shoulda scenarios with her. *If Nadine hadn't sidetracked me for so long, I could have convinced Tonya to stick around. Nah. She knows where she needs to be.* Taking a deep breath, he reactivated his MLC.com membership. He dove back into the maze of dating profiles, his skepticism boosted by the same disappointing results.

Over the next four weeks, he forced himself into at least one date per week off the dating website, struggling to maintain an open mind. Many women he met employed the same strategy as Linda Riley. They posted old photos, feeding the fantasy that surely the cognitive skills of any prospective suitor had diminished as much as theirs. After the first date, he adapted a strategy for cutting the date short when the revulsion meter went off within a half hour. Without him noticing, a behavior pattern developed where he followed each repulsive date with visiting Mandrake's, where he experienced more boredom and melancholy. Later at home, his experiences led him into the same silent rant as he went through his front door. *How could they be so unaware? Who would ever show up for a first date wearing a hang-around-the-house dress, resembling a sloth? And who had the unforgiveable audacity to understate their age by ten years or more? Why would anyone post photos of themselves engaged in an activity in which they could no longer participate?* Returning to further profile plowing before bedtime, his exasperation amped up from viewing the same fraudulent profile activity in perpetuity, chipping away his hopes for uncovering a compatible connection. His disgust with the unrelenting pattern guided him to a new plan, which he coined as "forced dating."

The first six women, who he intentionally met for happy hour, he classified as 'one and done,' but the seventh one piqued his interest. On their first date, he took her to a decent restaurant where she impressed him as a truthful woman, since she matched the attractive photos and perky profile she posted online. After agreeing to a second date, he left with renewed spirit the pattern was broken. Two days later, the second date moved in the right direction after a talkative, enjoyable meal at an outdoor restaurant near the coast. He kissed her goodbye, then said he would call her the next evening. While he parked Pearl at home, he received a text from her stating succinctly, "I don't feel a strong enough connection with you. Good luck." He recognized euphemistic codes when he saw them; "I can't see myself getting naked with you," or "You don't have the financial resources I hoped for," or "I just found someone else better." He headed straight to the side of his unmade bed and sat. Leaning forward, he put his face in both hands, as a familiar desperation clutched his mind. Residing in the Golden Years life stage meant he had acquired a dating reject affliction, making him unsuitable for meeting women in bars or attracting a romantic relationship anywhere. Moreover, he let himself mutate into a sucker for outdated pictures or embellished profiles online. Even his friends numbered too few for getting new introductions. Believing no substitute existed for a face-to-face encounter, he came up empty identifying his next step to find a life companion.

As he wallowed in bewilderment, a sudden jolt of inspiration intervened. Could he be ready to meet Barbara Conley? For months he deliberately avoided any chance for meeting Donna

Alvarez's older sister. In his fragile emotional state, seeing any resemblance of Donna risked his crumbling into a sobbing heap in seconds. But why not meet the woman Kevin reported shared so many qualities he cherished in Donna? Anxiety gripped his core as he picked up his phone. "Kevin?"

"Hi Chase, how's my surrogate stepfather?"

"Actually busy, tired, cranky, and hopeful you can help me. Thanks for asking. Kevin, would you please give me your aunt's phone number?"

"Most definitely. I take it you're ready to meet Barbara?"

"I don't know what I'm ready for, Kevin, but I'm ready to initiate the process for contacting your mom's sister. I can't run from this forever. She might not even care about me, but I feel she and I should at least have a conversation. Besides, I could get answers for the questions I've brooded over far too long. Meeting her could be all I need for closure. From her side, she might find clarity about your mom's most recent life by asking me questions. I'm feeling there's a chance our talking might move us both forward past our having lost Donna."

"As I've mentioned, she wants to speak with you whenever you're ready." Kevin read off Barbara's phone number. As Murdock jotted it down, Kevin sent him a text with her contact info.

"By the way, Nadine Curtis is not the lady you think she is," Murdock counseled using a fatherly tone.

"I know. I noticed her at the Carousel more than once after her so-called 'mistake' with me. We both ended up better off, right?"

"Yep. Hey, thanks for the number, Kevin, and please, don't tell your aunt I'm planning to call her. I still haven't decided if it's the right time yet." Ending the call, he yelled at the ceiling, "Who's the BS specialist here? Does the master Murdock know how to shovel it?" He went in his kitchen for a beer, fantasizing as he opened the bottle how the first call might go. He dialed her number but got her voicemail. Without leaving a message since he suspected a Kevin breach, he hung up, waited for five minutes, then tried again.

"Good evening, Mr. Murdock. How the hell are you? Kevin just called and gave me your number. Said you might be calling tonight."

"That rat bastard stepson of mine has no shame."

"Well, it's good he let me know. Otherwise, I wouldn't have picked up unless I recognized your number, junk phone calls being what they are. I really hoped I'd hear from you."

"I'm sorry, Barbara. I didn't intend to start off our first conversation like this. Kevin went level four bedwetter on me. If he'd been any worse, he'd have overflowed his entire condo causing flooding in the streets."

"Level four *what?*"

"I'll explain later. Being it's his first betrayal, I'll let it pass. I recently began wondering why I've waited so long to contact you. Early on, I had this fear I would break down or something."

"Perfectly understandable. I can't imagine what you've gone through. I thought I didn't love Donna until she got killed. I was wrong."

An eerie sense of déjà vu came over him as he sensed from her the same way Donna made him feel welcomed. She showed him compassion, not hesitating to share a very personal sentiment with him. Her voice projected a haunting likeness to her sister's same lilt, pace, and inflection. He felt nervous...captivated... conflicted. When he spoke, his voice softened, "I heard you and Donna had a falling out a long time ago. Probably a long story best kept for another time. I hope we feel comfortable enough someday, so we can talk about her and why I never even knew you existed until after her funeral."

"I think we'll get there, Chase, but you're right. Another time."

His phone pinged. A photo of Barbara Conley flashed on his screen in a text from Kevin. Having never seen a picture of her before, he became transfixed, powerless to take his eyes off her image. "Guess what your sneaky nephew just did?"

"Texted you a photo of me, at my request. This way, when we meet in person, you won't be caught off guard. He also sent me a photo of you before you called. Quite the looker."

"Aren't you the proactive one? I must say, the similarities between you two are not subtle. You have the same facial features, hair color, and..." his voice wavered, "sexy smile. You can imagine how disconcerting this is for me."

"Of course, I can. She was a little taller, I'm a little heavier. You won't be encountering an identical twin, Chase."

"Good. That would be completely unnerving. You're a beautiful woman, Barbara. How is it you're not spoken for? There must be men hitting on you constantly."

"I'm sure Kevin told you I was married before. My ex is a very decent guy. But we reached the point in our relationship where we regarded each other as roommates. Well, I want a stronger connection with someone than that. I won't settle for less. As far as men hitting on me, it doesn't happen as often as you suggest.

I must have a foreboding demeanor, a look in my eyes that says, 'proceed at your own risk.'" She laughed after saying it. "I don't know, Chase. We get picky when we get older, ya know? I have a far better idea of what I want in a mate as well as a much, *much* better idea of what I can't tolerate. Do you agree?"

"It's why I fell so hard for Donna. I felt so lucky I met a woman who could break through all the barriers. I have no quibbles about anything she did. She welcomed me in as-is condition into her life. It's a cliché, but what we had can only be described as magic."

"That's the word, it's what I want, too."

"Well, if you were some sea hag, I'd say good luck." Barbara giggled. "But you're the farthest thing from it. Have you ever heard of N.C. syndrome?"

"What's N.C. stand for other than North Carolina?"

"Good one. It originated from another stunner like yourself who's initials coincide with her lifestyle as a nympho cougar. She always hit up on youngsters disguised as men. If she hadn't been an insatiable, undercover, lying, club-hopping trollop, we might have made a go of it."

"Oh my. Well, just in case you're wondering, I can assure you I'm no cougar, nympho, nor have I ever been undercover about anything. And the boys can tell you, I don't lie. Truth works so much better."

"I have no doubt and I agree. But yeah, just when I thought I'd never be bowled over by another woman, she came along. She blindsided me, something I've never been adept at anticipating."

"I understand that. Pretty foul stuff. So... you're thinking maybe... Uh, wait, I'm getting ahead of myself."

"I have no expectations, Barbara. It didn't feel right for more time passing without phoning you. I will say this, however. We both have a strong connection to Donna, and yes, I want to learn more about Barbara Conley."

"I feel the same about you, Chase. Kevin and John think you are one of the coolest guys they've ever met, or as they say 'you're lit.' They love you, and that's good enough for me. So, I'll wait."

"For what?"

"For you to ask me out. We can't spend endless nights on the phone now, can we? We'll end up with cauliflower ear. Besides, my nephews filled us both in on each other while encouraging us to meet. I already feel as if I know you."

"Good point. Now that I'm not overwhelmed with trepidation, I'd love to get this moving. How about Saturday night?"

"You're on."

He ended the call feeling energized, alive, ready to meet Donna's only sister. He plopped on his bed cooing, "I haven't felt so calm and sure about anything for too stinking long. In fact, I feel lit. Hello, Barbara, goodbye blues."

Meanwhile, Barbara danced like a dervish around her house, feeling great things were in the making.

CHAPTER 23

STICKY SITUATIONS

With Saturday three days away, Murdock consumed his morning by obsessing on Conley. He yanked a printout from a stack of sales reports, shifting his focus toward work. Before he made it through the first page, Bodine slumped into his office staring at the floor. Murdock figured his boss's usual upbeat mood never made it out of his house. "You've got consternation, or maybe it's constipation, written all over your face, Bo. What's the problem?"

Bodine responded by dropping into a chair across from Murdock's desk, slouching, face down. "The doctor is ramping up the pressure to procreate. At age 37, her ticking clock drowns out our time together."

"I can understand that, Bo. Honestly, if you two weren't so damned good looking and so much in love, I'd keep my mouth shut. However, look at all the years you've squandered your superior seed. Think about bringing another Bodini or Bodette into this world. And what a brilliant mother Talia would be. I don't see any downside in you two having a kid."

"Chaser, I'll turn fifty on my next birthday. Don't you think I'm way past the age to contemplate fatherhood? I mean, Jesus, by the time my kid can buy me a six-pack, I'll be shopping for a retirement village."

"Only if your age controls your state of mind. Look, you come from a long line of healthy, vital, robust lineage. You'd make a great dad, too. Why deprive some little boy or girl from the benefits from your heritage or the economic advantage you guys would provide? Your kid could be the next U.S. President. Or win an Academy Award. Or become an astronaut and colonize Mars. Just look who's providing the gene pool; we're not talking about any shallow, skank baby here. Consider all the fuck stains who procreate more *and more* of the same lameness into this world. You and Talia could contribute someone much more meaningful. And, may I ask, what happens if you decide against it?"

"I lose Jenna. She's hellbent on becoming a mom."

"Are you sure? That sounds like one shitty option. What would you do, Bo, take a giant step backwards into the grade-A poon wrangler you once were? Haven't you had enough *strange* in your lifetime? Hell, in hindsight, I'd be thrilled if I faced your decision. I reckon the good doctor threw down the gauntlet, and I say, good for her."

"Yeah. I have zero desire for club-hopping anymore. Like I told you before, I can't picture my life without Jenna. I still have my ridiculous fear of being hurt or betrayed again. Honestly, Chaser, I don't think Talia could ever put a hurt on me. It's not her character."

"Then think on this like your life depends on it, Bo, because it does. You could comb the countryside for an eternity before winning over another jewel like Talia. Did she give you a deadline for a commitment?"

"No, but it's where we're headed unless I step up pretty soon."

"Well, since last night, I have my own complication. I'm meeting Donna's sister, Barbara Conley, this Saturday."

Bodine perked up, "Attaboy, Chaser. The time is right, eh?"

"I have no idea what I'm tackling here, but I'm ready for the game. Shit, Bo, what if I start crying when I see her? Seems we both find reasons for not going with the flow in a new direction"

"Yeah, I would second that. In your case, Chaser, it's a no-brainer. Meeting Barbara is well worth the risk. Even if you become a sobbing mess, I'm sure she won't think you're a pussy. She knows how deep your feelings for Donna run."

"She does, and if she were some semi-skank or the runt of the litter, I wouldn't think about putting myself through this. Get this, I called Kevin for her number, and the little sphincter sent me her picture while I was on the phone with her. I completely froze. Turns out she's as lovely and spirited as I remember Donna. I've gotta suck up my fear so I can move past Donna and meet her sister. Bo, I'm convinced Barbara holds the keys for my having closure. And as for you, Boss, formalize your commitment to Talia. You'll be a new brand of kickass once you become husband to Talia and daddy to mini Bodini."

———

Barbara graciously had offered they meet at her home. Since Murdock wanted no distractions, nor did he want to start bawling in public, he immediately accepted. She mentioned wine and finger food, which he supposed included lively conversation. She lived in a well-maintained white stucco house on the north end of Thousand Oaks. When his GPS went off with, "You have arrived at your destination," he snapped to, having no memory how he got there.

Stepping toward her front door, he had no awareness of his feet touching the ground, missed smelling the pleasant fragrance emanating from her manicured flowerbed, and overlooked the first step on her front porch. He landed on his right knee, dropped the glass bottle of wine he brought, and watched the glass shatter into smithereens as it smashed onto the concrete slab. The front door swung open. Barbara put both hands on her face, staring at the roadkill sprawled on her welcome mat. He looked up at her. "Good evening, Barbara. How do you like my method for breaking the ice? Whaddya' think?"

"Oh God, Chase, are you alright?"

"The good news is I'm too pissed to start crying, so that's a plus. Nice to finally meet you, Barbara. Got a band aid or three?"

"Come in, come in. I'll get some hydrogen peroxide and bandages. Don't worry about the glass. I'll sweep it up later."

He felt like a clumsy fool. No matter, it supplied the perfect distraction for disarming the brewing emotional meltdown. "Do I know how to make an entrance or what?"

She smiled. "From what I've heard, you pull this kind of crap all the time." They both cracked up.

"Yeah, but I don't usually injure myself in the process. Must be losing my touch."

He studied her face. Like Kevin Alvarez had told him, Barbara conveyed the same allure he loved about Donna, particularly the smile, the classic facial features plus no neck waddle, the flowing blonde hair, and a natural feminine appeal. *Nadine who?* Barbara made Nadine Curtis look like a cardboard impostor. She transmitted a genuine impression, sexy versus steamy, elegant versus glamourous. She wore soft blue slacks with a white blouse highlighted by stylish navy-blue flats. His eyes followed her gold necklace interlaced with light-catching crystals down the opening in her blouse. He flexed his knee to make sure the fall hadn't crippled him.

Catching sight of the blood seeping through his pants leg, Barbara reacted, "Can you stand yet?"

"Yes, I can. Just lead the way."

Once inside, Barbara took charge. "Sit down and put your leg up on the table. I'll be right back," she said with authority, a familiar tone he well remembered.

He looked around her pristine living room. It reminded him of the décor at Donna's condo, tastefully appointed and uncluttered. Her pastel rose and ivory colored couch offered floral pillows stitched to the back and sidearms. Its postured softness relaxed his back, giving him the few needed moments to unwind. The chestnut brown, slatted wood coffee table matched the wood frame and legs of the couch, matching pillowed chairs and slatted end tables. Fresh flowers in four crystal vases each displaying a mixture of pink, white, yellow and red fresh-smelling roses decorated her fireplace mantle, coffee table, and two end tables. Two ivory porcelain lamps with pale rose silk shades completed the look to Murdock's satisfaction.

After seeing Barbara in the flesh, he became more baffled why she chose a single woman's life. *Any man would be stoked to have a woman like her.* When she returned, he pulled up his pants leg to inspect the damage.

"Well, at least I still have the use of my leg. So sorry for the inconvenience, though, and introducing one of my body parts in the first five minutes."

She giggled, "It's not too bad. We'll have you patched up in no time." After a few minutes of swabbing, salving with ointment, and taping, she said, "There. You'll be good as new in a few days. Now, may I offer you a glass of wine?"

"Yes, yes. Better we use a glass instead of the porch." She giggled while patting his leg, then strolled across the room for the wine.

He marveled at her sexy backside. Her engaging demeanor relaxed him. He worried his comparisons with Donna would cloud his mind. Barbara distinguished herself in minutes. A fun evening with her required it happen without Donna in the room. While not yet smitten, he could see the path. He fancied she might be sizing him up as well.

Their conversation flowed unstilted, as if they were old friends. As the evening advanced, he finally cleared his throat and asked, "Are you comfortable yet for a conversation about the estrangement between you and Donna? So far, I can't fathom it, and I..."

"No, I need more time. Donna had a lot of wonderful qualities. She..." Barbara's voice cracked, "Chase, if we move with the flow, we'll get there, assuming you plan on knowing me better as well. I haven't even shared the story with Kevin and John yet so…"

"Fine with me, and very sorry if I'm pushing too hard. And yes, I hoped you would allow us time to earn each other's trust."

She smiled and leaned across the coffee table, her face inches from his. She whispered, "I'm hopeful, too, let's put it that way," then kissed his cheek.

When he felt her lips on his face and inhaled the full force of her beguiling perfume, he lost his composure. Without warning, tears filled his eyes. Having taken every precaution, or so he thought, her caring expression, tenderness, and sweetness overtook his composure. Seeing his red eyes with the sad look on his face, she got up and sat beside him, putting one arm around his neck. "I'm sorry, Chase. This must be so difficult for you."

"I promised myself I wouldn't compare you with Donna. Honestly, it's unavoidable. You're both such easy company, so lovely. It rocks me to the core."

"I'm sure it's temporary, but I know one thing for sure. The only way we can fight it is by not fighting it at all. Maybe after we see each other over time, you'll stop the back and forth."

Murdock appreciated her perspective on the situation. Despite the uncanny similarities between the two women, he found her unique; he considered her a *most worthy* pursuit. "I'm charmed at your interest in knowing me. When I first saw your photo, I figured some clever rich guy would sweep you off your feet before I had a chance."

"Clever I like, but rich doesn't always make the cut. At this point in my life, character and integrity mean more than money. Besides, Kevin and John tell me you're one of the funniest people they've ever met. A sense of humor is huge for me, too. If a man can make me laugh, I'm putty."

He chuckled, "You'd never know it by our conversation tonight, which started with my logjam on your porch, but I've been known for triggering a few guffaws."

Her smile gave away her amusement. "I'm very interested in your funny side, Chase, and everything else. Kevin told me you masterminded a promotion for your company causing an explosion of sales at an unprecedented pace. That category of brains is very sexy."

He looked at her without saying anything, not wanting to pound his own chest or fish for more compliments. The magnetism in her personality put a spell on him, much like the effect he experienced from her sister, only stronger. *I could talk to her all night.*

"Thanks, Barbara. Your kind words are appreciated. I'm sure we'll have a good time learning more about each other." He stood, still smiling, "I'd better get going."

They walked to the front door. She cautioned, "Don't step on any glass. I never got around to sweeping it up." She stood in the doorway as he stepped cautiously onto the porch.

He pivoted, "Would you please step down onto the porch with me?"

As soon as she took one step forward, he threw his arms around her, lifting her high off the porch, hugging her tightly. "You are such a peach. I'd like to keep this hug going for a day or so. Thanks for not rejecting me."

"You're awesome, Chase. Don't lose my number."

He gently placed her back in the doorway. "Don't forget the glass on the porch. I'm giving you an IOU for cleaning up all the mess. I promise I'll pay off real soon."

CHAPTER 24

HURRY UP AND WAIT

Sunday morning, Murdock strained to read the newspaper while drinking a cup of coffee. Although his eyes felt focused on each page, his attention centered on Barbara Conley. Frustrated he found every word incomprehensible; he threw the newspaper on the floor. He celebrated his relief from finally meeting Donna's sister, which morphed into a refreshing, optimistic outlook. As a bonus, Barbara seemed as interested in him as he was in her. *I'm attracted to Donna's sister and the whole thing feels like fate. No one could have scripted this.*

His phone rang. He jumped up from the table when he read "Barbara Conley" on the caller ID, whacking his sore knee on the coffee table. In racking pain, he grabbed his phone, squeezing out a normal sounding "hello" while disco dancing in agony. He put the phone on mute, cutting loose a window-rattling scream.

"Good morning, Chase. Thank you for such an exciting evening. Your injured knee showed up in a dream I had last night. You were a perfect gentleman as I struggled reattaching your lower leg back on the wounded kneecap." She kidded, "I couldn't get the aim right."

He chuckled. "Really glad you called, Barbara, and flattered I was on your mind last night. Funny thing, you've been on my mind ever since I opened my eyes this morning. I thoroughly enjoyed our time together, especially the part where I bombed your porch with the wine I brought." They both laughed.

"Well, if you haven't had breakfast yet and you can hobble to the car, I make a mean eggs benedict. Can you join me?"

"Say no more. I'll be there within the hour."

She greeted him at the door in white shorts and a turquoise sleeveless blouse, accented by black leather sandals showing off her perfectly pedicured toes. Her shapely legs exposed a modest tan; her blouse revealed just enough cleavage for an extra peep. Gold dangly earrings with a flat gold chain around her neck emphasized her beautiful blonde hair styled as if she just returned from the salon. He fought at keeping eye contact.

"You are a splendid sight for sore knees, Barbara. You're absolutely stunning this morning, and I'm suddenly so grateful the weather is warm." She smiled at the compliment, her radiance delivering the same warm effect as Donna's. While the sisters displayed obvious physical differences, their shared DNA included an innate sexiness. "And I'm grateful about that, too."

"Grateful about what?" she asked.

"Uh, did I actually *say* that? I thought I was only thinking it."

"Nice try. C'mon spit it out, Mr. Murdock."

"Well, since you must know, I was wondering how this ordinary, crippled man is sharing a gourmet breakfast with you this morning."

She chuckled, "Crippled *temporarily*, but ordinary? I don't think so. Anyone who can turn a company around the way you have is a far cry from common. And thank you for the compliment. Would you care for a Bloody Mary?"

"You betcha. Easy on the Bloody with an extra shot of Mary, please."

The delectable breakfast turned into an afternoon filled with non-stop conversation between occasional Bloody Marys. They both enjoyed a relaxed curiosity toward each other, encouraging their sharing more and more personal stories. The frequent hard laughs during the hours fueled their animated conversation. When she described her job in real estate, a bell rang in his head.

"Barbara, would you help me find a house? I've been in this small, one-bedroom apartment far too long. I need my own place. Business has been so good I'm ready to invest in a *real* home."

"You don't think that would be a conflict of interest? Since we plan on dating in the…"

"Nonsense. You know real estate, and I need someone I can trust. Where's the conflict in that? Besides, it'll give me a perfect excuse for seeing you more often."

"That's true, but you don't need an excuse."

"I like you more with each passing minute. It's a deal, then? When can we start?" He liked the way she slipped in the word 'dating.'" He confirmed his thinking the same way by continuing the conversation as if it were an assumed status for them.

"Give me an idea what you have in mind, including budget. I'll get on it tomorrow."

"I could kiss you."

"And you're waiting for what?" She pursed her lips. "Well, they can't kiss themselves."

He jumped up, took her hand and pulled her to him. She stood, wrapping her arms around him, smiling up at his face. They shared a long, tender embrace while their lips met, a welcomed first kiss. "God, woman. I never thought this could happen. I realize we've only seen each other twice. It's just, uh, well, that I feel like I've known you so much longer."

"I feel the same way. It's good, right?"

"*Good* doesn't begin to describe it. Hey, I'd better get going, not that I want to. It'll take me a few hours preparing for the upcoming workweek. Ever since our sales started climbing, it's been one four alarm fire after another. What a perfect first date, Barbara. I can't wait until the next one. I loved our spending the day together."

"Same here. Don't keep me on the hook waiting for a phone call or text, even if it's only for a quick hello."

"Count on it." They held each other for another long hug followed by a final kiss before he headed out the door. The kisses and upgraded dating status changed everything for him; it was no longer *if* he would fall for Barbara, rather, it was how hard. During the drive home, the estrangement between the two sisters gnawed at him. Advancing his involvement with her hinged on her telling him the entire story. *Who was the bad girl here? I can't imagine either woman putting hurt on their only sister.*

Bodine called him just as he was getting ready for bed. "Hey Chaser, when's the last time you picked up a golf club?"

"Hell, it's been at least two years. Why?"

"Hwang and Woo requested a visit here while the weather is still perfect, *and* they want a round of golf."

"Okay, then. It can only help strengthen our ties with their factory, right? When do we play host?"

"Next Friday. They'll be at the office Thursday. They have more new revisions on their production schedule. We should invite Chairman Davis to sit in on the meeting. I'd like him to see how we handle these guys."

"Couldn't hurt, but do you think Davis will be receptive? He oversees his own business, plus I'm pretty sure he's a teetotaler without any golfing interest."

"I'll extend the olive branch. If he can make it, fine. If not, I'll ask him to send James Terwilliger. James is much less uptight than Davis anyway."

"As long as he doesn't send Nadine Curtis," Murdock growled.

Bodine sniffed, "No worries there, Chaser. She's persona non grata around here now. I promise you she's aware of our serial-cougars-not-welcome-here doormat."

As Murdock predicted, Larry Davis begged off attending, suggesting they invite James Terwilliger instead. Terwilliger informed Bodine he welcomed the chance for learning more on how the two men ran the business, graciously thanking him for the invitation.

The meeting started right on time Thursday morning. As Bodine extended the introductions among Messrs. Hwang, Woo, and Director Terwilliger, each man bowed. They presented new product samples for consideration on Eye Cue's next orders followed by the cursory shipping schedule review. Bodine and Murdock nixed the sarcasm or coarse language they used on their first meeting with them. Terwilliger joined in on the conversation posing welcomed questions. When their presentation concluded, Mr. Hwang asked, "We go Mandrake's tonight? Get shit-faced?"

Bodine and Murdock laughed while Terwilliger eyed them while he smirked, "You already have a routine with these boys, it appears."

Murdock replied, "They love Mandrake's. More tits and ass than they ever see back home." Everyone had a good laugh.

Bodine interjected, "No shit-face tonight, Mr. Hwang. Can't stay up too late. We have a 7:00 a.m. tee time tomorrow morning. We'll go to Mandrake's tomorrow night."

Mr. Hwang, while disappointed, nodded. "Maybe we see Raura tomorrow night?"

Terwilliger asked, "Who's Raura?"

Bodine clarified, "They're both crushing on a waitress at Mandrake's named Laura. Pretty stunning six-footer hauling a substantial front porch." Terwilliger just grinned. "You're welcome to join our celebratory cocktail after the golf game, James."

The foursome gathered on time at the first hole tee box. Murdock prepared his tee-off by standing next to his ball, leaning on his driver. Mr. Woo asked, "Why you not take practice swing, Mr. Chase?"

"Mr. Woo, golf is like riding a bicycle. Once you've done it, you never forget." An announcement from the pro shop bellowed, "The Chip Wedgeman foursome to the first tee, please." No one moved except Murdock as he strode toward his ball.

Mr. Woo said, "Somebody erse, Mr. Chase, not us."

Murdock replied, "I'm Chip Wedgeman around here, Mr. Woo. They don't know me by any other name." The answer befuddled Mr. Woo as Murdock addressed his ball. Taking a huge swing, he promptly sliced his drive far right clear off the fairway. The ball landed less than 50 yards from where they stood.

Bodine, witnessing the pathetic effort mocked, "Not like any bike I've ever ridden." Murdock turned his back on Hwang and Woo to throw Bodine a meaningful scowl.

Throughout the round, Murdock flailed pitifully. After the 5th hole, he stopped recording his scores. Adding to his chagrin, the remaining three men each had respectable scores. Finishing the 18th hole, Bodine couldn't help but dig, "I'd say your bike needs a tune-up, Mr. Wedgeman." Murdock grimaced without comment.

"We go Mandrake's now, Mr. Bo?" Mr. Woo asked.

"It's only 11:00 a.m., Mr. Woo, and your friend Laura works the evening shifts. We'll go tonight. If we're lucky, she'll be on the work schedule. Chase and I have messages and fires to put out back at the office."

"Fire in office?" Mr. Hwang asked.

Bodine clarified, "Problems, Mr. Hwang. No fire."

Murdock wanted the day over. He hadn't seen Barbara since the previous Sunday, only a hasty phone conversation arranging an upscale dinner the following evening. He obsessed over whether she might discuss her rift with Donna. *Our entire evening could be at risk if I bring it up. Better I wait for her.*

Their post golf party at Mandrake's emerged as low-key. Fortunately, tall, lovely, and stacked Laura appeared at their table, thrilling the visitors from Taiwan. Bodine made sure their party was seated in her station. He gave Laura the requisite twenty-dollar handshake ensuring their table received special attention. Hwang and Woo followed Laura's every move around the room, scarcely taking their eyes off her. Worried they already crossed Laura's line, Bodine cautioned, "Gentlemen, if you don't stop staring at Laura, she'll get freaked out."

"What freaked out?" Mr. Woo asked.

"Feeling something or someone is creepy, scary. She won't like you if you make her feel uncomfortable." Bodine noticed both his guests had ordered four drinks each, six of which sat untouched still on their cocktail napkins.

When Laura made her next pass by their table, Hwang stopped her. She glanced at the neglected collection of full drinks, remarking, "Well, I don't think you need another round. Can I get you something else?"

Mr. Hwang acted like a shy schoolboy, obviously nervous. "Miss Raura, would you rike visit us in Taiwan? We pay expenses, make it good time for you."

Bodine's tolerance toward the foreigners' misplaced behavior hit its overflow button. Before Laura could respond, he blurted, "Okay, gentlemen, drink up. It's getting late, and Mr. Murdock has a hot date tomorrow." Laura smiled, walking away from the table without answering Hwang's question. Murdock mouthed an amen.

Murdock fought distraction all day and into the evening by guessing every five minutes the time he would get home for an uninterrupted round of music and dreams of Barbara. At one point, his frustration hit a boiling point, urging him to admonish their guests at Mandrake's when Bodine finally put an end to their visitors' disturbing harassment. His upcoming 'hot date' was indeed more pressing. It demanded his undivided attention. Exhilarated as he crawled into Pearl for the short drive home, he cried, "Sweet Barbara... tomorrow night. Just can't wait."

CHAPTER 25

THE COLD TRUTH

Murdock selected Barton's Steak and Seafood restaurant in Simi Valley for their special night. It fit the image he intended; he envisioned the elegant atmosphere, sitting beside Barbara in a quiet, mellow space where they would enjoy stellar food with impeccable service. Although located at a nearby strip mall which could mislead her take on its reputation, he would watch her surprise unfold as they entered the restaurant's tasteful interior. The well-known gourmet entrees attracted connoisseurs within a fifty-mile radius.

He picked her up a half-hour early for their 7:00 p.m. reservation. When she opened her front door, he stared, studying the ensemble she chose for their third date. She wore his favorite female wardrobe fetishes: a modest above-the-knee, low-cut black dress garnished by four-inch black patent leather heels. Her multi-chained silver necklace holding a braided silver pendant of concentric circles glistened from the setting sunrays, spotlighting her stunning décolletage. Contrasting her against Nadine Curtis, his gold standard for bountiful bosoms, he judged Barbara every bit as enticing. First Donna, then Nadine, now Barbara. In the male kingdom of female racks, he certainly had a string of luck going on. *C'est la vie.*

During the drive, Barbara started the conversation. "So how was golfing and Mandrake's with your Taiwanese colleagues?"

"Awful and terrible," he answered. "My rusty golfing skills left me humiliated from my first swing, such that I quit keeping score after the fifth hole. What made it even worse, Bodine and our visiting duo showed me how the game is played while Bo rattled off public one liners about my performance. Then our Taiwanese friends went over the goalposts with sexually harassing comments to our waitress at Mandrake's, ending with their inviting her for an all-expenses-paid trip to Taiwan for a good time with the two munchkins. By the way, our waitress, Laura, tops out at six-foot tall. Those guys were so drunk and out of control, Bo put them in their place abruptly, and we left. Hopefully, they follow the contract we have with them and we never meet with them again."

Having stayed silent through his story, Barbara let out a hefty laugh. "Not laughing at your misery at the golf game but at the out-of-bounds characters of these guys. Outrageous! Good for Bo for letting them have it and good for you for staying out of it. You did stay out of it, right?"

"Yeah. But if Bo hadn't spoke up when he did, I was ready to work them over. I had already broken out with my warning sweat." Barbara giggled hard, causing Murdock to giggle with her.

When they pulled into the strip mall's parking lot, Murdock kept a peripheral eye on Barbara as he said, "There's our destination on the right."

He watched as she stared silently at the restaurant's nondescript front. Finally, using the well-known, 'I don't like it' monotone mode, she said, "Oh, I see it." Murdock swallowed a laugh.

With his eyes focused on Barbara's face, Murdock opened Barton's plain, wooden double door. She blurted, "Wow, I certainly didn't picture this elegance from the outside. Those breathtaking chandeliers and cozy leather booths ready with the wine and glasses waiting are spectacular. Did you set me up or what?" They both chuckled together as Murdock took her hand.

After the hostess seated them side-by-side inside their booth, he crooned, "You know, Barbara, you look so spectacular I may have a difficult time ordering my meal. Really, you've stirred a part of me I believed disappeared forever."

She smiled, kissing him on the cheek. "I haven't dressed up in quite a while. I wanted to look my best for our date. I'm glad you like what you see."

186

"The word *best* doesn't do you justice. More like phenomenal."

"You're taking flirting into another dimension. I'll give you a half hour to stop."

"That obvious, huh?" They both laughed as they toasted their wine glasses. "I never mastered the art of being coy."

"Before I forget, I found two houses which meet your criteria; single stories, well maintained, good sized yards in nice neighborhoods. They're both offering open houses tomorrow. Open houses are the best starting place so you can compare and contrast."

"Fantastic. I'll visit them early before the tire kickers descend on them and catch the listing agents while they're still fresh."

"What? I'm the agent on one of them so you can get fresh with me... I mean, I'll be fresh for you... I mean, oh hell, Chase, you know what I mean." He refilled their wine glasses, loving every one of her laughs.

Witnessing her tongue-tied for the first time transcended cuteness. Her desirable qualities seemed endless, heightening his crush on her. As they chatted, two middle-aged men with their younger dates walked by their table led by the hostess. Murdock saw both men's shameless eyes glued on Barbara as they passed. He glanced over at Barbara, noting her ruffled expression as she observed their indiscretion as well.

What welled up in him provoked his response, "You gentlemen forget your cameras?" Both men glared at him as they kept walking. "It's okay, I'm sure you didn't see me sitting here. Happens all the time when I'm with my homely companion."

On cue and loud enough to entertain the dining room audience, Barbara snarked, "Unless you can afford a four-digit credit card charge this evening, you'd best keep your eyes on the lovelies you brought in." Several patrons burst out laughing, including Murdock.

As the two men continued walking, their dates bristled from their tactless conduct. One of the women complained, "You couldn't be any more obvious, Jack."

The other woman simply said, "Ditto, *Dick*."

Murdock smirked at Barbara. "Impressive comeback. It confirms my suspicions." He paused when she raised her eyebrows. "You're not a cheap date."

"Well, I just let them know what losers they are treating their dates and me that way."

And you did a good job. I guess at some point I'll simply raid my piggy bank," he teased with a raised eyebrow.

"Oh, sure, like I believe that, Mr. Murdock. Besides, I'm not for sale." She smiled. He winked back at her.

Their romantic pace moved faster than he anticipated. He recalled Donna's reluctance toward him at the beginning from the confounding emotions her husband's suicide caused. However, Barbara's mind seemed free and clear, just not ready to tip her hand. His gut reinforced going with the flow, not rushing her in any way.

When their meal finished, he signaled their waiter for the check. He put his arm around her. "Hey, I feel like our time here went by way too fast. Would you like to take a drive along the coast? Malibu is enchanting at night."

"Count me in. We can take a stroll along the shoreline. There's nothing like an old-fashioned romantic beach walk."

Did she really suggest romance at the beach? He pictured himself rolling on the sand with her, thrilled he always kept a thick, warm blanket in Pearl's trunk. When they neared the coast, he stopped at a liquor store, picking up a cheap white wine in a screw-top bottle. As they arrived at the beach, she leaned across the seat, pulling him close, holding his head in her hands, giving him a long, heartfelt kiss. His pulse rate accelerated as she ran her hands over his neck and down his arms. The uncertainty left him; he was smitten with her and she with him. Through just a twinkle in her eyes before the one sweet kiss, she tipped her hand.

While they walked toward the sand, Murdock scanned the beach for other people, especially law enforcement types. He made sure the wine bottle stayed wrapped in his beach blanket. After kicking off their shoes, he said, "I hope you don't mind drinking from the bottle. I spaced getting plastic cups."

"We've already tasted each other's spit, so no complaints here." Murdock snickered.

The rising moon spotlighted her loveliness. Her image in the nightfall matched the upscale beauty he fantasized about most of his life. She leaned over, rolling up her dress until it reached no more than an inch below her crotch. The process gave him a free view of her pretty legs and a yearning for the unseen.

"C'mon," she implored, "Let's see how the water feels."

"I like the way you think. Did I tell you this is my favorite place in the universe?"

"Mine too. I'm here often. Very cool sharing it with a kindred spirit."

Murdock rolled up his pants just below his knees. He held her hand while they walked into the shore break, the small waves crashing at their feet. He noticed a few waterdrops had sprinkled her face, hair, and dress, giving her context in the shoreline's landscape. His breathing became shallow as he savored the scene, regarding Barbara more fetching than before. As he drew the air slowly back in his lungs, he smiled at her. Her serene grin back implied her contentment matched his. The moments were theirs to seize, meant only for them.

He broke the tranquility with an off-the-wall comment, "You told me you were heavier than Donna. I'm not seeing it."

"Hey! I said a *little* heavier. Its more because I'm a *little* shorter than her, not that I weigh more."

"Well, you look downright irresistible. So, is tonight a good time for *the talk?*"

She laughed, "You didn't bring enough wine. Oh alright. I trust you anyway, although I'd rather have more kissing and hugging time."

"I'm totally up for that. I just need enough clarity for a broader, more accurate perspective of you and Donna. I'm sure you agree our situation isn't an everyday one, and I definitely don't want anything showing up down the road. You understand, right?"

"Yes, Chase. When you put it that way, I get it."

He drew her closer. "Honestly, without your input, I'm left with my own imagination how two such intelligent, fun-loving sisters could have been at odds so long. I've been having this good sister/bad sister internal dialog ever since Kevin told me about it. As much as I loved Donna, I prefer her as the scoundrel in the rift. It may sound coldhearted, but I can't imagine you as the reason behind it."

"Okay, let's unroll your blanket, have another few sips of wine, and I'll tell you what happened."

"Do I have to wait for our make out session until you tell the entire story?"

"Yes, because you might not feel like sucking face after I tell you everything."

"Ah, so *you're* the bad girl?"

"Depends on whether you think I've been overly judgmental about what took place. Just set your assumptions aside for a bit and be patient."

"Ok, I promise," he said with a soft kiss.

They spread the blanket on the sand. Sitting across from each other trading swigs from the bottle of cheap chardonnay, he noticed her dress remained rolled up. He grinned, "I never thought I'd ask you to show me less of your superb gams, but if you don't roll your dress back down, I'll be better off calling you from the car so I can concentrate."

She complied with his request by slowly pushing him over from his seated position on the blanket until he rested on his back. As he relaxed, she straddled his body with her knees while pinning his arms with her hands. With a sultry voice, she whispered, "Since you're being such a gentleman about things, I guess I'll have to take charge." She lowered herself onto him, pressing her lips on his as he covered her with his arms. With her lips still against his, she gritted her teeth as she spoke, "You sure you want to talk about this tonight?"

Murdock with lips still touching replied, "No, but yes, I have to know the story. I'm now praying that you are not the villain." She released her grip, rolling off him, releasing an audible sigh.

"Your restraint is sickening." They both laughed as she continued, "Okay, this is what went down. I regarded Donna's husband, Michael, as the most honest man you could ever meet. He took immense pride in his business, running it with the integrity of a saint. This I know because my ex, Will, worked for him. Will said Michael wouldn't cut a corner, wouldn't think of cheating someone out of a dime. He considered the plumbing supply business his legacy, a testament to his character. Michael's accountant passed away unexpectedly about four years ago. Although Donna became a highly respected psychologist, she also minored in business management at college. She volunteered to take over the accounting job while Michael located a replacement, doing all his bookkeeping during the evenings and on weekends. Over the next year, she overbilled Michael's customers to the tune of $150,000. Since the volume of business stayed enormous, and every one of Michael's customers trusted him without question, the extent of her cooking the books went unchecked for over a year. Then, a couple of customers started complaining followed by a few more and a few more until Michael confronted Donna, demanding she tell him what the hell was going on. To her credit, Donna didn't lie or play dumb about the accusations, admitting she'd gotten carried away by the prospects of nicer cars, a bigger house, finer clothes, etc."

Murdock's mouth fell open as he stiffened, stunned to the bone. The woman he thought perfect in every way was instead a conniving thief, willing to hurt loyal customers and undermine her husband for her own gain. "No wonder you didn't share this with Kevin or John. They would have been devastated. So, what happened after Michael confronted her?"

"Being a complete gentleman, adamant about his personal honesty, he visited, in person, every slighted customer, vowing he'd make things right. He made Donna correct every single overcharge, while he worked 16-hour days until he repaid each account in full. During all this, my ex, who was very close to Michael, and I, who loved him like the brother he was to me, suffered in silence. Right before the suicide, my ex told me Michael never acted the same after that, as if Donna's treachery permanently tarnished his reputation. He viewed her misstep as a fraud which cast a lifelong shadow on how his customers would regard him. Even though he left no note or communication when he took his own life, I knew exactly why he did it. From the moment I heard about his suicide, I couldn't stand the thought of Donna, seeing her, or communicating with her at all. Her actions were despicable, completely unnecessary, fueled by her own greed. I had a sick feeling inside my stomach long after Michael's death and still do when he crosses my mind. Something else you should know; Donna and I were close during the years prior. Soon after she took over the accounting, she hardly ever contacted me. Where we often threw parties, had dinners with my nephews, or evenings out together, that last year turned into a different story. We only had cocktails and appetizers two times that entire year, one of which happened at Christmas. Our close relationship really suffered. After Michael's funeral, I phoned her once, but she never returned or acknowledged my call, which worked just fine for me. So, you see, Chase, Donna was not a model citizen or the perfect woman you loved. Honestly, although we had the usual differences between siblings over the years, she wasn't near the woman I thought she was either."

Murdock could scarcely speak. He closed his eyes, letting slip a groan as he absorbed the news. Not only did it involve another character betrayal from someone he trusted, but also it came from the "perfect" woman he chose as his life partner. Barbara's information yanked him from a romantic high to a paralyzing gloom. Helpless to control his tears, he started sniffling. Barbara put an arm around his back, resting her head on his shoulder. She said, "C'mon. We'd better get you home."

CHAPTER 26

HOUSE HUNTING

Visibly shaken from the disturbing story about the woman he believed beyond reproach, he lost his voice. Driving Barbara home, Murdock fretted she noticed his agony. When they reached her front door, she offered, "Do you feel like coming in for coffee?"

He stammered, "Not a good time, sweetness. I wouldn't be very good company. Uh, just text me the address of the house you're showing tomorrow, and I'll meet you there." Her distress showed in teary eyes. She hugged him, then went inside the house, closing the door behind her.

Uncovering Donna's secret sucked out all sensations other than the torment racing through his thoughts for most of the night. Emotionally spent and in a state of exhaustion, he fell asleep heartsick. After less than three hours sleep, he hurried toward the shower. He drank day-old, reheated coffee while he finished dressing. The caffeine kicked in as he piloted Pearl to the open house in north Thousand Oaks.

The events from the prior evening haunted him as he revisited each scene. Following a classic romantic dinner, he ruined their intensifying intimacy when he nagged Barbara for specifics on the sisters' dispute. She kindly relented, exposing the grizzly details of the rift. He remembered emotionally breaking down in front of her, then leaving her with a troubled expression and teary eyes at her doorstep. She deserved better from him. The whole situation clawed at him, bringing on blistering remorse. He sang the refrain from a Garth Brooks song of the same title, "'Cause I've got friends in low places, where the whiskey drowns, and the beer chases my blues away, and I'll be okay." Adding his own words, he warbled the same tune, "Well, so much for the perfect lady, if there even is such a thing, in this cruel world, there's no such girl."

When the singing stopped, clarity found an opening. By dragging around the baggage from Donna, he jeopardized the chance for growing a strong relationship with Barbara. She didn't deserve feeling Donna around him when they were together. "It stops today," he proclaimed.

He found the open house she tagged for him within a section north of Olsen Road, a few blocks from Cal Lutheran University. As Barbara described earlier, the well-situated property boasted a manicured neighborhood without the extravagant price, which suited him fine. He wanted his own place; however, seeing her again remained the reason behind his interest. When he entered the house, he heard a younger couple drilling Barbara on questions about the schools, traffic, and how many families with young children lived on the block. He gawked at Barbara as the scene came into view. Dressed like the consummate professional in a navy-blue tailored suit offset by a classic white silky blouse and taupe pumps, he conceded Barbara made a traditional outfit fetching. He caught her eye, hopeful she overlooked him leering at her as she beamed a welcomed smile. When she finished with the couple, she headed straight toward him, pointing at the laundry room off the kitchen. When they got there, she closed the door behind them, immediately giving him a long hug and matching kiss.

"You worried me last night, Chase. I guess the story became way too painful."

"It definitely shocked me, Barbara, but I'm thankful you told me the story. Now, where's the master bedroom? I can't seriously consider a house unless the master turns me on."

She pointed at the living room which was in the middle of the house. "It's on the other side. Follow me." When they entered the master bedroom, she closed the door, swaying toward him while whispering, "I regret we didn't do this last night. Let's see if the master turns me on, too." She guided him to the king size bed, kicking her shoes off as she joined him in a horizontal embrace. She kissed him with a sense of urgency. When their lips parted, her audible breathing accelerated. "It's been so long, and I'm tired of waiting."

"Barbara, I'm as excited as you are, but, uh, well, we can't do this here," he sputtered, amazed she even thought about it.

A male voice resounded from the living room, destroying the moment. "Hello, is Barbara Conley here?"

She blurted, "Oh shit," while scrambling for her shoes, her face a rosy shade of lust pink. "Damned clients."

He said, "Yeah, what a nuisance. The nerve of some people." They both laughed while she straightened her suit.

She yelled, "I'll be right with you," then asked Murdock, "How do I look?"

"Including the glow emanating from your face, fabulous. Thanks for bringing back my ability for intense arousal. Oh, and I'll need a few minutes." She eyed the lump distorting his slacks as they both burst into laughter.

"What a waste," she cried. "Okay, I'll see what Mr. pain-in-the-ass wants. You gather your, um, composure and come out when you're ready."

Murdock confirmed, "Oh, one other thing. Raincheck?"

"You don't even have to ask."

"I think I'm in love."

"Hold that thought and bring it to my place tonight, 6:30. I'll fix us dinner." She hugged him with a tender kiss, rolling her tongue over his lips. "…we can enjoy each other for a night cap."

When his swelling subsided, he walked back into the living room. During a prospective client's ear-bending session with Barbara, he interrupted, "Thanks so much for the tour, Ms. Conley." Facing the man, he said, "This lady knows her stuff. Actually, I'm pretty sure my wife and I will be making an offer." Then he addressed Barbara, "I've got your card. I'll call you after I have the chat with my wife."

She replied, "Mr. Murdock, I hope I hear back from you soon."

The man standing beside her said, "My wife's in the car. I'll get her and be right back. I'll hate it if this is the one, and we lose to another buyer right ahead of us again." He walked out the door right behind Murdock, swirling past him as he reached his car. Murdock slowed down, smiling as he watched the man swing open the car door, help his wife out, then hustled with her to the house. As they swished by Murdock, the man grumbled something resembling how he didn't want another buyer getting the jump on the house because of her chronic indecision.

As Murdock got into Pearl, he heard a ding on his phone. Barbara texted him, "If that poor man and his wife only knew what we were up to in the master bedroom. I'm off to straighten the bedspread. Hahahahaha."

He let out a loud hoot. *This is surreal; I may have helped her with the sale of this place.* He felt euphoric. Over the last few days, he gained a new girlfriend, a lover, and hopefully, a chance for a lasting relationship. He went from not knowing if or when he had a chance with Barbara to having her almost doing the deed with him inside a stranger's house. The series of events boggled his senses; things were moving fast again, exciting him about the pace she just set.

Killing the hours before the evening at her place presented a problem. He attempted to overcome his eagerness for their date by driving Pearl through the neighborhood searching for other potential properties. He made it almost six blocks before he turned Pearl around. He sped toward the beach where he could better process the fortunate changes moving into his life and lose focus on the time.

The hours breezed by at the beach and gave him the overall refresh he needed. When he arrived at her place, she greeted him at the front door barefoot wearing shorts and a sleeveless top. She held a tequila gimlet which he accepted as she closed the door. He kissed her softly, saying, "You look even more ravishing than you did in the business suit. So glad you chose something less cumbersome to remove."

She grinned widely, "Glad you noticed. I always feel so confined when I dress to meet the public. Dinner should be ready in about a half hour. Let's go out on the patio. The weather is perfect for an al fresco meal." They sat at her round, glass patio table, each sporting grins as if this were a pregame ceremony, anticipating the main event. His stomach filled with butterflies. She stopped the grinning session, leaning into him as she said, "I'm sorry I got a little carried away this morning."

"I'm not sorry whatsoever. In fact, I'm hoping you're not having second thoughts about finishing what you started inside a stranger's bedroom."

She gazed into his eyes, her face softening with an affectionate smile. "Not at all. I've been counting the minutes until you arrived. I felt like a randy harlot today when I first saw you. I feel the same way now."

"We better change the subject until after dinner. Otherwise, I'll be laying you down on the dining room table, flinging food all over the floor."

"Ooh, sounds like a steamy movie scene. Okay, now it's my turn. Tell me the story how you met Donna."

He jolted upright in his chair, a flash of dread piercing his psyche. No one but his best friend, Ted Zachary, knew the details of his planned suicide. She caught him off guard, unprepared for divulging the sensitive details to anyone else. A quizzical grin appeared as she cocked her head awaiting his response.

"Oh hell, Barbara. Maybe this should wait. It's extremely personal, not that I don't trust you. Only my best friend in the entire world and Donna knew how it came to pass."

She showed herself as a quick study. "You called Donna on that suicide hotline where she worked as a volunteer?"

In a mild state of shock at her powers of perception, he reasoned she deserved an honest response. "Not exactly. She called me at the behest of my best friend, the only other person who knew my plan. Please, nobody, and I mean nobody else can know about this. Not Kevin, not John, not mom, not your BFF, nobody. Can you understand how raw this subject is for me?"

"Yes, I do. Oh man, Chase, I'm clueless about what I should say now."

"I'm not asking for a sympathetic response. Just listen. For over a year, I felt so down and out. I was divorced, unemployed, deeply depressed, at the point where I concluded the only answer was checking out, permanently. I couldn't leave my closest friends without giving them advance notice. My twisted logic convinced me the notice would avoid their feeling shock or rage from being blindsided by my sudden suicide. Telling my best friend, Ted Zachary, transpired into the game changer because he's the reason I met Donna. He called her on the suicide hotline and gave her my number. She provided the lifeline I needed to re-enter the world. When she eventually fell for me as I did for her, my life became worthwhile again. Even with her ill-advised accounting crimes provoking her husband's suicide, I'll be forever grateful she loved me, especially the inspirational ways she believed in me. When she got killed, I lost my will to live again and quickly revisited my suicide plan. If Ted hadn't monitored my every move immediately following Donna's memorial service, I'd be a goner by now. His intervention obstructed my attempt long enough until my other best friend, Richard Bodine, came through with the offer to help him run Eye Cue. Teddy's intervention and Bodine's job offer happened on the same day just minutes apart. Truly, their unwavering friendship during my crisis reversed everything. Today I value my life and all it holds in store, good or bad."

Murdock stared at Barbara, who was wide-eyed. She smiled as he spoke, "Until a short time ago, I never thought I'd meet another woman I could love who also appreciated me. I'm not making any assumptions about you. It's important you know that I'll be your man pal, boyfriend, or whatever you want unless you tell me to get lost. You've got me hooked hard, Barbara, like no one else, and I mean *no one* else. I can see myself becoming certifiably crazy about you."

He glanced upward, then cleared his throat, "I might as well put this on the table with hope you can digest it without any side effects. Can you, I mean, *will* you live with the fact that my memory of your sister always will be one of love and gratitude?"

Standing up, she clasped his hand, leading him into the kitchen in silent mode, carefully turning off the oven and a burner on the stove. She covered a salad she made with a paper towel then slid it into the refrigerator. "Dinner can wait," she declared while she guided him down a hallway, into her bedroom.

As she turned down the bed, her green shorts fell on the floor. She removed her hoop earrings before lifting off her yellow top. He stood transfixed, temporarily dazed by the irresistible vision before him. Her sea green bra and matching thong beckoned him as she laid down on the cool sheets. She chided, "You have way too many clothes on, Mr. Murdock. Get yourself certifiable before I count to five. One, two, three..."

CHAPTER 27

GLITCHES AND BITCHES

Murdock strolled into the office Monday morning, smiling ear to ear while his thoughts replayed the short version from the prior night's events with Barbara. Before he reached his office, Sullivan flagged him down, "We've got trouble, boss."

Murdock cut Sullivan off, "There's nothing you can say that will put a damper on this Monday, Rexuality. I just spent last night in paradise."

Sullivan cringed. "I'd love to hear the details, but we have a defective product crisis. The phones have been lighting up all morning. Seems Mr. Hwang's factory developed a QC problem, and the reps are panicking."

"Goddamnit. That's the last time we get talked into a *big order* from Hwang and Woo." He reversed course, storming into Bodine's office.

Eye Cue's President already heard the news, pacing around his desk. He screeched at Murdock, "Did you hear that shit, Chaser? Those Taiwanese horndogs might unravel all the momentum we've achieved. Now we're dealing with massive returns with unnecessary shipping charges. I'm so glad we licked Larry Davis' boots when we did, or he'd be all over us the moment he gets wind of this. I can just hear him..."

Murdock interrupted, "Calm down, Bo. First, get Hwang on the horn. Tell him we're not taking the hit from their fuckup.

Give him two options; A, they absorb all the processing and shipping charges on everything returned to his factory, *or* B, he flies a team of technicians out here immediately. Hwang's techs then fix the shit on site at our biggest customers' warehouses."

Bodine cracked a smile. "Oh, yes, they can," he shouted. "I like the way you think, Chaser. Let those bedwetters clean up their own mess. And I prefer option B. Much cleaner. What happens if Hwang refuses?"

"Tell him we cancel all future orders with his factory on top of looking for a new supplier starting today. That should put a knot in his knickers. Make him understand, if he likes riding this successful wave we've been on, his product *must* meet our standards."

Bodine caught on, "I'm on it. While I'm grinding Hwang into granules, you and Group Rex determine the extent of this cancer. Get me the top ten, no make that twenty, account names along with the quantities, by model, right now. I'll rub Hwang's nose in it. Then I'll let you know the dates the techs are arriving so Rexual Healing can notify the accounts. We could even be considered heroes by our customers, since I'm damn sure none of our competitors offer a concierge resolution with onsite repair service. That's the angle I'll use on the Board."

Murdock raced into Sullivan's office with the directive, whisking by colleagues until he reached his desk. The steamy memory from the night before with Barbara briefly masked his irritation. He came away from Barbara's delayed dinner party with a fervent belief his yearning for a good woman had ended. *Ah, last night. What an incredible, fascinating woman. It just sucks I have this crap-cluster, four-alarm fire now.*

The full-blown crisis caused by two pushy, horny, overzealous factory owners replaced the reverie of his previous evening with fierce resentment. When the emotionally strained Bodine advises the Board of the QC trouble, they might realize how clairvoyant he and Bodine were at their earlier presentation with the QC concern. Otherwise, they could have a Board-'splaining session appear on their calendar. With the pressure on, he refocused his thoughts toward gathering all the resources he needed, so their clients experienced nothing more than a minor delay.

Barbara popped into his mind. He shook his head not knowing when he could see her again. Drawing in a deep breath, he grabbed his phone and texted, "Hi sweetness, still reeling with pure pleasure. We have a crisis at the office, so don't know when I can request an encore. Tell all other would-be suitors to go to hell." He punctuated the message with an emoji, a pair of red lips in kiss mode.

She responded, "No worries. I only have your name on my dance card, babe." She included a smiley face with hearts for eyes.

Ecstatic from her instant reply, feeling like a kid who just got a 'yes' after asking a schoolgirl to go steady, he jerked when the phone rang. He furrowed his brow as he spoke, "What's up, Bo?"

"Guess what the hell else just happened? Talia called... she's pregnant." Murdock heard a boyish, frightened sound in Bodine's voice. "Now I *really* don't know what I should do first."

"Sorry, I have to ask. An abortion is out of the question, right?"

"Completely. She's having this kid with or without me."

He lowered his voice. "Calm down, Bo. You've got time to think about this, but not much. You know how I feel about you being an ultra-daddio, plus you've already admitted you're finished chasing skirts. You also love Talia, you know, with the right kind of love. In reality, you have an obvious decision here."

Bodine puffed his cheeks letting go a long sigh, "I can't handle this with her through a phone call. I'm leaving right now so I can be with her. She's hysterical with joy but terrified I'll wet the bed. I left a message for Hwang with instructions to ask for you if I'm not here. Work him over, Chaser. Don't let him wriggle out of anything."

"I'm licking my chops, Bo. Thanks for the opportunity. And, oh, do the right thing."

With Bodine out of the office, Murdock took charge. He had the warehouse manager suspend all shipments until they could determine which models were impacted by the factory's shoddy quality control. He put Sullivan on the phone running a courtesy call blitz for every account which complained. Murdock emphasized Sullivan would acknowledge their QC problems and assure them Eye Cue gave the issue top priority on each call. During his discussion with the managers, he conveyed the urgency for getting the issue fixed.

Late afternoon, he received an email from Sullivan containing a list of accounts with the specific data Murdock requested. In preparation for his confrontation with Hwang, he confirmed all departments and tasks were secured by 5:00 p.m., which matched the Taiwan time of 8:00 a.m. the following morning. He expected the call any minute. Armed with enough information and attitude to ruin Hwang's day, he received the call shortly after five.

"Herro, Mr. Chase. Dis Hwang in Taiwan. Mr. Bo reft bad message. He not der?"

"No, Mr. Hwang, but I am. The 'bad message' means we're not happy. My team dropped everything today wasting valuable overtime hours for compiling a list of our accounts, model numbers, and defective quantities received from *your factory*, which I forwarded to your e-mail address. Let me know when you are looking at it." After a long pause, he heard moaning on the other end of the line.

"Oh, dis not good, Mr. Chase. You send back to us right away. We fix."

"If we take this product back from our customers, you will pay all round-trip expedited shipping and processing charges."

"We pay one way; you pay one way."

"No, Mr. Hwang. You pay both ways, and I know that's a lot of money. However, I have a better idea. Just send your technicians directly to our accounts suffering the largest number of defective quantities and have two come here for the defective product in our warehouse. It will be quicker and cheaper than returning the product for repair then shipping again after it's fixed. This way, we and our customers only have a minor delay versus a long business disruption, something no one can afford. Bottom line, all parties involved have the least cost and inconvenience."

"Oh, Mr. Chase, that too 'spensive."

"Are you saying no?"

"So sorry, Mr. Chase. That too 'spensive." Hwang dug in, unprepared for Murdock's next missive.

"Personally, I think it's more expensive if you lose our business. How about this? We cancel all future orders and send back all defective product at your expense." Murdock raised his voice, "We absolutely *will* not do business with a factory whose owners won't take responsibility for a quality control problem of this magnitude."

Murdock heard a long silence followed by several voices shouting at each other in Taiwanese. When Hwang came back on the line, his tone changed, "We send five technicians tonight. Prease ter us which accounts see first."

"That's more like it, Mr. Hwang. I'll e-mail you the names, locations and contact people for the top ten accounts. Have your technicians schedule visits for two accounts each. I'll notify the customers your men are on the way. Thanks for addressing this like a pro, Mr. Hwang. You just saved everyone a lot of money." Murdock let out a loud sigh, relieved Bodine wouldn't return to a shit storm. "Oh, and don't forget, Mr. Hwang. Have two technicians plan on temporary residency here at Eye Cue at your expense until all remaining defective products have been repaired. I'm sure we have more accounts who will return defectives plus we have bad product inventory in our warehouse. I won't know the extent until we receive all requests for return authorizations. And you'll pay the shipping costs, both ways."

Hwang groaned, then after a long pause, practically whispered, "I understand, Mr. Chase."

Murdock indulged his urge to bait the man. "If everything goes smoothly, I'll send you two large, color photos of waitress Laura from Mandrake's." He grinned as he pictured drool running down Hwang's chin.

"Ooh, Raura. Van nize, Mr. Chase. I take care everyting."

"Great, tomorrow I'll send you the confirming email from our discussion listing all agreed upon terms. Good evening, Mr. Hwang."

He gathered his things ready for a peaceful night at home. As he walked toward the front door, he spotted Sullivan still sitting at his desk pounding the computer keys. "Go home, my Rexually transmitted friend. Hwang came through. We don't have to worry about taking the defectives back."

"That's great news, Chase. I guess my numbers crunching can wait until tomorrow." Before the two men could exchange goodnights, Bodine came charging through the front entrance.

"Chaser," he hollered, "Will you be my best man?" Murdock and Sullivan looked at each other, then burst into laughter.

"Well, I'll be. You *did* do the right thing. Hell, yes, I'll be your best man. All I ask is you show me any nude photos of Jenna Talia you might have before the ceremony." He hugged Bodine as Sullivan offered a handshake.

An animated Bodine waved his arms in the air, smiling like he won the lottery. "As if, Chaser," he said. "Even if I *had* any nude photos, they'd be for my eyes only. But nice try. Hey, what happened with Hwang?"

"Handled. He's got five techs bound for the states later tonight."

"Oh, thank Christ. I've juggled two high-intensity stressors all day. You just made it much easier for me to grab some shuteye tonight."

The three men entered the parking lot, carrying on about the wedding news. Walking toward his car, Murdock noticed an expensive black sedan with the motor running sitting beside Pearl. Bodine and Sullivan pulled out of the parking lot in the opposite direction. As he got closer, the driver's side window rolled down, revealing Nadine Curtis at the wheel. "Nadine, what the hell are you doing here?"

"Chase, I've been thinking non-stop about you lately. I'm sick of the nightlife and hooking up with random partners. It's not who I am, but it is what I became. Would you consider giving us another chance? You'll have my full commitment in an exclusive relationship, a promise you can trust." Her sorrowful tone sounded sincere, obviously repenting for her distasteful behavior.

In a voice dripping with sarcasm, Murdock retorted, "Ya' know, Nadine, if you'd mentioned this offer three weeks ago, I'd probably have given it consideration, not that I'd ever believe a word you said though. Look, I met a gorgeous woman who's every bit as appealing as you are, except...," he smiled, moving closer, "she's not an insatiable sport fucker. She's genuine, not a phony. I'll *never* worry about her being unfaithful or dishonest because she's got real character and values. Unfortunately, with you I'd always be wary, looking over my shoulder, wondering if some young cougar-trapper had caught your predatory eye. You're not trustworthy, Nadine. Understand what I'm saying here. I don't think you are even remotely capable of honoring any such commitment." He watched as she started trembling, teardrops rolling down her cheeks, eyes closed as she sobbed. "And oh yeah, Bo's getting married. Bitchen, huh? Goodbye, Nadine."

Murdock hopped into Pearl, driving away without a glance in her direction.

CHAPTER 28

PROGRESS

Seeing Nadine in her sad state the night before had been unnerving for Murdock, but also cathartic. Having freed himself from past sorrows and set himself into an exclusive relationship with Barbara, his energy level soared. For the rest of the week, he reassured Eye Cue's major customers by telling them the quality control steps Eye Cue management took to squelch the defective product issue. To Murdock's amazement, all the accounts appreciated his personal response with some customers increasing their pending orders. Bodine expressed his relief and gratitude, giving him an attaboy pat on the back.

Over the next two days, his romance intensified with Barbara. All the relationship indicators were on fire, showing remarkable progress while maintaining a head-spinning pace. During a lengthy, often X-rated phone conversation with Barbara, an inner peace settled in.

On Thursday morning, Murdock arrived early at his office eager for a status update on the recent product disaster. After making coffee, he scanned the end-of-day status reports, pleased at the advances made. The quiet in the office relaxed him. Letting his thoughts wander, he reflected on his return to Eye Cue several months earlier, recognizing how much time had passed without necessitating any field visits. Although managing the unusual product demand took priority over travelling, the daily convenience he had being near his office and home felt awfully satisfying. He reasoned the highly successful ad campaigns seeded the escalating product demand, landing him in his current enviable position. The existing reps were too busy hiring new reps and fielding orders for scheduling unnecessary, time-consuming account meetings with him. They had turned to Sullivan for day-to-day guidance and perhaps account conference calls. The glad-handing and back-slapping events sat on the backburner for now. Best of all, the new reps wanted the line so badly, they were happy making the trip for a meeting at his or Sullivan's office. He cautioned himself, remembering how nothing stays the same, and knowing that included this wind at his back. *I've been here before. Avoid complacency and overconfidence, whiz kid. This can't last forever.*

Eye Cue's receptionist, Gina Morgan, asked him earlier in the week if she could organize a small surprise party at noon on Friday in the conference room to congratulate Bodine on his engagement. When she first told Murdock about the event, he insisted on providing the cake.

He called the local bakery, inquiring about a custom creation for the occasion. He needed strawberry pink cake with vanilla and chocolate icing in the shape of a baby sleeping on its belly with its oversized butt up in the air. He further advised the baker, "Use a skin-toned vanilla icing for the baby's head and body, saving the chocolate icing for its butt." When the baker asked what he wanted written on the cake, he instructed, "On the vanilla icing across the baby's body, write 'Congratulations' in blue and pink. On the chocolate butt cheeks, write two words on each cheek, the first two in blue icing and second two in pink icing so that it says, 'Shit Just Got Real.'" He and the baker laughed for a bit before he finished, "The cake should serve around 80 people, so make this a big-assed baby."

The entire office buzzed with preparation for the party. Bodine entered the conference room greeted by applause, smiles, loud whistles and hoots as he headed straight for the cake. As he lifted off the large cover, the crowd went silent. "Now who else other than our Vice President of Sales would have the audacity placing an order for this hilarious cake?" Everyone in the room howled in approval.

Rex Sullivan marveled at Murdock's daring, "Wowser, Chase, this ain't like any other company I've ever worked for." Pulling out his cell phone, Sullivan pleaded with Bodine, "Please don't cut that until I can get a picture." Everyone else in the room followed Sullivan's lead, parading by the cake, snapping a souvenir.

"My husband won't believe this," one of the women blurted.

One of the men shouted, "Does Murdock have brass huevos or *what*?"

Everyone laughed as Bodine stared at Murdock, shaking his head with disbelief on his face. "Good thing you're officially banned from advising on the wedding cake."

Murdock chuckled, "I just wanted a special moment you'll never forget. You guys have been bombarded with a barrage of stress clusters lately. This cake indeed represents your next adventure, an expression of endearment, if you will."

Sullivan asked, "When's the big day, Bo?"

Bodine grinned, "We haven't nailed that down yet. I just know I'm going to be a father, and I'm stoked about that." The crowd clapped in approval.

Murdock brought in a few bottles of champagne and miniature plastic cups. "Just a couple of sips, people. We can't have anyone falling asleep on the job, especially anyone driving a forklift."

Surprising everyone, Dr. Jenna Talia walked through the door, escorted by Ted Zachary. Murdock started clapping, everyone else in the room joining in. He hugged Talia, giving her a kiss on the cheek, then Zachary, giving him a hug as well. "Thanks, Teddy."

Bodine appeared as surprised as anyone at the special guest appearances. "Hey baby, so nice you stopped by. This is your party, too. Hey, Ted, we appreciate your straightening us out about the decorum when we deal with the Board."

Zachary gave Bodine a hug, pointing a thumb at Murdock, "I had a premonition that you and the loose cannon here might smart-mouth your way into trouble. Glad you smoothed things over with your Board."

Several women surrounded Talia, escorting her straight to the cake. She laughed, saying "I know who had a hand in this, for sure. Chase Murdock, get over here right now."

Murdock, Bodine and Zachary walked over as if they were on a screenshot from "Top Gun." Talia hugged Murdock and told him, "Best cake ever, Chase."

Murdock shouted, "Okay, who wants the first piece of ass, 'er cake?" Laughter erupted followed by murmurs about Murdock's freewheeling expressions.

The head of HR, Brenda King, sidled up to Murdock, whispering an admonishment. "You'd better be careful, Chase. You never know who could take offense."

Murdock protested, addressing the entire group. "I've just been advised that there *could* be some people here who might be offended by my custom, and I might add, expensive cake along with the subsequent salty language. All those who feel I've crossed the line, please raise your hand."

A chorus of boos followed his announcement without anyone expressing distaste in his mock trial. He looked back at King, pointing to the cake's baby butt. "We'll save you a turd, Brenda." King giggled, slapping his arm while giving him the stink-eye.

Gina Morgan joined Talia, offering her a slice of cake along with a cup of champagne. "Si on the cake, but no gracias to the champagne," she said. "Can't imbibe for about nine months."

After the celebration, Zachary followed Murdock to his office, closing the door behind him. Taking a seat across from his friend, he asked, "I'd like a quick update on your state of mind. Everything with you okay?"

A huge grin appeared on Murdock's face. "Things are more than okay, Teddy. I haven't had a chance to tell you about Barbara Conley."

"Oh, wow, you finally met her?"

"Better than that, Teddy. I'm falling hard for her, and she's not interested in anyone else either. Can you believe my luck? She's a gift like none other, including Donna." He gave Zachary the details on Donna's poor decision concerning her husband's business.

"So *that's* why they weren't speaking to each other?"

"All along I was wondering who caused the stonewalling between them, praying it wasn't Barbara. Turned out, Donna wasn't quite pedestal-worthy after all. I guess I was so blinded by her love. Teddy, I never would've suspected her possessing the capability for doing such an awful thing. Her crime hurt many people and provoked her husband's eventual suicide. It's mind-boggling."

"Fascinating. So where are you at with Barbara? Another engagement celebration party around the corner?"

"Get real, Teddy. I've only known her less than a month."

"Well you've pulled some pretty impulsive shit over the last year. I had to ask."

"Touché, but no. We both want things moving at their own pace." Murdock held back from revealing how quickly the relationship became an exclusive one, afraid he might jinx it. "Teddy, Barbara gives me every quality I loved about Donna and then some."

"I'm excited for you, buddy. Just stay focused so it can all fall into place."

Barbara called him early Saturday morning. "A new property just hit the market, and I arranged a showing right away. It's well within your budget with all the amenities you want. Can you meet me there at ten? Since they scheduled the open house for Sunday, I did some quick talking, so I could do a private showing today. No other looky-loos allowed, and the owners won't be home."

"Sounds perfect. Shoot me the address. Can't wait to see you at ten."

When he knocked on the door, she greeted him wearing a much more casual outfit of red capris, a black, short-sleeved blouse, and black espadrilles. He noticed she was braless, her generous attributes straining against the confines of her blouse. "You're the sexiest real estate agent I've ever seen," he chirped with a smile. She locked the door behind them.

She smiled, locking her arms around him. "Well, had it been for anyone else, I would have worn my monkey suit." They shared a long, slow kiss. "And the master bedroom should meet with your approval. Follow me."

Walking down a hallway, she kicked the shoes off her feet. He asked, "Is this going to be a *custom* private showing?"

She replied, "I got so excited at the last place I showed you. Thinking about having my way with you in a stranger's house turned me on like you wouldn't believe. We can check the place over later."

Before he could take his shoes off, she stood before him, stark naked, face flushed from excitement, clothes strewn on the floor. They both tore off his clothes in seconds as they tumbled onto the king size bed. He practically squealed, "You really know how to make a presentation, lady. I'll take it."

"Take me first. I'm so ready. Ever since our first time, I haven't been able to think about anything else."

His voice had a breathless tone, "God, I adore your spontaneous lust." He loved how quickly she aroused him, reacting by covering her with wet kisses before she pulled him on top of her. He could feel the heat emanating from her entire body. She locked her ankles behind his back, rocking with the rhythm until she tightened up, quivering, holding her breath before letting out a loud gasp.

"Oh Chase, yes, *please*, keep doing that," she begged while keeping up with his accelerating rhythm. He looked skyward, as if she were a gift from above while they continued the manic pace in satisfying their primal desires. When they were finally at rest, both were covered in perspiration.

He put his hand over her heart, placing hers over his. Their pulse rates felt the same as that from a one-mile run. He smiled, giving her a soft, sweaty kiss as they both giggled. "I must inform you, sweet face, you'll have a helluva time getting rid of me now."

A splendid bliss covered him when she put her lips an inch from his ear, whispering, "No way, baby."

Those three little words gave him a profound sense they were on the same page, a reassurance he craved since the moment he fell in love with her. Just like Barbara had done early on, he would not tip his hand just yet. Things had ramped up so quickly between them, he needed time for reaffirming the validity of his emotions toward her. Ultimately, he sought a more objective mindset, one where he could judge her feelings about him as well. When she asked if he had interest in touring the rest of the house, he balked. At that moment, he fancied the possibility for them moving in together. More pointedly, he also could use the extra time to observe the two of them together should the chance of sharing a residence ever become a reality. He wanted proof any commitment this time led him in the right direction rather than making an impetuous gamble.

He smiled while giving her a hug. "I've seen all I need, Ms. Conley...and I'll certainly never forget the master bedroom. Thanks for the tour."

CHAPTER 29

ROMANCE CALLING

Mr. Hwang's technical crew quelled the uprising among Eye Cue's major accounts in five business days. The culprit, a defective capacitor on one of the circuit boards, proved an easy fix for the factory techs. Hwang called Eye Cue with the good news. When the call came through, Murdock sat across from Bodine.

After Hwang bragged about his techs' speedy job completion, Bodine responded, "Great work, Mr. Hwang. When will your two men arrive here and secure our inventory? I haven't shipped one piece of your product in over a week and won't until I know every piece has been thoroughly examined."

"No probrem, Mr. Bo. Maybe I come see you, make sure everyting ok."

Murdock muffled a laugh, knowing Bodine's probable response.

Bodine rolled his eyes. "That won't be necessary, Mr. Hwang. I'll make sure your techs experience a comfortable stay." He and Murdock knew Hwang's real motives involved playing golf then stalking the waitresses at Mandrake's while getting hammered. "We'll show them a good time." Hwang let out a groan.

Murdock, still chuckling, whispered, "What a horny little perv. Tell him Laura got fired. That should rewire his fantasy."

After Bodine ended the call, he smirked at Murdock, "So how's it going between you and Barbara?"

"Exclusivo and magnifico. Now I'm working on convincing her *not* to show me anymore houses."

"That's curious. I thought you despised living in your one-bedroom apartment." Then the Murdock brand of rationale hit him. "Oh, I get it, you're thinking about cohabitating. Jeez, *already?*"

"Yes, *already*. It has to be her idea, so I'll wait her out. In the meantime, I'll go with the flow. Mi amigo, she's the one, I'm sure of it."

"And what if she cools off?"

"Then I'll kill myself." Murdock forced a laugh, then shuddered at how haunting his answer sounded. He would never go there again, with or without Barbara. "Seriously, though, I will do everything in my power to earn her love, so we can stay together...forever."

Bodine raised his eyes. "Doesn't it feel pretty impulsive for *what*, barely a month since you met the woman? You don't need another rollercoaster ride."

"I know, but when it's staring me in the face, I fear missing out on the moment she brings it up more than I worry about us rushing things. Barbara checks off all the boxes for my ultimate life companion. She embodies all I ever wanted, even though I don't deserve her."

"I thought Donna was all you ever wanted."

Murdock realized Bodine held him on the hook, not buying his sales pitch. "She was but..." He hesitated without going into detail about Donna's thievery, feeling he shared enough on the subject when he told Zachary the story. "Donna's gone. Can we leave it at that? While I've got your attention, may I take a few days off? I'm thinking a four-day weekend with Barbara at an ultra bitchen resort on the coast where we can spend a long weekend together."

Bodine nodded yes, "You have earned it for sure. Have fun, and don't get carried away. You both need more time together before any big step, Chaser."

He located a getaway place online, the FogCatcher Inn nestled within the coastal town of Cambria. The beach setting supplied the picture-perfect atmosphere for isolated quality time with Barbara, giving them both the chance for round-the-clock time together.

She cooed at the invitation, "Oh, Chase. How romantic. Do the rooms have a fireplace?"

"I think so. It may even have oversized bathtubs with massaging jets. It's just a few yards from the shoreline, too."

"I can't wait. This will be so good, you know. No distractions. We really can learn more about each other."

"My thinking exactly. I'll keep my hands off you long enough for meaningful conversations, but my hands have a mind of their own."

Her tone became impish, "I'm sure we'll have ample time to explore both options. Hey, you should spend Wednesday night at my place, so we can leave early Thursday morning."

Amidst their first full night together, Murdock loved how the evening flowed unrestrained without any nits to pick. Their instinctive intimacy comforted him such that he found it incredible they had known each other only a few weeks rather than a few years.

Early the next morning, Barbara woke first, then woke Murdock using her cold foot kicking his butt. He jumped out of bed in a daze. Laughing at his weird expressions, she directed, "Get your ass moving, babe. We need to be on the road in fifteen minutes."

"Uh, yeah, sure thing." He moved toward his duffle bag, not yet fully awake.

They each wore shorts, flip flops, Hawaiian shirts, sunscreen in hand, eyes covered with shades, topping off their vacation garb with straw hats. Although unplanned, their outfits matched. Before he left for Barbara's the night before, Murdock loaded Pearl's trunk with beach chairs, an umbrella, and towels, all nestled beside a pre-stocked cooler with water, beer and white wine. While loading the trunk, he spotted his old frisbee, the same one he and Donna played with when they dated. Seeing it tugged at his heart, but he threw it away before he left. His excitement about his and Barbara's long weekend left no room for reminiscing.

While they tooled north on the 101 freeway, she sat quietly, soaking up the ocean views on a spectacular day. He tagged her contentment as a positive sign she accepted him as a full-time mate. The inner peace he experienced from her the week before wrapped him again in serenity, removing any leftover nervousness about their trip.

They stopped at a diner halfway toward their destination. After the waitress took Barbara's order, she glanced at Murdock, who responded nonchalantly, "I'll have a steaming hot real estate agent with nothing on it, open-faced."

Barbara, quick on the uptake, jumped in, "What he means is he wants that order to go, and I'll take care of it. Now, Chase, give the woman your order." They both giggled. The waitress's deadpan face showed zero reaction, revving up their entertainment. Barbara picked up the pace, "Just give Mr. Horns here the same as I ordered."

Having taken their order, the expressionless, silent waitress walked away, leaving them near hysterics at the table. A different waitress brought them their orders. They chattered and giggled about the zombie waitress during their lunch. Their high spirits carried them through the rest of the drive.

After checking in at the hotel, the bellhop escorted them to their room with the couple chatting about the striking accommodations the entire way. Barbara wolf-whistled with approval as she spied the fireplace and oversized bathtub. Murdock relished her pleasure, giving her a schoolboy grin for each comment she made. As soon as the bell hop left, he swooped her up into his arms and carried her across the room, gently laying her down on the king-sized bed. She sat up, smiling while unbuttoning his shirt. He complained in mock protest, "Are you taking advantage of me, madam? We just got here."

She hurried to remove her clothes when he joined her on the bed. He loved seeing her naked in broad daylight, her sumptuous body defying the aging process. After another session of knee-buckling lovemaking, he collapsed in her arms. Minutes later, they both fell into a deep sleep.

He awoke nearly two hours later as the sun rested high above the picturesque town. Staring at Barbara sleeping on her back, snoring faintly, he welcomed how he experienced both desire and peacefulness at the same time with her. He recalled how sexy Nadine Curtis excited him with her insatiable kinkiness and over-the-top looks, leading him into the belief he found love with the ideal woman. However, Nadine never awarded him any inner peace, just sexual satisfaction and warning signs of imminent betrayal. He considered Barbara in a different league altogether. She shared his sexual proclivities yet brought the highest standard of character and respect to the relationship. He knew how she felt about everything instantly since she never hid her emotions. Honesty dwelled in her core; she showed her contentment with him by just being herself. The reason why hit him like lightning. *I was never in love with Nadine, ever. Everything is different because this must be how true love feels.*

He leaned toward Barbara, snagging off her covers in one yank, waking her with a start. She looked at him with a smile, then glanced at the sunshine over the beautiful view outside the hotel window. She sat up, then implored him, "C'mon, get ready so we can take a walk on the beach, babe." He appreciated how she never called him honey or sweetie; he loved the occasional babe. "C'mon, I said." She put her cold feet on his belly, bolting him out of bed.

"Ok, I'm ready. How do I look?" He stood profiled in the nearby window, showing off his waking maleness.

Barbara grabbed her phone, threatening a photo session. "Get dressed, porn star."

The salted breeze rejuvenated them as they walked toward the water. She took his hand, smiling into the fading sun, floating with him in the serenity they shared. As they strolled down the sand, he stopped and faced her. "It's time I tell you something, Barbara. I never imagined any woman could ever touch me so profoundly, but..." He hesitated, his eyes searching her face, not finding the words he needed, restricting himself from letting go with "I love you."

She followed his eyes, waiting for the rest of his thought. As he stood tongue-tied, she offered her version of the moment. "It's special, isn't it? I can't say I ever lived through the brand of love you had with Donna. I *can* say I've never had the powerful feelings I have for you. Our relationship is so precious, Chase. I hope we build a love that lasts."

Overcome with emotion, he trembled, tears welling in his eyes. "My love for your sister rescued me from becoming just another pathetic statistic. Meeting another woman I could love so intensely again seemed impossible. Yet, here you are. You have my word. I'll never take you for granted. Like I said before, my taking a hike would happen only if you made the request."

She pulled him against her, staring into his eyes. As he lowered his head to kiss her, she whispered, "That'll never happen, so stop saying it."

He squeezed her tighter than he ever had before, holding her as if he would never let her go. "I'm sure this sounds like a tired cliché, sweetness, but..."

She interrupted him, "I know, because I feel the same way about you."

———

Their dinner plans included another walk on the beach. After dining on scrumptious fresh seafood and tropical cocktails at a beachside seafood restaurant, they kicked off their shoes, starting a long walk on the sand under a glittery rising moon. Barbara broke the silence, "This was such a great idea, babe. It's like being in another world. I'm already fretting about it ending," she giggled. "I can't wait to reciprocate."

He playfully responded, "Anywhere you pick works for me, Ms. Finecheeks." They continued walking, arm in arm, when his phone rang. "Shit, I knew I should have left this thing at the hotel. Uh-oh, it's Bo. He knows we're together. It must be urgent. Shit." He put his phone on speaker mode. "Hi Bo, you know I'm on vacation, right?"

"Yes. I wouldn't have bothered you except we have a tragic situation. Nadine Curtis committed suicide last night." Barbara put her hands over her mouth, her eyes wide in shock.

Murdock felt like a baseball entered his throat, blocking all the air. He gasped, then pressed Bodine, "Oh Jesus, Bo. Tell me you're drunk out of your mind, and you're just fucking with me."

"Sober as a nun, sorry to say. It gets worse. Her brother called to tell me she left a note. She's blaming it all on you and me. He told me about his plans on filing a wrongful death suit against us *and* Eye Cue. I hate to do this, Chaser. However, I need you back here right away."

"Shit, Bo. Have you contacted our attorney?"

"We're in between representation. I let the last firm go because they sucked. I don't even know who to call right now."

"Call Ted. He knows more than one top notch legal gun. Tell him we need one rabid son-of-a-bitch for this situation. I'll head back to the office first thing in the morning." As soon as he said it, he turned to Barbara, whose crestfallen eyes told him everything. Her weekend in paradise, shattered by his prior psychotic girlfriend's senseless act, sent her joy straight to anguish. Her pain flowed through his body like wildfire.

Her eyes welled with tears, "Oh God, what terrible news. I know there was no love lost with you the way things ended, but I can't imagine the pain she must have felt inside before she took her life. Of course, I can't help feeling disappointed being gypped out of our amazing vacation. Just know I totally understand we have to cut this short."

Murdock hugged her, hoping she didn't feel his panic or see his wet eyes. The shock formed from the news about Nadine; the tears appeared when he felt her pain from losing their resplendent weekend.

As they prepared to leave, his last conversation with Nadine flashed through his mind, including the manner he caustically admonished her at the Eye Cue parking lot where she came to him, heart in hand, pleading for another chance. He called her untrustworthy, then even worse, an insatiable sport fucker, finally rubbing her nose in the insults with updates of his new, solid relationship plus Bodine's engagement. Sadness overshadowed by shame gripped him. He may have been the one who pushed her over the edge.

CHAPTER 30

GUILT

The ride back Friday morning proved a miserable trek for Murdock, even with the soothing encouragement from Barbara. She became quiet eventually, obliging his silence. He scarcely slept the night before, spending hours standing at the picture window near the bed overlooking the dark sea, questioning if his callousness served up the final straw for Nadine's tragic suicide. He agonized incessantly over her reaching the point of no return knowing the torment she experienced must have been excruciating. Afterward, he replayed his own despair from the prior year where he made the same dreadful decision, saved at the last minute when Zachary outsmarted him by tapping Johnny Dunne's help. Nadine must have faced the same unbearable heartbreak from inescapable hopelessness. Even in anger, he never could have wished such deep pain or tragedy on her. No one deserves punishment that severe.

He parked the car in Barbara's driveway, took her hands, and focused on her eyes. After clearing his throat, he told Barbara about his last moments with Nadine, giving her the full backstory and clarity surrounding his concern. Barbara cringed, "Oh God, Chase. You called her *that*? Still, it would have simply been a wakeup call, maybe followed by an argument, for most women. But the poor thing must have been emerged in self-loathing. How would you have known her life hung by a thread, especially since she portrayed herself as being so formidable?" Barbara tried consoling him as he apologized for her ruined weekend, but she waved him off. "I'm not worried about me. I just hate your being put through such an ordeal. We can always reschedule."

"I know. I'm just dreading what's waiting for me at the office."

"Well, it's Friday. If you feel like company, just stay at my place tonight. I'll give you whatever space and time you want for hashing this out. At least we can spend the days we planned together."

"Appreciated. I'll know my role in this mess more after talking with Bo. Who knows? Maybe he'll have encouraging news for me. I'll call you as soon as I can." He helped her with her bags, then gave her a quick hug. She waved as he backed down her driveway.

The somber mood, especially on a TGIF morning at Eye Cue, caught his attention as he walked toward their receptionist, Gina Morgan. Noticeably still shaken from the news about Curtis's death, she simply pointed toward Bodine's office with no chirpy greeting for him. All morning he focused on having a prompt arrival at the office without any consideration for changing clothes at home after dropping off Barbara. Brenda King's disapproving glance as he entered Bodine's office woke his awareness of how outlandish he looked dressed in shorts and flip flops for an executive-only office meeting.

Zachary, invited by Bodine for defense options advice, greeted him first with a handshake, then a personal swipe to lighten up the heavy atmosphere, "Man, did we cut your surf's up moment short?"

Not amused, Murdock moaned, "Not funny, Teddy. First off, please pay very close attention to this story." Bodine and Zachary leaned back in their chairs, both studying his face. In distressed tones, he recounted his surprise encounter with Curtis in the Eye Cue parking lot followed by his last conversation with her.

Bodine leaned forward in his chair. "Chaser, your angry words are understandable for anyone who's been betrayed repeatedly as you were, but you *cannot* repeat this story to anyone else other than our new attorney. Do you clearly understand everything stays in this room with no exceptions for any of us?"

"Yes I do, but I already told Barbara."

Zachary offered advice, "Then, unless Barbara wants a subpoena for her testimony in court, you must impress upon her to catch an acute case of amnesia about it. Here's hoping Nadine's suicide note didn't quote your scathing critique of her lifestyle."

Murdock acknowledged, "I get it. That kind of condemnation could be damaging. So where are we with our defense?"

Zachary spoke first. "I've advised Bo about an attorney who will treat a wrongful death suit as a nuisance case. His name's Justin Arluck, a tenacious member of the legal tribe who has a reputation for shredding those who arrive unprepared. He's smart, experienced, very successful, and always goes for the jugular first. If Nadine's brother survives long enough for the Discovery phase, Arluck will treat it as a personal afront. By the way, he's known in law circles as Just, a well-earned nickname given him by opposing attorneys. When one of them learns they will face him in the courtroom, their lament is 'Just Ourluck.'"

Bodine offered another point. "Look, Chaser, Nadine's brother, Kelly Landsman, thinks we'll cave in right away. Wrongful death suits are iffy at best. I'll suggest Arluck browbeat Landsman well in advance of any actual suit he may file. For starters, we'll expose Nadine's character flaws right away. If she and Landsman were close or he's worried about his family's reputation, maybe he'll rethink her plight enough to back off. If he's just looking for a big payday, Arluck will dig into Landsman's background as well. From what Ted's told me, this attorney doesn't play nice."

Zachary added, "Arluck *is* a pit bull. He won't hesitate to peel back the layers on someone's character or lack thereof. I'm convinced he's the right man for the job. And, Chase, make sure you're respectful. Check your smart mouth at the door, understood?"

Murdock again bristled at Zachary's tone, which this time made him feel like a child being scolded. "Yes, dad. Jesus, Teddy, you're talking to me as if I'm some fucking kid."

Zachary reassured him, "Sorry it sounded that way, amigo. It'll be fine. Just a little heads-up for you and Bo in the event you boys actually take the stand."

"When will we know?"

Bodine answered, "We just wait until Landsman follows through on his threat. I can't sick Arluck on him legally unless he files suit. However, there may be an opportunity for him to sniff around Landsmen before he files. I'll know more after I speak with Arluck."

"You called me back early from what would have been a four-day love fest with Barbara just to advise me to hurry up, shut up, and wait?"

Bodine replied, "Take it easy. I wanted your advice as second in command on how I should handle the news. I had no attorney at the time plus I've got this guy, Landsman, threatening me on the phone. If you hadn't suggested I call Ted, I'd be hiding in the men's room, for God's sake. Lighten up, Chaser, we're in this together. Just keep your phone handy over the weekend. We'll see if anything happens. Now go home, my friend, get some sleep. You look like shit."

Murdock took out his phone, punching Barbara's number while still sitting in Bodine's office. He stared at Bodine as he spoke to Barbara. "Ms. Finecheeks? Hi. I'll take you up on your slumber party invite if it still stands. Bitchen. Be there in a half hour."

Murdock patted Zachary on the shoulder as he walked to the door where Bodine met him, "Look, Chaser, I know you're pissed off at me for my suddenly ending your well-deserved vacation. Consider it from the company's point of view. You're the number two executive for Eye Cue. As CEO, I would've been negligent not bringing you back for immediate availability in a liability event this size. Goes with the executive territory you cover, so to say. Let me be clear, your edgy attitude may make sense to you, but it's totally inappropriate for the position you hold. Clearly, you have plans for extended brooding over recent events this weekend rather than focusing on your blooming relationship with Barbara. Suck it up, Chaser, take charge of the moment, keep moving forward. Leave the past where it is. It's important you are vigilant, proactive, firing on all cylinders come Monday. And yes, I am a royal chicken shit without you."

Murdock bit his bitter tongue, "I understand Bo. Glad you torqued my perspective. I'll see you Monday." He gave his two friends a tiny smile before he left.

Zachary added after Murdock left, "Great job covering the rules with him, Bo. Let me know if I can help in any way."

"Thank you, Ted, for dropping everything to help us find Arluck. I firmly believe Chaser and I both needed large doses of your confidence and wisdom."

———

Murdock's weekend at Barbara's started out subdued, though better than sitting at home alone mulling over the scary litigation threats on top of Nadine's grim suicide. He took credit for both situations, tying his stomach in knots while fueling his thoughts in a spiral of self-blame. Watching Barbara make the extra efforts for his comfort, hoping he would pick her over the Curtis related issues he faced, inflated his guilt. Not much changed with him throughout Saturday morning and afternoon. While moping, he fiddled around watching TV between grabbing cold brews throughout the day. Barbara stayed occupied in her many interests, advising him late afternoon they were staying home for the evening.

After Murdock dished up a boring, tightlipped dinner, Barbara abruptly disappeared into her bedroom, leaving him alone in the kitchen. He robotically rinsed their dishes, placed them inside the dishwasher, then turned on the TV. When she returned, she wore a sheer white negligee, nothing underneath, and cooed, "Perhaps a special therapy session would help get your mind right." She produced a pink velvet bag wielding a familiar shape in one hand and a cherry- flavored lubricant in the other. "Can little Chase come out and play?" His arousal door swung wide open. Not only ready for playtime, he also snapped back into the real life he and Barbara were living, a very happy life.

Monday morning, Eye Cue received Nadine's funeral information, advising it would take place on the upcoming Friday afternoon at a Simi Valley chapel. Murdock fumed, "Jesus, Bo. Why can't they have a memorial service instead? This means her casket will be on display, and if it's open, I don't think I can look at her. An open casket will also make it a much worse tearjerker for her friends and family, all of whom will glare at both of us with daggers in their eyes. It won't even end until after the procession to the burial site where everyone puts a flower on the coffin, then begins a final sobbing session while the coffin is lowered into the ground. It's way too much for me."

Bodine seemed resigned to their fate. "Again, I'll remind you, we will all suck it up, Chaser. There's no avoiding this one. Remember, the entire Board will be there. I only hope Larry Davis didn't get the details in her suicide note before us, whatever they may be. I'm dying for the info myself. By the way, it's okay if we skip the procession."

Each day they waited on news whether Kelly Landsman filed the lawsuit. After briefing Justin Arluck on the phone as to Murdock's last conversation with Nadine, Bodine requested he attend her funeral as a precaution to document any questionable behavior while providing lip service to any unhinged hecklers.

With Arluck present, Bodine prayed the unstable Murdock, who stood as the most vulnerable, would trust the razor-tongued attorney to disarm any legally sensitive situations.

By Thursday afternoon, no one had any news on the lawsuit. Murdock went into Bodine's office, saying, "Maybe Landsman scrapped the whole idea after having a chance to think it through. Maybe Nadine's note didn't go into enough detail."

Bodine, still skeptical, replied, "Or… maybe his attorney will be lying in wait. We can just show up, pay our respects with solemn faces, and keep our mouths shut. Remember, our new attorney will be there to run interference for both of us."

Bodine's words of reassurance had no effect in soothing Murdock's shattered nerves. As he walked into his office and shut the door, he called Barbara, semi-pleading for her to attend the funeral with him. She responded, "Of course, Chase. I'll be beside you every step of the way."

"Ok, I'll pick you up at noon. We can grab a quick lunch on the way. Thank you, sweetness."

With a line outside the modest-sized church entrance, Murdock figured the seating as standing room only for Nadine's funeral. As they rolled into the parking lot, Barbara commented on how plain the church's pale beige, squarish building looked, noting it must be jammed over capacity. The next scene pulled an "Oh brother, her we go," out of Murdock when he saw people already weeping before they entered the church. Bodine and Murdock wore dark shades to avoid eye contact with anyone they didn't know. Barbara kept an arm around Murdock's waist as they went through the entrance, taking the printed funeral program card with Nadine's picture covering the front. Bodine pointed out the third pew from the front center with instructions for the couple to sit in the middle and wait for him. Then Bodine whispered to them, "I don't think Nadine would have picked this old shoebox of a church."

"Seriously, it doesn't match her style at all," Murdock answered.

After a glimpse around the entrance, Bodine checked inside the church as he entered, eager to verify Justin Arluck's arrival. He heard a voice behind him, "Richard Bodine?" He spun around facing a tall, slender, handsome black man wearing a black business suit Bodine priced at over two thousand dollars.

Bodine asked, "Are you…"

Before he could finish the question, the man responded with a handshake, "Justin Arluck. Pleased to meet you. Where's the squirrel?"

224

Confused, Bodine asked, "The squirrel?"

"The rodent," Arluck replied, "who's threatening to waste your time and money."

"Oh, Kelly Landsman. Well, I don't know what he looks like. We haven't heard a word from him all week."

Bells rang signaling the ceremony's commencement as a priest herded the attendees inside the entrance, encouraging them to find their seats. Bodine had Arluck sit directly behind Murdock and him as a vantage point to identify which faces glared at them.

Murdock eyed Nadine's solid bronze, purple, velvet-lined casket surrounded by white lilies and purple irises centered with the pulpit, then stifled a groan when he saw it wide open. Surreal emotions erupted when he saw her lying in a lilac colored dress, her hair perfect, makeup impeccably applied, just the way she would have primped herself on any given day. He fought believing the lifeless form embodied the same woman who nearly turned him inside out only a couple months before. Such an incredible beauty, such a misguided soul. Bowing his head, the sorrow overtook him. As tears dripped from his cheeks, Barbara gave him a tissue from her purse, which he dabbed at his face until he regained control.

All the Eye Cue Board of Directors assembled in attendance off to their left, no one gazing toward his or Bodine's location. Murdock feared they knew something he didn't. He nudged Bodine. "Look at the Board members. None of them have given us a glance."

Bodine shrugged, "I'll query Terwilliger on what he knows, if anything, when we're in the parking lot."

After the endless procession of friends, family, and work associates spoke their peace, the scruffy, white-haired, bespectacled priest in a white robe with a gold braided belt started his final statement. Staring through a hellfire frown directly where Murdock and Bodine sat, he spoke using deep, pious tones, "God's child Nadine was a tortured soul. Insensitive acts coupled with harshly cruel words pushed her fragile state into a dangerous place of shame and hopelessness. Why would a mindful person ever treat her with such disregard? When someone needs caring or compassion only another human can provide, why do we humiliate them, shun them, insult them?" The priest's chilling gaze remained fixated on the two men as several attendees searched for whom his pithy last words were directed.

A lump formed in Murdock's throat as his mouth went dry. It seemed rather ungodly how the priest's rhetoric contained a single callous admonishment of two men attending the service, whom he never met before yet deliberately chose to stare down. Barbara put a hand on his arm. She whispered, "You know, the priest's eulogy felt very weird and grossly inappropriate." He squeezed her hand. A final song, "Will You Meet Me In Heaven Someday," began playing on the church organ, sending Nadine a traditional farewell.

Following the closing refrain, everyone except Murdock and Bodine rose to vacate the church. Justin Arluck stood and leaned forward to Bodine, "Give me a three-minute head start to locate the opportunistic parasites in the parking lot before you leave the church."

Murdock asked Barbara, "Would you mind waiting outside, sweetness?" He handed her his car keys.

After the three-minute quarantine, the two men walked out of the church. They spotted two people talking with Arluck. Nonchalantly, both men walked past them, avoiding eye contact with anyone. Arluck called out, "Mr. Bodine, Mr. Murdock." They turned around, heading back where the three people stood. "Gentlemen, this is Kelly Landsman and his attorney, Ms. Theresa Meyer." No hands offered a proper greeting. "Mr. Landsman believes he has grounds to file a wrongful death suit against the two of you." Landsman said nothing, fixing his eyes on Arluck as Meyer acknowledged their presence by nodding.

Bodine asked, "Based on what, exactly?"

Arluck responded, "Based on a frivolous, unfounded notion they can squeeze the two of you out of a quarter million dollars. Based on the fact Mr. Landsman's precious little sister publicly acted like a wanton tramp with zero consideration someone could call her on it."

Landsman bristled, "That's pretty cold, Mr. Arluck. I'm sure when all the facts come out, you'll have a different tone."

Arluck smirked, just warming up. "Oh really? I think Ms. Meyer will agree that wrongful death is a pretty flimsy assertion." Meyer started a response when Arluck cut her off, "In most cases, a jury shows little or no sympathy toward a woman who sustained a lifestyle overshadowed by a flaunted proclivity for random sex with relative strangers; a woman whose sexual desires could not be satisfied; a woman who practically begged for eventual rejection based on the way she openly conducted herself. Your sister was a frenzied cougar on the prowl daily, who serviced youngsters from a local bar. She became a well-recognized, middle-aged nympho among the regular young barflies, who simply went along for the *free ride.* "

Landsman exploded, "That's a cheap shot considering we're burying her today. Who the hell are you passing judgement on a woman you never even knew?" Theresa Meyer froze, stayed reticent, unprepared to match Arluck with a rebuff.

Arluck pursed his lips before continuing, "I'm someone who's already garnered the first three witnesses in less than an hour, young men who will attest to her unsavory behavior. I'm someone who has witnessed multiple nuisance cases far more authentic than this never make it to court because a judge simply issues a pretrial dismissal. Most importantly, I'm someone who never has lost a case involving these unsubstantiated types of claims. You, Mr. Landsman, are typical of everyone who feels they deserve compensation for any grievance they conjure up from the irresponsible actions perpetrated by an unbalanced relative. I've been an attorney over twenty years, plus I have a 94% success rate, which is unheard of, by the way. Before you charge forward only to incur court costs plus attorney fees, which I guarantee will be your responsibility, I suggest you and your counsel have a serious chat about a reconsideration of this matter. I understand you're sad, shocked, and definitely hurt. Someone has to pay, right? Well, Nadine existed within an unstable mental state, a ship without a rudder if you will. I won't relish facing a jury calling her every name she unwittingly earned, or parade one witness after another who will verify in detail her deviant behavior. Let the woman rest in peace. Your family surely doesn't deserve the kind of publicity you're apparently begging for. It *will* get ugly."

Bodine and Murdock nodded their heads toward Landsman and the two attorneys, then walked away, eyes wide, trying not to squeal or fist-bump.

CHAPTER 31

INTIMIDATION

Despite Barbara's enjoyable companionship, a refreshing balm on Murdock's tattered nerves, he stayed preoccupied over whether Kelly Landsman would pull the trigger on the lawsuit. Her positive spirits also helped alleviate his jitters by imparting generous displays of her physical affection he craved since the day they met.

During their Sunday morning breakfast, he told her, "You are the most sensual, affectionate woman I've ever known, a true masterpiece from heaven. I'm so thankful I'm here with you. It seems preposterous some superman never swept you off your feet long before we met."

"Chase, are you being coy?" she teased. "I'm very picky, and I mean *very*. After the divorce, it's taken me a long time to consider having sex with anyone, the 'anyone' being you. I truly longed for intimacy, so I feel lucky we connected the way we did."

"I'm the lucky one, my divine temptress. You could have any man you desire."

After they cleared the breakfast table, Murdock asked, "Ok if I use your computer for about an hour? I should prepare for work ahead of time in case any other surprises show up tomorrow."

Barbara led him to her computer, signing him on before she left the room. Within minutes, guilt coursed through him as he realized Nadine might still be alive if he hadn't met Barbara. Nadine begged him for another chance. Had he not made the impulsive decision on meeting Barbara at the moment he did, he may have granted Nadine her wish. *It's so tragic, yet, in the scheme of things, I really have to purge this guilt I carry around. If I don't, this knot in my stomach will drive a wedge between Barbara and I, which is unthinkable. Bodine was spot on; the past is behind me. The only move I have is forward.* He signed off his work screen, then headed for Barbara's arms. Her love would keep him focused on the one thing he cherished most, their future life together.

Late Sunday afternoon, he received a call from Bodine. "Chaser, Theresa Meyer called me about an hour ago. She requested we meet at our office at ten tomorrow."

"That's all she said?"

"No. Apparently Landsman still wants a lawsuit filed. She said she tried discouraging him, but he can't be consoled. He wants someone paying for Nadine's death."

"Any chance you can have Justin Arluck show up?"

"Working on it. I already left him a message."

"Shit. I hoped Landsman would back off after the tongue-lashing Arluck gave him at the funeral."

"Apparently, it only fanned the flames. See you tomorrow."

He looked at Barbara. "It appears we're heading into deeper waters with Nadine's brother."

Previously at Nadine's funeral, Murdock fixated on the conversation between Arluck and Landsman, scarcely noticing Theresa Meyer, Landsman's attorney. With no conversation or distractions yet as he sat with Meyer in Bodine's office, he turned on the Murdock evaluation meter. He clocked her at early to mid-50's, short blonde hair, a pretty face toned with high cheekbones, a turned-up nose, penetrating green eyes, no etched wrinkles, and well-tanned from head to toe. Meyer reminded him what his junior high school flame, Linda Riley, might have looked like had she taken better care of herself.

The three of them made small talk while giving Arluck more time for making an appearance. Ten minutes later, Arluck walked through the door and shut it. Murdock could see relief on Bodine's face as the dapper attorney took a seat.

Arluck took charge immediately. "Ms. Meyer, have you ever visited a nightclub in town called the Carousel?"

Meyer hesitated, "Yes, I have. Is this personal or is this something about the matter at hand?"

Arluck continued, "Then you know very well the scene there, correct?"

Meyer asked, "What *scene* are you referring to, Mr. Arluck?"

"It's known as the 'den of cougars,' isn't that right? And I'd say you're a vintage cougar, at least age-wise. Judging from your admission, you probably know that fact all too well." Meyer shifted in her seat, not offering a response. Her face blushed, revealing her concern. Arluck continued, "How often do you patronize the Carousel, Ms. Meyer?"

"Oh, once in a while, I suppose."

"The head bartender, a Rudy Vilardo, said you're a regular with once or twice a week being more like it."

Meyer became flustered. "*What's your point*, Mr. Arluck? More specifically, how does my private life connect with Mr. Landsman's lawsuit?"

"Because you live the same lifestyle Nadine Curtis did. You know how fleeting and disposable the relationships are. You know what to expect, such as rejection, triumph, bad dealings, good ones, great sex, horrible sex. Any woman who spent the amount of time you have in that particular nightclub could be considered well-versed on the cougar lifestyle."

Meyer's face turned redder. "What's your point, Mr. Arluck?"

"The point being the Carousel is a breeding ground for fast hookups, broken promises, nasty breakups and disparaging language between impassioned parties. Occasional name-calling comes with the territory, wouldn't you agree?"

Meyer stood her ground. "Even if I do, we're not here to discuss my personal life."

Arluck bore a wicked grin on his face when he responded, "You're not exempt from taking the stand, Ms. Meyer. When I unravel Nadine's lifestyle for everyone in the courtroom, I'll need an expert witness. According to Rudy Vilardo, a man who will sign an affidavit or even take the stand if lunch is provided afterward, you'd qualify as an authority on the subject. He will attest seeing you dozens of times leave his establishment with a different young man each time. He even recalls a couple of rowdy mishaps between you and your youngsters du jour."

Meyer, visibly shaken as she stood, excused herself for a restroom break.

Bodine smirked at Arluck, "Very impressive offense. Apparently, you've been doing your homework, Justin."

Murdock asked, "How do you come up with all this information?"

Arluck replied matter-of-factly, "I had a hunch about her. I use a big shovel when scooping up character flaws. She's as randy as Nadine was. Her testimony won't paint a flattering portrait of the late Ms. Curtis. Even more damaging, it would expose her own proclivities. She'll avoid publicizing her own lifestyle at all cost. It wouldn't be enough for disbarment, but she probably would lose her job. Law firms won't tolerate attorneys exhibiting promiscuous behavior simply because it risks public exposure damaging to the firm. After what I put her through, she'll most likely run back to Landsman with a huge stop sign in her hands."

When Meyer returned to the office, she stood in the doorway without entering. She declared, "I'll take another run at Mr. Landsman. I don't think anyone wishes to know so much about Nadine." Without saying goodbye, she left the building.

Relieved, Bodine commented, "Looks like Landsman picked the wrong attorney for his cause."

Murdock added, "But the perfect one for us." With a Cheshire Cat grin, Arluck gave them a thumbs up.

They heard nothing from Meyer by day's end. The next afternoon, Bodine danced into Murdock's office. "Meyer just called. She talked him out of it, Chaser. Landsman's walking away."

Murdock, relieved from the news, blurted, "Oh Christ, Bo. Did we dodge a bullet or what? I can't wait to tell Barbara. Hey, we should celebrate at Mandrake's."

"My thoughts exactly. Call Ted and tell him to bring Cindy if she's available. He deserves the celebration as much as anyone. I'll have Talia meet us there. I feel like getting wasted."

When the Eye Cue executives swaggered into Mandrake's, they observed Talia, Barbara, and Zachary seated at a large table. Talia wore her customary low-cut blouse. Naturally, Murdock studied her already large breasts spilling out of her bra due to her pregnancy. "Jesus, Bo, Talia could probably balance two martinis on her massive fun bags."

"Don't give her any ideas on such a photo op, Chaser. She'd probably try it. The AMA frowns on that kind of publicity."

Barbara greeted Murdock with a hug and short kiss. "Congrats, you two. I guess your friend, Ted, knew exactly who to call."

Murdock shook Zachary's hand. "Thanks so much, Teddy. You were right about Arluck. He reduced Landsman's attorney to tears."

Zachary smiled, "Yes, the man has an uncanny knack for bringing out the worst in everyone."

Bodine announced, "Everyone here is on my tab. Since Talia can't drink, she'll be the designated driver."

Talia smiled, "Drink up, kids. Momma Talia will make sure you get home without incident."

<hr>

Murdock followed Barbara to her place after the party. Walking in her door, he said, "This is becoming habitual, me staying at your place. I hope I'm not wearing out my welcome."

"No way. I love every minute you're here. It's a thousand times better than being by myself thinking about you."

Her message hung in the air, the implication unmistakable. Still, he sensed the timing too soon to say out loud what he was thinking. She must be the one who broaches the subject of living together. Since he had fallen irreversibly in love with her, he had no appetite for a potential lukewarm response from her if he suggested a permanent arrangement first. He would stay patient, not posing any risk of rejection.

"So, have you found more houses I might be interested in?" he asked, testing the water.

She hesitated, then admitted, "No. Honestly, I haven't been looking very hard. When's the lease up on your apartment?"

"It's month-to-month, so I can bail almost any time. If I find the right place, I can jump on it immediately."

"Chase, I don't mean to sound presumptive or pushy in any way. I realize we haven't known each other very long, but, uh... what if you're standing in *the right place* this very moment?" She left it open ended, giving him time to grasp the weight of her question.

Huge smiles appeared on both their faces. "Sold. Whaddya say we seal the deal with a kiss?" he chuckled as he nestled her in his arms.

CHAPTER 32

WHEN IT'S RIGHT

In Murdock's mind, the love he shared with Barbara never surfaced as a knee jerk reaction to temporary lust or infatuation. He recognized the real deal. Any uncertainty he experienced happened when he recalled how his love for Donna grew over time. By comparison, his love for Barbara developed at warp speed. Yet Barbara's clever approach showed him patience, offering him an opportunity to think things through. As a result, both reduced risking a rushed relationship brought on by temporary emotions. Instead, they enjoyed mutual peace in their romance leaving any doubt behind.

As they lay in each other's arms Monday morning after a most gentle lovemaking session, he confided, "You said what I've been thinking all along. Things have happened so quickly between us. Honestly, it seemed so all-consuming I feared it might be fleeting. But it isn't, Barbara. I feel stronger and stronger about you every day. I'm just still in shock we've already reached this point."

"I feel the same way. We're only in the honeymoon stage of our relationship, yet when something is so obvious, I can't keep questioning it. The idea of us cohabitating, so we can both keep moving things forward, just came naturally. We have no deadlines here, and we can set our own pace. It's my way of showing you how much I love you, even though it's only been a couple of months."

"Cliché or not, I fell in love with you the first time we met. I literally became tongue-tied, sweating, the whole bit. Any doubt I had about our having a future dissolved when you told me what caused the rift between you and Donna. Since I already loved you then, I couldn't imagine you being the problem. Even though it's a heartbreaking story, I'm thrilled I was right about you." He lightened up on the topic, "Does this mean we're going steady?"

She laughed, slapping him on the arm. "So, now it's my turn. I won't stop saying yes until you stop asking."

As he rolled out of bed to start his workday, he revisited Donna's legacy. The belief he could feel serenity again left him on the night of Donna's fatal accident, the same night he planned on kneeling for her hand in marriage. Since Barbara filled in the details of Donna's life before he met her, he had all he needed to make his peace by simply loving her as his saving grace during the lowest point in his life. His genuine love for Barbara brought him full circle, healing the near-mortal wounds from Donna's tragic death while restoring his clarity. She would have his devotion until he died, a vow she would hear at the altar one day. *How can one man have the fortune of being saved so completely by the love of two sisters?* He pledged a daily grateful attitude, never falling into a jaded or unappreciative disposition, but rather, maintaining a rock-steady resolve. Too many people never find true love in their lives; he found it twice. Whatever it took, Barbara would remain the most precious person in his life, without his ever wavering.

Before heading to work, he drove home for a shower and fresh clothes. He felt awkward as he opened the grungy front door, wondering how much longer he would call this apartment home. He called Ted for his trusted advice. "Teddy? Can we have dinner tonight? I need a consultation."

"You're not visiting the dark side again, are you?"

"Not at all. I'm as stable as can be and living in paradise. I just want to share some thoughts since you're without peer as my ultimate confidante."

"Mandrake's?"

"No, too noisy. How about the steakhouse? You deserve better than burgers and fries. Plus, you can't shove a steak up your nose."

Zachary snickered, "Try me," reacting to Murdock's reminder from another 'consultation' dinner at Mandrake's over a year ago. During dinner, Murdock painstakingly had described his original dirt nap plan as Zachary stuffed a fat steak fry up each nostril to tone down the drama.

They met at the steakhouse at 6:30 p.m., promptly ordering drinks once they were seated. Curious what merited a dinner meeting, Zachary queried, "So, why are we here?"

Murdock answered, "Nothing heavy, mi amigo. I just have a simple question. How long did you know Cindy before you realized you were in love with her?"

"Five minutes"

"C'mon. Be serious."

"I swear it's the truth. I actually experienced the proverbial love at first sight. She knocked me out. Still does."

"That's fan-fucking-tastic, Teddy. You just validated what I once considered a high school kid's mentality. You see, I felt the same way about Barbara. Too good to be true, too soon, not enough time for the relationship to develop, blah blah. So how long before you moved in together?"

"A month."

"Are you shitting me? We've only been seeing each other for about two months. This morning we discussed the possibility of living together. I guess things can ramp up pretty quickly when…"

Zachary interjected, "When you know. I must say, Barbara is a daisy. If she feels the same way you do, you're one lucky man."

"I'm betting she does since she is the one who brought up the idea." Ted gave him a silly grin, nodding.

Their waiter arrived, "Good evening gentlemen, are you ready to order?"

Murdock nodding yes with a straight face, joked, " Yes we are. My partner here will have the porterhouse. Just puree it in a blender so he can suck it into his nostrils to cheer me up, not that I need it. Two straws, please." Zachary rolled his eyes at the waiter. The waiter looked at them, then chuckled. Once they placed their real orders, he walked away still laughing.

Zachary continued, "Don't question it, Chase. You're in your mid-sixties, she's in her what, late fifties? A woman like Barbara should put your shopping days behind you."

"And she most certainly has, Teddy. I'm just so in love with her, I can't see straight."

"Your vision problem will pass. She's got keeper written all over her. Did you see how the other men at Mandrake's stared at her? Just so you know, I'm not only talking about the older dudes. Several younger bucks gawked at her as well. She is summarily hot."

"Don't I know it. When we go out together, I become invisible. Men hardly acknowledge my presence."

"Just remember 99.99 percent of them would kill to walk in your shoes. Cherish her, Chase. You've been inconceivably lucky between her and Donna. It won't happen again. Of this, I'm certain."

He parked in the space near his apartment after dining with Zachary. Even though Barbara welcomed his company anytime he liked, he decided sleeping in his own bed this particular night would give them both space for processing their earlier discussion. He kept asking himself, "Why not? What could go wrong?" His phone ringing stopped the internal dialog. Seeing it was Barbara, he smiled. "Hey, sugar cheeks, how did you know I was missing you already?"

"Chase, something's come up. I have to know how you feel about it right away. I couldn't sleep tonight without giving you full disclosure on this."

"What, you're bisexual? I can work with that."

"I would laugh if this weren't so serious. You met my mother, Margaret, at Donna's memorial service. Well, Margaret's having health problems. Her doctor diagnosed her with Alzheimer's. As you know, it never gets better, only worse."

"Does she live by herself?"

"For now. When I attended the doctor visit with her today, he told me mom had reached a fairly advanced stage of the disease, so I should consider putting her in assisted living, the sooner, the better. The problem is she can't afford a facility offering the special care she requires."

His head dropped, understanding what this meant. Barbara had no choice except to take care of her ailing mother. The dream arrangement they discussed only hours ago faded into stark reality. He recovered, "Barbara, I understand clearly what you're implying. Our plans for playing house certainly have to take a backseat to making sure your mom gets the proper care."

"Oh Chase, I don't know any other way to handle this other than to bring her here. She's been a widow for a long time. Ever since her appointment today, I've been dreading how you might react."

"My reaction? Love you more than ever. If there's *anything* I can do in the help arena, promise you'll just tell me. After we talked this morning, I knew…no matter what, I will always want you in my life, even if it includes having your mom as a roommate."

Barbara sobbed, unable to keep the emotions at bay any longer, "God, Chase, you melt my heart. I assumed you'd say something like 'All bets are off' or 'Give me time to think about this.' You really must love me if you can accept this additional burden in our lives without hesitation."

"It's not a stretch, sweetness. You've made me happier than I've ever been in my entire life. I'm not throwing away all we have or our dreams over this…or anything. Besides, your mom is a saint as far as I'm concerned. She brought the two finest women I've ever known into the world. I've been a bit selfish my entire life. It's time I do something for others. I can't imagine a more worthy recipient than Margaret. You tell me what you need, and I'll bring it. Please, don't hold back."

"Ok. What I need right now is a big dose of you. Can you stay with me tonight?"

"On my way."

Walking up her steps, she threw the door open, still clutching a tissue. Her big smile canceled out her puffy eyes. She threw her arms around him, blurting, "Oh, sweet man, I worried I might lose you."

"Look at it this way. When Margaret's here, I'll be considered a young man again, a rebirth of sorts."

"Agreed, Mr. Reborn. Let's celebrate with a cool drink, a hot shower, and a big hallelujah."

CHAPTER 33

DEMENTIA? FORGET ABOUT IT

With the expanded warehouse almost finished, Murdock enjoyed a few days of diminishing chaos. He daydreamed how the new warehouse guaranteed Eye Cue pulling off their sales growth target by year's end, rewarding he and Bodine substantial gains in their personal income. Seeing Barbara regularly as they planned his move into her home kept him motivated at work. While he worked, Barbara finished arrangements relocating her mother. Once Margaret settled in, Barbara invited Murdock over for dinner. She planned on reintroducing her mother to Murdock, then mention he would move in with them later.

Upon meeting her for the second time from the year before, Margaret's advanced frailty combined with her degenerated cognitive condition blindsided Murdock. Barbara put her arm through his as she walked him toward Margaret. "Mom, this is Chase Murdock."

The diminutive woman's eyes lit up. "Of course, I remember you, Chase. You own the dry cleaners I use. How's your wife, that cute little oriental woman? I forgot her name."

"No, Mom. Chase is my boyfriend. He once dated Donna, remember?"

Margaret looked confused, shouting, "Well how can Chase be your boyfriend, too? It doesn't seem right, Barbara. Does your sister know?"

Barbara, with a calm voice, reassured her mother. "It's okay, Mom. Remember, Donna's gone."

Witnessing what a struggle they faced in the near future, Murdock fought off discouragement. Telling Margaret about him moving in appeared futile. He smiled at her, gently taking her small hand. "Hello, Margaret, I'm Chase Murdock. We met at Donna's memorial."

Murdock's remark sent Margaret into a lucid flashback. She bent over in her chair, putting her face in her hands. "I'm so sorry, you two. Of course, I remember that awful day."

Murdock excused himself, smiled at Barbara while pointing at the kitchen. He made them each two strong cocktails, placing the four glasses on the table, then taking a seat strategically positioned for careful monitoring of Barbara's progress handling her mother. In four gulps, he finished his first drink. Amid downing his second one, Barbara walked in the kitchen, taking a hefty swig of the first cocktail as she sat down beside him at the table. She glanced at her second waiting cocktail.

Raising her eyebrows while smirking at Murdock, she gave him a thumbs up as she chugged the rest of the first drink. "You know, Chase, it's like this all the time now. One minute she's with us; the next, she's so forgetful she can't remember which gender she is."

In mock disbelief, he asked, "Do we even have genders anymore?" Barbara muffled a nose laugh. Putting down his empty glass, he said softly, "I figured telling her about me living here might be an arduous process. Seeing how she is, however, makes me believe it won't matter much if or when I move in. She'll just wake up to a brand-new day, every single day. Seeing me around here will either be a surprise, or it won't. Her accepting me won't be a problem. You can tell her I'm renting a room because we're cutting expenses by living together, or whatever you think is best."

Barbara advised, "I set up her room on the other side of the house equipped with a hospital-style bed and a baby monitor. She should spend most of her time there, although I worry about her roaming around late at night."

He envisioned a lot of evenings staying in, making sure Margaret received the care plus the supervision she deserved. "With the two of us romping around, I hope her bedtime is early, and she is a sound sleeper." He paused, then leaned toward her, "You know, sweet cheeks, judging from your mother's state of rapid decline, you shouldn't work full time anymore. It's fine with me if you totally quit work. You won't have any money worries because I make more than enough for all our expenses. Besides, I'm sure we'll be spending more time at home. Let's just focus on getting settled, so we can develop our new routines. Whenever you find the time, just give me a rough budget of what your bills are along with what you think our food, etc. might be. I can just transfer money from my paycheck into your account twice a month. I'll also put you on my health plan at work, which eliminates that expense from your monthly bills. Do we have a plan?"

She threw her arms around him, her words blocked by her crying for a few moments. She regained control, sputtering, "Oh, Chase, it's amazing you're offering me this, but I hate you having all the financial burden. I do have savings left from the divorce settlement and an IRA."

He assured her, "It's no burden. Keep your savings and retirement. Compared to my buying a house, living here will still be a bargain and a helluva lot more fun. Plus, I won't be incurring any more of those pesky charges I accumulate from self-pleasuring." He loved hearing her laugh out loud. "Barbara, we'll make this work. I'm ready for dedicating myself to you and whatever comes with you. Rest easy, sweetness."

She got choked up, her eyes welling up again, still smiling through her tears. He gently dabbed them using a tissue he had in his pocket, softly asking, "Do you think it will make any difference if you mention to Margaret I'll be moving in?"

"If I catch her in the right moment, yes. I should at least try. There always will be the possibility she won't remember me telling her. Until you actually *do* move in, your coming around as often as possible should help, so she can feel more comfortable seeing you and hearing your voice. How much notice does your apartment require?"

"Thirty days."

"Then just give notice right away. I can start talking about it with mom. Maybe she'll grasp what's happening over time."

"Okay. Let's walk around your house soon, so I can figure out what I keep and what gets donated or tossed. I'll give notice tomorrow."

"Good idea, but let's get Mom and have dinner first. I'm starved."

Early the next morning, he handed his onsite landlord the liberating rental termination notice. He felt the shackles of his tiny apartment slip away, bringing on his thrusting both arms in the air "Rocky" style, then jumping up and down singing out loud to the film's theme song. Realizing how early it still was, he stopped by Johnny Dunne's place.

Dunne showed his surprise after opening the door. "Well hello, Chase. Haven't seen you around in a while."

"I know, Johnny. I apologize for not stopping by. A lot going on at work and personally as well. I wanted to thank you for helping Ted keep an eye on me after Donna got killed. It kept me from doing something stupid." It touched him when Dunne gave him a knowing glance, showing he understood.

"I was happy to help, Chase. Glad everything is going okay for you now. It's really good you came by."

"There's one other thing I wanted to ask you, Johnny. I just gave notice here at the compound because I'll be moving out in thirty days."

"Oh? You find a better apartment?"

"No. I'm moving in with a lady I met a few months ago. We hit it off so well I'm making the ultimate commitment." He stopped himself from sharing the detail about Barbara being Donna's sister. Rather than face a bunch of questions, he kept Dunne's knowledge at a minimum.

"Sounds great, Chase. Congratulations. Anyone I might know?"

"No, Johnny. Just a very special lady. I'll introduce you sometime. Speaking of which, how would you like to make some extra dough by helping me out again?"

"I'm always up for that."

"Good. I need your skill in loading my stuff into a rental truck. I'll have one load for the Salvation Army and another load for the place I'm moving into. Interested?"

"You bet. Just call me when you know an exact date and time. I'll make sure I get the time off from my job. But you know, Chase, I only make about fifteen bucks an hour as a security guard, so I hope you do a little better."

"How does fifty bucks an hour sound, Johnny?"

Dunne's eyes lit up followed by a gasp then a huge smile. "Wow, more than fair, Chase. I can't believe it, so appreciated, wow, really great."

"Excellent then. I'll call you in a few days when I have the particulars."

"Wanna celebrate later with a couple of beers?"

"Wish I could, Johnny, but I have chores piled up that must get done in a very short amount of time. I'll be in touch."

He walked away, leaving Johnny yammering to pin him down for a beer date. Back at his apartment, Murdock began a list of items he could purge versus the essentials he would keep. Staring at his audio system and record collection, it dawned on him Barbara knew nothing of his passion for music. *How could she? She's never been here.* He wondered if his hobby might turn into an issue, since his intentions involved full retention of the audio system and every single record album. One thing for sure, his approach on this critical subject must avoid any possible conflict between them. He only needed a fix on how flexible she might be in housing the second love of his life. Eager for a fast resolution, he called her.

"Hey, bombshell of my dreams, I need your thoughts on something."

She said, "Ask away, sweet man."

"Since you've never visited my apartment, you wouldn't know I own a sophisticated music system I need mingled among your living room décor. It has a pretty large footprint, not to mention my record collection. I hope it won't be a problem."

"Oh. Well, it sounds a lot more substantial than my music system. You know, it's one of those all-in-one tabletop jobbies. You've probably seen it. It sits on the side table near the dining room. Maybe we can just use mine, and you can get rid of yours, or we'll put it in the back bedroom."

He cringed, quickly conjuring up a slick sales job for securing her understanding. "It's not quite so simple, sugar cheeks." He then described every component in his audio system, including the floor-standing loudspeakers plus the extent of his record collection. After telling her how much space the entire group would entail, her long pause on the phone worried him.

Then Barbara threw questions at him, "You still play those big records? Plus you have tall floor speakers? Well, babe, it sounds like you're one of those hi-fi fanatics to me."

"I didn't pick this hobby, you sweet thing, it picked me. Look, maybe you should come over here and see what I'm talking about."

She chuckled, "Nah, no need. Just messin' with ya. Bring it all. Since I better understand your hobby, and obviously how much you love it, we'll just figure out a way to make it work. The living room may be a bit more crowded, but so what? I have extra space. Don't worry about it. Come to think of it, I have the perfect spot for my tabletop system in the bedroom. We'll make your system look stunning in the living room."

Thankful she skipped through any pushback or making a big deal about it, he purred, "I'm smooching you through the phone, cuteness. The understanding you have for me is incredible."

"Just bring all those kisses home to me, babe. Sugar cheeks here is feeling frisky."

"Well, I am certainly up for a frisking session. However, with Margaret on board, our spontaneity will be compromised, so meet me in the laundry room in fifteen minutes."

"Ooh."

CHAPTER 34

JUST ARLUCK

Bodine initiated planning a ribbon-cutting celebration for the new warehouse by calling on Rex Sullivan, "Consensual one, I'd like you as the lead event planner for a splash in the trade media trumpeting our modern warehouse expansion. Make sure all the Board members are invited as well. Oh, also invite Hwang and Woo. Tell them we don't expect their attendance, but you never know, since they use any excuse for a trip here. If they ask about a party, tell them cake with champagne... in the parking lot. Maybe they'll think twice about making the trip. Then again, maybe we should throw a huge bash at Mandrake's." After briefly mulling the idea over, he recanted, "Nah. There's too much margin for error. The press would have a field day with some of our shenanigans. Oh, and make sure Justin Arluck and Ted Zachary are invited."

"Got it, boss." Sullivan cleared his calendar, then dug into organizing the event. He arranged a media blitz promotion featuring Eye Cue's dynamic success and highlighting their two leading men. Less than two days later, Sullivan walked into Bodine's office. "Okay, Bo, we're set for two weeks from this coming Friday."

"Thank you. Your efficiency is exemplary, Group Rex. Advise the media pros all pieces, and I mean *every* single text article plus every photo, require your personal approval before anything goes to press. We can't have a maverick reporter going rogue on our reputation, right?"

"Understood. Offhand, I don't think anybody would risk losing our business over a poor judgement call."

"Well, we prefer believing that, but rogues slip through, nonetheless. Just stay vigilant."

After Sullivan left Bodine's office, the Human Resources Director, Brenda King, walked in. "Sorry to bother you, Bo, but we received a legal complaint filed against Chase."

"About what, Brenda?"

"About the baby cake he bought for your engagement party in the conference room along with the language he used."

"You've got to be shitting, er, kidding me. I can't imagine even one of our employees complaining about something so tame."

"Well, she's not exactly an employee. She's a temp."

"Who the hell let a temp attend our party?" Kings eyes opened wide while shrugging her shoulders.

Disgusted, Bodine growled, "What's her name, and is she still working for us?"

"Sonia Genovese and no. She only worked here for a week filling in for a vacationing administrator."

"That's just great. So, what the hell does she want?"

"Money, naturally. Claims the company's lack of professionalism made her feel threatened."

"Threatened my ass. How much money?"

"Fifty thousand dollars."

"Fifty grand... what a snake. This, after Chaser asked anyone in the room who might be offended by his actions to step forward. I only heard boos. This Sonia what's-her-name can't be serious. She's taken subterranean to a new low."

"We must respond quickly, Bo. How should I proceed?"

"We have a new attorney on retainer. His name's Justin Arluck. I'll find out if this is even worth wasting his time. Thanks, Brenda. I'll call you after I chat with him."

Bodine called Arluck, describing the entire scenario in between his exasperated comments over the issue. Arluck chuckled, "Get me the woman's full name, a copy of her complaint, and the temp agency she works for. She and I will have a little talk." Bodine called Brenda King who relayed the information Arluck requested. With such a competent lawyer in the fold managing the burden, Bodine moved with ease onto his next scheduled task.

Just when Bodine clicked on his computer screen, Murdock walked into his office. "What's shakin' with the soon-to-be daddy and husband of the tantalizing Jenna Talia?"

Bodine didn't smile at the greeting. "Someone complained about your baked goods selection and 'piece of ass' reference. I just chatted with Justin Arluck. He'll discover if she has a leg to stand on."

"She who?" Murdock sat down, leaning forward.

"Some temp who shouldn't have attended the party."

"She can't be serious. She also didn't step forward when I asked if anyone had an issue with the cake or my salty language. Remember?"

"Doesn't matter. All these opportunistic sponges want is a quick buck. I'm hoping Arluck rips her a new one like he did on Theresa Meyer."

"Ya know, Bo, I'm getting sick to death about watching every miniscule thing I say or do to avoid offending someone. All these phony, leeching, toddler-minded slackers have their hand out, claiming entitlement for compensation from their manufactured pain and suffering during normal socializing, like a baby shower. Have you ever heard the foul things women actually say at baby showers? It makes *me* blush. This is bullshit of the highest order, goddamnit."

"Yes, Chaser, we live among the hypersensitive PC population, for sure. Next thing you know, we'll require new employees' signatures on an everyday slang and baby-butt cake disclaimer."

"I don't know about you, but I'm royally pissed off, enough so I'm sure it'll put a damper on my entire day. Let me know when you hear from Arluck."

Two days later, Arluck called in, "Hello, Mr. Bodine. May I schedule a meeting at your office tomorrow at 10 a.m.?"

"Sure, Justin. What's the progress?"

"I'm having Sonia Genovese meet us there. It shouldn't take long."

"Sounds promising."

"Let's just say, no worries, Mr. Bodine. But be prepared to offer an apology for Murdock's behavior, okay?"

"Let's do one better. Murdock himself will attend. Since he's the one who offended the woman, he can be the one who tells her he's sorry."

"Fine. See you at ten."

Sonia Genovese arrived at the office promptly at 9:50 a.m. the next morning, entering the building right behind Justin Arluck. The receptionist, Gina Morgan, escorted them to Bodine's office where he and Murdock waited impatiently. Murdock pegged Genovese in her late twenties or early thirties, average height and weight, long brunette hair surrounding a pretty, makeup-free face, wearing jeans a little too tight with a dark-blue blouse. After introductions were made, Arluck took the lead.

"Ms. Genovese, do you have legal representation?"

"No, I don't need it. According to my sources, this is a black and white issue of hostile profanity in the workplace, something which makes me feel unsafe. There are no safe zones in Eye Cue. *That* alone creates a hostile environment. Why should I waste my money on a lawyer for something I can handle myself?" Bodine and Murdock focused on Arluck, both squinting to keep from busting up.

"Ms. Genovese, since you are a temp, can we assume you have other jobs, sometimes running concurrently?"

Genovese put a 'gotcha' smile on her face, as if the offer she came for was forthcoming. "Yes, I do."

Arluck leaned back clasping his hands together. "Would you mind telling us about your evening job in the hills above the San Fernando Valley?"

Her smile disappeared as she crossed her arms. In a defensive tone, she carped, "How do you know about *that* particular job, Mr. Arluck?"

Arluck leaned forward. "I have several law students, who are only too happy to help me run errands I don't have time for myself. From the information I received, it appears you also work in the adult film business. Is that correct?"

The glow on Genovese's face faded into a scowl. "Look, I'm not an actress, if that's what you're implying. I'm a Director's Assistant. That's all. Anyway, what does this have to do with the complaint I filed?"

Like a shark smelling blood in the water, Arluck narrowed his eyes, "You're complaining about something extremely mild compared to what you must witness or *hear* in the porn industry. In fact, my assistant had a bird's eye view from a hilltop street overlooking the property where you worked during a recent outdoor shoot. She went armed with high-powered binoculars along with a parabolic microphone. She heard and recorded quite a bit of foul language, all in the spirit of passion, I assume, during the not-a-Disney scene she witnessed. My point is, judging from what you observe at these porn shoots, unless you request ear plugs and blinders to create your own safe place when the cameras are rolling, you must have pretty thick skin behind your willing participation in this sort of activity. Am I right?"

Murdock homed in on the discourse, enthralled at the way Arluck meticulously picked apart his target while maintaining a self-confident demeanor as he delivered his facts in perfect order. He admired the manner the attorney confirmed the pesky woman as a slimy money grubber. At the other extreme, Genovese's remarkable failure to connect the dots between her own bawdy behavior and the complaint she filed mystified him.

Genovese's cocky attitude and smug expression evaporated. Murdock and Bodine exchanged glances, both knowing Arluck wasn't finished. "It would be a shame if your other employers learned about your job as a Director's Assistant, wouldn't it? I expressly did *not* request your boss at the temp agency attend this meeting in order to protect your privacy, although legally, it would have been appropriate. Perhaps, you missed that little item during your legal research on the internet." He slid a document across Bodine's desk where Genovese sat, holding a pen in his outstretched hand. "Therefore, I suggest you sign this document rescinding your complaint against Eye Cue, so we can all go about our business with no harm done."

Genovese took the pen, scribbling her name on the document. When she stood, Murdock delivered one last jab. "Ms. Genovese, I am so sorry if I offended you in any way with the baby-butt cake or any coarse language which may have followed."

Genovese, not amused, sniped, "Go fuck yourself, Murdock."

As she stomped out of the office, he shouted, "Now *that's* offensive." With Genovese out of earshot, he and Bodine burst into laughter, while Arluck flashed a mischievous smile. Murdock walked over where the attorney sat. He shook his hand, extending a compliment, "I'd describe that takedown as sub-zero, Justin, like you slapped her parasitic face with a verbal ice pack. Cool justice if you will. May I call you Just Ice?"

Arluck snickered, "Only between us boys if you don't mind. I don't need the press discovering *another* one of my monikers."

Bodine spoke, "It's not like fifty grand would have broken the bank, but I'm really glad that opportunistic weasel got her comeuppance. Thanks, Justin."

Arluck turned to Bodine. "This wasn't difficult, but if you guys continue bringing me these time-wasters, I'll have to jack up your retainer fee."

Bodine nodded. "Hopefully, we can classify this incident as an aberration. We will take every precaution necessary so something like this never happens again. However, if we require more pesticide from you in the future, we'll accommodate a reasonable retainer fee increase. We have no intention of seeking other counsel in our affairs, I can assure you."

"Works for me." Arluck tucked his papers into his briefcase.

Murdock wanted to know, "Did your assistant really have high power binoculars and a parabolic microphone?"

Arluck answered, "What assistant?"

CHAPTER 35

CELEBRATION

Bodine paced in circles during the morning of the ribbon-cutting ceremony until Murdock entered his office. "Everything set, Bo?"

Bodine replied, "Yeah, except now I've got another celebration on the table. Talia wants our wedding well in advance of the baby's due date, preferably, she said, before her baby bump grows sizeable."

Murdock asked, "What's the rush? Does it really matter when you make it official?"

"She's a little old school in that regard, Chaser. She doesn't want the kid born out of wedlock. Me? I didn't think I really cared, but I've changed my mind. I'm sold on marrying Talia. It's more important she experiences complete comfort with this, so I'm starting on these plans today."

"Let me know if you need any help. I'm sure Barbara would pitch in, too. She's become pretty tight with Talia, so she'll jump at the chance. One caveat, since Barbara's mom lives with her now, she'll be picking her spots."

"Good idea. Thanks, Chaser. By the way, aren't you moving in pretty soon with the divine Ms. Conley?"

"Yeah, but I hadn't planned on another roommate. I'm just so crazy about Barbara, I'll make whatever comes along work. The woman makes life worth living, you know?"

Bodine became reflective. "Thinking back about all the years I spent prowling the bars, getting involved in one empty affair after another, I appreciate how Talia formed a whole new perspective for me. Even though I'm pushing 50, Talia's brand of love keeps me feeling like a young buck again. You know, Chaser, since I learned about the baby, my baby, I finally understand what having a purpose and a legacy means. I have the perfect life partner to share all the love and guidance raising our budding fetal wonder, who will reside at the White House one day. It's meaningful and badass all in one."

Murdock concurred, "Look at us. Two former horndogs who finally embraced adulthood. I formerly thought maturity meant hanging out with kowtowing wimps ruled by their women. Whodathunkit? I'd say we've transcended into the bitchen dimension, a state only known by the rare few."

Bodine chuckled, "It's amazing how an attitude toward the opposite gender changes if you change yourself. If there's a downside in this direction I've taken, I can't imagine what it is."

"I can't either. Let's get moving, time for flashing your studliness."

Eye Cue employees loved the casual dress code Bodine implemented when he became President. However, this event revolved around an unusually special media-driven day. Under a directive from Bodine, every man and woman dressed in formal business attire. Since Sullivan invited several photographers from the industry press, Bodine wanted everyone at their professional best. When the newly expanded warehouse ribbon-cutting ceremony commenced, Bodine beamed at Murdock, "We're on, Chaser. Let's go impress the hell out of these folks."

As the two executives stood behind the makeshift podium staged at the edge of the loading dock, Murdock gazed at the gathered crowd. Including Eye Cue's top 20 percent national sales reps plus all the Board members, the audience contained more people than he anticipated. As he reflected on Nadine Curtis's tragic absence, he winced upon realizing she missed celebrating the success she personally fostered. The purposeful scattering of the media confirmed Rex Sullivan ensured several reps, including sought-after photographers, worked the event. Eye Cue re-entered the promotion stage again, but this time primed for a significant ramp-up in business. He detected a few unfamiliar people, which set off his curiosity if they might be spies from the competition or just Bodine groupies.

Murdock stepped toward the microphone donning a big smile toward the gathering. In his best radio voice, he announced, "Ladies and gents, please take a seat. I'm happy the press is well-represented here today, and we appreciate your accepting our invitation. After Mr. Bodine and I say a few words, everyone is welcome for lunch, which includes a delicious cake, although somewhat more on the conventional side." Several employees, having witnessed Murdock's baby-butt cake only a few weeks earlier, laughed at the aside, prompting quizzical murmurs among others.

Murdock spied Justin Arluck in the audience, stoked at seeing Theresa Meyer, the attorney Arluck skewered during the lawsuit fiasco from Nadine's brother, seated beside him. He waved at Arluck then blurted, "Hey Just Ice, er, Mr. Arluck, glad you could make it." Arluck glared at him, shaking his head. He gritted his teeth upon realizing his gaffe, hopeful the press didn't catch the slip. Without skipping a beat, he continued, "Let me introduce Eye Cue's unrivaled President and CEO, Mr. Richard Bodine." The crowd stood, clapping and roaring their approval.

Bodine, dressed for thrills in a tailored, tropical wool black suit, black shirt, and pink silk tie, took the podium during the applause. He carried an oversized pair of scissors using both hands. "Thank you all for joining us today. This new warehouse represents a huge leap forward for Eye Cue. By constructing a cutting edge, state-of-the-art facility designed for managing substantial product demand surges, we can fast-track our market share, showing substantial gains in much less time. The cash saved from paying rent on those overpriced, offsite storage facilities will be redirected into building our inventory levels. Relying only on our dedicated carriers will increase our daily shipment rate using real-time product inventory software." The Eye Cue faithful applauded, cheered, even whistled for several seconds. "Thank you, folks. We wish to acknowledge and thank Eye Cue's Board of Directors for giving this project their blessing and our steadfast employees, who expertly kept control despite the breakneck pace established from our last media blitz." Enthusiastic employees ignited another round of applause. "And, most of all, I can't say enough about the man who brought Eye Cue the talent and vision for a largescale marketing plan, making all this a reality. Please welcome our Vice President of Sales, Mr. Chase Murdock."

Murdock, not expecting Bodine's accolades, got a lump in his throat causing a puddling of tears in his eyes. While the audience clapped, he turned away to gather himself. Bodine eyed him, eyebrows raised, giving him the finger hook to say a few words. He approached the microphone, while still dabbing his eyes with a handkerchief. "Jesus, Bo, you could have given me a heads up about this."

Bodine leaned into the mic. "Aw c'mon, Chaser. That's no fun. I love catching you when your guard's down once in a while. It doesn't happen very often." A warehouse man screamed above the cheers, "Murdock rocks!"

Murdock spoke into the microphone, "No one knows this, but Bo rescued me from the scrapheap of this industry. He gave me the opportunity to thrive in a business I thought had abandoned me. I believed in his talents as a powerhouse President, so I jumped at the chance. He requested my help in re-engineering Eye Cue to become a major force among our peers. Indeed, quite a daunting task... but not really. It simply required my spreading the word about Eye Cue's gifted President among the leaders in our industry and beyond. Clearly, we've transformed the way the business community at large regards Eye Cue by spawning awareness about Richard Bodine."

As the executives stepped back from the podium, the crowd jumped up clamoring for a better view, their applause quickly became a roar. While the adulation continued, Bodine displayed the humungous scissors as he stepped toward the new warehouse doors, which sported two six-inch-wide black and pink ribbons. The photographers all jockeyed for position, flashes already popping as Bodine beckoned Murdock to join him. Each man took a scissor handle then sliced the ribbons. Bodine had the honor of opening the massive steel doors. Murdock stood back, allowing the photographers a clear view of the sparkling new facility. Once the doors fully opened, cameras continued flashing while the crowd oohed at the pristine new warehouse, complete with shiny steel shelving spotlighted by high tech lighting. The dazzling new forklifts delivered only the day before gleamed, awaiting their first assignment. Even the concrete floor flashed a spotless sheen. The crowd stayed on their feet straining for a better view, launching another ovation at the impressive sight.

Inspired by the crowd's energy, Bodine again took the podium, announcing, "Let's kick some butt, Eye Cue. Now everyone, enjoy lunch."

As if on cue, three eighteen-wheel cargo trucks rolled down the street, loaded with new product for the waiting shelves. The warehouse personnel scrambled to remove chairs staged below the loading docks as the first truck entered the freshly paved lot.

People filed up a stairway into the warehouse where lunch was staged. Forklift drivers fired up their new rigs in anticipation.

"I'd say the commemoration is a masterful success," Bodine said to anyone within earshot.

Murdock answered, "Yeah, excluding your impromptu words of love. God, Bo, the public adoration you showered on me really stunned me. You could have waited until cocktail hour."

"Wrong, Chaser, and don't chastise me for giving you credit. Everyone in this company along with the media should know you're the catalyst, the reason we're leading, not floundering. I wouldn't change a thing."

Murdock tapped him on the shoulder. "Check out Just Ice over there sitting beside Theresa Meyer. I wonder how long those two have been lunch buddies."

Bodine cracked up, "I bet having her ass handed to her in my office was a massive turn-on. If she's recognized the error of her ways, maybe she'll drop the prowling. Cozying up to Just Ice could only boost her career. Really, could you imagine Arluck's female equivalent?"

"That would be double jeopardy against any adversary. I'm really grateful Teddy knew about this guy."

"No shit. He's already paid for himself five times over. Let's get going. My wedding plans can't wait any longer. No interruptions starting now. Also, please call Barbara asap because we need her help getting started."

"Right behind you, Boss."

<hr />

The attending industry media produced the splashy publications of the ribbon-cutting event faster than everyone's expectations. It threw Eye Cue into another sales explosion. A mere two weeks after the ceremony, Murdock went into Bodine's office shouting, "You media darling. Once again, you've ignited Bodini mania. We can't answer the phones or handle the PO's lighting up our e-mail fast enough. The press kissed your ass like you're the second coming."

Bodine, preoccupied from constant phone calls and e-mails about his wedding plans, stayed glued to his computer monitor. "Ain't it great, Chaser? Coolest of all, the publications feeding this frenzy can't bill us a dime for their special coverage. We never hired them; we invited them to the ribbon-cutting, remember?"

Murdock was pumped. "How bitchen. All these circumstances have played right into our hands. May I offer a suggestion?"

Bodine answered, "Chaser, can't you see I'm busy here? Please go throw your line back in the water."

Murdock persisted, "Bo, you should capitalize on your media persona they've successfully created and promoted industry-wide. You are what sets Eye Cue apart from the also-rans. People inside and outside our industry, men and women alike, dig you, which means they crave learning everything possible about you. Don't forget, there are a fair number who are crazy about Talia, too. They don't even give a shit about you. It's the proverbial win-win. Your mandate as President requires you to fan the fire, Bo."

"What are you proposing, Chaser?"

"Even though we just now expanded the warehouse, I foresee us outgrowing this facility altogether, believe it or not. If we promote the shit out of the Eye Cue Prez plus the occasional Talia cameo, we'll blow our growth projections into the ozone. The Board will consider you the Cajun Clark Kent. With our compensation package, we could come into more money than we ever imagined. Once we're both rolling in dough, we can give Eye Cue an adios with free reign to develop a brand new, dynamic company where only you and I comprise the Board of Directors. Your status as the industry's stud master general will follow you. Can you even conceive the possibilities? You're now entering your peak career time which arrives only once, but in your case, includes a wide-open window."

Bodine finally glanced up. "Ya know, for a guy knocking on the door of geezer-hood, your drive for achieving a higher level than we've already accomplished, well, uh, blows me away. It's downright motivating." Bodine pushed away from his computer.

Murdock walked around the desk facing his boss. "Look at the possibilities, Bo. This is how all those snot-nosed punks get rich. They flip businesses, then use the proceeds to start another. Why wouldn't we try the same thing? We already have the prime industry contacts plus a track record the younger bedwetters can never match."

"Chaser, very soon I'll become a husband and a father. I don't know if I'll have the energy or the time for shooting off in a whole new direction."

"That's the cool thing, Bo, you won't need to invest that much time. You'll be the new Chairman of the Board, swimming in amenities and benefits, including a handpicked personal assistant, or two, who will perform all the work you choose to avoid. Your responsibilities would include presiding over quarterly meetings, plus showing up at annual shareholder meetings in between flitting to exotic locales worldwide, *with family*, commanding attention to our company. Simply put, Rexual Healing and I will run the companies, while you just *figurehead*, so to speak, as a master hobnobber. The industry leaders will welcome you with bootlicking homage."

Bodine stared toward the ceiling with chin cupped in his hand. "It bears consideration, Chaser. The factories will be only too happy supporting our efforts. Hey, what about all the folks here at Eye Cue who depend on us?"

"We'll do what any ruthless company would do; we'll pirate away the best ones. How does Bodine Enterprises sound?"

CHAPTER 36

THE BODINES

While business remained strong amid the aftereffects from Eye Cue's latest media exposure, Bodine's and Dr. Jenna Talia Gorman's nuptials pushed closer. Murdock tried asking Bodine multiple times about starting their own enterprise after flipping Eye Cue. No matter how clever Murdock shaped his approach, Bodine dismissed him for a time after his pending marriage. Every time Murdock even casually broached the subject, Bodine's response usually sounded like, "Not now, Chaser. Let me get this handled first. Then we'll talk."

Having been rebuffed numerous times before Bodine's last rejection, Murdock focused on his upcoming move into Barbara's home. His approaching shared responsibility caring for her withered, erratic mother weighed heavily on his mind. Unannounced, he stopped by Barbara's house one evening after work. When he walked inside, Margaret sat motionless on the couch watching TV, holding a teacup, stark naked bearing a serene look suggesting this was perfectly normal. Shocked at Barbara's absence, Murdock ran into Margaret's room, frantically searching for her bathrobe or a towel. Finding her bathrobe, he shot back waving it at the elderly woman.

"Hello, Margaret, would you please put this on for me?" Margaret remained catatonic, oblivious to his voice or presence.

As Murdock threw the robe over her, Barbara burst through the front door.

Out of breath, Barbara panted, "Oh God, Chase, I'm so glad you're here. I left mom alone while I filled a critical prescription for her at the pharmacy since their delivery guy didn't show up for work. I couldn't coax her into the car, but I didn't think it would be a problem for just ten minutes."

He understood her mortified expression, pulling her over for a hug. As he nuzzled her cheek, he whispered, "Barbara, your mother greeted me by re-enacting a scene from Lady Godiva, only not quite as fetching, I might add. She could have wandered out the front door giving the neighbors a fright. I think we both should agree from this point on we never leave her alone even for one minute."

Barbara burst out in tears, "It's getting worse, Chase. I think she's already lost it altogether." While they talked, Margaret Conley simply stared at the TV, unaware of any people or conversation near her.

Murdock had seen enough. "Barbara, with Eye Cue thriving, I'm making plenty of money, more than sufficient for us and your mother. In other words, I can afford assisted living for your mom as well. Don't you see? Your caring for her here *all* day and *all* night will suck the life out of you. I can't bear you being a prisoner inside your own home."

Barbara put her arms around him, kissing him through her tears. "You're right. I'll get online first thing tomorrow, baby. Even if I could handle her myself, this shouldn't be your burden. She's going downhill so fast, we'll both stay miserable. Not a good start for our new life together. I'm in."

"Then I'm *all* in, sweet cheeks."

⁂

The next morning, he walked into his office with Bodine tagging along behind him. Standing in the doorway, he told Murdock, "Top secret, Chaser. The wedding will be exactly thirty days from today. It'll be a small ceremony with only Talia's family, you, Casual Rex, Ted and Cindy invited."

"What about Barbara?"

"C'mon Chaser, of course she's invited, but I thought she was shackled 24/7 with her mother."

"Not anymore. Margaret's getting so bad, Barbara's seeking out a facility with advanced supervision over her watching TV buck naked or shampooing her hair with toothpaste. The lights are on the *lowest* dim setting, but there's a big vacancy sign when you look into her eyes."

"Sad news, Chaser. You both have my sympathy. Here's some good news. Talia showed pure excitement at having Barbara at the wedding. She wants her standing beside her as bridesmaid at the ceremony and will ask her right away. Anyway, we'll party at Moonshadows in Malibu for dinner afterward. Tell Safe Rex no media can know about this. We don't need the circus atmosphere or any nosy reporter following us around."

"No honeymoon?"

"We agreed to wait until the season when Maui's weather becomes perfect. Besides, you and I should start finetuning your brainchild soon. If we strike out on our own, then it would rock if our honeymoon included celebrating the new direction as well. We also could make it a longer trip if we wait."

Murdock nodded, amused at his boss. *He's taking my idea seriously after all.* He suggested, "I say you have only one *solitary* media rep with a photographer at your wedding. Tell them you want the final say on what gets published. After the media selections are made in your presence, have the photographer hand you all the camera memory cards used at the wedding shoot to protect your privacy. The coverage will stoke more interest in Eye Cue, which should foster another sales spike. The personal exposure will keep your fans on social media drooling over the wedding pictures. Remember what I said about building your image. It can't hurt."

Bodine scowled, "Oh, alright, but just one rep plus one photographer. That's it."

When Bodine finalized the wedding logistics the next day, Murdock delivered the details to Sullivan, who took detailed notes. He described the reasoning behind the couple's 4:00 p.m. ceremony on a Saturday the following month inside the main chapel of St. Mary Magdalen Church in Camarillo. Murdock read from a brochure, "Built in the early 1900's, St. Mary Magdalen's regal presence, sitting majestically on a hill overlooking the older affluent part of town, offers a scenic venue. The stained-glass windows, imported from Germany and skillfully inlaid in the early 20th century stone architecture, portray the church's solid reputation as a quality location for worship as well." He handed Sullivan the brochure, then complimented the wedding duo on their discovering the perfect setting for media coverage.

After reviewing the ceremony's scope, Murdock instructed Sullivan, "Unsafe one, please contact Billy Green at

MediaTronics. Have him send a rep along with a photographer to Bo's wedding." Murdock cleared his throat, "Let me be crystal clear, we only want *one* of each at the ceremony. If Green does things his way, it will turn into a cluster of flashing lights and unwanted people. Speaking of unwanted people, make certain he keeps his mouth shut about the event. Understood?"

Sullivan answered, "Understood, Chase. I'll have him put the piece in the publication offering the broadest reach. Don't worry, neither Green nor his tactics will get past me."

Between the work pace, monitoring Bodine and Sullivan on the wedding details, and helping Barbara locate an opening within an assisted living facility for her mother, Murdock lost all sense of time during the next four weeks. Two days before the wedding, after almost giving up finding someone, Barbara hired a caregiver for Margaret during the wedding day. Frantic from constant multiple task flurries at the last minute, Murdock trusted Barbara to keep him sane. Truth be known, his mood stayed nothing short of ecstatic over the upcoming wedding because Barbara, who he considered his number one reason for living, would spend the full day of activities by his side.

As a gift to his wedding party members, Bodine hired stretch limousines for the occasion. The plush transportation likewise eliminated worry about anyone going overboard at the Moonshadows reception. As their limos pulled up at the church, Bodine, instantly miffed upon spotting a gaggle of media reps and photographers outside the event, challenged Sullivan, "How the hell did *this* happen?"

Sullivan answered, "Sorry, boss. I suspect Green's guys had a few competitors tailing them. I'll make sure right away only the authorized rep and photographer make it inside the church." He exited the limo, bulldozed toward the interlopers, then requested I.D. from each, summarily dismissed those not employed by Billy Green, and advised each one the police had been notified about the intrusions.

When Sullivan rejoined the wedding party, Bodine told him, "Thanks for taking those reps by the reins. I hate asking you this, Rex, but after that scene outside, would you mind standing at the doors until the ceremony begins? I only want the *one* rep and *one* photographer inside the church with no one else sneaking in."

"That's a smart move, boss. I'm on it."

While Sullivan performed crowd control, the remaining attendees filed into the beautiful old church. Talia Gorman's Elvis rose-pink gown revealed no signs of her baby bump. Her blonde hair, luxuriously piled up in a French twist rimmed by occasional ringlets, spotlighted her facial beauty. Wearing a low-cut dress delicately framing yet emphasizing her trademark oversized bustline, Murdock watched the men in the room do a doubletake, then steal secret glances whenever Bodine's head turned away. Under his breath, he mumbled, "Wow, Talia is ravishing. If Bo sees what I see, these boys better have life insurance."

Bodine's silk-blend suit presented in a deep black finish, accented by an Elvis rose-pink formal shirt, pitch-black silk necktie, and pink rose boutonniere, all in perfect harmony with Talia's dress. Both ensembles in tandem, enhanced by an assortment of Presley's iconic love and gospel songs playing, staged an elegant nod to The King. As they walked toward the front of the church, Murdock clutched the ring Bodine would slip on his new wife's finger, while Barbara held Talia's new husband's ring.

The presiding priest faced the small gathering and spoke, "Richard and Jenna have requested I veer from my more conventional marital service. They assembled their personal reflections which I have combined and will now share. As you know, Richard and Jenna are two very special people: Richard, the successful businessman, overseeing the livelihood of many, and Doctor Gorman, a highly regarded obstetrician. They share a singular ideal, simply stated as no level of success is more important than the devotion they feel toward each other or the mutual commitment they cherish."

Speaking directly to the couple, he continued, "You two will have to balance thick with thin throughout your lives together. Although circumstances may blow hot, they might paralyze you later when the ice-cold reality of disappointment arrives. Celebrate the good times, as there will be many, while staying vigilant should turbulent storms arrive. Devotion is key, borne by respect. As long as you maintain devotion to each other, so many problems or mishaps will dissipate swiftly. Although romance is a fascinating, powerful force, love develops from deeper roots. True love involves unwavering support at all times for your loved one, defending them when others are critical or failures arise."

Murdock reflected on how the priest's deliberate tone delivering tender words hit home with him. From his peripheral sight, he witnessed Barbara's tears pool, then run down her cheeks as she dabbed at them with a tissue clutched in her hand. Murdock leaned toward her, giving her a knowing smile. *That's going to be us up there one day. I can't wait.*

The priest added his own perspective, "You two have arrived at a marvelous place in your lives now, abounding in achievements from your careers while expecting your first child. You deserve the best life can offer," the priest paused, "because you've earned it." He addressed those gathered behind the couple. "And now, Richard and Jenna will exchange their vows."

Bodine faced Talia, a soft, gentle gaze peering from his eyes. "Jenna, my life was an empty, meaningless mess until I met you. You've shown me what love can truly be, its wonder, its vulnerabilities, its miracles, through ways I never appreciated before. I will be forever grateful having you as my life companion. With all my soul, I love you."

Gorman gulped, overcome by emotion, letting flow her joyful tears as she stood trembling. Barbara moved closer, a fresh tissue at the ready for the bride, but letting her own tears flow freely. Murdock fingered a stray tear just as it left the corner of his eye.

When Gorman regained her composure, the priest smiled at her, "Jenna, may we hear from you?"

Gorman looked at Bodine, then glanced at the attending group. Turning back, she said, "Bo, I never dreamed I would meet a man like you. Beneath your occasional gruff exterior beats the heart of a warm, deeply loving person. I adore your sweet, gentle ways with me. You're a genuine, kind, no-nonsense man. You also crack me up." Those present chuckled as she resumed. "I've never known anyone like you. I'm so in love with you, so proud you are the man our child will call Daddy. I will love you forever or eternally, whichever comes last."

After her last remark, sniffling made its rounds through the guests. The priest turned to Murdock, pointing at the ring he held. Murdock opened the little box, handing the ring to Bodine at the same time Barbara handed Gorman the ring for her new husband.

The priest said, "Please exchange rings, then join hands."

Bodine fumbled the ring. Amidst the audible gasps, Talia dropped downward, snagging the ring before it hit the ground. She stood up giggling as she handed it to Bodine, who just shook his head.

The amused priest patted Talia on the shoulder, "I feel the two of you walk on sound footing. You display undeniable affection and commitment toward each other. No need whatsoever to ask if anyone believes you two shouldn't be joined in matrimony or pose the traditional question whether you'll take each other to be man and wife. Your love stares us all in the face. Therefore, I now pronounce Richard and Jenna Bodine man and wife. I'm sure they know what comes next." The camera flashed repeatedly as the Bodines shared a tender kiss.

Everyone in attendance rose to their feet, applauding among a wolf whistle or two. It was official. The new power couple's lives became intertwined forever.

CHAPTER 37

TRANSITION

The Bodines' reception at Moonshadows launched the moment their limo pulled into the parking lot. As the wedding party limos lined up at the entrance, they were rushed by an intrusive mob of reporters alongside photographers flashing their cameras at everyone. Bodine kissed Talia before he scrambled out of the limo. The force from the door he opened whacked a stalking photographer square on the camera against his face, reeling him backward into a spread-eagle on the ground.

Bodine stormed through the entrance, wading through waiting customers while staying laser-focused on the manager, Molly Quinn. "Hello, Ms. Quinn. The only reporter and photographer allowed at our party are inside our first limo." Handing her a folded $100 bill, he said, "I trust your security team can keep the intruders away from us during our dinner reception."

Quinn smiled, slipping the C-note in her jacket pocket. "Don't worry about a thing, Mr. Bodine. We deal with disturbances on a regular basis. My guys know the drill." She immediately pressed her walkie-talkie addressing her bouncers, "Butch, Mario, no press allowed inside except the one reporter and photographer who arrived in the first limo with the Bodine party."

"Which one's the Bodine party?" came the reply.

Quinn rolled her eyes. "Those three black stretch limos with the celebrity-like couple in pink and black. You *did* see them come in, didn't you, Butch?"

"I saw them, alright. Got distracted by the knockout blonde. Sorry."

Bodine smiled at Quinn who stammered, "I'm sorry, Mr. Bodine. Butch is a great security man, but not as refined as we would like."

"No problem, Ms. Quinn. Tell Butch I'm counting on him to keep those hounds at bay."

Among the many patron clusters waiting for a table, Ms. Quinn led the wedding party toward a long table beside a room-length window overlooking the Pacific Ocean. Flood lights shined on the breakwater beneath charming, well-heeled people dining on the outdoor terrace. Shortly after everyone was seated, a bold, non-authorized photographer appeared on the terrace, winding his way through the al fresco diners until he arrived at the expansive window. As he lifted the camera preparing the shot, Mario came up behind him, wrapping his left arm around the intruder's neck simultaneously grabbing the camera with his right hand.

Molly Quinn, alerted about the situation seconds before, reached the window in time to witness the burly security guard escort the frustrated paparazzi wannabe back into the parking lot. "Good job, Mario," she barked into her walkie talkie, "tell the rest of them I'll have the cops here in five minutes if anyone else bothers our customers."

As Quinn retreated into the reception area, another photographer approached from the opposite side of the terrace near the wedding party. While readying his camera for a shot, Butch, the other brawny security guard, stripped the camera from his grasp while shoving him away from the onlookers. As soon as Butch removed the trespasser, sirens could be heard advancing closer on Pacific Coast Highway. The local press party crashers swarmed the parking lot, all requiring physical removal by the police with assistance from Butch and Mario.

When the madness subsided, a woman approached the newly christened Jenna Talia Bodine chatting with Murdock, Barbara, and the Zacharys. "Excuse me, Mrs. Bodine. My name's Carla Green. My husband handles your husband's promotional work. I just wanted to tell you how impressed I am with your wedding gown." The woman then scanned the restaurant, hoping no one would notice as she leaned over with a Sharpie fine-point pen atop a recent trade magazine in her hand. The cover splashed a stunning shot of Talia beside her new husband promoting the revamped Eye Cue Technologies. Mrs. Billy Green sheepishly asked for the new bride's autograph. Talia smiled, obliging the woman without comment.

Murdock witnessed the scene unfold, making a mental note to call Billy Green on the carpet first thing Monday morning. "That was unbelievable," he carped as Carla Green left their table wearing an expression reminiscent of a manic schoolgirl who just bagged her first rock star autograph.

Bodine, as if reading Murdock's mind, snarled, "That Billy Green will hear from me on Monday. All we wanted was our privacy. His loose lips put a permanent stain on his credibility with me. I'm sure his crass wife drives him crazy, but his personal problem should not show up sniffing for an autograph at our one and only wedding reception. Chaser, I want you and Sullivan in my office during the call. From now on, both of you will squeeze him out of big money when pricing future promotions we throw him. If he doesn't comply, drop him off the go-to list."

After a grimacing Sullivan nodded, Murdock promised," No worries, we'll knock him down a notch or two."

Before the reception ended, Murdock and Barbara left for home in their return limousine for arrival by the promised 11:00 p.m. return time to relieve Margaret's caretaker. The couple crashed for the night, both hitting the bed seconds before they fell asleep. From early Sunday morning until early evening, Murdock witnessed firsthand what Barbara dealt with every moment Margaret lingered awake. As with the first incident where he caught Margaret watching TV nude, her "normal" indeed involved walking around the house naked. In fact, the only aberration in her behavior showed up when she displayed a short-lived cognizance of her surroundings. She refused dressing, eating, or speaking civilly to either Barbara or Murdock. Reasoning with her, eventually escalating into their forcing a needed action, resembled dealing with a toddler. The visible, rapid decline of her health kept Murdock and Barbara in perpetual disbelief. Even Margaret had no idea what she would do next.

After they coaxed Margaret into bed, Murdock sat down beside Barbara. "Okay, sweet face, it's time we let someone else deal with this. No one should face the ordeal you do daily. I know you've attempted searching online for places with immediate openings, but it's time we both get *your* life back. If Margaret's demands keep you from the phone, just call me. I can make a few calls during breaks." Barbara leaned on him, emotionally spent from exhaustion. He suffered Barbara's anguish, finding intolerable the toll it already took on her. "I've watched all I can stomach, sweetness. Your gutting this out is not worth losing your health or sanity. What I don't understand is, since we know how advanced her disease is, how your mom sustained herself living alone until the time you took her to the doctor."

Barbara explained, "She has three neighbors who live in her apartment complex, all of whom she's known over many years. They're probably her only friends and watched over her every single day and night by rotating their supervision in shifts. Each one had a baby monitor in her home. Without them, Mom would have been here with me a long time ago, I guess. I visited her every week plus called her almost every day. When I took her to the doctor, I noticed how different she seemed from my prior visit a week earlier. We had a long wait at the doctor's office in a crowded room. It was like she went rigid, appearing very withdrawn shortly after we got there. Who knows how many close calls she's had without any of her friends bothering to call me?"

Murdock lifted her off the couch, walking with his arm around her to the bedroom. He brought her a glass of milk, then lay beside her until she fell asleep. After making himself a stiff drink, he pulled out his phone beginning his search for full time assisted living nursing homes in the area. He read information about the challenges in long term elderly care, gaining knowledge on the subject for more meaningful conversations with Barbara. After many articles and facility descriptions, he crawled into bed with Barbara, rolling her inside his arms.

On Monday, Barbara began phone interviewing assisted living facilities for her mother's 24-hour care. Throughout the conversations, Margaret sat staring out the front window in a vegetative state. After she finished the last call, Barbara told her mother, "I think I found a good one, Mom. Let's check it out." Margaret turned toward her daughter with a blank countenance. Tears welled in Barbara's eyes as she prepped her mother for the short trip across town.

Driving toward their destination, Margaret fell asleep, her head rocking back and forth against the passenger headrest. Barbara smiled at her mom resting, grateful for the peace during the drive. As she pulled up to the entrance of the Serenity Haven facility, she stopped the car. Margaret didn't move. Barbara unbuckled the elder woman's seatbelt. "C'mon, mom, let's find out what these folks have for us." A Serenity Haven assistant opened Margaret's door in anticipation to help her to her feet. Instead, Margaret rolled to her right side, partially falling out of the car. The assistant caught her, steadied her back into the car seat, then released her, assuming she would exit the car. Again, Margaret slid partially out the door, having departed for her permanent dirt nap during the ride.

The assistant, armed with a stethoscope, held the instrument over Margaret's heart for over a minute while an overwrought Barbara stood near him fighting back her tears. The assistant stood, facing Barbara, "I'm sorry, ma'am. I'm afraid your mother has passed."

Barbara froze, unable to react. She remained standing as her entire body began trembling. The assistant, who already summoned an ambulance, took her by the shoulders, slowly guiding her to a nearby chair. There would be no rest home tour.

As Barbara slowly regained her senses, she reached in her purse for her phone. "Chase? Mom's gone. No, no, I'm not searching for her, babe. She died in the car on the way to tour Serenity Haven."

Murdock choked up, feeling Barbara's pain. Taking charge of the situation, he arranged Margaret's memorial service for the following Sunday. Not knowing if they could reach Margaret's friends and showing support for Barbara, he invited the Bodines along with the Zacharys.

When they arrived early Sunday, Kevin and John Alvarez, wearing somber smiles on their faces, rushed over to greet their Aunt Barbara standing beside the man each considered their stepfather. Barbara found an old family photo, which she had enlarged and framed, then placed it on an easel at the entrance to the church. In the picture, Margaret sat beside her husband, George Conley, holding their two precious daughters, Donna and Barbara, on their laps when the girls were still preteens. Barbara clutched Murdock's hand, suddenly sobbing, "What a helluva way my mother's life ended. No time to appreciate her or say goodbye. Oh God, everyone's gone except me."

Murdock turned, wrapping her in his arms, whispering, "Thank God for *that*. Perhaps your Mom knew we needed privacy." Barbara stifled a chuckle. Unfettered, Murdock went on, "I love you, Barbara. As long as I'm breathing, you'll never be alone. I'm sure Kevin and John, who adore you, will never leave you alone because you are the only close family they have left."

Following the memorial service, Barbara held a reception at her home where her friends and family gathered. Margaret's three surviving friends attended the wake along with the Murdock invitees. As he met Barbara's closest friends and neighbors, he discovered himself feeling at home, seeking the approval from her dearest social connections.

Talia Bodine sauntered up to Murdock who stood beside Barbara. "So, this will be your new digs, eh Chase?"

Barbara put her arms around Murdock, answering Talia's question, "And not a moment too soon, Jenna." She faced Murdock, "Nothing left in our way, sweet man. When exactly will your eternal residence begin here?"

Murdock responded, "I've cleared up everything at the compound, so I can leave any time. I'll have my stuff here by next weekend." Perhaps inappropriate for a wake celebration, Mrs. Bodine clapped loudly, piquing Mr. Bodine's curiosity as he joined the group.

By Saturday noon, Murdock's belongings arrived at Barbara's home, an outcome created by Johnny Dunne working non-stop. Barbara came out to greet them following the instructions she received in a text from her man. "Please follow this request to the letter. I promise I'll explain later. When you greet us outside, put on your largest robe with a towel on your head. Wear your sunglasses. Use a British accent for your five-second hello, then go back into your bedroom. Don't come out until I give you the all clear. I'll tell Johnny you're not doing well since your mother passed. Love you for trusting me on this." An hour later, after unloading everything into the house, Johnny pulled away to return the small moving van with $300.00 cash he earned in his pocket. Murdock headed for Barbara in the bedroom. She greeted him with no towel on her head or robe. Murdock smiled, saying "It's most important Johnny has no inkling you're Donna's sister. I worried he would recognize the strong resemblance. Further discussion will continue later."

Setting up house with Barbara developed into a healing therapy the couple enjoyed. For the first time, Murdock savored going home each night after work welcomed by an eager, affectionate Barbara. Both often commented on the absence of effort or struggle between them. As he previously promised, he expressed his love for her daily, so thankful he loved and shared his life with an extraordinary woman. As deeply as he grieved Donna's loss, he equally embraced his crazy luck in meeting a lover even more kind, sweet, and unequivocally adorable.

CHAPTER 38

THE PLAN

With Margaret gone and the move into Barbara's home behind him, Murdock refocused his attention on cashing out of Eye Cue. Monday morning, over a week after the Bodine wedding, Murdock approached his boss. "Okay, Bo. Since you're officially off the market, let's schedule a time for the conversation about flipping Eye Cue."

Bodine, the stress of his wedding ordeal behind him, smiled at Murdock as he motioned toward the chair across from him and shut his office door. "Let's do it, Chaser. First thing, I'm pretty sure we're not well-versed enough for a solo flight. We need solid instruction on how we begin the process. Ask Ted if he'll share his expertise about corporate acquisitions so we head in the right direction."

"Already got Teddy on board with dinner at his place tonight. Are you available?"

"You're not fucking around, are you? Tonight is fine. I'll alert Talia."

Zachary had ice cold beer waiting after ordering Chinese food when Murdock and Bodine arrived. Murdock asked, "Where's Cindy? There's nothing we'll discuss she can't hear."

Zachary answered, "Yeah, but it doesn't mean she wants to. Besides, shoptalk is *not* on her priority list. She took a girlfriend to a movie. Now, until the food gets here, grab a beer so you can spell out this venture to me."

The Eye Cue executives glanced at each other then back at Zachary as they both sat on the leather couch in the family room. Zachary sat in Murdock's favorite chair on the side of the extravagant coffee table. Murdock took the lead, describing the justification to sell Eye Cue. His description included both he and Bodine taking a few personal months off before drawing up plans on their new venture. "Frankly, Teddy, we don't know where to begin."

Zachary eyed them both. "Have you thought this through? Is this the best time for starting such a labor-intensive move without guarantees of success? I mean, Bo, you *just* got married with a kid due in a few months. Chase, you and Barbara *just* set up house, and most notably, Eye Cue is on fire right now."

After glancing at Bodine, Murdock responded, "Over the past few months, our trade media marketed Bo as the most visible, successful, charismatic leader in the industry. The most recent coverage only enhanced his standing. There's not another CEO or corporate President around who can claim anything near the recognition, or may I add, fan base. He's a celebrity, for God's sake. Eye Cue's product demand remains steady at fever pitch showing no signs of slowing down anytime soon. If we give this direction a thumbs up, we'll move quickly to overcome the pricing risk before business plateaus then drops off."

Zachary took a pull from his beer, then set the bottle down. "Got it. Well, the first thing I'd do is get Justin Arluck involved. You'll require an investment banker to underwrite the sale after they find a buyer. Arluck knows countless reputable ones. Good thing he mentioned mergers and acquisitions as included in his practice. He'll translate all the legalese while staying focused on your best interests. Since you both witnessed his results-driven skills, it goes without saying he'll get the highest price."

Bodine cracked, "I'm sure his retainer fee will escalate in the process, but a proper buyer bringing the right price overcomes the cost. After witnessing him firsthand shred the bedwetters who tried their hand at hosing us, I'll welcome the additional expense."

Zachary continued, "When you're ready and before you call Arluck, call a Board of Directors meeting to announce your intentions. They shoulder the shareholder fiduciary responsibilities in analyzing all the facts and validating your plan, which must include a sound profitability factor for shareholders. Bottom line, Arluck and the Board must get the numbers right so everyone benefits fairly. Next, let's go over how you will spin your justification for selling the company."

Murdock replied, "Bo and I have a vision. We see ourselves getting involved with something bigger, more diverse. Although Eye Cue commands a strong standing in the industry, we envision tackling a product line expansion over and above electronics. Besides, if we sell Eye Cue now at the right price, we'll both walk away with a buttload of cash."

Bodine cracked, "Think boats, Chaser. Boats are much bigger than butts."

Zachary's eyes got big. "You never, never can use personal benefit for you or the Board as a justification. You'd get an immediate thumbs down on the sale from the Board. You could advise you both believe Eye Cue's revenues show a rapid trajectory toward a peak growth rate, plateauing at higher levels over the next year, even sooner. When the plateau hits, the growth rates and earnings will level off then diminish, which will send the stock price down, perhaps a significant amount from its peak. Therefore, the perfect selling window starts now with an objective of your hitting higher earnings and growth rates to amplify pricing power. Pricing a business based on *projected* revenues, earnings and growth data is standard practice. Again, if the growth and/or earnings plateau is followed by a downtrend, there goes your price plus any outside interest. Bottom line, I agree 100 percent the time is ripe for placing Eye Cue on the bidding table."

Bodine reached over, patting Zachary on the shoulder." You just gave us the perfect justification. Quite impressive, Ted. Thank you."

Murdock chimed in, "I knew you could show us the way, Teddy."

A knock at the door paused the moment. Zachary declared, "Food's here. Hold that thought."

They munched on Chinese food while swilling cold beer. Zachary asked, "How soon can you call your Board together?"

Bodine replied with a mouthful of fried rice, "I'll call Larry Davis first thing in the morning. I assume it'll take at least a few days. It'll be weird not seeing Nadine there, you know. She's the one who started us thinking about spreading our wings. She told Chaser we could 'write our own ticket.' It opened my mind about the possibilities. Such a waste. The woman had so much going for herself."

Murdock smirked, "Not including the psychotic behavior, of course."

After finishing every food morsel plus a couple more beers, Bodine and Murdock both stood up, each giving Zachary a hug with thanks for his straightforward advice. Zachary requested, "Keep me in the loop on what transpires. I'm quite interested in how you two fare on this. I've got this excitement tingle going on from anticipation. Guys, this is once-in-a-lifetime stuff."

The next morning, Bodine stared at Murdock across his desk as he called Davis. After Bodine described why he wanted a Board meeting, Davis sounded shocked. "Why in the hell would you want to do this now, Mr. Bodine? Eye Cue's sales pace sets a new record every week. Your stock trades higher than anyone imagined before you implemented your promotional strategy. I don't understand your motivation." Bodine and Murdock smirked at each other in recognition of Davis's first response coming in as predicted.

"Mr. Davis, we believe it's a straightforward strategy. Mr. Murdock and I understand how growth happens in this company. As it turns out, I hired the most dynamic marketing persona in Chase who brought us the marketing success we enjoy today. Because of his techniques, our growth almost tripled in less than six months from a new product demand rate moving far faster than we consider sustainable. Plus, selling Eye Cue when the demand enters a plateau stage, which I consider a reality in the not-too-distant future, would diminish the advantage we carry now for attracting the highest price. Now's the perfect time for using our success story to snare a buyer while the Eye Cue fan mania irons are still hot."

Davis admitted, "Well I can't fault your logic there. However, I am concerned the shareholders might not feel comfortable with the risk in turning over the reins to not only a new management team, but new Board members from the buyers." Murdock gave Bodine a thumbs up after Davis hit the second objection as projected.

Bodine countered, "If we get the proper price, the shareholders' concerns will be overcome by the benefits they realize from the sale. Concerns about who the replacements are will dissipate after they get a whiff of the green they'll make, especially if we land a cash deal. Mr. Murdock and I will go over the strategy with the Board, assuring them we will require and request their guidance along the way. With your permission, I'd like Justin Arluck's legal services from the acquisitions side of his law practice. His input is a mandatory element in our Board presentation."

"Alright, Mr. Bodine. I'll call a special meeting right away for Friday afternoon. Good luck."

The second the call ended, Murdock punched Justin Arluck's number on his phone. "Good morning, Just Ice. This time we've got something up your alley." He briefed Arluck on the project before inviting him to attend the upcoming Board meeting. Murdock continued, "Ted Zachary says you might know a quality investment banker to manage the deal."

"I know a few. Let me determine the best fit in your particular industry, then I'll call you back. One last thing, may Theresa Meyer attend the meeting with me?"

"Is she working at your firm now, or is this some wacky attorney dating ritual?"

For the first time since he met the man, Arluck let out a laugh. "I hired her away. I identified certain characteristics in her when we went one-on-one, which I believe could mold her into a key player at our firm. Her previous employer didn't have a clue about tapping into her potential."

"It doesn't hurt she's so damned attractive either. Having you two at the meeting will show how serious we are as well. I'm sure most Board members are familiar with your reputation."

"And that reputation is?"

"How filthy you can be considering your track record and propensity for laying the competition to waste."

"I'm taking your misuse of the word filthy as a compliment."

"Of course, it's a compliment. You're the quintessential master of legal takedowns, Justin. There's no better person who can protect us against getting screwed. This is a *huge* deal for us bundled in a golden harvest opportunity for you and your firm. We trust your guidance will bring home the prize. I'll await your call after you select an investment banker."

"Okay, I'll accept your definition of filthy assuming it stays between us. Thank you." Arluck's tone sharpened a bit. "And just so we're clear, I didn't hire Theresa for her looks."

When Friday afternoon arrived, the Eye Cue executives strode into the conference room at Davis's office, both sighting a tray of goodies, small water bottles, and coffee in the center of the table. The buzz of lively conversations between the Eye Cue Chairman and Justin Arluck while another Board member chatted up Theresa Meyer uplifted Murdock's mood. Judging from the voice tones interspersed with chuckles emanating from the parties involved, Murdock recognized the disarming behavior the two attorneys used provided the perfect stabilizer before the meeting.

As Eye Cue's President, Bodine presented the company's sale proposal to the Board of Directors, choreographed in no small part by Murdock. At first, the plan met with strong resistance from many members. The questions and comments centered around Davis's initial concern on the timing of the sale. Selling Eye Cue right now bordered on frivolous, many grumbled, since the company just achieved its most dramatic sales spike ever.

As Murdock prepared to reiterate the timing rationale, Lawrence Davis addressed his fellow members. "I thought the same thing when Mr. Bodine first approached me. In simple terms, it makes more sense taking this step now rather than waiting until things peak, then watch it all diminish back toward business as usual."

Justin Arluck stood up. "If I may interrupt, I have an investment banker from Imperial Capital Markets waiting in the wings. With Eye Cue's current sales pace versus their prior year, we should have no problem finding a promising buyer right away. Delaying the sale risks facing a substantial reduction in the current price potential Eye Cue commands now."

Murdock looked at Theresa Meyer while Arluck spoke. Meyer's admiring gaze at her new boss suggested more than just boss-employee status simmered between them. Murdock elbowed Bodine to catch her adoring smile. Bodine whispered, "Tell me they're not touching pee-pees."

Chairman Davis allowed a few more comments before he put forward the motion to vote on the sale of Eye Cue. Every member said "Aye," approving the sale to proceed. Larry Davis exposed a wide grin as he announced, "The motion to approve the sale of Eye Cue Technologies is passed unanimously." Richard Bodine and Chase Murdock advanced one step closer to lifelong financial freedom.

CHAPTER 39

CRUNCH TIME

In less than a week, Imperial Capital Markets, the investment banker Justin Arluck retained, submitted prospective buyers for Eye Cue Technologies. Bodine had Arluck in his office scanning the potential buyers on his computer screen when he called Murdock. "Chaser, you better get over here."

Murdock spotted Bodine and Arluck huddled at the computer, studying the list while making notes on the most viable candidates. As he sat down across from them, Bodine asked Arluck if he recognized any names. Arluck replied, "Just one. Destiny Prime Holdings located in San Francisco. Very dynamic publicly traded company, owns an array of exceptional assets. Diversification has been their key for success. They avoid heavy bets on any single type of business. I know their CEO, Evan Buchanan, from a previous client. He is a *very* bright guy, negotiates with aggressive, sometimes extreme tactics. However, to his discredit, his reputation includes being a public boozer and skirt chaser. His righthand men, while matching his acuity, participate heavily in his established party culture."

Bodine repeated the words, "Skirt chaser, huh?"

Arluck smirked, "Sounds like a job for Theresa Meyer."

Murdock bristled, responding, "I'm concerned Buchanan may be too heavy duty for Ms. Meyer, don't you think, Just Ice?"

Arluck gave the scenario perspective, "Not when he's downed a few cocktails after a woman like Ms. Meyer comes on to him."

Bodine sounded shocked. "You're not suggesting she..."

Arluck raised his hand. "No, no, no. She would only be on a fact-finding mission. As Buchanan's lips get too loose, he'll unwittingly spill some inside info. When Theresa hears the double beep I'll send her over a wire, she'll make a swift departure from the premises, leaving the hardball moves up to us tomorrow. Concerning Ms. Meyer's assignments, let me assure both you gentlemen, I'll never assign a job placing her in harm's way."

Bodine asked. "Ah, in other words, she's going undercover."

Arluck nodded, adding, "We'll set the stage by getting Buchanan away from his comfort zone with meetings scheduled here by giving him a tour of your operation. At the end of the business day, we'll direct him to his prepaid reservation at the Westlake Four Seasons. Later, after we've parted company, he'll head straight to the bar where Theresa will be sitting, all alone, wired for sound. My office will make all arrangements. I'll call Buchanan myself with the invitation when I get back to my office. We'll start to calibrate his interest based on how quickly he contacts you, Mr. Bodine. Just text me whenever you get the call."

Murdock whistled, "Without a doubt, you deserve the nickname, Just Ice, in the most professional sense, of course. I can't wait 'til I watch you play this guy. Oh yeah, and it seems Theresa's appeal absolutely played a prominent role in why you hired her." Arluck responded by glancing away with a sideways smile.

Within three hours, Bodine received a phone call from Thomas Carlton, one of Buchanan's underlings, inquiring if Bodine would consider a visit by Destiny Prime executives at the Eye Cue headquarters. Bodine needed clarification, "Who will attend?"

Carlton replied, "Myself plus a gentleman named Willis Day. We oversee the strategic acquisitions area with direct reporting to Evan Buchanan."

Bodine answered, "What about Mr. Buchanan?"

Carlton, using a snooty tone, replied, "Mr. Buchanan never attends the first negotiation round."

"Then we're not interested," Bodine shot back. "We have no plans for a long, drawn out process, Mr. Carlton. As Eye Cue's

CEO, I'll be involved in every stage throughout this process, and I expect the same from the CEO of any potential interested party. If Mr. Buchanan declines an appearance for this occasion, he can witness Eye Cue being sold out from under him."

Carlton backpedaled, "Hmm. Well, may I call you back, Mr. Bodine? I'll personally let Mr. Buchanan know your stance and ask if he will make an exception."

"Very well, Mr. Carlton. I hope we hear from you soon because I'm sure you've already heard about the interest in Eye Cue growing by the minute. It would be a shame if your CEO's *protocol* becomes the reason a competitor aces Destiny Prime out."

Evan Buchanan, annoyed about the ultimatum, yielded to Bodine's checkmate. Harboring a fervent curiosity toward Eye Cue to fill an industry gap within their holdings, he had monitored Eye Cue's stock performance plus press releases daily. He agreed on a meeting at Eye Cue set for the following Thursday with Bodine, Murdock, and Arluck.

With instructions from her boss, Theresa Meyer received a carte blanche shopping spree at the nearby high-end mall. The mission, a perk earned from her new position at the law firm, included her purchasing the most provocative cocktail dress, high heels, and perfume available.

Bodine instructed Rex Sullivan to enlist three female temps, stressing a dazzling appearance as a requirement. Sullivan asked, "What exact duties will they perform?"

Bodine replied, "Window dressing. Just make sure they're seen as often as possible during Evan Buchanan's visit. He's a womanizer. I want his horns quivering while he's here."

On the meeting day, Messrs. Buchanan, Carlton, and Day arrived at the Eye Cue offices by 10:00 a.m. Buchanan, a large man weighing over 250 pounds while standing under six feet tall wearing undersized glasses perched on a plump, bland face, showed patchy signs of balding gray hair. As they waited for the meeting, his contrived expression conveyed, "this better be worth my time," while his two lieutenants took turns kissing his ass.

During the tour of the Eye Cue facilities, Bodine and Murdock picked up cues from the Destiny Prime team, signaling each other by checking their watch, a code they selected before the tour. Both encountered a stream of positive mutterings, which escalated when they entered the new expanded warehouse.

Buchanan himself commented, "I've never seen a warehouse this modern or so clean. You could eat off the floor, for God's sake."

While the tour continued, Sullivan's fetching temps paraded to and fro, capturing the Destiny Prime men's attention by making eye contact with them. After a catered lunch from the finest Italian restaurant in town served by the three stunning temps, the six men assembled in the conference room.

Bodine opened the meeting. "Gentlemen, Mr. Murdock, Mr. Arluck and I are meeting with Destiny Prime to advance our deliberation on your potential acquisition of Eye Cue. We selected your company first over other interested parties based upon your considerable success as a Fortune 500 entity. Should an offer from you be forthcoming, we have no concerns it would be in earnest with the resources necessary to consummate the sale."

Buchanan asked, "Just how much do you think Eye Cue is worth, Mr. Bodine?"

Bodine glanced at Murdock, next at Arluck before addressing the question. "Rather than offer you a biased estimate, we would rather commence fielding offers. Care to make one?"

Recognizing the first volley in the cat and mouse game, Buchanan didn't flinch. "We *know* what Eye Cue is worth, Mr. Bodine. Why don't you forego the fishing trip by accepting our firm offer of $400 million?"

Murdock swallowed a gasp before it escaped. With a $400 million price tag, he would earn in excess of $20 million based on his stock options plus his ownership percentage in the company. Arluck remained deadpan, being the far superior poker player. Bodine, staring at the floor, peeked at Arluck, who delivered the prearranged cue for Bodine's response.

After a lengthy pause, Bodine answered, "That sounds very reasonable, Mr. Buchanan. It's obvious you've been monitoring our progress. We'll take the remainder of the day for evaluating your offer. We reserved rooms at The Four Seasons in Westlake with an open tab covering all your expenses. Please make yourselves comfortable there. We'll reconvene at 9:00 a.m. tomorrow morning. Does that work for you?"

Buchanan nodded, "We appreciate the fine accommodations, Mr. Bodine. We'll wrap up the deal here first thing tomorrow morning." Buchanan along with his two minions rose from their chairs, exchanged handshakes with the Eye Cue team, then filed out from the conference room.

As soon as the door closed behind them, Murdock exploded at Bodine. "Bo, what an *insane* amount of dough. When I first came back here a few months ago, Eye Cue was worth about $250 million. Why didn't you jump at the offer?"

Arluck said, "Not so fast, Mr. Murdock. In these negotiations, the first offer is almost never their best. Let's find out what Theresa draws out from Buchanan tonight. Plan on meeting here at 7:00 a.m. tomorrow. By then, we'll know if Buchanan's offer is indeed their maximum number."

Theresa Meyer sat at The Four Seasons Hotel bar with her shimmering ebony cocktail dress hiked to mid-thigh, her lovely legs complemented by four-inch, beaded silver heels. Her image personified an expensive $$$$ rated call girl. She nursed a twenty-dollar chardonnay, making one last check on the microphone nestled at the bottom of her bra between her well-exposed bosom. An internal earpiece concealed by her blonde hair confirmed the system's perfect placement. Testing the system for Arluck, she whispered, "Just talk to the hooters, Mr. Buchanan." She heard a crystal-clear chuckle from Arluck.

In the manner Arluck predicted, Evan Buchanan entered the bar upon arriving at the hotel, leaving his bag with the bellman. One glance at Meyer had him walking straight toward her. He bragged as he placed his large rump atop the barstool beside her, "This must be my lucky day. I'm about to fleece some unsuspecting gomers on a big deal, then I run into you." He extended his hand. "I'm Evan. I'd be delighted if you'll help me celebrate."

Meyer flashed a radiant smile, taking his hand. "My name's Teri. I'm *always* happy when I run across a successful man. A good day, huh, Evan?"

Buchanan, mesmerized by Meyer's tantalizing figure, fixated on her beautiful face. "I'll know first thing tomorrow morning." He ordered a double Macallan 1926 scotch rocks while Meyer mimed sipping her wine. While the bartender unlocked the case of rare liquors to retrieve the scotch with a $5,000 per double shot tab, Buchanan snorted, "I can't go into details. Let's just say these boys are about to leave a pile of money on the table, and they gave me an open tab here tonight, so I feel like celebrating with a worthy scotch." Arluck whispered the estimated price of the double shot to Meyer.

Meyer probed, "How big a pile?"

Buchanan replied, "I'd estimate about twenty percent of an even *bigger pile*." He drained his scotch with one swill, signaling the bartender for another the second his lips parted from the empty glass.

Meyer inquired, "So how much money are you talking about, Evan?"

"I can't say too much," he responded while swigging the second double scotch. "By the way, Teri, what brings you here all alone?"

"My date canceled at the last minute, so I figured I'd at least have a drink before heading home." She held off pressing him on the money issue, figuring by the third double cocktail, Buchanan's loose lips would flap. "I'm not into high finance, Evan, so tell me your definition of a successful a man." She turned on her stool, crossing her legs, giving him an unobstructed view of her tanned thighs just below her enticing cleavage. "So how much could you save from this deal you're talking about?"

Buchanan, sipping on his third double scotch, lowered his voice, "Take the number 100 then add a bunch of zeros. That's as much as I'll say. Use your imagination, Teri."

"$100,000?"

"Not even close."

"Oh my. You *are* into high finance. Very impressive." She heard two beeps in her earbud, the signal Arluck snared the vital information he sought. "Evan, I'd love to learn more about you, but I need a lady's room break. Be right back. Save my seat please." As Buchanan ogled her sashaying away from him toward the restroom, she gazed back shooting him a flirtatious smile. When she reached the area blocking Buchanan's view, she detoured straight into the self-parking area behind the hotel.

At 7:00 a.m. the following morning, the Eye Cue executives absorbed Arluck's every word as he broke the news. "This means Buchanan will pay $500 million for Eye Cue, gentlemen. After the sale finalizes, he'll assume you both stay in charge of the company for another year or so until his management team is in place."

Murdock, beyond awestruck, clamored, "Holy shit, Bo. Another $100 million?"

Bodine replied, "Thank God for Just Ice and Theresa Meyer. Great job. Please give Ms. Meyer our gratitude for her stellar performance. Next we reel in Evan Buchanan. He may balk at our caveat, however, because Chaser and I won't stay one day after the sale closes."

Arluck remained matter of fact. "No problem, we'll make it a condition of the sale. There's a very slim chance Buchanan will walk. By flapping his gums, he all but guaranteed that $500 million *is* the fair value number. Because you want a quick sale closing, I do not suggest we go for a cash *or* stock premium, although the company warrants them. Include your personal conditions plus make this a cash-only, no stock deal. Those two provisions will be a respectable premium."

Buchanan, Carlton and Day entered the reception area at 9:00 a.m. sharp. Buchanan, still grousing over Theresa Meyer ghosting him the night before, complained to his two colleagues, "That's never happened before." Oblivious to Meyer's beguiling con job as she extracted inside information from him, he boasted, "That bitch had no idea how happy I could have made her." Gina Morgan, overhearing his demeaning language but not reacting, escorted the three men into the conference room where Bodine, Murdock, and Arluck waited.

After an exchange of handshakes, Bodine asked. "I trust you found the accommodations at The Four Seasons acceptable?"

Buchanan sneered, "Except for a gorgeous barfly who ditched me, yes. But I definitely enjoyed several shots of their rare scotch offering." Everyone but Bodine chuckled.

Bodine continued, "Okay, let's get down to business, shall we?"

Buchanan replied, "We trust you've digested our offer, Mr. Bodine."

"Yes, we have, Mr. Buchanan. First, so we all understand just how serious you are about acquiring Eye Cue, I'll share with you this little number on our micro recorder." Bodine pressed the play button, exposing Buchanan's conversation with Theresa Meyer where she asked him about his expected windfall in clinching the deal. When everyone heard Buchanan say, "not even close," the color drained from the large man's face. He snatched a water bottle off the table, downing half of it as he struggled to regain his wits.

Incensed to the nth degree, he roared, "That's low, Bodine, real fucking low."

"So, it appears, is your offer, Mr. Buchanan. By about $100 million, as stated during your cocktail banter. FYI, we don't appreciate being labelled as gomers. We'll accept a $500 million cash-only deal for Eye Cue with the provision Mr. Murdock and I walk away the day after the sale is closed."

Buchanan sat motionless, flushed, unmistakably seething at the public exposure of the pompous, loose-lipped wretch he was. He stood, gesturing Carlton and Day to do the same. "I don't care for your business tactics, Mr. Bodine, but we remain interested. You'll hear from me personally one way or the other by the close of business this afternoon." Offering no goodbye handshakes, Buchanan, with his men lined up behind him, showed themselves out.

Minutes after the Destiny Prime team left for the airport, Bodine and Murdock stewed over whether they would get good news before the whole day passed. Arluck encouraged them, "Look, guys, we red-faced him in front of his top lieutenants, yet he didn't storm out, nor did he offer up an argument or refusal. He wants Eye Cue. He wants it bad before another suitor swoops in. He's well aware of the value his organization will gain from this acquisition. I'm betting you'll get the good news later today. Kudos to you, Mr. Bodine. You played Buchanan like a concert violin. That was no easy task."

Bodine grinned at Arluck, "Thanks, I had a superb teacher."

Time dragged by as Bodine and Murdock watched the clock. A short time before the promised deadline, they still had no response. Murdock convinced himself the deal must be dead. He barged into Bodine's office, "Goddamnit, Bo, I knew you should have taken the $400 million. How much money do we need, anyway? We have no assurances another buyer will pony up more than that."

A stoic Bodine sat at his desk. "Maybe you're right, Chaser, but I trust Just Ice's instincts. Besides, both companies require shareholder approval. Based on what Just Ice told us, a proper price must be presented on both sides. We'll just ride this out. Buchanan may be caught up in another big deal, or just couldn't find the time today to finish this. On the bright side, I bet they're using the time for locating lenders for the cash deal. Remember, we're small potatoes for them."

Murdock couldn't mask his frustration. "A $500 million acquisition is small potatoes? Buchanan must wipe his ass with gold flecked Alder leaves imported from the Himalayas."

Before Bodine could respond, his phone rang. When he heard Buchanan's voice, he turned on the speakerphone while smirking at Murdock. "Well good afternoon, Mr. Buchanan. Hope you had an uneventful flight home."

"Cut the pleasantries, Mr. Bodine. I'm still pissed at the way you ambushed me. By the way, who is the stunning blonde you sent to entrap me?"

"Just a talented associate, Mr. Buchanan."

"Well she's just a slithering snake as far as I'm concerned. Nevertheless, I'm overnighting a formal offer to you at your asking price of $500 million cash… begrudgingly, I might add. All things considered, though, with what your team accomplished attaining Eye Cue's superior growth rate in record time, I can't lose. After you read it over, call me with any questions."

Bodine replied, "Just to confirm the offer's other specified condition, Mr. Murdock and I are released from all Eye Cue duties when the deal closes, correct?"

"Yes, it's all spelled out in the offer. Good day, Mr. Bodine." Buchanan ended the call while Murdock started writhing in ecstasy on the carpet by Bodine's desk. Bodine joined him.

CHAPTER 40

DESTINY

With Murdock in his office, Bodine received Destiny Prime's formal offer hand-delivered the following Monday. After a small high-fiving frenzy with expletives exchanged, Bodine requested Justin Arluck's presence at the office right away. When Arluck arrived, he entered the office rubbing his hands together. Wearing a toothy grin, he declared, "Okay, boys, let's see what we've got."

Murdock, more nervous than his usual high anxiety, paced back and forth, choking down two blueberry scones while watching the meticulous Arluck study the papers spread over Bodine's desk. Sitting opposite Arluck, Bodine's body became motionless, budging only to sip coffee as he kept vigilance on Arluck's every move.

Following a slow-motioned, tortured half hour, Arluck declared, "It's all legit, guys. $500 million plus you both walk away with your respective cuts after fees the day the sale is recorded."

Murdock pumped his fist in the air, shouting, "So fucking *bitchen*." Bodine, overcome by emotion, covered his face with his hands. Murdock asked, "Just Ice, how long will the transaction take?"

Arluck responded, "About six months."

Murdock picked up his phone. He awarded Barbara with the first call on the news. "Sugar cheeks, Bo signed the papers and we're almost very rich. Please have a cocktail at the ready and put on some baby-makin' music! We're gonna have some fun tonight."

Bodine howled while Arluck's face broke into a wide grin. Bodine called Talia, leaving a similar message on her voicemail. After hanging up, he said, "She's in her third trimester, so we may have to improvise."

⁓

Reaching his new home after driving on the freeway like a maniac, Murdock discovered a note taped on the front door, "Ready when you are, hot stuff." He entered the house, expecting Barbara would rush into his arms. While searching for her in the living room, he caught the sweet fragrance of her perfume. He heard the strains of "I Want to Know What Love Is" by Foreigner wafting from their bedroom followed by a shout from his beloved, "I'm on the work bench, baby. Bring all your special tools."

Dazed from his lust, he tried to unbutton his shirt while kicking his shoes off as he headed straight toward the sound of her voice. Ripping out the last two buttons of his shirt as he entered the bedroom, he snickered when he realized Barbara followed his directions with a bonus. She laid on her left side facing him shrouded in a black, see-through negligée set off by six-inch red patent-leather stilettos. Her blonde hair cascaded down past her shoulders pointing his eyes at his favorite gold hoop earrings framing her face. As she handed him a tequila gimlet, she cooed, "Is this good enough for you, baby?"

His newfound wealth coupled with Barbara's seductive ensemble proved a provocative aphrodisiac. Throwing the last of his clothes on the floor, he set the drink down on the nightstand. She took one look at his manhood and chirped, "I guess we can check foreplay off the list."

"No short-changing for you, my precious," he replied. "As cool as you are and as hot as you look, you have a much-deserved warmup coming." With a tender kiss, he pulled the negligee away from her body. He whispered, "Please, leave the shoes on." After taking a sip of his cocktail, he kissed her again. From his perspective, their lovemaking solidified their passionate feelings for each other, something he sensed she experienced as well. His desire for Barbara coupled with the sizzle of financial freedom reached fever pitch as he collapsed in her arms, both satisfied and spent.

294

When he awoke, she rested alongside him, showing him a loving smile when he looked at her. "You're incredible, Chase. I feel light as a whisper. I love you so much."

He propped himself up on one elbow. "Let's get married, Barbara."

Her smile widened. "Of course, my *sweetest* man. Took you long enough." They broke into laughter. "Do you have a date in mind?"

"Actually, I do. We should have our wedding as soon as possible before Jenna Talia's baby is born. The Bodines must attend, and Talia's in her third trimester. So we have a mere two months, maybe less."

The next morning, Bodine anticipated announcing the news to Eye Cue's employees before they heard it from anyone else. After signing the document sealing the deal, he called an emergency meeting in the warehouse for all employees right before the lunch hour. Murdock stayed chatting in Bodine's office all morning after he witnessed Eye Cue's President signing the official sale papers as a final reality check. His chatter describing his wedding plans darted in between multiple questions and assertions about his and Barbara's new life. Bodine, listening off and on, took in Murdock's animation while remaining silent, enjoying his friend's happiness. Bodine interrupted the chatter by advising Murdock about the upcoming employees' meeting. Murdock cringed, "Jesus, Bo, it'll be a sad, maybe shocking event for these folks. Are you sure I have to be there?"

Bodine looked at him in disgust. "Yes, I'm sure, weasel king. There is absolutely zero chance you get out of being front *and* center with me. And, if you keep whining like a bedwetter, you'll be the one who tells them. Stay here while I call the Chairman of the Board, so we can schedule the Board approval meeting along with getting the Chairman's signature. We'll seat Just Ice beside us to field questions or challenges. We can accomplish both the calls before the employee meeting starts."

"I'll give Just Ice the heads up while you're on the phone with Larry Davis."

An hour later, Bodine, Murdock and Arluck headed for the warehouse, joining up with the Eye Cue employees filing inside. Bodine detected concerned looks on the workers' faces wondering why he called the meeting. Holding a microphone, he waited as the last stragglers found a seat. When Brenda King signaled she accounted for all employees in attendance, he walked with an uncharacteristic hesitance toward the front row seats, surveying the crowd.

He began, "Folks, I'm not sure what's the best approach for this message, so I'll just dig in. As you know, our company became highly successful in a relatively short time." The audience stirred restlessly. The previous light-hearted banter among them ceased. "We received a lucrative offer for the acquisition of Eye Cue by a mega corporation called Destiny Prime, and this morning I accepted the offer." A few groans with grumbling echoed, while most in the crowd sat stunned.

An employee asked, "But it'll be business as usual, right Mr. Bodine?"

"For the time being, yes. However, after the sale is finalized in about six months, Chase Murdock and I will leave the company." A few employees booed as others displayed surprise or hurt, as if betrayed. Some women sniffled, while a burly warehouse man lost his composure, breaking down among his colleagues.

Murdock gestured at Bodine for the microphone. "Folks, you have nothing to fear. When the new management team takes over, *you* will be the ones who show them how it's done, not the other way around. These people are money managers. Initially, they won't hit the ground running because they will depend on your know-how and exceptional operational skills. If a buyer takes over when things aren't going well, they'll clean house, but that is far from the case here. Eye Cue is kicking ass clearly because we have you working here." A mild, less than inspired applause followed. "Just keep performing at the level you have, and it will, in fact, be business as usual."

Bodine stepped back into the conversation. "Mr. Murdock is spot on about all of you. We have provisions placed in the deal which secure your jobs under your current productivity metrics. All you have to do is *be* you." The employees interrupted with avid applause. "Over the next few weeks, we will clear this transaction through a formal vote from our shareholders, working hand-in-hand with our Board of Directors. Although it may feel disruptive at times, our goal is to stay the course. The smoother the transition, the better for everyone." Most workers nodded in agreement as Bodine signaled the caterers to bring out the surprise luncheon for everyone.

During the luncheon, several employees approached the soon-to-be-ex Eye Cue executives, extending congratulations. Some asked what the two had planned once they left Eye Cue. The men offered handshakes; the women wanted hugs.

Back in his office, Murdock became aware how the team transformed before his eyes into a family of sorts. He choked up as he recalled the women who cried when they congratulated him. It would be a long six months, or maybe not. He remembered his marriage proposal to Barbara and the short time available for making their arrangements. He set the wedding plans as his number one priority. After their stay-at-home honeymoon waiting on the Eye Cue sale closing, the nuptial's travel celebration would commence. Murdock leaned on his elbows putting his forehead in his hands, shut his eyes, and smiled at his good fortune.

As his reflection progressed, he discovered a conflict with who his best man should be. At his lowest point, Bodine threw him the support line, giving him an escape from near destitution when he offered him the rare opportunity for an executive level position. From the moment where he had nothing, to standing on the verge of becoming a millionaire had transpired in less than a year. On the other hand, he credited Ted Zachary for saving his life. Zachary teamed up with Johnny Dunne, who ran enough interference at the hardware store to end his suicide plan using Pearl's tailpipe. He approached Bodine with trepidation over his heartfelt decision.

"Bo, I have to tell you something, and I really hope you'll understand."

Bodine, seated at his desk, looked up at him with a question mark in his raised eyes. "Spit it out, Chaser. Whatever it is, you know I will."

"Ok, well, you allowed me the profound honor to serve as your best man, which thrilled me to the bone being that guy for you. You also brought me the career chance of a lifetime, not once, but twice. As far as my amigo, you're a champion. I owe my confidence and livelihood to you. However, you may recall Teddy and I have been friends since high school. As you know, he's gone through everything imaginable with me."

Bodine proved gracious with clear insight. "Chaser, I think it's only right you pick Ted as your best man. You guys gave me my first exposure inside this industry. I know damn well how deep your friendship is rooted with him. Don't give it a second thought. However, I would love being a groomsman at the altar with you and Barbara."

Murdock, grateful his friend said the words for him, let the tears run down his cheeks. "Of course, mi amigo."

Although the moment tempted him to confide more reasons for his decision, he stopped short, swearing again Bodine never would learn about his original DIY checkout plan. His face shining from stray tears still running down his cheeks, he partially extended his hand, then bent over instead to hug his boss. "This was an impossible decision for me, Bo. Thanks for showing so much class, making it easier on me than I deserve."

Bodine smirked, "A simple handshake would have sufficed, Chaser. I know how much this means to you. Wipe off your face and regroup before anyone sees you."

Barbara spent her day stressing over the wedding plans. When Murdock walked into the house, she sat writing in a notebook at their dining room table. He leaned down to kiss her, noticing several pages of scribbled notes. She looked up at him with a crooked smile. "Hey, baby, how can we pull this all together in less than two months? Most folks take a year or more planning a wedding."

Murdock put a hand on her shoulder. "We should prioritize, uber cheeks. What's first on your list?"

"How about *where* we say, 'I do?'"

"Remember where we held Donna's memorial service? I think it's fitting we use the same church. It can be our final goodbye to Donna before we usher in our new life together."

Barbara dropped her pen, then leaned back in her chair. " Ooh, I don't know. That feels a little eerie, Chase. Then again, it is rather symbolic." After mulling the idea over for a long minute, she agreed. "Okay, let's do it. I'll call them first thing tomorrow. I just hope we can get the date we want."

"If they say they can't accommodate your request, call me. I'll go into full bribe mode."

The next morning, Murdock received a call from Barbara at his office. "The church is pushing back, Chase. They're claiming a conflicting event for the day we want."

"Give me their number. Let's find out just how significant this other event is." The receptionist connected him with the church's event coordinator, Kathryn Rinaldi.

"I'm so sorry, Mr. Murdock. We have a special event planned for that afternoon. It's a fundraiser for the underprivileged elderly."

Murdock inquired, "Just how much money do you expect from this event, Ms. Rinaldi?"

"Well, the one we held a year ago raised $2,500. We're hoping we top that."

"How about I donate $5,000 to your cause, which gives you a stronger reason to free up the date for my wedding? You can reschedule the fundraiser for another time as well."

Shocked, Rinaldi uttered, "$5,000? That's extremely generous, Mr. Murdock. Let me make a phone call and get right back to you." *Money talks, even in the spiritual realm.* The phone rang less than a minute after he hung up. "Mr. Murdock, with gratitude, we accept your offer. Perhaps you can give me your bride-to-be's phone number, so I can get all the details for the wedding."

Murdock texted Barbara the news from his call plus a heads up to expect the call from the church lady. She texted back her relief at his removing her worry about their special venue. Once they set the date, everything started falling into place. Barbara texted again, "What do you think about holding the reception at The Four Seasons in Westlake? The hotel is first rate with beautiful surroundings."

Since he never shared with her how the Evan Buchanan ambush happened at that location, the karma struck Murdock as funny. "Too perfect, my mesmerizing goddess," he texted, chuckling.

Having received Bodine's blessing over the best man quandary, he called Ted Zachary. "Teddy, I have something super important to ask you."

"Sure, Chase. Shoot."

He choked up, then swallowed hard. "Well, I'd be honored if you'd be my best man. I can't imagine anyone else who means more to me or who I'd rather have standing by my side when I marry Barbara. After all you've soldiered through with me during our friendship over these many years, you are without question my best man in every way."

"I'd be delighted, Chase. But what about Bo? Does he feel slighted?"

"Nope, Bo understands. I explained why I felt you were my first choice. He's not offended at all. In fact he told me you were the right choice before I told him I chose you. He'll stand as my groomsman at the wedding."

Zachary's voice cracked, "Wow, that's outstanding and awfully good of him. Now give me the details so I can get started on my duties. I assume the event will occur before Jenna Bodine gives birth."

"That's the plan."

Having assembled the most important aspects of the wedding plans, Murdock discovered his relieved fiancé in an amorous mood when he got home, since she greeted him in her black negligee and red stilettos in anticipation of his arrival. He embraced her with a lingering kiss, then said, "Barbara, you know how your spontaneity electrifies me."

"Baby, I'm so glad you like it. After wading through all these wedding details, I realized how much I missed our little sessions. So let's not rush. I feel like loving you slow, starting with a simmer." She handed him a shot of his favorite tequila.

"Fine with me. One request, I want you completely naked for me this time, sweet cheeks. And don't mind my clothes. I won't waste a second taking them off."

Barbara's eyes twinkled. She inched closer to him placing her lips beside his ear, "Not so fast, Trigger. Just stay dressed so you and I can share a steak and lobster dinner near our favorite spot on the beach. After dinner, we'll need a blanket, two crystal champagne glasses, a bottle of terribly expensive champagne, topped off by an all-nighter in the moonlight with your most lustful creations. Can you handle it, and can we leave as soon as I've grabbed my long coat? I'm famished. By the way, I'll be wearing this outfit under the coat at dinner to keep our body heat high."

Murdock bolted to her closet, snatched the coat, and helped her slip into it. He swept her up in his arms, keeping the stilettos intact, then took off in a labored gallop toward the finish line at Pearl's side door, hauling a limp Barbara delirious with laughter.

CHAPTER 41

NEW BEGINNINGS

Once they established the wedding date, Murdock worked with Barbara on the guest list, both desiring a modest number of attendees. Outside of Barbara's immediate family, closest friends along with the Bodines and the Zacharys, Murdock's special requests, Johnny Dunne, Dr. Howell Bronson and Rex Sullivan, made the final list. Dunne earned his wedding invitation from his role in preventing Murdock from killing himself. Dr. Bronson had been his doctor since Murdock's middle thirties; he loved the old guy and considered him a lifelong friend. Sullivan, his righthand man, established himself as a key driver for Eye Cue's ascent into prominence within the electronics industry, plus his diligence at work freed up Murdock's personal time for romancing Barbara.

With the wedding date two weeks before Dr. Jenna "Talia" Bodine's due date, Barbara remained adamant about asking Talia if she would consider serving as her matron of honor. Talia gave her an instant answer, "I would be honored, Barbara. You were my rock when we got married. Bo and I consider you such a treasured friend, and so will the little sprout. If you're okay with furnishing me seating at the altar, I'm your matron."

Barbara responded, "I'll make sure Chase arranges a throne placed at my left side for you and the precious newbie." Barbara crossed her fingers trusting the baby held off making a surprise appearance before or during the wedding day.

Talia focused on throwing a surprise shower for Barbara; Bodine aimed at having a bachelor party for Murdock. After everyone filtered through the multitude of schedules, both parties ended up falling on the night before the wedding day.

Bodine, the future groom, Ted Zachary, and Rex Sullivan comprised the bachelor party. When Bodine and Sullivan approached him about the date, Murdock's stress took charge. "Okay, boys, let's just make sure we keep a limit on the imbibing. I will *not* show up at my own wedding plagued by a hangover."

They all agreed upon a four-drink limit. Murdock scowled at Sullivan after he quipped, "No one says they can't be doubles."

Though Talia hosted Barbara's shower at her home, Mandrake's accommodated the bachelor party. The four compadres pulled up at their familiar haunt in the limo Bodine supplied. Murdock observed, "Having this party at Mandrake's is a bittersweet adios, since we won't be hanging out here anymore."

Bodine responded, "Yeah, amigo, but we both have something so much finer at home waiting for us. I won't miss Mandrake's. Besides, we can take the wives out for a sentimental journey here once in a while."

Murdock chimed in, "That'll work," with Ted nodding in approval. Sullivan felt the exclusion.

To catch Barbara off guard, Talia had invited her for a visit at the Bodine home under the pretext of preparing her a special meal with the traditional spicy girl talk the night before the wedding. Barbara accepted without hesitation, welcoming the diversion from her frazzled nerves. Barbara stepped into the house. A group screaming "Surprise" greeted her, causing her to jerk into a wide-open smile. Her best friends beside her new friends from knowing Talia stood clapping, the scene bringing Barbara to a surge of happy tears.

Barbara spotted the party's theme banner, *Daily Sex Before Senility.* She wiped her eyes before she hollered, "Ok, bring on the wine and the porn. I'm ready."

On the wedding day, Murdock arrived in a nerve-racked state. He agonized over everything and anything, pacing back and forth in front of the church. Bodine, Zachary and Sullivan failed to calm his anxiety. Murdock queried Zachary for the third time, "You still have the ring, Teddy?"

Zachary maintained his soothing tone, "Right in my pocket where it's been since you handed it to me, Chase."

Murdock eyed Bodine. "How do I look, Bo?"

Bodine rolled his eyes. "Chaser, you look exactly the same as you did the last time you asked me, which was five whole minutes ago. Chill out, amigo. Everything will be fine."

"Yeah, it's just that my pits are getting all batchy. Is it showing through the tux?"

Bodine reassured him, "Out of sight, so get it out of your mind, Chaser. Jesus, you're acting like the first rooster to make it into the henhouse. Relax."

Murdock eyed Sullivan. "Rex, do the limo drivers know they can't go anywhere during the ceremony?" For the first time in Sullivan's memory, Murdock called him by his actual name, no cutesy off-color nickname. Sullivan grinned, "I'm with Bo, Chase. Best you get married in a more serene state, so you don't miss the special moments. The cars won't move an inch unless you tell them."

Bodine reached in his pocket, pulling out four airline-sized bottles of Jameson Irish whiskey. He doled out three bottles to the rest of the men. "Okay, boys, let's all help Chaser regain his footing here. We've got fifteen minutes until showtime."

Murdock downed the whiskey in one gulp. After a few more minutes had passed, a renewed peace enveloped him. "Ah... much better. Thanks, Bo."

The ceremony began promptly at 2:00 p.m. Barbara wore a mint-green, form-fitting wedding gown plus shoulder-length veil trimmed in matching ribbon. Murdock selected a white tuxedo, white ruffled shirt trimmed with a mint-green silk bowtie and cummerbund set. Zachary, decked out in a pale taupe tuxedo accented by a mint-green dress shirt and tie, and Jenna Talia, radiant in her sleek, pale taupe dress under a loose, mint-green lace wrap covering her shoulders and prominent belly, flanked the celebrated couple. Barbara kept glancing at the elegant Talia perched on an overstuffed chair two feet away on her left. A beaming Ted Zachary stood at Murdock's right. Bodine, also in a light taupe tux, white shirt accented by a solid mint-green tie stood beside Ted, monitoring Talia at frequent intervals.

The preacher began, "Mr. Murdock and Ms. Conley acknowledge everyone in this church for their unshakeable loyalty, love, and honesty. They proclaim how life without you would be an empty one indeed. You're all here to honor Chase and Barbara making the ultimate commitment to each other. They're grateful having you as their support group and humbled by your quality contributions to their life."

Barbara heard a groan slip from Talia. She glimpsed peripherally at her matron of honor squirming in her seat. She whispered, "Are you okay, Jenna?"

Talia grimaced, "I don't know. I just felt a rumbling down there and..." She shrieked, "Oh God, I think my water just broke!"

Bodine rushed over followed by Dr. Bronson, who garnered Talia's permission to examine her. Within seconds, he announced, "This baby is ready, so we must prepare for delivery right away."

Bodine gasped, "Right here? Shouldn't I call an ambulance?"

Bronson chuckled, "No, not yet. We're doing this right here, right now, son." He glanced back at Talia who's rapid breathing continued accelerating. "She's already gone into the final stage of labor. Some women are just lucky that way. Now, *run*, and get me plenty of clean towels and a couple jugs of warm water plus some bottles of drinking water." He located Murdock, tossing him a set of keys. "Chase, get the medical bag out of my car. It's carrying everything I need thanks to your heads-up note in the invitation. It's the only red '57 Chevy in the lot." Facing the mother-to-be still clinging onto Barbara's hand, he directed, "Young lady, please stand up so we can get you on your back. We'll make do with this carpet." In seconds, he whipped off his jacket, spreading it on the carpet. Barbara assisted Talia, as she cautiously stood up, water running down her legs. While Barbara held onto her, Talia slowly kneeled. Bronson swiftly positioned her on the floor. Barbara rolled up Talia's wrap, placing it under her head. Bronson hiked up her dress, removing her panties all in one motion.

Murdock and Bodine sprinted back carrying the items Bronson requested, arriving nearly at the same time. Bodine, out of breath, wheezed, "I brought a sheet, too, you know, for privacy, Doc."

Bronson waived him off. "No time for modesty here, son. Besides, it'll just get in my way. You can use it as a shield from the audience for your wife." He raised his voice, "Now, if everyone will please stand back, I'm ready to prep the lady." He slid a towel under Talia's bottom, then reached in his bag, producing the items for delivering the newest Bodine into the world.

While Bronson treated Talia, Murdock engaged the preacher. "Ever seen a wedding like this, Padre?"

The preacher answered, "It's actually happened twice. Both times, it was the bride, however. Talk about cutting it close."

Murdock asked, "No pun intended, Father, but is it possible we just cut to the chase?" He brought Barbara over where the preacher stood, saying, "I, Chase Murdock, take Barbara Conley to be my lawfully wedded wife and…"

He pointed at Barbara who took the cue. "I, Barbara Conley, take Chase Murdock to be my lawfully wedded husband."

The preacher smiled, declaring, "Well alright. I now pronounce you man and wife."

The gathering cheered. Talia writhed in pain. Still clutching the wedding ring in her hand, she maintained the presence of mind to scream, "Barbara! Come take Chase's ring! Ooohh shit, this hurts."

Barbara ran over, kissing Talia on the cheek when she took the ring. Ted Zachary trotted over by Murdock, handing him Barbara's ring. After the couple exchanged the bands, the preacher announced, "Ladies and gentlemen, please welcome Mr. and Mrs. Chase Murdock." The fresh-minted newlyweds gave each other an abbreviated kiss, then swiftly huddled around Talia across from Bodine.

Barbara knelt down beside Talia, dabbing her forehead with a damp cloth. Bodine crouched then held his wife's hand. Cindy Zachary offered ice chips. Bronson broke up the huddle, "She's crowning, folks. I'll need all the elbow room I can get."

Talia's breathing became rapid, her face distorted in agony. Bodine choked up, feeling his wife's pain. Bronson stood over the new mother, his face inches from hers. "Alright, darlin', time to start pushing like there's a freight train coming out. Richard, hold one of her hands. Barbara, hold the other." He positioned himself again between Talia's legs, giving her an order, "Okay, Jenna, give me what you've got and *push* hard. C'mon harder, like you're having the biggest bowel movement in your life. Let's not keep this youngster waiting."

The heavy breathing together with the moaning-pushing routine played out over several minutes. Bodine watched his wife become exhausted from the ordeal. He felt utterly helpless, thinking he should call an ambulance. His knees wobbled from a wooziness overtaking him. Talia made one more concerted effort to push, inching the child's head into view. Bronson yelled, "One more push just like that will give us that beautiful baby." Jenna cut loose with a screech such that folks covered their ears. Applying gentle precision, Dr. Bronson coaxed the tiny body from the birth canal. The doctor crowed during which baby Bodine worked up a yelp, "Don't know if you knew the baby's sex, so let's just welcome your new gorgeous daughter into the world."

Everyone clapped, yelling their congratulations. Talia, Bodine, Barbara, Cindy Zachary and Murdock cried. Bronson addressed Bodine, "Congratulations, Richard. Hand me a clean, dry towel, please." Holding the umbilical cord, he reached into his bag lifting out the surgical scissors. He offered them to Bodine. "Care to do the honors, Dad?"

Bodine took the scissors. "Where do I cut it?"

Bronson pointed to a spot on the cord, "Right about there should be perfect."

Bodine started to cut, blurting, "Damn, this thing's like cutting a garden hose."

Bronson replied, "That's because it's a lifeline, son. Okay, make the cut and stand back. I'll finish up. Call the ambulance now. Jenna and the baby require hospital care plus your help to have the baby's vitals documented and a birth certificate issued. Got a name for her yet?"

Bodine shouted, "This is Daisy, everybody. Not sure about the middle name yet, but we both picked Daisy." He squatted alongside Talia, tears running down her cheeks, a wide smile on her face. "Be right back, baby. I just have to make this call so you and Daisy can get to the hospital quickly. Don't leave this spot." The overwhelmed admirers laughed, clapping their hands in relief.

Murdock threw his arms around Bodine. "I'm so happy for you, Bo. Makes me wish I had a kid when I had the chance. See what a great decision you made? We're all richer from you literally growing a pair. You might call her Daisy, but she'll always be my little Bodette. And hey, after you get your girls settled in at the hospital, expect a delivery of two Four Seasons gourmet dinner plates with cake, naturally. No sense eating bland hospital food on Bodette's birthday and my wedding day, right?" Bodine smiled and nodded in appreciation.

Hearing the sirens from an ambulance and fire truck entering the church grounds, Murdock turned to the crowd. "It won't be the same without the Bodines at the reception, but let me say through a grateful heart for my new wife and little Bodette, LET'S PARTY!"

"Hey Chase, can I ride with you and Mrs. Murdock?" It was Johnny Dunne, jumping, waving and yelling at the Murdocks.

"Hell yes, Johnny. I wouldn't even be here if it weren't for you."

THE END

ABOUT THE AUTHOR
BOB MOODY

- Bob's a Southern California native, grew up in the San Fernando Valley, graduated high school by the skin of his teeth

- Made the unconscionable decision to volunteer for the draft during the height of the Vietnam conflict in 1968, serving until 1969 in the Mekong Delta as an Army Communications Specialist

- Studied broadcasting, journalism, and marketing, then used the knowledge working 40+ years in sales management within the consumer electronics industry, employed by Sony and Panasonic among other name-brand manufacturers

- Married at 35, thus skipping a generation before he had two sons now young enough to be his grandchildren, divorced when boys were young adults

- Followed comedians Jonathan Winters, Steve Martin, and Bill Hicks, his own sense of humor evolving into an acquired taste, hovering around warped irreverence

- Lifetime beach lover, laid back, perhaps as far from Type A as a man can be

- Music lover starting with Elvis, regrets not learning to play an instrument

- Baseball aficionado, loves the game, hates the business

- No wanderlust, doesn't care if he ever sets foot in another airplane

- Seasoned navigator of the internet dating scene, so far a futile hobby

- Now living in Camarillo, Ventura County, California

- Discovered late in life he wanted to become a writer

- Wrote and self-published with Contributing Editor and Muse, Diana Howell Gallagher, "Dirt Nap Chase" in 2012, then wrote and self-published "Serial Dating...at 60," on his own in 2013, bringing in Diana again in late 2018 to work with him on "Bitchen Chase," the sequel to Dirt Nap Chase

- Bob claims five true friends, each of whom he's known for over 50 years

www.ingramcontent.com/pod-product-compliance
Lightning Source LLC
Chambersburg PA
CBHW020539020726
47494CB00006B/1834